ALL
DESIRES KNOWN

ALL
DESIRES KNOWN

TANYA VAN HASSELT

Matador
9 Priory Business Park
Kibworth Beauchamp
Leicestershire LE8 0RX, UK
Tel: (+44) 116 279 2299
Fax: (+44) 116 279 2277
Email: books@troubador.co.uk
Web: www.troubador.co.uk/matador

ISBN 978 1783062 669

British Library Cataloguing in Publication Data.
A catalogue record for this book is available from the British Library.

Typeset in Garamond by Troubador Publishing Ltd
Printed and bound in the UK by TJ International, Padstow, Cornwall

Matador is an imprint of Troubador Publishing Ltd

MIX
Paper from
responsible sources
FSC
www.fsc.org
FSC® C013056

To all my family and friends

ONE

Secrets were always safe with Juliet.

'Another baby will make everything all right again.'

Nell tried to say this with all the confidence that usually and worryingly eluded her. It wasn't fair to talk about quarrelling with your husband like this, even to your best friend, and must be why Juliet was staring at her with an expression on her face Nell had never seen before.

'But Alastair's refused to have more children – Nell, you wouldn't cheat on him – '

'What's to stop me having an accident?'

Juliet said slowly, 'Then you're not already pregnant?'

'Not *yet* – '

Nell waited for the familiar complicit smile to return to Juliet's eyes. If you want something enough, you can find a way of getting it. Juliet had said that often enough (even if Nell hadn't listened) ever since they'd first met twelve years ago in what felt like a never-ending queue for the ladies at a London theatre.

Juliet ought to be egging her on. She was *always* on her side. Instead she was jumping up from the kitchen table to make more coffee, when both their mugs were still half-full.

'So what's going wrong between you then?'

Not even to Juliet could Nell repeat what Alastair had said

when she'd asked him about trying for a third child. Immediately afterwards he'd gone out and bought her a ring of deep green emeralds, which must have cost far too much, but Alastair's overspending showed how sorry he was.

'If Alastair understood how much I want this, don't you think he'd give way?'

'He ought to understand already. Have it out with him. He says he loves you. Here's your chance to test him.'

It was more than three months since Alastair had so inexplicably lost his temper with her but Nell hadn't buried a lingering soreness. She glanced down at the daisy-shaped ring on her hand, the brilliant centre diamond with emerald petals embedded in sharp spikes of gold. There was something of challenge in Juliet's tone she couldn't follow and which made her uncomfortable.

Oh God, am I being crass going on about having another baby to Juliet when she's only got Vail?

Juliet's son Vail was born nearly a year after Nell's Sebastian. Her boyfriend Newland – a university lecturer in American literature from Boston steeped in old-style courtesy and culture – disappeared from Juliet's life soon afterwards. Juliet said she didn't want Newland either as a lover or as Vail's father, and she was tired of being told to read Henry James.

Nell was sorry. She'd admired what she'd taken to be Newland's high-mindedness. But then you couldn't expect someone like Juliet, four years older and smarter than Nell, as well as being edgy and funny and contradictory, to see that as enough.

'Please forget what I've told you. I don't mean any of it really, or else I don't know what it *is* I want,' Nell said, hating herself, wishing she'd never opened her mouth and was anywhere except in Juliet's kitchen. 'For myself, I mean. But if only you – '

'Nell, not that again. Listen to *my* secret instead.' Juliet shook the shining dark strands of fringe which always fell into her eyes, pushed a froth-filled mug across the table and slid back into her seat. 'I've decided to send Vail to Wharton.'

Five years ago, Alastair had unexpectedly landed the job of heading up the politics department of the boys' public school which dominated the ancient town of Wharton in East Sussex. They were given one of the school-owned houses just outside the grounds, but Nell missed the old unconstrained days of their shabby London basement – and Juliet.

Now it ought to be coming back, that careless happiness. In May this year Juliet had announced she was joining them in Wharton at the start of the summer holidays, renting a tiny house near the station. Nell had almost given up persuading her. Wharton might be in reasonable commuting distance of London but Juliet was building up a successful career in government think tanks concerned with education and mental health. Nell was ashamed to admit that her own highly enjoyable job, part-time in the school's art department, could hardly be called real work.

'No objection, is there? There's no need to look so disbelieving.'

'But you've always laughed about Wharton being for spoilt little rich boys – '

'Only because I meet so many ex-public school types at work who've never quite got over where they went.' Juliet picked up a silver teaspoon and examined the hallmark. 'I've changed my mind. Haven't I done that before?'

Nell hesitated, afraid Juliet was reading her thoughts. How on earth was Juliet going to afford the astronomic Wharton fees? She said, knowing how lame it sounded, 'I thought you had to go on the waiting list ages in advance.'

'That ridiculous snobbery about saying you put your son's

name down at birth. People do like to drop it into conversations. Along with their old Oxbridge college. These establishments have to promote the myth, but actually it's all about getting enough bums on seats – they'd go bust otherwise.'

'So is Vail pleased?'

'I told you it's a secret. I've got two years to save up,' Juliet smiled as she watched the swaying teaspoon she was balancing on one forefinger. 'Then there are bursaries for single mothers. I've checked it out and got it sorted.'

Isn't so much confidence alarming? The headmaster's wife Eleanor Hunstrete had said to Nell after meeting Juliet for the first time this summer. Nell had laughed. Confidence was catching.

'It's brilliant news,' Nell said, disconcerted to find herself remembering Eleanor's question. She adored Vail. With his dusky hair and vibrant blue eyes he looked exactly like Juliet. He wasn't her godson – Juliet didn't believe in godparents – but he was the only child of her closest friend. She'd looked after him when he was a baby so that Juliet could work.

It's because I'm disappointed Juliet didn't say what I wanted her to. I'm being mean, I've everything compared with her, a husband and two children. Being beautiful and having all these men asking her out doesn't make up for that.

'Oh Juliet! I feel awful – I haven't asked you about last night. Do tell me.'

'Last night?'

'Your date. With the psychologist. Imagining how it was all going was the only thing that kept me sane all the time I was driving the children back from Buttery Barbara and trying not to agree with their complaints about her being so sugar-sweet and controlling.'

'Oozing out of her tin like treacle. Weird that Alastair's mother's like that, isn't it? Okay then, the psychologist guy was thoughtful and interesting and available. More than available. But at the end of the evening he went weepy on me. So much for emotional literacy. I can't bear men who cry.'

'Could you trust a man who *never* cried?' asked Nell doubtfully.

'Oh Nell! Why must you always make excuses?'

'Do I? How annoying of me. Sorry, I will try and stop.'

'There's no point in taking on other people's torment – and you're not helping them.'

Confused images rushed into Nell's head: the old ladies waiting for death in the nursing home where she volunteered to do art therapy, the patiently hungry eyes of the dogs trailing behind homeless people, even the sight of cows grazing in the water meadows around Wharton and who were going to be killed one day. These and all the other countless miseries of the world haunted the edges of her thoughts, and people telling her that such pity was useless never made any difference.

'Anyway, go on about him,' she urged, to show Juliet she wasn't hurt, though she was, secretly.

'I can't now. I said I'd pick up Vail from tennis.'

'Aren't all three of them walking back with Alastair? Actually I ought to go home anyway,' Nell said, getting up. 'With the new term starting we've got the dreaded Common Room meeting this afternoon. But we've had such a summer – and Vail going to Wharton means you'll definitely stay here.'

'Definitely,' Juliet agreed, more seriously than was usual for her. She shot a glance at Nell. 'Alastair doesn't *mind* me coming here, does he? He hasn't said anything to you?'

'Alastair? He's as delighted as I am – ' Nell broke off. For the first time it struck her that Alastair hadn't wanted Juliet to move to Wharton. Not that he'd said anything against it. She hurried on, ' – but he'll be home in a minute wanting lunch. Promise me you'll fill me in on last night another time – '

'The next heart-stopping instalment…but he's not getting his Freudian hands on me on any permanent basis. Shrinks are generally half mad themselves or those that aren't soon become so, which isn't exactly surprising.'

'I wish my life was full of exciting new men like yours is,' said Nell, trying to atone by repeating what she'd often said before, and which they both knew was untrue.

Alastair wasn't waiting for her when she arrived home. Instead, Rachel was circling the kitchen with an accusation ready.

'We've been back ages. I thought you were only getting the papers and stuff.'

'Sorry. I called in on Juliet – '

Rachel rolled her eyes in the amazed manner she was learning to do rather too well.

'And you only talked for *two hours*? Not like you.'

'Mum, when's lunch? Vail's staying – '

Sebastian and Vail appeared in the doorway, both of them hot and shiny-faced.

'You boys look as if you need a cold drink before that.'

Sebastian brushed this aside, but Vail gave her the enchanting smile that mirrored Juliet's.

'We've already helped ourselves, but thanks. Are you sure it's okay about lunch? Mum says it is with her – '

'Vail won the end of summer tennis club award,' interrupted Rachel. 'He won't tell you, so I will.'

'That's great. Was it a prize, or just honour and glory?'

All three children looked at her with the pitying expression Nell was growing used to.

'*Mum*! We're not at your stupid old Malory Towers. Of course Vail got a prize. What's the point of winning otherwise? Twenty-four tennis balls and a sweat-shirt. I came second in my group so I only got a tee-shirt. Seb can have it if he likes.'

'Where's Dad?'

'In your room. On his mobile.'

Nell ran upstairs two steps at a time.

'I've got the most inspired plan.'

Alastair, pulling on a clean shirt, grinned at her with the teasing affection that spread all over him like sun-warmed skin.

'Your plans are *always* inspired. Out with it.'

'You know we had to pay a deposit to reserve Sebastian's place at Wharton? It's got to be a secret from everyone but us, but Juliet's just told me she wants to send Vail here, so couldn't we do the same for him? I'm sure she's going to find it hard to find the money for the fees, but he could try for a scholarship, you know how brilliantly clever he is, far more than Sebastian. The newspapers are always going on about how private schools should offer more of them to disadvantaged children or they'll have their charitable status taken away.'

'Darling Nell, Vail's hardly disadvantaged – '

'Wouldn't it count that he hasn't any grandparents as well as no dad? It jolly well ought to.'

'He does have Juliet's parents – '

'A fat lot of good they are. He practically never sees them since the quarrel – which wasn't Juliet's fault.'

'It was her fault to refuse any support from them when Newland went off. They'd already bought her a house remember, very few parents can do that, only child or not.'

'They didn't have to be so sniffy about Juliet leading her own life. We're her dearest friends, so if we don't help her who will? It'll show her how glad we are she's moved here, she was worrying you thought I spent too much time with her. I'm sorry, it's been a frenzied summer with helping her settle in and then we'll be having Vail here after school some days when Juliet's late back.'

'I'm used to being the neglected husband,' Alastair said, laughing at her, and swinging his arm into an imaginary tennis forehand.

'Everything's going to be so easy for us with getting such a big slice off the fees because of you teaching here. You're going to say she'd feel awkward about accepting it, but I'm sure we can get round that somehow – you could anyway.'

'We've agreed to it already, have we? I'll tell you what, to prove it to you, I'll do it today. And later I'll prove something else to you as well. Or now – '

Nell responded to his kiss whilst gently stopping the hand that was undoing the zip of her jeans. Her husband was – almost – everything she wanted even now, thirteen years after they'd married with such romantic haste in a London white and muffled in freezing January snow. She'd been just twenty, still at art school and Rachel already on the way. But of course that hadn't been the reason for either of them.

She drifted downstairs with Alastair, reassured that the distance keeping them apart this summer had all been in her head. Didn't he always want everyone around him to be as happy as he was himself? He would change his mind about a baby once she was pregnant.

TWO

That the singular beauty of the Wharton chaplain had acted as a double-edged sword in his earlier life could hardly be doubted. Clement Hunstrete asked no questions, persuading himself that curiosity in such matters slips too easily into prurience. He was a gentleman – and he liked to think he lived like one.

Clement watched his wife lean forward in the unforgiving wooden seat to get a better view. No cause for anxiety there. She was past the age of admiring an attractive man for any unsuitable reasons and should be allowed to enjoy one with scholarly detachment.

Just as he was. After all, Wharton was a highly academic public school in the best English tradition. Surely he deserved any consolations offered him for the unnerving business of finding himself its headmaster?

If any of the other women attending this inaugural chapel service of the Michaelmas term had designs on the chaplain, Clement suspected they were wasting their time. Not that they would be guilty of nursing forbidden desires for someone else's husband. Martin Darrow had been a theology tutor at Oxford and a curate in his native Midlands before returning to his old school as its chaplain, but he had never married.

Noli me tangere – the words strayed into Clement's head as he contemplated the luminous purity of Martin's face. There was something unreachable in the man's bearing which might serve to fend off the attention which must otherwise make his life complicated. Don't touch me – the warning was there for those who chose to see it.

But it was not old master paintings of the newly risen Christ in a dawn garden that Clement found himself picturing. It was those of the martyred Saint Sebastian, his white flesh pierced by arrows, flawlessly beautiful in his suffering. Clement, a medieval historian, was reminded that plague victims had prayed to Sebastian since he could understand their pain and would help.

Clement glanced past the pews crammed with teenage boys to those which were reserved for Common Room and visitors. From his headmaster's seat near the chapel's high arching doors he saw that Nell Garwood, his favourite among the young wives, was fixing her wide-eyed scrutiny on the chaplain.

This could be excused, Clement reassured himself, for Nell was an artist – even if she disliked calling herself one – and was painting Martin's portrait. If anyone was entitled to look at him like that it was Nell. All the same, Clement hoped nobody else had noticed: it would be so easy for people to get the wrong idea! Nell was both ingenuous and fatally warm-hearted; a disastrous combination, Clement considered, and likely to land her – or still worse, the school – in a whole load of trouble.

Without meaning to, Clement shifted his gaze to Alastair Garwood, sitting next to his wife, his summer-bleached hair flopping across his forehead. An easy-going fellow in his mid-forties. He'd been in charge of the politics department and run the school tennis for five years now. There wasn't a Common Room member, male or female, who had a critical word to say about Alastair.

Nothing surprising about that. But Clement wasn't convinced. A man shouldn't try to be universally popular; it suggested a certain superficiality of mind. Or conceivably something to hide. Just now Alastair was apparently listening to St Paul's remonstrations to the over-sexed Christians at Corinth, but Clement guessed his mind was more pleasurably occupied. He hurriedly adjusted his own face into the absorbed expression with which he'd convinced parents and boys during a dozen years as Wharton's headmaster that he could remember who they were.

At the entrance to the Turner Room, his personal secretary Meredith stood poised to avert any hiccups in the smooth stage management of the reception for first-time parents which followed the chapel service. Clement was fond of calling the event a graceful commencement to the academic year; he was less explicit but equally conscious as to its effectiveness in demonstrating to parents that by choosing Wharton for their sons they were guaranteed membership of an elitist club.

For the Turner Room, with its massive dimensions and ornate plaster work ceiling, was the school's undisputed showpiece. Above the rococo marble fireplace hung a magnificent seascape, boasting a triumphant brass plate inscribed Joseph Mallord William Turner. Glasses of wine and orange juice glinted on mirror-polished oak tables. In this gilded and cultured setting parents could forget that their direct debits for the term's fees had already come out of their bank accounts.

Clement greeted each batch of parents with a judicious mix of courtesy and authority, and got rid of them by gesturing towards the refreshment. He looked approvingly at his deputy Jim North, introducing an earnest-faced couple to the chaplain. They were the type who liked to be reassured that the school took pastoral care seriously – an expression Clement regarded with scarcely veiled contempt but was forced to subscribe to in this climate of government meddling – and would probably make a nuisance of themselves during the next five years.

Martin was certainly an invaluable asset. Clement was

11

comfortably aware that he was envied by fellow headmasters: a decent chaplain was a rarity. Martin's loyalty to the school was indisputable, for he'd been a scholarship boy here some thirty years ago. He was as solid as a rock theologically – by which Clement meant no happy-clappy triumphalism – and had a first class degree from Balliol. Yes, Martin had been an inspired appointment. You'd never suspect his Coventry working-class origins; he spoke with barely the trace of an accent. There was only that pale skin to suggest he'd had a bad start in life. Poor nutrition, not enough fresh air, or whatever it was places like that lacked.

A benign smile at the sea of parents and a glance at the clock. It was time for the welcoming address. As Clement mounted a dais on which a lectern was placed, he spotted his chaplain staring at a tall man of rigid posture that usually signified the army. Distaste stirred in his mind at an unpleasant recollection. Piers Benson, a Wharton old boy with an unsavoury smell about him; the son was coming into the sixth form this term. He hadn't cared for the boy at interview and yet he'd been obliged to give him a place. It had been contrary to his better judgment and he was still annoyed. But what else could he have done?

Martin looked so suddenly white and ill that for a moment Clement hesitated. The fellow ought to have a drink. Why the devil did he feel the need to wear a hair shirt all the time? He scanned the room for his ever-reliable secretary Meredith, and saw she was indeed carrying a glass towards Martin. Just as she reached him, Martin appeared to utter something, his face distorted with uncontrolled passion. He swung clumsily towards Piers Benson and nearly fell against Nell Garwood.

Good God, Nell was flinging her arms around him! Just the kind of emotionalism to draw attention to Martin's extraordinary behaviour. He prayed Meredith would have the wit to ring the bell for silence, adding an aside to the almighty that the incident might go unnoticed. Clearing his throat, he prepared to speak with the compelling integrity of an incorruptible headmaster. Public schools couldn't afford the faintest trace of scandal. Weren't the press always waiting to pounce and make his life even more precarious than it already was?

THREE

Rachel ate breakfast all right, Nell saw her doing it. Then there was school lunch. Was Rachel eating that?

'Don't be stupid, Mum.'

'I'm worried you aren't eating enough.'

'You're always worrying about the wrong things. Why don't you give it a break for once?'

'Darling, you don't want to lose any more weight.'

Rachel jerked up her shoulder.

'I'm not. You really can't see it, can you? You ought to sort your own life instead of mucking up mine.'

At thirteen Rachel was fast losing the open, affectionate responses of her childhood, and was cultivating a surly argumentiveness that whipped up into storm clouds for no reason at all. Nell thought she could cope with walking on eggshells – friends protested their daughters were exactly the same – but Rachel's attitude at mealtimes was starting to frighten her.

In the evening Rachel pushed her food around the plate, eating very slowly, cutting food into tiny pieces. One pea on her fork at a time, and each one taking forever to reach her mouth. Supper was now a nightmare with Nell afraid to make an issue of how little Rachel was actually consuming. She found herself stealing covert glances, noting how much thinner Rachel was becoming.

'Go easy on the spending front, will you? We ought to tighten up.' Alastair's mouth was full of toast. It was a Friday morning, three weeks into term; the children had left for school and Alastair was as usual cutting it too fine for chapel.

Nell turned round from the kettle, frowning. Alastair rarely troubled himself or her about money. Their life was cushioned by the Wharton public school system; even their house was provided for them. All the Wharton facilities were on tap for members of the Common Room and their families: swimming pool, tennis courts, acres of playing fields. The economic difficulties of the outside world could be easily forgotten.

'Don't take that the wrong way.' Alastair jumped up from the table, wiping butter smears from his mouth. 'Must dash, I'm running late.'

Nell watched his disappearing back, her thoughts flying to that night in May, in half-term week, the first and only devastating quarrel of their married life. Was Alastair remembering it too, with this casual reference?

'Leave it, Nell, can't you? We've got two perfect children already, we've everything we want.'

'You may have, but what about me? I want another baby.'

'For Christ's sake, Nell, we can't bloody afford another child!'

The row ought to have ended in passionate lovemaking. Instead they'd lain in oppressive silence, on the edges of the bed, not touching. The next day he'd gone out and bought her the daisy ring.

It still didn't make sense. Loads of the Common Room families had three or four children and they got by. Alastair had always been a man who liked to give, making little of it, enjoying other people's pleasure. She and Alastair didn't do stand-up rows; she'd teased him that he couldn't be bothered, could he, and really there had never been any need.

But she *had* been shelling out cash at an alarming rate

recently. Almost all of it on Rachel. Another pair of those illogically expensive boots which had become an essential item of teenage life, gorgeous new curtains and a designer duvet for her bedroom, a furry white jacket like the one her friend Rosie had. All of it to try and shift their daughter out of the black mood in which she'd wrapped herself.

None of the extra money spent on Rachel had made an iota of difference, but when your child was changing into a stranger and starting to treat you as public enemy number one, you tried anything, didn't you, and so what if it was spoiling and bribery, Buttery Barbara's comments were always irritating and why should she take any notice of her anyway?

Nell grabbed her lesson diary and hurried into school, resentment and excuses to herself jostling uneasily with anxiety over Rachel. It was just conceivable Alastair was beginning to worry about how they were going to manage the fees they would have to pay for Sebastian when he started at Wharton. It was nearly two years away and they would get a substantial amount off, but it would still be a frightening chunk of their income.

She had her own account, into which her salary went, and anything she made from selling her paintings, which was practically nothing. Apart from her clothes and presents, the money in her account paid for family holidays, and just now was earmarked for their holiday to America in the summer. Otherwise everything else went through their joint account which Alastair looked after, or said he did. It had occasionally occurred to Nell to wonder whether he checked it or scanned for mistakes, but then she rarely did this more than cursorily herself, and never bothered with the joint account statements at all.

Nell had only three lessons to teach that morning, but she couldn't give her mind to any of them. Was it her fault Alastair was suddenly twitchy about cash flow? She came back to the house at lunch time, and ran upstairs into the little study which Alastair had to himself for all his politics books.

'Not that you've got very many,' Nell had teased him as they arranged the furniture when they first moved in.

'There's no need,' said Alastair, 'I teach at an elitist establishment – and who wouldn't with the fantastic long summer holidays – but I've no desire to turn into a clone of Clement Hunstrete. God forbid.'

'Yes, poor Eleanor has to endure almost every wall being filled with history books, not just his study. I know how fortunate I am having a husband with a taste for minimalism.'

'Not when it comes to comfort I don't. I like it when you put on that sarcastic voice. I'll need a decent armchair for in here. You might choose it for me, darling, you're so much cleverer at these things than I am.'

Nell looked at the armchair as she went into the study. It was bulky and covered in rusty-brown leather, a classic example of the furniture found in men's clubs and they were supposed to appreciate. Not a good choice. It was unsettling the way you changed your mind about things. She'd wanted it for Alastair, more, she realised afterwards, than he'd wanted it for himself. It had cost a great deal more than they ought to have spent, and hadn't really proved its value as Alastair from the very beginning spent very little time in his study.

'I prefer to do my marking in the sitting room beside you on the sofa,' he protested, when she commented on this. 'Then I can console myself in various ways in between essays.' He pulled her towards him and slid a hand up her jersey.

It was impossible to find fault with this point of view. At least she hadn't then. Recently a small part of Nell wondered if the room might have had more use as a painting studio, but she kept this to herself. Proper artists who got their work recognised and made money needed studios, not someone like her, still struggling to find time in the day for everything that crowded in, with hardly a moment to be creative on her own account.

There was a pile of files in the cupboard. Nell rifled through them, but they contained only old exam papers and coursework schemes. At the bottom of the heap there was a yellow folder without a label. She pulled it out and put it on Alastair's desk. It was almost empty, containing only the most recent bank statement. Alastair must have been having a throw-out. Maybe he was thinking of switching to banking online, something he'd always resisted. Her eyes ran down the columns of figures, of money going in and out of the account. It looked all right; although there wasn't much balance at any time, they weren't overdrawn.

She saw a payment for a thousand pounds. That must be the deposit for Vail's place at Wharton. She was glad they'd done that, even though Juliet – but here Nell stopped herself. She'd never thought about it before, she'd never had to, but she was beginning to realise that the giving and receiving of money between friends wasn't as uncomplicated as it ought to be.

Nothing could have been sweeter than the way Juliet had thanked her. She'd come running into their house the following morning, hugging Nell, eyes full as though she was going to cry, only Juliet never did.

But something had jarred. Nell almost wished the whole thing undone. Had it awakened comparisons between their situations, or even regrets for Newland, which were safer buried?

She was about to close the file when she noticed the date of the transaction. It was the thirty-first of August, several days *before* she'd asked Alastair about giving Juliet the money. She stared at the print, remembering. It had been at the beginning of term and Alastair had nipped round to Juliet's that evening. Yet here it was in black and white that the money had already left the account.

It was an error, the bank's computer had got it wrong.

The explanation almost satisfied her – and then didn't.

She saw again Alastair's face, when she'd asked him about giving Juliet the deposit money, heard again his voice when, with his usual relaxed generosity, he'd agreed and said he'd see to it, his smile making everything easy. Why hadn't he admitted he'd done it already? She'd have understood, wouldn't she?

She remained quite still, trying to take it in, her attempts to make sense of it all tripping over the accusing fence that had reared up in her head. However hard she tried to reach over it she couldn't see beyond it – or make use of the pop-up excuses toppling around its base.

He'd never lied to her before. She was certain of it. It had never occurred to her he'd ever do so. Why should he? Alastair was always transparent, straightforward.

She moved away from the desk and leant against the back of Alastair's armchair, hearing only her own breathing in the quiet room. For a long, cold moment she stared at the red wine stain the shape of Sicily on the oatmeal rug. Rather appropriate, Alastair had joked when she'd scrubbed at it ineffectually, for the wine had been Sicilian, one of those rough Italian country wines he loved to drink, and Rachel, Nell liked to remember, had been conceived in Sicily during their first proper holiday together.

She and Alastair had spent dizzy days and nights in a tiny mountain village near Mount Etna, and when they weren't making love she'd painted everything she could see, drunk and revelling in the intensity of light and strong contrasts of colour in the landscape around them.

The wine stain had been part of their home, a familiar old friend. Now it was an ugly, dirty mark which ought to be properly cleaned.

FOUR

Nell stared at herself in the long mirror of her bedroom, expecting to see the different person she'd turned into in the space of ten minutes. But guilt and the beginnings of small poisonous seeds of suspicion left no mark. Her face appeared as it always did. Wide apart grey eyes looked back at her uncertainly under thick brows that were too straight, a smudge of violet from the morning's painting class lingered on a nose that wasn't straight enough.

She too was keeping a secret. At the end of the summer holidays she'd stood in front of this mirror with her hands on her stomach and imagined it swelling with the beginnings of a much-longed for baby. She shivered, no longer seeing her image, but telling herself that what Alastair had done was as nothing compared to what she'd been getting up to.

It was a sneaky thing to do. She was trying to get what she wanted by deceit. Worst of all, the person she was deceiving was her own husband. She must give up the idea immediately, put it out of her mind. What had she been thinking of?

But then she wanted a baby so much! Why couldn't she have this thing when she was so sure Alastair subsconsciously wanted it too, if only he knew himself better? He might protest that he'd like to have her more to himself, but she was only thirty-three, they had years ahead of them for one another.

Having Rachel so early on in their relationship had been hard in one way because Alastair wasn't ready to share her with a baby. But to her it had been even more miraculous than finding herself married to Alastair. She'd been careful never to betray this. She'd known from the beginning that Alastair, a lot older and more experienced than she was, liked to feel he was being put first.

Then Sebastian too had come sooner than planned. Alastair had minded this; she knew his face by then too well to miss the mixed feelings it expressed when she told him she was pregnant again. She was still breastfeeding Rachel, and Alastair, always vague about these things, had thought it was impossible, while she'd been too dazedly full of joy – and short of sleep – to think at all.

But they'd managed with two babies so closely spaced; they'd been happy. Juliet's Vail had been quick and advanced for his age. Soon he and Sebastian had become like twins. Life with Juliet and the children had been one long tea party. Sun-filled, chaotic days, whirling past in bright colours like balloons in a high wind. No complications, no doubts.

As she remembered all this, her resolve hardened. She wanted to have another baby – and why shouldn't she at least try to get what she wanted? What was the value of vacillating? If Alastair could go behind her back, she could do the same.

And if she'd already conceived without yet knowing it! Yes, then she wouldn't have to make a decision. Tomorrow she would buy a pregnancy testing kit. After all, wasn't it all part of marriage, these little deceptions for overall harmony and long-term happiness?

The doorbell rang and she froze. She would pretend to be out. Then the ring came again, and she realised it must be Juliet who always did a double ring. It was their familiar signal. 'So that you know it's only me,' Juliet had explained. 'And you

21

needn't answer the door if you're in the middle of something else, I know what it's like.'

Juliet always did know what it was like. She was also the last person in the world whom Nell wanted to see at that moment. It wasn't her fault Alastair had acted as he had, but he'd made Juliet deceive her too. When Juliet had confided that she'd decided to send Vail to Wharton, she must have been already expecting a thousand pounds to land in her bank account any moment and to say nothing about it. She'd been playing a part and had never admitted it.

It wasn't Juliet. Two large women with benevolent faces were filling up the doorstep. Nell's heart sank.

'It's not a good moment, I don't want to be saved and I'm really sorry but I haven't got any time to talk – '

The telephone rang as she slammed the door. She ignored it. It might be Juliet or it might be Alastair. She would go out, just as soon as she could be sure those women weren't still loitering in the road ready to pounce.

Juliet's voice over the years: *dearest Nell, you don't need to be so afraid of conflict.*

She looked at the big clock in the hall. Only half-past one. Martin. She could go round to his flat, there was still enough time before she had to go to the old people's home for their art therapy. She mustn't be late for them, they were all such darlings and she loved the way they looked forward to the sessions. She wouldn't tell Martin about the money business – that would be disloyal to Alastair – but it would be enough just to be with him, to be close to whatever it was in him that made her feel the world was all right after all. Goodness? Not exactly. That was the wrong word, but it was the nearest.

The telephone rang again and it struck her it might be one of the children's schools trying to get hold of her to tell her something dreadful. Serve her right for snapping at those women. She snatched up the receiver and held it to her ear with a shaking hand.

'Nell? Is it all right to talk? I mean, you are alone aren't you?'

It was Hilary, Rosie's mum, one of the more chatty mothers from Rachel's school. Nell liked Hilary, and she liked Rosie. She liked all of Rachel's friends and their mothers, but they weren't real friends, they weren't like Juliet. She forced herself to sound welcoming.

'Hi – is everything okay?'

'Sort of. Only there's something I ought to tell you and I feel bad about it. I was going to come round – '

Oh please no.

'About Rosie?'

'No – at least only partly. I'd better come straight out with it. You know Rachel's stopped doing Facebook?'

'She only started in the summer, after her birthday – '

Nell fought the inevitable urge to defend herself. She hadn't known. Part of letting Rachel have a computer in her bedroom had been that she and Alastair knew her password and could check up on her at any time. It was a warning to Rachel and a sufficient safeguard – so Nell had thought. She'd never actually put it into action. But then Hilary was a mother who thought she was entitled to snoop on her children's online activities. She was probably right. Another layer of Nell's disintegrating confidence in herself flaked away.

'She told Rosie she'd been getting comments – things said – '

Hilary sounded unusually diffident as if she didn't know how to express something. Nell gripped the phone.

'What things?'

'I can only repeat what Rosie said to me and that's likely to be an edited version.'

'Online bullying? Is that what you're saying?'

The words came automatically. Nell had read a stream of newspaper articles and watched a television documentary about teenagers who had been the victims of personal abuse on the internet. But she'd never thought about it in connection with Rachel.

'Rosie didn't call it that. More like jokes about photos, you know how they send them to each other – and to boys.'

Oh God, she'd been living in cloud cuckoo land, imagining that because they'd brought their children up in safe middle class Wharton this kind of thing couldn't touch them.

'Hilary, you don't mean nude stuff – '

'Might have been getting that way. Rosie wriggled out of being too specific – and something that's a joke to one person can come as a cruel attack to another, can't it?'

'She's been on edge all summer. What exactly did Rosie say?'

'That she's cutting herself off from her friends. Skipping lunch. Rosie says Rachel will never forgive her if she lets on to anyone. You know how they watch each other, and are obsessed with what they look like, comparing how much they weigh, thinking they have to have bodies like those absurd creatures parading up and down catwalks. That's all Rosie would tell me, and obviously I had to pass it on to you straightaway.'

'Yes, of course you did. Thank you. I'm sorry, it can't have been easy for you. Having to tell me, I mean.'

'Well, we mums have to stick together, don't we? Maybe you should check she isn't going on those anorexia websites you hear about. This won't be much comfort, but I caught Rosie exchanging tips on how to give a blow job the other day which is pretty worrying too. Not that I believe she's actually – all the same I had a heavy talk with her. Teenage girls – you never know what's really going on.'

You never know with anything. Friends, husbands, children. I've been going around with my eyes shut.

'Say thanks to Rosie for me,' she said. 'If you can do it without making difficulties for her. And you.'

'It can happen to any of them. Saying all this to you, it's not what I'd choose, but I couldn't just sit by and do nothing. You'd do the same for me if it was Rosie.'

But it never would be Rosie, Nell told herself, after she'd thanked Hilary again and put the phone down. Rosie was sensible and uncomplicated, like her mother. Why wasn't Rachel like that?

Because she's like you.

Upstairs in Rachel's bedroom she logged on to the computer, sick at heart at what she might find.

The history of sites visited was blank.

FIVE

'What a wanker – '

'Think he's tried it on with Oliver Benson?'

'Bet you the Hun doesn't – '

Martin Darrow heard the snatches of conversation from boys trooping along the corridor outside his classroom.

A chill premonition had crept over him when he'd seen the boy's face in the chapel at the beginning of term. He'd gone straight to the notice boards in the cloisters, his eyes darting down the lists of new boys. Dear God, here it was. Sweat pricked at his hairline and ran down into his dog collar. Benson, Oliver, coming into the lower sixth form. Piers Benson's son.

Martin eyed the pile of essays from his A level Religious Studies class that lay on his desk waiting to be marked. He didn't see them. He saw only a boy's face.

Oliver Benson had already been taken up by a couple of boys in the year above him. For more reasons than the obvious one. Chris Parrish and Zachary Shilling – manipulative boys with vicious minds. Oliver Benson was just such another. So arrogantly clever, rotten to the core, sealed within a slippery surface.

Like father, like son.

'Just one moment.'

Coming out of his classroom Martin caught sight of Oliver

loitering by the notice boards. He ought to be in class if he didn't have a free lesson time. If he did, he should be working in his study bedroom or the library.

Martin shot him a sharp glance. The boy's eyes looked dull and unfocused. Drugs? Possibly. Like the rest of the Common Room he knew the signs to watch out for, guessed just which boys took drugs. Expulsion on possession in school; that was the Wharton line. Schools had to turn a blind eye about the holidays, or they'd risk losing too many boys – and their fees.

Should he search his pockets, turn out his study? Was this his chance? His jaw tightened as saliva filled his mouth.

'I'm going to see the school nurse, I don't feel too good.'

Martin measured the boy's face slowly and deliberately before turning away.

'I don't suppose you do. Another time then.'

Martin watched him across the quad and out of the arches which led to further buildings and the school's medical centre. He'd already developed the Wharton walk. One hand in jacket pocket, the other arm hooked round books and files. A combination of adolescent shuffle and man-about-town swagger.

Why had he let the boy go? He couldn't answer himself.

Back in his chaplain's flat he turned to hang over a table cluttered with jigsaw fragments, slamming the door on his memories. The tangle of coloured cardboard fragments would become Brueghel's painting of Icarus' fall from the sky when the wax in his wings melted in the heat of the sun.

He usually began with the straight-sided pieces, the clear defining edges which contained it all, boundaries which offered a safe cradling. It might be childish, but a man needed to be a child in one part of his life if he was to be an adult in the rest of it.

Nell didn't start like this, going round the edges. She'd come to his flat on several days over the summer to paint his likeness as part of the exhibition of Common Room portraits. She'd begun with rough strokes of his features, dark shadows in the eye sockets and under the jaw line. The painting was propped up on an easel borrowed from the art department in the corner of his sitting room, still not finished.

If he'd started with the sky he might feel safer now – not from what had once happened to him, that stain could never be wiped clean – but armoured against the clamour of desires crowding into his head like harpies. Instead he'd completed just one small detail. He stood staring down at the white legs disappearing into the green-blue water. Icarus, who had flown too high.

Part of his chaplain's job over the years was to support boys with worries over their sexual leanings. It was his hardest task. Boys were often unsure beneath their bravado; some were unhappy and confused. They almost all knew and understood a lot less than they pretended. The boys' trust in his absolute discretion made his responsibility heavy; the inadequacy of the help he could offer left him sad. For how could he say anything to offer hope? Why had Christ said so little? And others too much?

There was a knock at his door. There always was. The boys dropped in at all times and he was thankful for it. A religious faith worth its name couldn't be taught en masse; it would be howled down in the need to save face. Giving boys time on their own to talk and letting them feel they were interesting and mattered – this was probably the most worthwhile part of his day. He did it as much as he possibly could.

It wasn't a boy; it was Nell Garwood, red-eyed and with a smudge of paint on her nose. He looked down at her canvas bag bulging with twisted tubes of oil paint, brushes and smeared rags.

'I had a feeling you weren't quite done with me.'

'Is it an okay moment? You don't mind being interrupted?'

He made some tea and wondered about the red eyes while she studied the portrait on its easel.

'I'm not sure,' she said. 'Martin, can you *ever* really know another person – be certain of things about them? Or even of anything?'

'No,' he said. 'But the scared child in us craves it. That's the whole problem with fundamentalism – it wants to have it all clear. Certainty – God the great consoler – it's time we left all that behind. But you're not talking theology are you?'

Instead of answering, Nell picked up the lid of the jigsaw box. 'You're doing *The Fall of Icarus*! You haven't done much yet.'

'I only started it yesterday.'

'But you've concentrated on this one fragment, the whole subject of the painting. It always makes me sad – how nobody's noticing Icarus' death, as if it was irrelevant. That's what's so awful about people's secret suffering. We don't see it.'

He tried to read her expression without appearing to, but she was turning over pieces of the jigsaw and didn't meet his eyes.

'You're someone who picks up on what matters.'

Was this true? As he looked at Nell's troubled face he began to question the value of what he'd said. Or what it meant anyway. The reckless hug she'd given him in the Turner Room at the start of term was part and parcel of her intuitive grasp of someone else's emotions and immediate sympathy with them. But when she *wanted* to believe something! At that point she might well lose herself in doubts about the worth of her own perceptions and a reluctance to ask any unsettling questions.

'We'll probably never be entirely confident we're doing – or have done – the right thing when it comes to relationships of all kinds.'

'Mmm. Is it like that with the boys?'

'Teenagers need to be cagey at times. Just when they're thinking most, they can be flippant and cynical on the surface. You can only offer suggestions, which might or might not take root, and hope they send a boy down a more sunlit path. You can't be sure anything has happened. Most likely you'll never know. But *something* has.'

'It's not exactly encouraging,' said Nell in a resentful tone he hadn't heard in her before. 'You're going to say it's no use asking God to change things – and people.'

'We pray for others because it's part of Christ's way of living and loving. I imagine it's a waste of time instructing God with precise details as to what we want him to do.'

'Okay, you've got a point there. Anything's better than feeling pressurised into getting Answers to Prayer – I have quite enough of that from my mother-in-law.'

'Whom I'm never going to be allowed to meet.'

'She'd only say things afterwards which I couldn't bear.'

'I've missed you coming to paint,' he said, choosing not to examine what she meant. He *had* missed her. She'd only fitted in a couple of sessions this term, but they'd been a time of escape for him; safe, cool hours. Her presence offered him respite; it helped him recover the self she'd painted over the summer. Nell must never know about the thoughts which stalked his days. He wouldn't be able to bear the disappointment in her eyes. She still believed in him.

He'd believed in himself – or thought he had. But he'd lived without confiding his troubles or his joys to others. He wasn't that kind of man. He'd kept the secret long enough, hadn't he? He wasn't about to come out with it now.

As he covertly studied Nell, he understood he was failing her too. He said, to change the subject, 'It's the Wharton lecture tonight – a Dr Lewis Auerbach. Have you remembered? Some eminent psychiatrist. Could be interesting.'

'I'd forgotten about it – but thanks. Actually, I don't feel up to it. I hate leaving the children in the evening, and I've got to get up at crack of dawn to go on the sixth form art trip to Paris.'

Martin didn't press her. His suggestion to Nell was careless enough. He had no intention of going himself, even though the headmaster liked to see a decent showing from the Common Room.

'You know, I don't think I can do any more to this.'

Nell had given up fiddling with the jigsaw and was looking critically at the painting on the easel.

'Does that mean it's finished?'

'No – yes – it isn't the same thing. I thought last time there was still something I was missing. I might just have to stop.' She turned round to face him. 'You said in the first sermon I ever heard you preach that all human beings were unfinished works of art – that God doesn't give up on what he's made but waits for all eternity for its completion.'

'Did I? I was quoting someone else,' Martin said, conscious of speaking more mechanically than he meant to.

'But even if you believe it, finding things out about people – and yourself – is hateful, isn't it? You discover you aren't a very nice person. And they aren't either.'

SIX

Dr Lewis Auerbach looked around the cavernous school hall, appreciative of a certain irony. Above his head, massive oak rafters soared, as if to symbolise the immeasurable scope of scholarship and the timelessness of high culture. The setting was all it ought to be: a compelling and unmistakable demonstration of Wharton's assured place among England's leading public schools.

Lewis might be one of the country's experts on adolescent psychotic illness but he was not at Wharton to exercise his profession. He'd been invited to the school to lecture to the sixth form and Common Room on the past, present and future role of psychiatry, a brief which might mean almost anything, and in Lewis's hands probably would. He was not a man who tolerated constraints placed on his work, though he faced so great a one in the other half of his life. It was an uneven distribution of discipline and may have accounted for something contradictory about his mouth and eyes.

From their portraits on dark panelled walls, past headmasters viewed the proceedings with a stately detachment. Their Victorian values of godliness and good learning had been swept away by two world wars and the pervasive tide of educational reform. They had been in their graves for more than a hundred years and what a twenty-first-century psychiatrist said could be no concern of theirs.

The portraits at the far end of the hall were evidently of more recent incumbents, for they were painted in increasingly differentiated styles, as if each subject wished to assert his own personality and record his contribution to the school. Sombre drapery of academic gowns, piled-up leather-bound classic texts and bibles gave way to bright familiarity against backgrounds resplendent with ambitious building projects. Lewis decided that the final painting must be of the current headmaster's immediate predecessor. His upraised hand was stretched forward to break out of the canvas, possibly protesting against his retirement to a Dorset cottage and the governorship of the local prep school.

Lewis watched his audience carefully as he waited to speak. A sea of wary teenaged expressions, wilting white shirts with crumpled ties, a smell of adolescent sweat and Lynx body spray. Well over a hundred boys in the cruelly uneven and haphazard process of becoming adults. Within the next few years perhaps a dozen of them would be knocking on a psychiatrist's door. Depression, obsessive compulsive disorders, schizophrenic illnesses – all these destroyers of the human mind could alight on any one of the unscarred young faces in front of him. For a moment his wife's image swam before him. Ursula had been just a year or two older than these boys.

He stood up. He must for this hour forget Ursula, his own fatal error of judgement, his guilt and endless responsibility.

'I'm a psychiatrist. Mostly viewed as dubious doctors with strange names – I've got one myself – pushing theories down gullible victims lying on couches. You'll be familiar with psychiatrists in films – they're usually dodgy charlatans or sinister mind dictators, the ruthless agents of a controlling state.'

He saw the teenage mask of assumed indifference lift as though acknowledging that he might be worth listening to, if only for a few minutes, but he found himself hesitating.

'So is a psychiatrist someone who tells the difference

between people who are mad and those who are sane, who decrees what is normal? But what *is* madness – and is sanity all it's cracked up to be?'

Easy rhetoric. Too easy. The stuff of journalists writing in the colour supplements, and here he was, churning it out to these boys. They deserved something more from him than this. For if Lewis was sure of anything, it was of the overwhelming value of his profession, and all that it might do to push back the darkness and confusion in human hearts. It was only at the end of the day, when he went home to his wife, that his own contribution to psychiatry changed colour and became futile.

'Why do we fear psychiatrists? Is it because we're frightened of ourselves?'

The sounds of Rachmaninov came into his head. *Rhapsody on the theme of Paganini.* Ursula sitting at the piano, her white-blond hair falling over her face, a tumult of sound and emotion, beautiful and drowning.

'The myth of mental illness,' he heard himself say. 'Isn't this what we all want to believe in?'

*

Clement Hunstrete settled back in his seat. The evening was going well, more than well. He'd introduced the lecturer and made his little welcome speech. Now his part in the proceedings was largely over. He breathed a sigh of relief which included a nod of congratulation to himself.

The Wharton Memorial Lecture was a long-standing tradition in the school calendar, being an annual event for the governors, Common Room and sixth form, together with a sprinkling of the town's intelligentsia or chattering classes, and each year featuring a different theme delivered by a so-called expert in the field. The occasion promoted the cultural prestige of the school, especially when someone particularly well-known could be enticed to 'give their time to inspire the youth of today', a phrase Clement often found useful. In these years he was able to enjoy a heightened sense of being part of the great and the good. Since Clement understood, at times too well for his peace of mind, that he must above everything else strive to bolster Wharton's reputation as a model public school, the evening had come to be a favourite with him.

Dr Lewis Auerbach was not a household name, but psychology was becoming one of the most over-subscribed of university degree courses, and was therefore regarded as a fruitful subject for the sixth formers. The success of last year, when the school had secured a popular politician, had been subsequently clouded by press allegations of his irregular private life. The local paper had thoughtfully reminded its readers that he had been a recent visitor to Wharton school, where fees were so much per year. The bursar, inclined to be sensitive since the fee-fixing scandal, had been especially annoyed; as usual they'd got the figure wrong.

It had been Alastair Garwood who'd pushed to have the wretched man, and he was a lightweight if ever there was one. Too busy charming everyone – no hinterland you could get hold of! Well, that was politics for you. It was impossible to touch pitch and not be defiled, and sleazy politicians were surely pitch.

This man here tonight was undoubtedly among the best of his profession, according to the inquiries he'd made. Lewis Auerbach had written a host of contributions to medical journals as well as having a best-selling book to his credit – Clement hadn't looked at it but had been reassured it wasn't written in the easy access style for which he entertained an entrenched distrust – and was evidently much sought after as an occasional lecturer at conferences and universities.

It had been a good move to get him down here, if he could

hold his audience. Sixth formers knew how to make things difficult. They had a way of covering up their own vulnerability by exposing other people's. Compassion wasn't yet in their repertoire.

Clement ran a headmasterly eye over particular boys who could be relied on to be tiresome. No funny business going on there. They were listening, and not even bothering to pretend they weren't. Dr Auerbach certainly had an impressive manner all of his own. He looked relaxed enough, though his watchful posture and clipped speech suggested both energy and an abrasive intelligence. He was of medium height only and unusually dark-haired, while his eyes as they scanned the audience appeared to be almost black. Well, that was after all the classic colouring of his Jewish ancestry. Add a beard, and Christ himself would have had much the same…even if artists throughout history had painted him with a pink skin and golden locks.

Britain had good reason to be grateful to the influx during the thirties of intellectual and highly-educated Jews, Clement reflected. They'd enriched the country in every branch of art and science and among them had been Jacob Auerbach, a refugee doctor from Holland who'd got away from the Nazis while he could. He'd lived to pioneer the work among the thousands of traumatised children in the post-war years, and become one of the most illustrious thinkers of his time. Now here was this man continuing in the same line as his grandfather. God's chosen people, you might well say.

Clement glanced again at the rows of sixth formers. Their attention – so often wayward and prone to heedless cruelty – was fixed on the speaker. Yes, Dr Auerbach had won the respect of the boys. He had the powerful presence boys always picked up on, and a good dose of unselfconscious authority. Questions had started, and he was cutting through the old chestnuts. Vincent van Gogh was coming into it, as he always did, a magnetic and romantic example of the casualties resulting from the world's attitude to madness.

The ubiquitous business of recreational drugs too. Was Dr Auerbach against cannabis? Clement took note of the boy who'd had the effrontery to ask that one. Oliver Benson, who'd hardly been at the school a month. He hadn't even stood up and was speaking in a drawl deliberately assumed, Clement told himself, to annoy the lecturer. Still, he'd miscalculated. Dr Auerbach cut the question off; he kept his voice disinterested and avoided being hijacked into repressive adult negativity versus creative and open-minded youth. Full marks to him.

Once again, Wharton's headmaster congratulated himself. This man was able to deal with any of the trickier and lewd questions that would inevitably follow. As far as Clement was concerned, Freud had a lot to answer for.

SEVEN

Lewis drove home, asking if he'd wasted the evening. He was reaching the age when he was becoming more aware of the shortness of time – and perhaps the limits of his own energy. A man in his twenties may sample the delights of life on offer, and yet not feel he is wasting a precious resource. Taking things up and then discarding them when they brought no rewards of fulfilment or pleasure was part of being young. The advancement of self-knowledge lay along these paths.

But Lewis knew this was no longer the case with him. He was at the end of his thirties, and had reached the top of his profession. His work both absorbed and fuelled a fierce energy and ambition. He must always learn more, understand better, forbid any frittering away of time spent on anything that didn't directly contribute to the demands made on him by the life he'd chosen. Twenty years of hard graft lay behind him, and there were perhaps another twenty ahead.

They would not be less hard because he was a consultant, established and secure of earning more money than for some years he'd known properly what to do with. Nobody in any branch of medicine could afford to sit back for one moment; change was happening too fast. As to the money, he'd found a way out of that and trusted it was the right way – and the necessity of keeping it secret.

Psychiatry itself was challenged on every front, with the expanding roles of psychologists and therapists as well as the flood of new mood-changing drugs eroding its position within modern medicine. It was having to fight its corner. Lewis believed passionately in the fight – and the cause. It was the reason he accepted invitations like the one tonight.

General practitioners couldn't be expected to spot mental illness in their crowded waiting rooms and rushed appointments. They didn't have the time or the knowledge. People needed more attention paid to them, and they needed it from doctors who had made a special study of the mind.

It was the terrifying pressure to respond to so much need, this was what haunted him, what drove him on. Where were the hours to see all the patients trapped in wretched, despairing lives? To give even the beginnings of enough time to them, he must live in such a way that he wasted none of his own.

Had any of those spiky adolescents got anything from their two hours in that lecture hall? Only a handful had spoken up at the end, but this was to be expected. There would have been other boys relying on someone else asking their question for them, not wanting to risk mockery in the harsh spotlight of the occasion.

Certainly they'd cared enough to listen. He'd an idea, mined from his own childhood, that this was enough at their age. To learn to recognise some signals about what was worth finding out in life. His job was to create the kind of ferment in their minds that led them into asking questions, and to go on asking them. It wasn't to give neat answers. That meant leaving out too much.

Finality always made Lewis uneasy.

He was later than he'd meant to be. That reception after the lecture with the headmaster wanting to parade him about! It had been a tiresome affair. He'd have been better talking to some of the boys. But it never went like that at establishments like Wharton – or anywhere at all come to that. There always had to be a social show tacked on, an occasion made of the thing. Lewis wished there wasn't. Too much eating and drinking in the grand manner was another distraction that swallowed up too much time. Time he hadn't got.

Lewis put his foot down hard on the accelerator. He was driving too fast, but the roads were almost empty. He must get home to Ursula. Only just over the limit. Some rules he broke – and told himself it was in order to keep the one big one in his life.

She was waiting up for him, wearing the dusky pink dressing gown he'd given her last year. It clung round her slim body, adding to the waifish air which she'd never lost. Once that look had held a gamine charm; now it was disturbing, like a child with a premature aging disease. She was more than four years younger than he was, but her blue pool eyes were those of an old woman peering into the next world.

He took her into his arms, looking down into her face for the usual signs.

'How have you been?'

'Watching *The Hours*. Feeling the cold of the river when she drowned herself. I played the music – '

She wanted to punish him, to make him afraid. He'd grown used to it. It shouldn't hurt any more – but it did.

'Tomorrow will you play me the Schumann sonata instead? It's beautiful and you know how I love hearing you. But let's go upstairs – '

'To make a baby! Don't think you can trick me like that, I can hear your plans, all the lies you tell me, they talk to me in my head – '

Without warning she twisted away from him and started screaming.

'Darling, it's very late.'

'You have to listen to my music *now*.'

Argument was impossible with her, he knew well. If persuasion didn't work – and its success was usually random, defying his attempts to systematise the occasions of failure – no amount of reasoning would alter her course. Her illness had made her entirely self-absorbed; the feelings of others didn't enter her calculations. As she sat down at the piano, he brooded over this phrase, which was all wrong, for surely Ursula didn't make calculations at all.

He watched her languidly picking out the notes. In the early days of their marriage she'd played not with the trained care of the diligently-taught child who has worked her way through the grades, but with a passionate intensity he knew now he'd mistaken for something like musical genius.

He listened with the attention he was always careful to show, wanting to believe in the healing power of the music, but not really doing so, for he knew she didn't believe in it either. That too was being taken away from them. She played randomly, erratically, as if the concentration needed to read music was too much of a demand. He saw her wavering fingers trying for an elusive chord, and was ready with his comfort when it evaded her. She tried again, and then again, drooping on the piano stool, before slamming both hands on the keys with a crash of discordant sound.

'If you hadn't come back,' she said, her voice becoming flat and disconnected, 'I would have killed myself. I was counting the ways I could do it – '

'I always come back.'

'One day you'll find I've gone. Run right away from you. You'd like that, wouldn't you?'

He'd heard it all many times.

'My darling,' he said. 'I never want you to do that.'

'You try to control me, to get power over me, but you're waiting for when you can get rid of me, you'd like me to vanish out of your life – '

She began to weep but almost noiselessly, and he stroked her white-blond hair, murmuring endearments into it. After a few minutes her body became less rigid, and she leant her head against him. One finger picked out an arpeggio, the notes plaintive and despairing.

He took her hand in his and closed the piano. Every part of him was tired. Her hold on reality often wavered; the evening had clearly contained those murmurings of the threat that lay heavy over them, dark clouds gathering over their days and nights. Monday would come; he would leave her with a renewed twist of fear in his heart. Yet mixed in with his fatigue he was thankful for the present moment: he could be at home with her tomorrow.

Lewis never blamed his wife. He'd seen in his own patients over and over again how a suicidal individual will take no account of the effect their actions might have on other people. The breakdown of the normal functioning of the mind closed off understanding. Patients might appear callous, careless about hurting the people they professed to love. Lewis knew about these failures of empathy. He knew that the patient has little control over them. He also knew they were sometimes catastrophic, for they might remove the last barrier to suicide.

Schizophrenia attacks around one per cent of the population worldwide… Schizophrenia is where the mind splinters inexorably into fragments….Schizophrenia is not the split personality of popular culture but the destruction of the mind… Around ten per cent of sufferers will eventually kill themselves…

'We'll have a good day together,' he said.

They climbed the stairs, his arm around his wife's shoulders, his mind returning to the Wharton lecture hall. Had he done something for those boys? In his tiredness he told himself he'd wasted his time. Trying too hard – shouldn't he of all men know it was unavailing? Then he remembered the boy who had asked the last question, afraid of being laughed at, but speaking out all the same. It had been the most important question of the evening. If nothing else, he thought his encounter with that boy made the visit to Wharton worthwhile.

Beside him, Ursula murmured something, but Lewis was back at Wharton and heard only the boy's voice, arranged to sound casual: 'Is suicide always selfish?'

Lewis registered the faintest hint of a stammer. He too had once stammered. These days he had almost total control. Months might go by and then suddenly, unexpectedly, he would be caught out and interrupt a surprised expression on the face of a patient or colleague. Now there was this question he would have wished to avoid. He must not do so.

'Suicide can be understood as a way of expressing what is experienced by the person concerned as unbearable pain. When someone is in that kind of pain he becomes incapable of seeing anything beyond it. Can he be called selfish for that?'

He considered the boy's shuttered face, checked for signs. Take this slowly, keep it detached, he needs you to make it clear to everyone that this is just an intellectual debate.

'Studies show that about half the population have suicidal thoughts at some time in their lives. So such thoughts are not unusual.'

'They're in Dante's circles of hell –'

A ripple of adolescent mirth. Lewis ignored it. He'd noticed the chapel leading off the quad. There must be a resident chaplain at a school like this. What line did he take, what kind of help did he give to the boys? Did they talk to him, really talk to him – or could he only offer them the inadequate fare of so much religious teaching? How many of them suffered, silently and desperately, within the privileged world they inhabited?

It'll be worse if I talk down to him. He's one of those anxious, clever boys, thinking about too much for his age. Don't run away from the truth because that's what he's asking for.

'Medieval writers like Dante thought of suicide as self-murder, prompted by the devil. We know better than that now, we know that many people who commit suicide are suffering from some form of mental illness. That's the problem, the real tragedy – people believing no change for the better is possible, that there's no other escape. Good mental health care might have helped them to see that their feelings come from a distorted view of their own past life, which makes them feel trapped and hopeless about the future.'

Lewis stared around at these teenagers, still on the edge of their childhood. His heart ached for the boy with the stammer. What was he, sixteen, seventeen? He could be his son.

'For the storm does eventually pass; doctors *can* help and there *will be*, in time, a way out of the darkness.'

Now he tightened his arms around the girl he'd married when he'd been little more than a boy himself, and kissed her very gently on the forehead.

A psychiatrist is a doctor of the soul, his grandfather had believed. It was too late to argue with him now.

EIGHT

Nell shut her eyes, longing to go to sleep altogether, so that the rest of the journey would disappear into oblivion and she could wake up just as they arrived back at Wharton around supper time. The forty or so boys sitting behind her in the coach wouldn't notice, being wholly taken up with stuffing themselves with chocolate bars and bursting crisp packets in each other's ears.

But Trevor Faversham was brooding silently beside her. As the head of the art department he was likely to feel aggrieved if she didn't pretend to be doing her bit in watching out for any excessive bad behaviour. It had been nice of him to have asked her along to help on this trip when she was only part-time.

She certainly hadn't pulled her weight over discipline. She ought to stay awake now and keep a firm eye – even though firmness was usually beyond her. The boys knew it, but Nell didn't mind. They were good-hearted boys. Most of the time.

'Go halves on this with me, Mrs Garwood?'

It was Oliver Benson. A half-wrapped Mars bar was thrust over her shoulder. She turned round to smile at him. It was impossible not to find Oliver endearing even though it was quite clear that despite considerable talent he was doing AS level art because it was seen as a soft option. He'd only come on the trip because it was less boring than a weekend at Wharton since the most recent crackdown on under-age drinking in local pubs.

'No thanks, Oliver. It's very sweet of you though.' She looked him in the eye and tried to sound like the rigorous and effective person she was not. 'I hope you feel you learnt something from the weekend. I'll look forward to seeing some results in your work.'

Oliver bit off a mouthful of chocolate. With those light blue eyes and gleaming blond hair he was impudently good-looking, and quite certainly knew it. 'I expect you're feeling tired,' he said kindly.

Nell giggled. She liked it when the boys teased her. That was another thing Trevor couldn't understand.

'I'm back!' she called, something over an hour later, as she pushed open the front door.

'Hello darling.' Alastair stood in the kitchen doorway carrying a half-empty glass of wine. 'You should have let me pick you up from the coach. I've opened the bottle at just the right moment. I'll pour you a drink.'

'Where are the children?'

'Upstairs – give them a shout. I'm afraid Rachel's in a grump. Doesn't want anything to eat.'

'What happened? Is Sebastian all right?'

'He helped himself to something and went up to do some work just a few minutes ago. You go and find them, and then come and relax. I've put that pie you left – it looks very exciting darling – into the oven, so you haven't got to do anything about supper.'

'Except clear away lunch and lay the table,' said Nell, glancing around the kitchen and laughing, because she was so pleased to be home and the kitchen was hardly ever tidy anyway.

Alastair laughed too and poured her a glass of wine. There didn't seem to be much left in the bottle.

'You've been a quick drinker. Didn't you say you'd just opened this?' Nell teased, leaning over to give him a kiss.

'Well – 'Alastair gave her the delightfully sidelong grin he handed out so easily. 'I was waiting for you after all.'

'I'll go and see the children. Why have I been imagining them running down the stairs to greet me, like in an old-fashioned film? I suppose I ought to be cheered they've missed me so little. I'm not as indispensable as I thought I was.'

'Far from it,' said Alastair, pushing her gently towards the stairs. 'Hurry up and say hello to them darling, and then we can have supper. I'll open another bottle.'

Rachel's bedroom door was shut. Nell opened it slowly, as she always did, feeling that this was a reasonable compromise between knocking (smacking of obsequious parental timidity) and bursting in (violating what Nell saw as everyone's reasonable right to privacy).

'How was the weekend darling?'

Nell bent over the desk and kissed the top of her daughter's head since Rachel didn't swing round on her chair, or jump up to hug her. The computer screen, Nell saw, had gone blank.

'Shit.'

'Did you have fun having supper with Auntie Juliet and Vail last night?'

'Fun's not the word I'd choose.'

'I'm sure you got a good meal anyway,' persevered Nell, finding to her dismay she was adopting the bright tone she always loathed when other people used it. 'Auntie Juliet's a much better cook than I am. Did she make her amazing Italian chicken thing?'

'She's not Auntie Juliet. Why d'you have to keep calling her that? Just because she's your so-called friend doesn't mean she's our bloody aunt.'

'All right, point taken. You *are* getting too old – but it's a habit I haven't got myself out of.'

'You never do get out of stupid habits like that.' Rachel got up slowly from her chair, and went over to the window. 'I'm going to have a bath, if that's all right with you.'

'Yes, of course. But what about supper? Dad said you weren't hungry.'

'Well – so I'm not. What's it got to do with him?'

'Come down and have something after your bath then darling, if you feel like it.'

'Can I have my room to myself in the meantime?' Rachel yanked the curtains more closely shut, swerving away from contact.

'I'll go and say hello to Sebastian.'

It was silly minding about teenage moods. Nell went along the passage to Sebastian's bedroom. Rachel had obviously had a bad weekend. Probably a spat with one of her friends. For a moment Nell was tempted to snoop, but she put the thought away quickly. If Rachel ever thought she was being spied on, she would freeze her out altogether.

Sebastian must have heard her coming, because he came running out of his room. Nell clutched him to her.

'Darling! I've missed you! Tell me how you've been.'

'Hungry. Dad isn't such a good cook as you are.'

'I'm glad I have my uses,' said Nell, disentangling herself and smiling at the collection of mugs and an empty cereal bowl on Sebastian's floor. 'But you look as though you've scavenged for yourself okay.'

'What? Oh those. Well, I had to. I knew you wouldn't hassle. Last night we had a really early supper at Auntie Juliet's and around nine Dad said we should come back, so we did, and Vail came too to watch a film. But actually it was unfair because Dad stayed on for another drink. And I hope you don't mind but Vail stayed the night in the end.'

'You know I don't – I'm always pleased to have him. But I hope Dad roped in one of the sixth form boarders to keep you company. I don't like you being on your own late at night.'

'*Mum*! We're perfectly safe. Rachel'll be fourteen in May. And don't forget I'm twelve now.'

'Well, did he?'

'Yeah, Timothy came. The scholarship one who can't get his words out. He's nice but he just read all the time.'

'I believe he's terribly shy. What was the film – was it good?'

'It was all right.' Sebastian ignored the first part of the question. 'Vail brought it.'

Vail always did bring the films, the music, the computer games. Why was Sebastian so passive, always the one on the receiving end, never initiating anything for himself? He seemed so much younger than Vail in every way, but he was nearly a whole year older. Were friendships often like this, the leader and the led? Did it matter?

'And Rachel was okay?' Nell asked this hesitatingly, feeling it was unfair to interrogate Sebastian. She must never encourage the children to betray each other. Their close loyalty was one of the best things about the family. She added, to make it easier for him, 'Didn't she like the film?'

'She didn't watch it.' Sebastian piled a couple of mugs into the cereal bowl. 'She said she'd got her, you know, girls' thing.'

So that was it. Nell felt relieved. Rachel was still all over the place with her periods, becoming moody, tearful and most of all, angry with Nell. It was bad luck it had come the one weekend she'd been away. It would be no good trying to make her eat some supper the way she was at the moment, but a hot bath would help. Later she'd take her up a comforting drink with some painkillers, and maybe one of the chocolate sponge puddings which Nell still bought and Rachel left untouched.

Sebastian nudged her, evidently feeling the attention was no longer on him.

'Can I come down and have Rachel's share of the pie with you and Dad?'

'Yes, you greedy pig. Come on now or Dad'll have drunk all the wine.'

'He was plastered last night,' said Sebastian dispassionately. 'At least it looked like it.'

'Oh dear. Well, I can assure you I didn't get drunk in Paris, and Mr Faversham didn't either, though I suppose he might have wanted to.'

She thought back to the tedious hour they'd spent together after their dinner out at a Moroccan restaurant with the boys. They'd sat in the hotel lobby, spinning out a couple of glasses of cheap French wine and keeping one eye on the front door to make sure no boys sneaked out in search of more sophisticated nightlife.

Trevor was more unattractive than any man had a right to be, she found herself thinking, disappointment making her unkind. For the first time she thoroughly sympathised with his wife who'd run off a couple of terms ago. His regurgitated philosophy from his days at art school and clichés about post-modernism must have become too stultifying to live with.

She escaped to her cramped room and lay down on the hard single bed and tiny sausage pillow. Paris was for lovers, not humourless men boring on and paying graceless compliments. She remembered a weekend staying on the Left Bank when she'd first met Alastair. This wasn't a city for sleeping alone. You needed to be young and awash with romance, seizing your partner into your arms under the plane trees of the great boulevards, kissing with shameless and abandoned passion, oblivious of everyone but the person whose face was your whole world.

But now, as Nell trailed down the stairs with Sebastian, she asked herself if Trevor Faversham too felt unsure of where life was taking him, or even what it was he wanted. Was this the real reason why she longed for another baby – because babies and small children offered uncomplicated and uncritical love?

NINE

Eleanor Hunstrete, who ought to have been arranging the table for the dinner party for assorted governors and members of the Common Room at the headmaster's house that evening, was instead drinking tea with Sue North, the wife of the deputy head. The two of them were cosily ensconced in armchairs in Sue's sitting room and only very spasmodically giving any attention to the evening ahead.

Eleanor had been giving dinners of this kind for so long that the prospect rarely disturbed her. She wasn't even doing the cooking herself, having been persuaded by Clement that one of the few perks of the headmaster's job was to preside over a dinner table in perfect confidence about the food. If some wives would have taken umbrage at the implication behind Clement's decree, Eleanor was not among them. She was only too thankful and thoroughly enjoyed scrutinising lists of menus from first class caterers and feeling like a lady in an Edwardian country house.

'I need a buffer to keep the more tiresome elements apart,' she said now, half distracted by Sue's new Sanderson loose covers. 'Now why can't I make wonderful upholstery like you?'

'You do other things.' This was the kind of cheering remark Sue always came up with and she never implied – as she might have done – what other things? For although Eleanor had gained the top first in her year for English at Oxford, it hadn't led to anything more than writing for a literary journal on forgotten and neglected authors. With modern readers mostly preferring to leave them in obscurity, her work was dwindling to occasional editing, and tutoring Oxbridge candidates at Wharton's all-girls comprehensive school. Their eldest son Tom had started his second year at Oxford and George was away in Africa on his gap year. There was only Petrarch, their golden retriever, and Clement left – and perhaps only Petrarch really needed her now.

'I expect it's too late to learn,' she said comfortably. 'Another lengthy evening eating too much, and not being able to take one's shoes off under the table. Sometimes I wonder whether entertaining people achieves anything.'

'Public relations, oiling the wheels – '

'And the Morpeths are coming which is embarrassing. When I was put next to Neville Morpeth at last year's Sussex schools do and remarked that I didn't think we'd ever met, he said in a very sarcastic manner that actually they'd been to stay with us!'

'You could try learning one of those tricks which are supposed to help with remembering things.'

'It was also very unfair, as it was his wife who sent me a thank you letter which started off with *Dear* followed by a space. She must have meant to ask him what my name was, but then forgot and sealed up the envelope. So these things *can* happen to all of us.'

Sue scanned the list of names Eleanor had given her in the manner of a games mistress sizing up suitability for the school lacrosse team.

'It's quite simple if you go by the principle of allowing each guest pleasure on one side and duty on the other.'

Eleanor sighed.

'You would have made a much better headmaster's wife than I am.'

'Nonsense!'

'You'd have brought out the best in people like hostesses are meant to be able to do. And you wouldn't have had people looking at you as if you're not all there. Nor would you have a dog who disembowelled visitors' shoes.'

Eleanor didn't really regret this last, caring a great deal more for the pleasures of Petrarch than the sensibilities of guests who must take their chance with elderly retrievers.

'Still, I must do my duty in the sphere of life to which God has called me, like characters in Trollope are always being told.'

'Very sensible advice,' agreed Sue firmly, not bothering to argue with Eleanor's compliments, the truth of which had long since been tacitly acknowledged between them.

'But as to your scheme' – Eleanor reverted to her troubled dinner table – 'the mathematics don't always work out so easily, when there are far more duty than pleasure people to be fitted around the table.'

'Put the plainest and dullest ladies next to Alastair Garwood then. He'll make them feel they're the most attractive women in the room.'

'Mmm. He's certainly got that knack.'

'All things to all women. Not always a quality to be trusted in a husband,' said Sue, who having been head girl at her boarding school forty years ago had never quite lost the language of her years of authority. 'He's blessed with undeniable sex appeal and the kind of charm that gets him everywhere he wants without trying. People like that have never had to develop any more sterling qualities.'

'They may have them all the same,' protested Eleanor. 'We've never had any evidence that Alastair is anything other than just exceptionally nice.'

'Jim let something drop recently. One of his more ambiguous remarks. But he'd got it from Trevor Faversham, and we all know where his interests lie.'

'Nell?'

'He didn't have the wit to keep his own wife from running off, but that doesn't stop him hanging round hopefully after someone else's.'

'I jolly well hope you're wrong. I always feel I must look out for Nell since finding out I was at school with her mother. Nell's never said anything about Trevor – they went on the sixth form art trip together didn't they?'

'Even a man as obtuse as he is wouldn't push his luck then. Nell never sees what's under her nose. She doesn't pick up on men being attracted to her – or else she doesn't want to.'

'Isn't that what's rather appealing about her?' said Eleanor. 'Most women work hard to win admiration from all quarters, as though they're taking part in a competition. You'd be the first to say married women shouldn't notice such things, let alone act on them.'

'Exactly. It doesn't occur to Nell to misbehave and so she's entirely unsuspicious about everyone else.'

'It's to be hoped she is just now anyway, what with Rachel hitting teenage troubles. Don't show your surprise too obviously, but I did try to boss her into taking Rachel to see that Dr Auerbach who gave the Wharton lecture. She's worrying herself to death. I was suddenly inspired by the idea that he didn't come here for nothing, it must have been *meant*, in the way things are.'

'Did Nell agree? I can't see Alastair liking it.'

'Not sure. Mind you, her friend Juliet has probably been helpful. I have a feeling she works for some government body that advises on mental health issues. Don't you hate the way that word creeps into everything these days? And nothing coming from the government can be trusted, since the days of You Know Who. But did Jim say anything in particular? Don't tell me if you shouldn't – ' Eleanor added, in a half-hearted attempt to preserve the fiction that as Wharton's senior wives they were above petty Common Room gossip.

'Only about Trevor remarking that Alastair looked too pleased with himself and he could guess the reason. Jim ascribed it to jealousy.'

'I want to go on believing in Alastair as a hero. We do *need* them. Oh dear, why do people have to run after each other when they shouldn't?'

'We can't control our feelings but we can certainly control our actions. It's just that we don't want to.'

Eleanor made a face.

'People may be so carried away by passion they can't help themselves,' she said, but more to provoke Sue than from any conviction.

'Twaddle! And are affairs actually about love of the romantic high-flown kind you're talking about? I'd have said they're more from boredom and general dissatisfaction with life.'

'People meet and fall in love – even across a crowded room,' persisted Eleanor, 'I don't think they wake up one morning and think to themselves, I'm bored, I'm going to start an affair today.'

'Not consciously, no. But there must be a readiness, an openness of mind which then leads to something starting.'

'So why do perfectly nice people have affairs then?'

'Because they're greedy.' Sue put the cups back onto the tea tray with a firm hand.

'All the same, I do think it would be nice to be tempted,' said Eleanor in a regretful tone. 'There would be all the satisfaction of virtuously turning away like a heroine in a Victorian novel. Not that they always did. But nobody has ever *tried* to have an affair with me.'

'Be thankful for it. Think of all the unhappiness you're saving yourself. Stick to a few harmless daydreams and don't ever think you'd be happier if they became reality. I expect even safe husbands like Clement and Jim let their imaginations off the lead occasionally.'

Eleanor tried unsuccessfully to imagine Jim having fantasies of the obvious male variety. She pictured him in his winceyette pyjamas carefully washing his teeth before climbing into bed, and began to laugh.

'I ought to get back – '

'Yes, go and do the seating plan while the spirit is upon you. Why not put Nell on Clement's other side? It'll feel like a compliment to her and it'll do him good.'

'It's a little hard on poor Nell.' Eleanor pushed her feet back into her scuffed shoes and stood up reluctantly. 'Though Clement would certainly like it. And perhaps they could discuss medieval painters – yes, that would be it. There would be fertile ground there.'

TEN

'Take Rachel to a shrink? What on earth for?'

It was turning out as Nell had guessed – and why she'd put off asking Alastair.

The dinner party at the Hunstretes the previous week had been surprisingly enjoyable. The headmaster had subdued his customary vagueness, exerting himself to be more pleasant than she had ever seen him; they'd discussed favourite artists and books in a very satisfying manner. Eleanor had been as she always was, interested in everything, full of unceremonious scatty kindness, and asking her in a quiet moment if she'd thought any more about taking Rachel to Dr Auerbach.

Now Nell hovered by the kitchen worktop, half thinking about the supper she ought to be cooking and wishing she hadn't started the discussion. Alastair, drinking Merlot at the kitchen table, was already putting up that sheen of invisible armour about himself which was always a prelude to him sliding away from engagement.

'I can't bear to go on like this – seeing her *withdrawing* from us.'

'Darling, she's a teenager now. They all start to go off their parents, it's standard practice.'

'I don't mind that too much.' She knew this wasn't true as she said it. She did mind dreadfully. She hadn't gone off her own mother, she'd deserted her. It still hurt whenever she thought of it and just now she was thinking of it too much. 'But she's *unhappy* – '

'And isn't it likely that most teenagers go through patches of unhappiness? You told me you did yourself. She'll get over it.'

'How do you know? It's been too long already.'

'My sister was just the same at her age, always sulking, or so my mother maintains.'

Nell said nothing. She didn't like Alastair's sister, a merchant banker who was so aggressively successful and capable that she made Nell feel stupid. There was no way she was going to admit any family likeness to Rachel.

'It's more serious than a mood. I'm frightened by her at times.'

'Oh darling! If you feel like that, then take her to the doctor. No call for more than that surely. You don't need me to come along, do you?'

Nell opened the fridge and pretended to search for something inside it. She *did* want Alastair to come with her. More than that, part of her argued he ought to *want* to come with her. She said, trying not to sound sulky and childish, 'Not if you're too busy.'

'Why have you suddenly come up with this anyway? Nothing's happened has it?'

'No, of course not. But I can't go on worrying and not knowing what's going on.'

'Going on?'

'What she's thinking, I mean, and why she won't eat like she used to – and why she's so sullen and secretive. She's been deleting the history on her computer which makes me think she's been accessing things she shouldn't.'

I ought to have repeated to Alastair everything Hilary told me. But I can't. It's all mixed up with going into Alastair's study behind his back. Hilary's phone call was my punishment.

'Are you sure about that? Darling, you should have said. Though I don't see she's likely to talk to Dr Royce any more than you, except that he must be used to this kind of thing.'

Nell opened up a mixed bag of peppers and tipped them onto the chopping board. She steeled herself to be obstinate.

'She needs more than that. What can Dr Royce say that would help? GPs don't have time to deal with problems like this. They have ten minute slots, and if you take longer the next person is kept waiting, and glares when you come out of the doctor's room.'

'Why care about that? For God's sake Nell, why do you always look at things the wrong way? What does it matter if an old dear with a leaking bladder or a fatty mother with her overfed children have to wait?'

'Well, I know it doesn't much – ' Nell stared unseeingly at the peppers, aware that as usual she was losing her way with irrelevant details, and tried to retrace her steps. 'I just think it would be better to get a referral to see someone who knows about teenage depression and things like that.'

'*Does* anyone know? We don't want to get ourselves tangled up with some cranky pop psychologist.'

'No, not that certainly.' Nell saw her opportunity and took it. 'I want to take her to see Dr Auerbach.'

'The guy who gave the Wharton lecture?'

'Yes, why not? He's meant to be a brilliant child psychiatrist and – '

'Hang on. I don't suppose you can just get an appointment with a specialist of your own choosing. The NHS doesn't work like that.'

'I know. We'd have to pay. He has a private practice on top of his NHS work.'

There was a silence which she didn't like. Alastair poured himself another drink.

'Have you any idea what that would cost? You wouldn't get away with just one appointment. Don't tell me these people don't charge astronomic fees because I'll bet it'll be triple figures for every half hour they give you.'

It's not you, it's us, Nell wanted to say. But she was uncomfortably aware that she contributed far less than Alastair to the family budget and therefore had less right to say how money should be spent. Then she remembered the thousand pounds and something of resentful anger crept into her heart. Her knowledge dangled before her as a weapon which could be used.

'Alastair, did you give the money to Juliet for the Wharton deposit before I suggested it?'

Her face always let her down. She was never able to wrong-foot people. She wasn't quick-witted enough. Alastair gave her his rueful smile.

'Did Juliet give me away then? Darling, I'm sorry if I overstepped the mark. I was so sure it was what you would want to do for her that I just went ahead and did it. I can see I ought to have waited.'

'So Juliet told you about sending Vail to Wharton before she said anything to me. How do you think that makes me feel? The two of you sharing secrets behind my back?'

'She was only sounding me out on the quiet about Wharton scholarships, on the grounds that I'd know more than you – Nell, there's nothing unreasonable about that.'

'I wish I'd known,' Nell said slowly. 'And that you'd said something at the time.'

'I was stupid not to. Bad judgement on my part. You can imagine how relieved and happy I was when you came bursting into the bedroom that day suggesting exactly the same thing.'

'Did you ask Juliet to say nothing about it to me? Is that why she didn't think to mention it when she told me about Vail going to Wharton?'

'Darling, don't let's quarrel about it, I was really trying to do the best for you both. Please forgive me for jumping the gun and making trouble.'

It occurred to her that Alastair knew how to glide out of uncomfortable situations by pretending he was making things easier for everyone else. He carried it off with so much charm that you didn't notice until later. Rebellion rose up in her but she couldn't bring herself to probe any further. Husbands and wives had to get over discovering things they didn't like in each other and concentrate on all that was good and loveable.

'I suppose I'm just feeling hurt. More about Juliet than you.'

'She's *your* special friend darling, not mine. You might have felt you couldn't ask me to do this for her – and I was wrong about that.'

'You know I never feel I can't ask you things.'

'Well then. It *is* important to do what you can for friends. You were right all along.'

There was another silence. What else could she say? He'd taken the ground from underneath her feet. How could she ever tell him now that she'd searched through the bank statement? Their whole conversation had been like one of those dramatic irony scenes in a play when the audience knows something the actors don't.

What was the point of saying, part of me wishes we hadn't given the money if it means we haven't got it for Rachel? It was mean-spirited, and Alastair had never made her feel that. And she'd *wanted* Juliet to have the money. At least she had at the time. Wasn't she trying to have it both ways?

Alastair's reckless prodigality was one of the things she'd always loved about him. He always gave without counting the cost to himself and sometimes surprisingly. The right hand should give away money without the left hand knowing about it

– Martin had said something like that in a chapel sermon not long ago.

She remembered the way she'd dashed at sharing her idea with Alastair. Now she wondered at herself. Had she in truth been so eager to be open-handed to Juliet because she wanted to be the same to herself over having another baby?

'You're more generous than me,' she burst out at last.

'Now you're being silly. Come here. That's the kind of generosity *I* want.'

'Alastair – not now.' She rummaged unsuccessfully in the drawer for the little serrated knife to cut up the peppers.

'That super-sharp vegetable knife's disappeared – I must have thrown it away with the potato peelings last night. It's the only one we have with a decent pointed end.'

'Can't you buy another? Maybe you took it to scrape paint off Martin's portrait or something. It's a pity you're not getting paid for that. It's very good and you've caught the likeness all right.'

'Have I?' Nell was doubtful. She knew that there was something missing about the way the portrait had developed, something she wasn't seeing.

'Yes, it's got him to a tee. I've got a very talented wife. We must get you some more commissions somehow. Take your mind off worrying about Rachel.'

They were getting away from what Nell wanted to talk about. Alastair wasn't disagreeing with her or denying her anything, but he was distracting her until she'd lost track of her argument. She hardened her heart against him.

'Shall I see if I can get a referral to Dr Auerbach?'

'Sweetheart, I think we ought to give it a bit of thought before we do anything rash. We've got our summer holiday in America to pay for. We don't want to leave ourselves short for that.'

'There's still some of the money left from those sheep paintings I sold last summer.' Nell found another knife in the drawer, and began to hack at the peppers.

'Darling! That wouldn't begin to cover it. Once these people get hold of you, the bills will keep coming in. Do we really want to squander money on over-paid private consultants when a family holiday in America will do Rachel far more good? Do think about it rationally.'

'I *have* thought about it,' Nell said stubbornly. She and Alastair (almost) never had rows. She prayed this wasn't going to spiral into one.

'Then she's meant to be going with Rosie on their school skiing trip after Christmas, isn't she? That's something for her to look forward to.'

'Yes, but I'm worried about that too,' said Nell, distracted now by another anxiety which had occurred to her. 'Being away from home for the first time without us, and you know how she hates leaving Sebastian.'

'That's easily solved. Why don't we say he can go to Aviemore on that children's snowboarding holiday club that Juliet's sending Vail on? Rachel's hardly going to mind leaving him if he's not here anyway. Then both kids are sorted, and we can have that second honeymoon we've always wanted.'

He was looking at her with the expression she remembered from their first meeting, the one which told her how completely he admired and desired her. It never failed to lift her up into what passed for happiness and it did so now.

'You know what it is,' he said, draining his glass and coming to stand close behind her, 'you're too fearful. Some things are best left to sort themselves out without interference – ten to one they do without getting all stirred up.'

She wanted to believe him. He started kissing the back of her neck. Resistance to him melted as it always did.

'Too good a mother as well. Come on, why don't we give ourselves a treat? Leave those peppers or whatever you're making, and go for supper at that new Italian place in the High Street?'

'Rachel'll refuse to eat anything.'

But he took her in his arms and within a few minutes she found herself calling the children. He was both impulsive and extravagant and too often confounded her with his easy optimism. She knew this, yet still she responded to his embrace. Was this because she was afraid of where an open quarrel might lead? Nell shrank from the cowardice that had been her persistent companion for too long. She'd think about it another time.

Unanswered questions lay in the air between them, but Alastair was her husband and the father of her children, and she'd never yet allowed herself to question her love for him.

ELEVEN

Martin had gone to the Wharton lecture after all. Not because he wanted to, but simply because when the moment came, it was preferable to sitting alone with his thoughts.

He hadn't heard much of it. He'd chosen a seat near one of the doors, reserved for latecomers, ill at ease, poised to escape if he had to. He tried to make himself concentrate, and castigated himself for his inability to do so, for here was a man who ought to be listened to. But in the same room was Oliver Benson, and the air stale with old dirt and secrets.

Oliver Benson asked a question designed to wrong-foot the lecturer. That was all part of him, the ceaseless wish to make life harder for those around him, simply for the pleasure it brought. The sea of white shirts in front of Martin's eyes began to swirl like clouds.

'So where d'you live then, Darrow?'

' – that's where Clavering lives – hey, Clavering – '

'Darrow's the shoe shop in the High Street – '

'Your dad's shoes are common – '

He was back more than thirty years; he was in the dormitory his first night at Wharton, this terrifying hell where his brains had won him a free place. A local industrialist's philanthropic scheme to send a handful of gifted working class children to England's exclusive public schools offered dizzy pinnacles to his proud mother and father; to him it offered ostracism and having his head stuffed down the toilets. Fox, Vickers, Wentworth-Jones; they surrounded him like starlings jabbing at a crust. His pocket money stolen from him, his clothes stripped off him, his body beaten, burnt, cut, water tipped nightly into his bed; this was what his brains had brought to him.

All this – and the other thing, the thing Benson had done to him, which he could not think about even now without fear and shame. Glazed ice-cold blue eyes a few inches from his own, taut lips drawn back, muscled hands pulling away his games shorts. Quick, hot breaths which became his own and he was left alone until the next time. Then, at the end of the summer term, Benson left, covered in school honours, to go to Sandhurst and the army. After that the starlings found other younger crusts and the abuse so expertly and relentlessly instigated by Benson died out.

Why had he never told anyone? Why had he accepted such treatment as his due – never made any attempt to expose Benson, leaving him free to select future victims? He didn't know. He still didn't know. Could anyone understand the workings of the thirteen-year-old mind, when dormitory life was ruled by such rituals as who could sustain the longest erection?

A new headmaster had come to the school, an ordained academic, who overturned its culture of overdeveloped bodies and underdeveloped souls. Rugger Buggers were kings no longer. As Martin moved up the school he began his search for a different God; he found a place amongst boys who were as quiet and reflective as himself.

His parents, intimidated by his free place at Wharton, had hardly dared set foot in it themselves. They'd known they didn't belong and made no attempt to try. To their way of thinking Wharton was an awe-inspiring place fit only for people far above them.

For five years he moved between two entirely separate worlds. Home and his father's shoe shop, with its smell of leather and stacks of green and white boxes, slowly shrank in his mind as Wharton, deep-rooted in its historic traditions and scholarly ethos, consumed his imagination.

Above all, he fell in love with the chapel, its golden grey walls rising high and pure, upright as hope against the Sussex water meadows. He'd gazed up at its painted ceiling, dreaming that God himself had scattered the gold stars that glittered against the fathomless blue of eternity.

Oxford, his ordination, two curacies. Then the chance to return to Wharton as its chaplain. God was giving things back to him – and more.

Half a lifetime had passed. He had put away childish things. But his destroyer was here again at Wharton, and it wasn't any time at all.

Martin smelled again the sour adolescent sweat and felt his hair being yanked back. Piers Benson must be punished at last – through his son. He would be tortured and humiliated as he himself had been all those years ago, and ever since by his failure to speak up and save other people from what he went through.

He was going to bring ruin and disgrace on Oliver in some way as yet undecided, but he would do it and be glad of it. The boy *was* his old enemy. The laughing, callous smile, the swift, invasive hands.

Through a mist there was Dr Auerbach's intelligent and watchful face, but he couldn't make sense of what he was saying. He began to cough, and found he couldn't stop. Three minutes later he was back in his chaplain's flat.

Now it was half-term and he was weaving his way back to Charing Cross station after a day spent exploring London's City churches. It hadn't helped.

A man with any conscience left inside him would hand in

his notice and leave Wharton. What good was he doing here, turned in on himself, choking on poison? How could a man help teenagers get closer to a God who'd hidden his face from him? An ordained man had a duty not to allow his spiritual poverty to weaken the faith of those around him. Yet each day he remained at Wharton he was doing exactly that.

How quickly a man's thought processes become crooked! He was already losing his hold on the work at Wharton. No longer at ease with himself, all naturalness in his dealings with the boys was leaving him. He was offering stale bread. As the practice of listening and talking with God withers, so does the desire for it.

So it was with sex. He'd learnt the truth of that before he left Oxford. Total abstinence – he had done it. He'd kept the promise he'd made then to himself and to his God, and he had been rewarded. Sexual desires had long ago faded into nothingness and never returned, their place being taken by the daily beating consciousness of God alive within him.

Vive ut vivas. As chaplain he processed with the choir under the school motto, carved in stone above the great doors. In past Michaelmas terms he'd preached on what this might mean. Live that you might live. But the belief in his own worth, in his work for others, built up over the years in Oxford and Wharton, shrivelled into meaninglessness as he spoke empty words.

What was happening to him that he couldn't resist the forces that drove him downwards? Theology told him that a man who turns his back on God's grace cannot see his light nor desire his love. He *was* turning his back on it. He could know God's face only as wrath.

'If only they had a chaplain like you at Rachel's school!'

Nell had said this to him yesterday when she came late in the evening to take away the portrait from his room. The misplaced trust stung unbearably.

'You're troubled about Rachel, aren't you? You said she wasn't eating enough – biting your head off when she's not hiding in her room.'

'I think it might be something I've done. But I don't know, I can't get her to talk to me. Everything's been worse since I went away for the weekend on the sixth form Paris art trip. I wish I hadn't gone – though when I agreed to it, Rachel didn't look as if she cared if I was around or not. Now I'm scared that she – and telling myself I'm being silly doesn't work.'

Martin remembered Oliver Benson had been one of the boys who'd gone to Paris. He said nothing. His room was going cold.

She wanted something from him and he was turning her away. He helped her carry the painting and the easel down the flights of stairs and to the art studios in the new building leading out of the quad. He said, almost desperately, 'Nell, don't struggle on with Rachel by yourself. There are child psychologists, psychiatrists – that man who came to lecture even – you must get some advice, some help.'

'I have thought of it, but Alastair – '

'Thinks that things go away if you leave them long enough,' he interrupted. 'We all do it. But Alastair would never say no to anything you thought it right to do, when it was for the happiness of you or the children.'

That could be a bucketful of lies, he told himself. Alastair's not an easy man to know. It's hard to say which way he'd jump in a crisis or faced with a difficult choice. Kind-hearted yes, and demonstrably still in love with Nell, yet that might not go far enough with him. But then how much of human exchange was untainted by faint nuances of insincerity, of vanity, of hypocrisy? Self was always there, ready with its endless subtle colourings and coatings to sweeten the image reflected in the mind's mirror.

'Alastair doesn't do unhappiness,' Nell stated flatly. 'He doesn't understand it.'

Martin thought of this again as his eye caught the words *Steep Stairs* on the door of a shabby, stuccoed building in a little side street near the Strand. They were printed in distorted fonts and unexpectedly bold colour combinations, the letters falling against each other like dominoes. At the same time, a memory came back to him of Meredith, the headmaster's secretary, telling him of an article she'd been reading, about a charity set up for teenagers who were finding it difficult to access help from young people's mental health services provided by the state.

Meredith had wanted him to show more interest than he had done, he remembered now. How could she know that as they were talking, he'd spotted Oliver Benson lounging at the far end of the cloisters with Chris Parrish and Zachary Shilling. Those two – it would always be them. He'd made some excuse, impatient at Meredith's enthusiasm, ignoring the disappointment in her eyes.

But he needn't have cut Meredith off like that. They were old friends. Sometimes, these last few weeks, when he'd noticed her examining him with her habitual sharp percipience, he could have wished they weren't.

It was an unprepossessing building, squashed in between two nobler ones, but sleek surroundings were out of place for small charities, struggling to survive among the big giants fighting for the public's money. Martin stood irresolutely, taking in the peeling paint on the windows and wondering what was going on inside. Did the charity care for victims of abuse, did young teenagers make secret calls to the one place where their stories would be believed? There had been nothing like this for him as a child, nowhere that he'd known of, nobody he could tell.

The front door opened, and two men appeared at the top of the narrow flight of steps leading down to the pavement, absorbed in conversation. '*Einmal ist keinmal*,' Martin heard, spoken in a thick Irish accent. 'You of all men should have learnt that once is nothing. With Ursula now – but you won't want to be hearing the truth just yet – '

The speaker was a stranger to Martin; the other man was the child psychiatrist who had given the Wharton lecture.

TWELVE

Nell gave the tarragon sauce a final stir and licked the spoon. It didn't taste anything like the one that Juliet had made, so as usual she must have done something wrong.

'I'm afraid it's not as delicious as Juliet's, but I did try to remember it right,' she apologised, pouring sauce over chicken pieces and handing out plates.

'I'm sure it's a great deal nicer,' said Alastair, as she'd known he would. He took a mouthful. 'Yes, it quite definitely is.'

'You always say that whenever Mum tries to copy somebody else's recipes,' said Sebastian.

'And she's gullible enough to believe you,' snapped Rachel. 'That cow would give you the wrong ingredients on purpose.'

'Please eat some of it at least.' Nell saw that Rachel was sitting with her plate untouched and shot Alastair a warning glance. Don't pick Rachel up for using that word.

'Where did this come from?' said Alastair, fingering the unopened bottle of wine and examining the label.

'Oh, someone gave it to us, I've forgotten who,' said Nell distractedly.

'Not Juliet then.' Rachel glared at them both, her mouth an ugly line.

'Evidently not,' said Alastair in the light drawl he used when on the edge of the anger he never allowed to appear. He glanced at Rachel. 'Don't spoil supper for us all – particularly when's Mum's worked so hard to cook it.'

'If I was at boarding school you wouldn't be having your supper spoiled as you put it. In fact, I wish I *was* at boarding school.'

'Oh darling! Don't say that. But please eat some supper – I haven't given you much.'

'I meant it. Why can't I go? It's not just me it would suit, is it?'

Nell looked to Alastair for support, but he was concentrating on opening the wine, and the corkscrew appeared to be giving him trouble.

'Where on earth did this idea come from all of a sudden? You've never said anything about it before now.'

'I didn't want to go before now.'

'Dad and I would hate you to be at boarding school – we'd be miserable not to be all together.'

'Speak for yourself. Why don't you ask Dad what he wants?'

'You already know the answer to that,' said Alastair, pouring wine into two glasses. 'And it's irrelevant since we couldn't afford to send you. We wouldn't get a subsidised place like we will for Sebastian. If Wharton took girls it would be a different story. I wish it wasn't like that, but it is.'

'That's your excuse. You're still paying fees for Sebastian.'

'Yes, but not very much, so what he's doing is beside the point.'

'All the same, it *is* unfair that Rachel doesn't get a choice because of the money I mean, and me being the boy in the family.' Sebastian turned to Rachel with the apprehensive expression Nell saw too often on his face. 'But I don't want you to board and not be here – '

'It's not that.'

Rachel always responded when Sebastian looked like this.

Nell loved the way the children sided together. She longed to say the right thing for all three people around her, but knew she wasn't going to be able to.

'Darling, you've all your friends here – '

Rachel shrugged.

'So what? They're not exactly irreplaceable.'

Alastair took a sip of wine and passed the other glass to Nell.

'Sweetheart, whether you believe me or not, I'm with Mum on this one. We want our children with us. And talking of that, what's our family half term treat going to be? That's a tradition we don't want to lose.'

'Tickets for a *Queen* tribute band,' said Nell. 'And supper at the Japanese noodle place we all like.'

'Before you say anything, me and Vail chose the food part, and Juliet the concert,' excused Sebastian.

'A great selection all round. And if the concert's packed with middle-aged rockers, Mum and I promise not to embarrass you, though I can't speak for Juliet,' said Alastair, reverting to his usual easy tone.

Rachel slid her food to the side of her plate and put down her knife and fork.

'Why the fuck did you ask her?'

'I didn't – not especially,' protested Nell. 'We've always done something special all together, every half term I can remember.'

'It sounds crap,' Rachel said, pushing herself away from the table. 'You can count me out.'

'But darling – '

'I don't see why I should have to come if I don't want to, you'll be just as happy without me.'

'Have you filled in the forms for me and Rachel's skiing trips after Christmas?' asked Sebastian quickly.

Alastair smiled at Nell.

'That's all organised. Five days in Aviemore for Sebastian, and the inside of a week in the French Alps for Rachel – and a few days of peace for us.'

'Not much peace for me,' Nell pointed out. 'We've got Gran over Christmas, which takes days to recover from, I've got to frame and hang my Common Room portraits for the Turner Room exhibition, and after that get all the materials for when the girls' school are coming in for the three day project at the start of term.'

'Another of Clement Hunstrete's deluded efforts to build bridges and prove that Wharton deserves to keep its charitable status,' said Alastair.

'You're talking about my school,' said Rachel. 'The one you've just said I've got to stay at.'

'You know Dad didn't mean anything – '

Alastair stretched out his hand across the table.

'Don't make trouble. Sweetheart I'm sorry – '

'If I was your sweetheart,' Rachel jerked herself out of reach, 'you wouldn't – keep away from me.'

She shoved her chair away and flung out of the room. Footsteps banged up the stairs, a bedroom door slammed. Sebastian crept silently away without looking at either of them.

Nell turned to Alastair.

'What on earth was all that about?'

Alastair shrugged.

'My fault – sorry, darling. I put my foot in it.'

Nell examined Rachel's plate.

'And she's eaten nothing. Do you think the boarding school thing is all connected – getting away from being watched?'

'Don't ask me. But if she really wants to go to boarding school, we could ask my mother to pay the fees. She probably would, you know.'

'Yes, on her terms. And insist we send her to one of those

places with a fundamentalist foundation where a smug bossyboots tells you there's something wrong with you or you haven't got enough faith if your spiritual experiences don't match up to theirs.'

'Oh darling! It's not as bad as that.'

'Your mother is,' said Nell obstinately. 'She'd use it as a kind of hold over us. To control Rachel. You know what she is.'

'I'd like to see her try. And if it's what Rachel wants – '

'We are *not* taking any money from your mother.'

'I shouldn't have brought my mother into it. My mistake. But we could be throwing away an opportunity.'

Nell struggled to be honest.

'I don't want her to *want* to go to boarding school. Just to be happy here, like she used to be. Before – '

'Before what?'

'I don't know exactly,' said Nell, and she didn't. 'We're not asking your mother for any money – *ever*,' she reiterated. 'I know you don't agree, but we must get Rachel to see someone. Dr Royce might refer her to the local children's mental health services or whatever they are, for counselling or something.'

'Yes, and before long we'd have busybodies from the social services poking their noses in and sniffing about. You know how they're always itching to get at the middle classes. Give them an opening into a set-up like Wharton and they'll be in seventh heaven.'

'Why don't we go privately and try Dr Auerbach then? I googled him – he works mostly in London but he has a clinic at somewhere called Brookner House. It's towards the coast, not far away. Please, Alastair. It's that or the local people. Look how it's upsetting Sebastian as well now. We can't go on like this.'

Alastair drained his glass and reached impatiently for the bottle.

'For God's sake, Nell. Can't you shut up about the bloody man?'

Alastair practically never snapped at her. Nell got up from the table and opened the dishwasher. Neither of them spoke. He's waiting for me to give in, Nell thought, but I won't. She switched on the kettle to make coffee, the silence heavy between them.

'Oh, give it a try then, if that's the only way you'll stop going on about it. Do you want any more of this?' Alastair poured himself what remained in the bottle. 'I think you're wrong and you'll be going against me – but go ahead. Just be prepared for the flak. These people always say everything's the mother's fault. It's on the first page of their psychology textbooks.'

It wasn't often Nell won an argument, or even managed to see one through. Tomorrow she would phone their GP and ask him to refer Rachel to Dr Auerbach for the earliest possible appointment. She piled the plates into the dishwasher, hiding her relief. Such was her worry over Rachel that she didn't think to analyse why Alastair had given in so easily. She was conscious only of gratitude.

THIRTEEN

Nell ran upstairs to go to the loo, even though it was only ten minutes since she last went.

'Ready darling?' she said to Rachel, who was hunched up on the sitting room sofa apparently absorbed in the television.

'I've been ready for the last hour, in case you didn't notice.'

'You don't want the loo before we go?'

'It's not me who practically lives there,' said Rachel in a bored voice, not lifting her eyes from the screen. 'That's the trouble with you, you always think everyone else has to be exactly the same as you are.'

'Then I'm very sorry,' said Nell, as gently as she could. It wasn't the moment for an argument, however trivial. She had to get Rachel to the hospital.

'That's what you always say, but you don't do anything about it. If you were really sorry you'd change and stop being such a crap mother.'

'We'd better get in the car.' Nell picked up the car keys with a shivery hand. A half-hour drive in hostile silence lay in front of her. The route to Brookner House, the private hospital where Dr Auerbach ran his clinic, lay along country roads, and for this Nell was deeply thankful. She didn't think she could have negotiated the stresses of motorway turn-offs or busy roundabouts in her present state.

Getting their GP to refer Rachel to Dr Auerbach had been unexpectedly easy. Nell hadn't understood why, until it occurred to her that Dr Royce had two sons at Wharton, and had also attended the Wharton lecture. These connections had possibly smoothed the way. Since Nell was ignorant of the etiquette of private medical referrals, the apparent simplicity of it appeared miraculous. Within days of seeing Dr Royce she'd been offered this appointment for the following week.

It couldn't come too soon for Nell. Half term had been tense. Rachel had refused to come with them to hear the tribute band to *Queen,* electing to spend the night at Rosie's house. They'd taken a friend of Sebastian's instead. Juliet had delighted all three boys, laughing with them, drawing them out, teasing Alastair. Nell, all the time agitated about Rachel, couldn't shake off a mood of feeling dull and uninteresting. A Freddie Mercury lookalike pranced about the stage and the whole audience leapt to their feet and swayed ecstatically to *Bohemian Rhapsody.* Nell, stealing a surreptitious glance at her watch, prayed there wouldn't be too many encores.

A van pulled out of a side road too close in front. Nell slammed her foot on the brake, adrenaline flooding. *Keep calm. I need to speak coherently to Dr Auerbach even though he's going to be like Rachel and think I've done everything wrong. Alastair says psychiatrists always blame the mother.*

'You'll find Dr Auerbach's secretary in a waiting room on the left at the end of the corridor.' The girl at the hospital reception desk gave them a polite and impersonal smile. 'She'll take your details and tell Dr Auerbach you're here.'

Nell turned blindly away, stigmatised as The Bad Mother.

'She said left, not right.' Rachel spoke for the first time since leaving home.

In the waiting room there were comfortable sofas and armchairs not at all of the usual institutional variety, but covered in the designer chintz Nell associated with a country house drawing room. The carpet was green wool and the walls were papered in stripes of pale mint; evidently beautiful and tasteful surroundings were seen as part of the healing process. Or was it that people who were paying huge fees felt they were entitled to them?

She and Rachel ought to be sitting on a plastic chair in a waiting room full of other people ahead of them in the queue. Then she reminded herself of what Dr Royce had said, and boxed up the guilt. Rachel might have had to wait months before seeing anyone on the NHS. The ethics of it would have to wait. This was money she'd earned, and there could be no more important way to spend it.

Alastair's bitter words played round and round in her head like an insistent jingle. She shovelled them away. She'd taken this path, and she was going to go along it – as far as she could. But her stomach still churned at doing so against Alastair's expressed wishes. It was the first time she'd directly opposed him, and it gave rise to a strange mix of determination and resentment swirling around with fear of the new ground on which she found herself standing. Once words had been said they couldn't be forgotten, however much the person apologised. What was the good if Alastair said he hadn't meant it? He'd meant it at the time and there was *still* that time, it didn't go away, but stayed, alive and sharp.

'Rachel and Mrs Garwood?'

A man with hair and eyes so dark he looked Mediterranean in origin had come into the room. A doctor's smile, kind but detached. Nell leapt to her feet and knocked her bag onto the floor.

'I'm Dr Auerbach. Would you like to come in together first of all, and after that perhaps Rachel might like to have a chat with me by herself. Would that suit you?' With a swift movement, he picked up Nell's bag, returned it to her, and swung round to Rachel as he asked the question.

'I don't want Mum with me at all.'

Rachel didn't get up off her chair, but she flicked a glance at Dr Auerbach which was more than Nell had expected. All too often Rachel stared at the ground whenever adults approached her, or burst into tears without warning.

'That's fine. We'll leave your mum to have a cup of something here and come and fetch her after you've had a chance to explain things. Is that all right with you?' He was looking at Rachel but Nell knew he was talking to her. She began to feel unreal, as though everything was happening to someone else, and not to her, Nell Garwood, whose life had always been so undeservedly happy.

She sat down again on the flower-covered sofa (trailing roses, pink and bronze) and watched Rachel inch out of the room, one shoulder jerked mutinously upwards. Was she going to cooperate? Eleanor had been so confident about this man. She must trust Eleanor's judgement, and Martin's too. It had cost her a lot to get Rachel this appointment; the near quarrel with Alastair and getting Rachel to agree. That it might all come to nothing was too awful to face thinking about. She blinked back tears. She must *not* cry here.

'Would you like a cup of something, Mrs Garwood?'

A woman put her head around the door. She had greying ginger hair and tired skin like the apples in their fruit bowl at home that nobody got around to eating.

'Oh – no thank you, I'm fine.' Nell jumped up nervously. She wanted the loo again.

'I'm Dr Auerbach's personal secretary, Dilys Cole. I'll need you to fill in and sign this form for me.' The line of her thin-lipped mouth softened. 'Don't worry too much. Dr Auerbach will get your daughter better if anyone can. He's the best there is.'

'Thank you. Is he? I mean – '

'I've worked for him for over four years. He doesn't give up on anyone, though some clients try him hard enough.'

'I suppose he works incredibly long hours,' said Nell, abashed. An image of the tall Agrippa figure from her childhood copy of *Struwwelpeter* lingered.

'There's no stopping him. Does far too much and always makes himself available whenever and whatever. It's not surprising he gets taken advantage of.' She gave Nell a warning look, as if she too might prove to be a nuisance.

'People must often become demanding and obstreperous when they feel desperate,' said Nell. 'And their relatives too, when they have nobody else to turn to. He's very fortunate to have you,' she placated, anxious to persuade Dr Auerbach's secretary (would she ever call her Dilys?) that she at least would do her best not to join the black list.

She completed the form with nervous meticulousness. It might be counted as a step in the right direction. But even this was a struggle. Her hand shook and seized up so that she could hardly form the letters, and her signature was unrecognisable. In a few minutes, she was going to be called in to see Dr Auerbach. She didn't dare to imagine what Rachel might be saying to him.

'Please could you tell me where there's a loo?'

'That's all right dear, just the door opposite, and take your time.'

I am clearly a basket case and she means to take me in hand and be forbearing, thought Nell, as she came back into the waiting room to find a tray with a cup of tea and a chocolate biscuit wrapped in gold foil. She began to sip the tea which she didn't want, and then decided she did, the idea creeping into her mind that help might come from unexpected or even obscure places.

It was like when you needed to adjust a painting; moving trees between foreground and background, putting light into previously unnoticed details. The shapes of the people around her and the spaces between them were altering in relation to herself. Above all, Alastair, the central figure in her mental landscape, had shifted his position. Nell still couldn't quite admit to herself that he hadn't been the source of strength and support she'd automatically assumed he would be.

And Juliet – Juliet was *different*. Juliet was slipping away from her. Whole days went by when they hardly spoke. They'd been best friends year after year, telling of their joys and disappointments, sharing the intimate details of their lives. When Juliet had first moved to Wharton they'd lived in each other's pockets. They'd spent the summer holidays together, the two of them with the children, and Alastair whenever he wasn't playing tennis, which was whenever he could and so practically all the time.

Accusations stacked up in Nell's head. Juliet had never come clean over the deposit money. Juliet was too busy finding new friends in Wharton but was quite happy to make use of Nell when she wanted her to have Vail after school.

Then there was Rachel. Before, whenever she'd thought about her friendship with Juliet (which was almost never, because when you were friends you didn't have to) the idea of elastic came into her mind, which would stretch to encompass each other's failings or whatever was going on in their lives. It looked as if she'd pulled the elastic too far. Rachel apparently hating Juliet as well as everyone else hadn't helped. In the past she'd have confided worries about Rachel to Juliet. She hadn't done so, despite knowing that Juliet must be well informed about theories of mental health through her work.

Nell still couldn't think about it properly, in the coherent step by step way you were meant to think about things, the way articles in magazines told you to. The two people whom she'd relied on, whom she'd trusted entirely, had each in their separate ways let her down. She didn't want, just yet, to even try and work out what this might mean.

Neat piles of glossy leaflets were laid out on a highly polished mock antique table. Nell could see they had such titles as Understanding Bi-polar Disorder, Body Dysmorphia, Anorexia and Bulimia, Schizophrenia Management and Care. Others were less specific and included General Anxiety, Depression, and even plain Stress. It looked as though psychiatry was making a bid for the entire population.

She selected a leaflet on Obsessive Compulsive Disorder and began to examine it in a haphazard fashion. Freedom, pleasure, relief, confidence, she read, imagining the flow of text being murmured in a soothing tone by therapists. Happiness, vitality, rest, guidance – all these could be found if only you were shown how. There was help here, accessible and clearly expressed, but she couldn't concentrate, it was all bouncing off the surface of her brain.

Hope, healing and sanctuary. The words sounded familiar, and then it came to her that she'd read similar promises on placards outside churches, the kind she'd always shrunk away from. Did psychiatrists and psychologists and therapists offer a safer alternative to what religion had once given to people – and still gave to a lucky few?

FOURTEEN

Rachel Garwood. Thirteen years old. Middle class, one sibling, parents still married and living together. Refusing to eat, disrupted sleep, signs of depression and apparently angry with everyone and everything. A familiar story, right across the country, cutting its ugly swathe through all classes.

Lewis looked down at the letter of referral and thought about the child who'd sat, mute and uncooperative, twisting and winding a lock of hair between her fingers, for the best part of half an hour. Nothing unusual about that. It wasn't often you got much from the first consultation. Once in a while, yes, it all came out and the way forward appeared straightforward, although of course it wasn't, and then this illusory clarity sent you off in wrong directions.

'I don't want Mum talking to you in front of me,' she'd said at last.

'That's all right. She doesn't have to.'

She was sitting pushed back into the chair, putting as much distance between them as she could.

'And I don't need to come here.'

'Fair enough. Still, *I'm* here to listen if *you* want to say anything.'

'I'm not that bothered.'

Lewis waited. Then he said, 'Do you know why you're here?'

'So you can mess with my head. So Mum says.'

She had grey-green eyes which stared unfocused at the corner of the room. He'd seen the same expression – or lack of expression – in too many teenagers' faces. He saw how thin she was, much thinner than she ought to be. He'd seen at a glance (for instant assessments of this kind had become second nature to him) that the mother was slim, but the daughter was much more than that. His heart sank. He liked the look of this girl with her thick sulky brows, and he feared there might be a long hard road in front of her.

'Is that really what she said?'

'You know the answer to that question already, so why are you asking it?'

This was better. And she wasn't stupid. He said, 'You don't like wasting time. Nor do I. But I'm glad you're here. What about your dad? Would you like him to be around if you come to see me again?'

She looked him in the face for the first time.

'He wouldn't come.'

'Did you ask him?'

'There's no point, is there?'

I'm drowning, I want to escape, to disappear – her face told him all this. I'm too tired to answer your rubbish questions which mean nothing.

'Well, *I'd* like to see you again. I'll have a word with Mum and fix it up. Okay with you?'

A turning away of the head as if to say it would be a waste of time. And then something under her breath, just before he opened the door to take her back to the waiting room, which might have been, 'if you want to.'

She'd given him plenty to think about, though it might seem little enough on the surface. Something bad had happened to this girl. He'd noted her reaction at the mention of her father, and what she'd said about him – and not said. He needed to know more, and just for an instant she'd looked as if she might tell him.

He thought about her background, living in the shadow – could it be called that? – of the public school where he'd lectured only recently. He remembered the boy who had stammered and asked about suicide. The discreet enquiry he'd made after that evening had reassured him that Wharton had an exceptionally gifted and perceptive chaplain. The boys were known to turn to him when they were in difficulties. He'd been thankful. Now, he wondered. Was something happening within the school, and if so, was there any connection with this girl?

There would be nothing more from her today. The next session might pan out very differently. Or not. Adolescents always had the capacity to be surprising. Even classifying them as adolescents, as if they were some quantifiable species, was a misleading approach. To see adolescents as an entity – and inevitably they had become a marketable commodity – with fixed attitudes, codes and behaviour was loaded with dangers. Adolescence was best understood as an experience, different for every unfinished being going through it. It was a process without clearly defined boundaries or predictable outcomes.

And an extraordinarily difficult and painful time for far too many. Lewis knew the profession was still floundering when it came to adolescent mental health. Here was he, supposedly one of the country's experts, and half the time he was working in the dark.

Now he must get what he could from the mother. He checked the notes. Nell Garwood. A name he liked; he'd been brought up on Dickens.

She's too young to have a thirteen-year-old daughter was his first thought. The same serious eyes, though hers were a purer grey, the same luxuriant hair, the natural brown of a ploughed field in winter. It fell to her shoulders, pushed behind her ears as if to be out of the way.

He gestured towards a chair and she sat down quietly, shooting him quick glances of timid expectation. He went through the usual routine of family health and development questions and answers with her, jotting down notes on a sheet of paper. It was an exercise that gave him the structure he needed to build up in his mind a picture of the family and time to plan how he ought to approach the problem.

'If you can't decide what to do next with the patient, wash your hands while you think.' He remembered the quip from medical school. Psychiatrists didn't have reasons to wash their hands (wasn't psychiatry tacitly looked down on by the rest of the medical profession as the soft option where you didn't get dirty?) so they used other tactics. But they were for her as well as himself, for she was still looking afraid of him.

'Now that I'm clear about who's who in the family and so on,' he said, putting as much encouragement into his tone as he thought she would accept, 'I'd like you to fill me in with your own thoughts – try to tell the story as you see it.'

He bent over his notes so she wouldn't feel he was watching her too closely. She did try, he could see that, but her account was more confused than he would have expected from someone with so much overt quickness of understanding. She was hiding something – or protecting someone.

'You've given me a very good picture.' It wasn't true, but he could see this mother needed all the reassurance she could get. 'It's a great help. Forgive me now if I go over the main points. You've described what's been happening at school and with her friends. After learning she'd closed her Facebook account you've been checking what she's accessing online. Have you told her you're doing this? No? Are you sure she hasn't guessed? Still, you haven't come across any evidence she's been visiting any worrying sites. There's no trouble with her brother Sebastian to whom she's always been close. And you're happily married.'

He allowed a fractional pause. She didn't react.

'So we have to consider other aspects. Can you pinpoint the time when she began reacting or behaving in a way that was different, that made you concerned about her? Don't worry if something seems irrelevant – include everything you can. Don't be afraid of detail. There's no hurry, so take your time.'

'I thought it was just being thirteen and feeling muddled,' she stumbled, then began again. 'At least – I think I *wanted* it to be that. You know, being secretive and finding fault with everything at home. Especially me. It's as though everything came out of nowhere.'

'You mean the change was quite sudden? It can often appear to be. Small differences in behaviour can go unnoticed even by the most careful of parents.'

'The summer holidays were hectic and I didn't take enough notice…I think the not eating only started with the new term. Then at the end of September everything kind of tipped over, when I came back from a weekend in Paris. I hardly ever go away and maybe she resented it. She looked like she hated me and didn't want me there at all, that I might just as well have stayed away for good. It's as if I've totally failed her as a mother, and she's punishing me.'

'Withdrawing from you? Angry with you?'

'She shuts herself away in her room for hours – '

'Have you seen any signs that she's been deliberately hurting herself – what we call self-harming?'

She looked at him with so much shock in her face that he continued more gently, 'It can be very hard to spot these things. Teenagers become secretive and the family may be the last to realise.'

'Yes. I don't know. But I don't think so.'

Her face flushed scarlet like that of a guilty child. Why was she so determined to blame herself? Did she really believe she'd done something to cause her daughter's problems? And if so, what? He lolled back in his chair to encourage her to relax.

'The weekend away – was that – ?'

'It was a school trip – taking sixth formers to Paris.'

All above board there. Not that he'd doubted it. Relief, barely acknowledged.

'Go on. Do you know if something particular happened that weekend while you were away? A quarrel with someone, a party, was she unwell in any way?'

She didn't answer immediately but tugged desperately at her jumper, pulling it over her head and making her hair fly up and crackle with electricity. Only after she'd bundled the jumper into her bag did she look up and explain with a kind of apologetic ruefulness, 'I shrank it in the wash – and I'm used to living in a house without much central heating.'

He noticed that only the collar of her short-sleeved shirt had been ironed and he could see the white lace of her bra because a button was missing. He kept his face blank.

There were dark red marks on her bare arms. For a split second his mind lurched absurdly, before he realised that it wasn't scars or bruising but paint of some kind. He glanced at her hands clasped over her knees. They looked as if they'd been thoroughly scrubbed for they were very clean apart from the encrusted nails and cuticles. Was she an artist as well as an art teacher? Something in her face made him think she might be. But she hadn't said. She hadn't said much about herself at all. He would come back to that later.

'I'm sorry,' he said. 'This building's always too hot.'

'I suppose hospitals have to be, because of people having to undress. I don't know,' she hurried on, blushing faintly, 'at least, Rachel has been difficult – moody – whenever she has her period – she started last summer – and so at the time I thought it was that. My husband was at home looking after the children. She didn't go out at all during the weekend apart from having supper with a family friend.'

Lewis glanced down at his notes and scribbled: query friend – who? What was really happening in this family? Where was the husband in all this? It ought to have been both the parents coming, however bewildered and defensive. With one missing like this he only got half the picture, although that was often enough and occasionally too much.

'Does Rachel's father have any insight into all this?'

He felt rather than saw her withdrawal.

'I seem to have lost all faith in my own judgement. I keep saying things to her that don't help. Just recently I feel I'm making one mistake after another.'

Lewis caught the one after another, and was careful not to show it. What other mistakes did she mean? Why didn't she want to talk about Rachel's father? Men were often uneasy with medics, particularly those in mental health. It looked as though Alastair Garwood – and he would hardly be alone in this – preferred to leave this aspect of family care to his wife. So far he was no different to countless other fathers.

It was the obvious, on the surface, explanation for Nell's silence and Lewis told himself it was enough. But it didn't satisfy him. He couldn't have explained the reasons for his doubts even to himself. The instincts developed over years spent with troubled children told him that there was a secret somewhere that Rachel was party to – or involved in. There was something wrong happening in this family. Was it between the father and the daughter? Or was he imagining demons? His mind flickered back to the marks on the mother's arms. They were only paint. He was overreacting.

He stretched across for another sheet of paper, knocking

over the plastic beaker lying on his desk. He began to wipe up the water with tissues, but absently, rejecting Nell's proffered help, all the time thinking about Rachel and her mother and the father who was both absent and present in everything he had heard.

'The family friend she had supper with, is that a close relationship?'

'Rachel's known Juliet since she was a small child, going back to the days when we lived in London. Her son's much the same age as ours. She's a neighbour now as well as my dearest friend – she moved to Wharton in the summer.'

'Would Rachel be likely to confide in her?'

She shook her head.

'If she did, Juliet would pass it on to me.'

'Or in anyone else? Grandparents?'

'There's only my mother-in-law, and she thinks everything can be solved by praising the Lord.'

'Hardly much help to you at this juncture. Juliet's son. You say he's much the same age as your own boy Sebastian?'

'Yes, they're good friends – although they're very different.'

'No reason to think there's something going on between him and Rachel? Or there has been in the past?'

She looked at him in surprise.

'Not in the way you mean. He's more than two years younger than she is.'

'It was just a suggestion.'

He thought back to the sea of boys at Wharton in that great hall where he had given his lecture, seeing again the uncertain, changeful faces.

'You live next to the school, is that right? I expect Rachel knows some of the boys?'

'Yes, but there's no sign of a boyfriend or anything like that. She goes to an all-girls' school and there's a certain amount of mixing with the Wharton boys, especially among the older ones. Rachel's never had any kind of special relationship with a boy.'

'You're sure of that?'

She didn't look at all sure now he'd pressed her. Again he wondered what she was hiding – from herself as well as other people. He was used to parental evasiveness but it made his job hard.

'You've given me the impression she's not a child who would find it easy to confide in her friends – or in anyone – about what's going on in her life. Has she always bottled things up and felt she had to go through difficulties by herself?'

'Yes – always – but I don't think there have been any – serious difficulties I mean – '

He said, watching her face for any slight change in expression, 'Has Rachel ever said or done anything to make you think she is having suicidal thoughts?'

He hated this question but it had to be asked, and asked very directly.

'No – at least I never thought – did she say anything to you to make you think – ' her voice was so choked as to be almost inaudible.

'Nothing at all. I have to cover all possibilities – and I need you to answer me as best you can. It's an alarming idea, but that's all it is. My impression was that she isn't thinking along those lines and won't do so. But teenagers can feel they're being sucked into a void. There's an emptiness because they've lost their way – the secure ground and safe signposts they had in childhood have gone. They may no longer know who they are or why they're alive.'

'Is it because we – I – have done something wrong?'

'You don't want to think like that. It can happen to happy children with the most caring and attentive parents as well as ones who've had troubled childhoods. Or even for no apparent reason.'

He could see she didn't believe him. It happened all too often: the mother or the father falling apart from excessive anxiety over a child. He said carefully, 'Occasionally, if things get bad, and too difficult to manage at home, a child may benefit from a spell away from the family. That's why we have the child and adolescent unit here. I think Rachel will get better without that. But I want *you* to be all right.'

'Thank you,' she said, a break in her voice telling him that she was on the edge of tears. 'It must be so hard taking responsibility for all this – ' she gestured towards the door – 'all the hurts and sorrows of so many people – ' The words trailed away as she hung her head and soft strands of hair fell over her face.

Her words lay in the air between them. Other people had said much the same to him before, but none had said it with such unstudied sweetness. He caught his breath. This woman, this girl – what was it about her that without warning made his heart sing?

For one long moment he lost hold of who he was, of who she was. Surreal images of that shining hair drying the tears of the world raced through his head. He watched the pure curve of her neck in silence knowing he must let her tears go unchecked, for some part of him understood that she was crying not just for Rachel and herself, but for him, and perhaps underneath it all for the anguish that people with mental illness suffer everywhere.

'Sorry.' She dashed the backs of her hands across her cheeks in a childish gesture, and looked fleetingly into his eyes. 'It's your fault for being so kind. You ought to put on an enigmatic psychiatrist's face, then I wouldn't be so pathetic.'

She was trying to smile. A gleam of white teeth appeared and disappeared as her lips curled over them. He found himself staring at her generous mouth, into her reddened eyes. Some strange recognition of something longed for and never admitted stirred within him. All at once a wild surging joy flooded through him.

But it was only for an instant. A warning flickered across his brain. He must stop looking at her. He shifted his position in his chair and forced himself to look away, down at his notes, anywhere. His next appointment was already overdue; Lewis, like any other psychiatrist, could track the passage of time to the last minute without checking a clock.

'There's family therapy available, if you feel that would help. It can be useful in some situations.' He saw her stiffen and kept his voice smooth. 'But yours may not be one of them. Have a think about it all over the next few days. And I'd like to see Rachel again as soon as possible.'

He began to discuss details and arrangements with her, successfully retreating into the concerned but distant professional manner which served him so well, and told himself that the madness had passed.

Nell Garwood was just another mother, one of many. He would forget her altogether or confuse her with someone else, once her daughter was on the road to recovery.

He got up and held out his hand. It was his usual signal that the appointment was at an end, and it always got rid of people without difficulty.

FIFTEEN

'So how did the appointment with the great Dr Auerbach go? Have you time to tell me about it?' asked Eleanor, waylaying Nell halfway up the High Street the following day. 'That is, I'm assuming you managed to get Rachel there.'

'Yes thank goodness. In the end she was fine about it.'

This wasn't quite true but Rachel's intransigence was hardly relevant or worth remembering now. There was too much else going on. She leant down to pat Petrarch, standing patiently beside Eleanor, resigned to this delay in his excursion to the park.

'That's a relief. Well done you. Were you on your way to Waitrose? No? Here, let's sit down on this empty bench. I've been having qualms about turning into one of those aggravating Good Women of Wharton who like to run other people's lives.' Eleanor made a wry face at Nell. 'In other words, an interfering busybody. Advice can end up as very oppressive, can't it? I'm relying on you not to feel embarrassed if you're itching to tell me the whole idea was a disaster and you both hated him on sight.'

'I don't think you *could* be an interfering busybody,' said Nell, smiling at the permission offered to her. 'You never are. Yesterday's all a bit of blur.'

'But you're glad you went?'

Nell thought back to the previous evening. She'd been in the kitchen cooking supper and Alastair had come in late and gone straight upstairs. That was the first different thing. Almost always he came in and kissed her before he did anything else. She was tired, partly from the strains of the day, but more from the effort of quelling her smouldering resentment that at breakfast he'd forgotten she was taking Rachel to see Dr Auerbach. But then he appeared a few minutes later, carrying a bouquet of white roses, on long stems. He held them out to her.

'I'm sorry, darling. I ought to have come with you. I know that. Tell me how it went. But before you do, give me a kiss to show you've forgiven me.'

She buried her nose into the roses to hide her confusion, and then kissed him, the clouds on her mind's horizon lifting.

'It's only a first appointment – and I didn't – come next time if you like.'

'He wasn't one of those charlatans who sit staring glassy-eyed into the ceiling and never open their mouths?'

She began to tell him about Dr Auerbach while she arranged the roses in a cut-glass vase that her mother-in-law had given her last Christmas and which she'd never used. She pushed the tall stems into position feeling happier than she had for days. They were sterile, these out of season roses, entirely without scent and imprisoned in tight buds. In another day or two they would nod their heads and die. But Alastair had bought them and that was all that counted. He might not always agree with her, but his sweetness and generosity to her made these small differences unimportant, and even Barbara's hideous vase wasn't so bad now it was filled with flowers – and Alastair's love.

She said now to Eleanor, the picture of the white roses and Alastair's change of attitude still fresh in her mind, 'Yes, I *am* glad I went.'

'Did Rachel take to him?'

'I thought if I asked her she'd say she couldn't stand him. But she was okay about seeing him again so that was something gained. We've got another appointment next week.'

'And did *you* like him – or more important, is he going to help? Though probably that's an impossible question at this stage.'

'Yes and no. He was very polite and he followed what I said, you can see he's clued-up and knowledgeable. And insightful. But then at the end he went all aloof – as if he was bored.' Resentment, which she hadn't been aware of at the time, took shape as she recalled Dr Auerbach's parting handshake. 'I suppose he has to deal with some very money-no-object and smartly-dressed mothers and decided I was one of them.'

'It's unlikely he thought that,' said Eleanor, with a frank glance at Nell's paint-stained jeans. 'Was he very formally dressed himself?'

'I don't know,' said Nell, realising she didn't. 'He wasn't wearing a tie, I think, or a jacket. It was terribly hot everywhere.' She paused, as something came back to her. 'You know how you focus on an irrelevant detail when you're hassled about things? Well, I found myself noticing that the hem of one trouser leg was coming down. It was incongruous somehow, because everything else about the whole place was so immaculate.'

'Maybe he doesn't have a wife to see to things like that.'

'Oh, he does. There was a large photograph of a very beautiful woman on a bookshelf. He spent half the time writing stuff down, and I didn't like to just sit there staring at him so I looked around the room.'

'Was she all pearls and soft misty focus?'

'No – fragile with huge, haunting eyes. Very blonde and blue-eyed. She must be much younger than him, unless it was an old photo.'

'Then she's turned into a career wife who's above mending his clothes. Another brilliant doctor, medical people always marry each other. Though one usually thinks of doctors having romances with nurses rather than female surgeons or anaesthetists,' added Eleanor, clearly dwelling on childhood memories of reading *Sue Barton, Student Nurse*. 'Beautiful and blonde, like one of those impossibly glamorous nurses in hospital dramas.'

'I would have thought being married to a psychiatrist would be too unnerving for most people. They would see through all your wifely deceptions.'

'Nell! That doesn't sound like you. I can't imagine you having any. And don't women want to be seen through – and yet still loved?'

'But not analysed and labelled.'

'It's my older take on marriage. The difference between fifty-four and thirty-three. It has its advantages. I suppose he must be forty odd to be a top consultant.'

'He looks as if he can see through people at all events,' said Nell, wincing slightly as she watched women walking past and checking their reflections in shop windows.

'He probably keeps the photograph there as a reminder or even a warning – to himself and other people. You often see them in doctors' rooms. It's part of their armour. They tend to have them of their children too, to complete the picture of the untouchable family man.'

'There weren't any photographs of children, at least not that I noticed. Though I bet he has them. Successful clever ones, just like himself.' Nell heard with surprise the edge to her voice, and made an effort. 'I think the trouser hem only caught my attention because it didn't add up with the picture I had of him. You always imagine men like that have women falling over themselves to do everything for them.'

'Is that something feminism has missed?' mused Eleanor. 'Picking up a man's socks is a privilege in one sense. It means the woman *has* a man, and that's the main thing. There must be many women who would love to have someone to cosset.'

'It doesn't sound very liberated,' said Nell doubtfully.

'Your dazzling friend Juliet wouldn't think so, at all events. But you're a more old-fashioned girl at heart, the kind men are said to secretly prefer. Though that *may* only be in certain nineteenth-century novels.' Eleanor fell silent, as if pondering the successes or otherwise of various heroines.

'Strange his Christian name should be Lewis – with such a famous Jewish grandfather you'd have expected something more Old Testament, wouldn't you? At least he doesn't remind me of Lewis Dodd – the hero of *The Constant Nymph* you remember – one of those gifted and self-centred musicians who bring heartbreak to those who love them.'

'I definitely trusted him,' said Nell, seeing that Eleanor was beginning to lose herself in a literary reverie. 'In between the hard questions, and me getting muddled about things, he was kind in a doctor-ish way which made me – ' she broke off, not wanting Eleanor to know that she'd cried in front of Dr Auerbach. He must have thought her pretty unhinged, just like his secretary had. 'It's difficult to like someone when they make it clear they don't think much of you, isn't it?'

'I don't see why he shouldn't like you. Aren't you confusing detachment with dislike? Psychiatrists must have to separate themselves emotionally from their patients.'

'But I'm not a patient.'

'Mothers of patients then. It comes to the same thing. They have to keep clear of personal preferences and reactions. Their training would cover all that.'

'And he was *distant,*' persisted Nell. 'Quite deliberately so, at the end anyway. He fell into that ironic tone clever men slip into when they're talking to over-educated but still ignorant women like me.'

'Plus ça change,' Eleanor murmured. 'They can't help it.'

'Anyway, what does it matter? He's there for Rachel and that's the important thing. He can be as stand-offish as he likes.'

'He didn't say anything about what he thought?'

'Nothing at all.'

'Well, psychiatrists are meant to be silent most of the time aren't they?' Eleanor gave her a considering look and said inconsequentially, 'I wonder how they manage socially – it's to be hoped they distinguish between personal and professional behaviour, as otherwise it must make social gatherings very awkward.'

'You talked to him, didn't you, after the Wharton lecture?'

'Yes, it wasn't as unnerving as I'd expected. Psychiatrists must deal with difficult women all the time and so it would be surprising if they didn't become reasonably adept.'

'That smacks of being mechanical and insincere – and nobody could call you difficult.'

'Ah, those women who are meant to be fascinating to men, the Iris Murdoch types. It's unfair the way they get away with it. Nobody ever criticised *them* for being tricky. But stop worrying about Dr Auerbach liking you or not. I don't suppose he gave you a second thought.'

'No, I don't suppose he did,' said Nell. She got up from the bench, unaccountably forlorn.

SIXTEEN

'There's something I haven't told you.'

It was a month since Nell Garwood had first sat in that chair, and fixed her speaking grey eyes on him. A month during which he'd convinced himself – or tried to convince himself – that she was just another of the many mothers he came across in his working life. It was a crush, something he could deal with and get rid of. Sudden carnal desires for another person, however inappropriate, were part of being human. In time the chemicals in the brain settled down and the mania wore off. The emotions might feel overpowering, but they weren't. They were fleeting and could be overcome – and then forgotten.

Why was it that she'd hit him so hard? He thought of his wife whom he loved and tried to tell himself that Nell represented to him what Ursula had been – or what he believed she'd been – before illness had begun to destroy her. Now only a ghost remained. His obsession with Nell was nothing more than a predictable reaction, created out of a desire to get back the wife he'd lost.

He would get over it, this fantasy. He would keep her at a distance. Of all men he should know that first impressions could be disastrously misleading. The curious mix of naivety and perception in Nell's manner could be an engaging trick and no more than surface deep, just as the quick sympathy she displayed might spring merely from the desire to please. Even her friendliness and confiding ingenuousness might in some sense be artifice, half-consciously employed because she'd learnt it was expected of her and worked to her advantage.

He told himself all this with a sense of the futility of his own struggles. She was none of these things.

But still he ploughed on. Hadn't he seen the careers of colleagues destroyed by giving in to unguarded desires which they ought to have known would burn themselves out if only they could learn to wait? To betray the trust between patient and doctor was both dishonourable and destructive. If he gave in, if for one moment he allowed himself to go down this path, he should forever despise himself. He must put Nell Garwood altogether out of his head – and he *would* do it.

He'd seen her only to exchange a few words at the beginning and end of the three appointments with Rachel. He'd kept these times as brief and impersonal as he knew how, and he assured himself that he did know how.

But now he needed to talk with her about what he'd learnt during the last session with Rachel. Or to ascertain whether it was merely a product of a teenager's fantasy, a made-up focus for angry confusion.

He was going to have to tread very carefully. If what Rachel had said was true, was Nell aware of it? Rachel had claimed she hadn't a clue, but she might be wrong and certainly couldn't be relied on. And if Nell did know everything, why had she insisted there was nothing wrong within the family? He remembered the bewilderment in Nell's face at the initial appointment. He was sure she had no idea, no suspicions then – and it wasn't because she was dense. She wasn't.

Ideas dived and swooped like clouds of starlings massing into changing patterns as he regarded Nell sitting on the edge of her chair. All of them complicated by the questions he couldn't ask and the desires he must keep hidden.

What was she going to come out with? He'd asked her to come and talk about how things were going with Rachel, and had been careful to convey that this was a routine meeting, an opportunity to review progress. She probably hadn't believed him. Even so – but as he tried to rearrange his thoughts, a streak of brilliant turquoise in her hair caught his eye and he reflected that he'd never seen her without paint marks on her body or clothes.

'I should have told you before.' She put up her chin for a second. 'But I didn't think Rachel could possibly have guessed what I – '

So she did know. A stab of pain and pity for her shot through him.

'I always wanted lots of children,' she fixed her gaze on the pale green space between them, 'we had the two and I knew I was terribly lucky. Some of my friends haven't got married or had any at all. But then I found I did desperately want another baby, and my husband – Alastair – didn't feel the same. So I – I decided to try and have one without telling him. To become pregnant I mean.'

Colour had flooded her cheeks and she bent her head so that her hair fell over her face. Lewis watched her in silence, his mind racing ahead to what might be coming. What she'd just told him was entirely different to what he was expecting. He tried to gather his thoughts. Was the mess going to be even worse?

For one horrified moment he wondered if she was going to tell him she was having an affair. He shrank from the possibility; she was to him something sacred. She wasn't his and never could be. Not only was she somebody else's wife, she was the mother of a child in his care.

But still she was *there*, she existed, the hope in his life. What he felt for her must remain forever hidden, worship never admitted and at a secret shrine; to have that image of goodness smirched, of innocence destroyed, to find she was not as he knew her to be – this would make his life altogether dark.

He must say something but no words were possible to him. He stared at her hands pressed against each other on her lap, the wedding ring on the third finger, the smudge of dark blue across one thumb.

'I was so sure he'd be pleased really to have another child that I thought – I thought it would be all right to make the decision myelf. So I stopped using contraception.'

The blackness receded in Lewis's mind. She might be deceiving her husband in one way but not in the way he had imagined. He said mechanically, 'And your husband knows nothing of this?'

Her voice was almost a whisper.

'No – nothing.'

A baby! Ursula's yearning face swam in front of him. Her desperation for a child had become part of the illness which pursued her, and which he feared would one day overcome her altogether. She wasn't fit to bring up children yet did he – or anyone else – have the right to deny her the chance? But he had.

So Nell too wanted a baby. And so much so she was prepared to deceive the husband whom she appeared to love. This was all wrong, from whichever way you looked at it, but he couldn't bring himself to express his thoughts. How could he trust them anyway, feeling the way he did towards her?

He watched her in silence, waiting for her to continue. She was going to tell him she was pregnant. The humiliation stung as he discovered that among the emotions jostling for position in his head, jealousy was uppermost. He felt he hated Nell's husband, this man who had a right to give Nell what she most wanted, and yet denied it to her. All this – and what he'd done to Rachel.

'Are you pregnant?'

The words came out before he could prevent them, his voice sounding harsh and unreal.

'No!'

Already he was angry with himself for the indiscretion. He had exceeded his brief; it was inexcusable to push her into further explanation. He made a strong effort, and said more temperately, 'Mrs Garwood, are you sure you want to tell me all this? You know you don't have to.'

'I do because of Rachel. I think – I'm certain – that Rachel's realised. I've given it away somehow, doing something pathetic like gawping at prams in the street.'

'She hasn't said anything to you?'

'Nothing. But it must be why she wants to punish me. I've made her feel she isn't enough for me, that she's being replaced with another child.'

'Resentment made worse by being kept in the dark?'

'Yes. Don't you think it might have started something, might be the reason for the way she is?'

Lewis acknowledged the question without answering it. Instead he asked another.

'Rachel hasn't said anything to her dad, as far as you know?'

'She hardly speaks to him. She used to be closer to my husband than to me. She's always adored him. But that's all changed. She would think that it's both of us wanting a baby, so you see I've turned her against him as well, when it's not his fault.'

Not his fault. Lewis turned the words over in his mind. The question of whose fault things were never ceased across the whole muddle of human lives. Apportioning blame was rarely helpful. It was never as simple as people wanted to believe.

'Can you go on?'

'It must be my fault about Rachel. If I'm right about it being to do with the baby, and you believe I am, don't you?'

She was searching his face.

'We've no real reason to think so.'

This wasn't enough, her expression told him. He was going to have to be very careful.

'Anxiety is making you blame yourself. It's likely there's more affecting her state of mind than a possible reaction to what you've just described. But I'm glad you've felt you could tell me about it.'

'So am I.'

He could see her eyes were bright with tears. His hand moved to reach across the desk. He fought the urge to take her into his arms and kiss away the hurt and guilt. In his imagination he breathed in the smell of her skin, buried his face in the softness of her hair.

'Have you told anyone else?'

'Only my very best friend – Juliet.'

'When was that?'

'When I first – at the beginning of term, in September. I shouldn't have done, it wasn't fair on Alastair. But I used to tell her almost everything. Not so much now.'

He caught the *almost* and wondered where the boundaries had lain. He guessed they would be around her husband, despite this one lapse she obviously regretted. She was a woman who would keep quiet about the more intimate side of her marriage, thinking it disloyal to betray a husband's weaknesses to a friend, however close. What she was doing was silly and childish, and didn't say much for the communication between husband and wife. It was however a small matter and none of his business.

'Any reason for that?'

'It must be wonderful,' she said, appearing to shy away from some disturbing memory, 'to make people better – to reduce some of the grief and confusion in the world – to feel you are able to do some good, instead of feeling useless.'

'Psychiatrists can't cure people. As a boy I thought they should be able to, but I was wrong. Often they can only alleviate, or just contain. In some cases it might be best seen as an exercise in damage limitation.'

The familiar rage and pity that men and women must suffer so terribly flooded through him, as it always did at such moments, before ebbing away. Hadn't his forefather Job been given an answer of a kind which had been enough for him, and conceivably could still be enough for a psychiatrist God knows how many centuries later? He switched his attention back to what Nell had said.

'The longing to produce the miracle, to feel the divine spark within us, we all crave that. It's built into human beings, if indeed we are made in God's image.'

'People expecting you to be like God and to work miracles must make your life pretty impossible at times.'

'Don't we all have over-high expectations of other people? Ones that they cannot possibly deliver? Then we blame them, or run away from them when they inevitably fail to live up to them. And we do it to ourselves.'

'Blaming yourself for things you can't help?'

'Demanding that we *are* more, and do more than we are capable of. To be gentle with themselves is one of the most vital steps that people with severe mental illness have to take. But it's not easy, unlearning damaging ways of thinking, and they may come to it too late.'

She was silent, taking time to work out what he'd said. He'd caught her earlier use of the word 'useless', and now he came back to it.

'You could say the ability to love and work is what defines mental health. Work might be any kind, paid or unpaid, looking after people or being a good mother like you are.'

'I wish I'd come to your lecture at Wharton.'

'I was speaking more to the boys – '

A camera shot flickered in his brain and he saw again the face of the boy who'd stammered, and in the shadows behind was Ursula, out of focus and ephemeral, asking something of him that he couldn't give her.

'My husband – Alastair – says what head doctors don't know is a whole lot more than what they do know.'

This was unexpected coming from her. Was she in some sense testing him? Was she beginning to guess at the truth but refusing to admit it?

'Much of psychiatric medicine *is* a leap in the dark and hoping for the best,' he said, smiling at the apologetic look she was giving him. 'It's necessarily years behind – we still know very little of how the brain works. Your husband's right, if you look at it from one side. After all, it wasn't until the end of the eighteenth century that doctors saw the need to treat the psyche rather than the body in cases of mental illness. If you look at it from the other, you can be excited about how far we've come in a relatively short time.'

His eyes rested on the streak of turquoise in her hair.

'The answers – though they will always be necessarily incomplete – don't just lie with chemistry, what's called the biological approach. The problem of human depression, the sense of loss, of our endless unfinished sadness – it's a spiritual question, and it's the arts, among other things, that offer us hope.' He pointed towards her paint-stained hands, trying to end on a lighter note. 'So you're doing your bit.'

How would it have been if I'd met the husband that evening I lectured at Wharton, he asked himself. If I'd met *her* then, at his side, as his wife! Would it have been any different?

'I want you to know that if you're worried about Rachel at any time you can phone me. In the middle of the night if necessary. This is my mobile number and it will always reach me.'

She made a gesture of dissent to the card he held out to her.

'Thank you – you're very kind – but I couldn't possibly disturb you, I wouldn't think of it. Your wife, your children – '

'I give this number to all the parents. Mrs Garwood, don't blame yourself,' he said quickly, seeing the uncertainty in her eyes. 'I'm quite sure Rachel's troubles aren't about you or anything you've done – or not done.'

Her face cleared like a child's let off a punishment. She said, 'Would it be okay if you called me Nell – is it allowed? You can't imagine what a relief it is now you know about everything. It isn't trying to evade responsibility, is it?'

'It's what I'm here for, after all.'

'I expect you think I should be telling Alastair but – it's just that you know what men are.'

'Yes.'

'Sorry. I sort of forgot you *are* one.' She smiled at him with unstudied friendliness. 'You don't think of doctors as being men somehow, ordinary men I mean.'

There didn't seem to be anything he could say to this. She'd shown him unmistakably and with ludicrous simplicity that she viewed him simply as the child psychiatrist who was being paid to do his job. Surely this was what he wanted, or ought to want. He looked down at his notes and then at his diary.

'You've got another appointment booked, haven't you Mrs Garwood? I'd like to talk to you again then.'

He could have enlightened her then and there, but where

did his duty lie? Problems of confidentiality came up all the time in his work and always required careful navigation.

He stood up, wanting her to leave him. He needed to be alone to work out in his mind what he should do – and whether he was going to be able to bring himself to do it.

SEVENTEEN

Nell drove home light with relief. Telling Dr Auerbach hadn't been as humiliating as she'd dreaded. He hadn't criticised her. There had only been a curious expression on his face which he'd quickly erased. Far more importantly, he'd said that he didn't think what she was doing was connected to what was going wrong with Rachel.

All this meant (a nicely encouraging voice in her head assured her) that she didn't have to give up on trying for another baby. Over the next few days she turned up its volume, greedy for its encouragement. It was so hard to make yourself not want things!

'You young people think you have a right to be happy,' declared her favourite old lady when she went into the nursing home for their art therapy session. 'It's not until you're old you find there's no such thing as rights. Or that you'll get what you're foolish enough to think you want either.'

Arguing with herself only added to Nell's confusion. It was with a sense of relief that she found herself on her thirty-fourth birthday at the beginning of December getting out of the train at Charing Cross station.

'You ought to have a decent birthday treat this year,' Alastair had said, climbing into bed and reaching across for her on the night of her talk with Dr Auerbach. 'You've been worrying too much. Why don't you go on a shopping spree in London and I'll jump on a train after my last lesson? Then we can have dinner somewhere and maybe the theatre?'

It wasn't his fault that his generosity was coming at the wrong time, or was for the wrong thing. She didn't care about buying things for herself just for the sake of it, she wanted him to give her another child. He ought to know this, instead of thinking he could fob her off with a visit to the shops.

'I should be getting on with art stuff here.'

'Look, it's your free day isn't it? There's nothing that can't wait.'

'What about Rachel and Sebastian? They're probably expecting all of us to do something together.'

Alastair sighed and then kissed her.

'You always think of them rather than us. But as it's your birthday I'll give in. How about this: you have a day in London, meet up with some friends or whatever, and when you get back we'll have a celebration family dinner at that French place we read about?'

'I could go to the Rembrandt talk at the National Portrait Gallery,' said Nell, suddenly brightening. 'Or I could see if Juliet would come out to lunch. She's been a bit funny recently, almost off with me.'

'I hadn't noticed.'

'You don't think we shouldn't have done the deposit money for Vail? I've sometimes thought it's made a *thing* between us.'

It's also made a thing between you and me, but we've colluded to pretend it hasn't. Are all relationships held together by shutting your eyes to small deceptions and discoveries? You're told that tolerance and realism should see you through, but they aren't doing it for me, I haven't got enough of either...

'Oh darling, I'd forget about it if I was you. Why don't you ask one of your old art school friends to go with you to the lecture? Anyway, isn't Juliet always saying she can't get a proper lunch hour?'

Alastair said this with such careless complacency that Nell almost believed he *had* forgotten. Some idea that his happiness in some measure depended on this ability to forget anything unpleasant or disturbing was edging its way into her everyday consciousness.

'Oh, I don't know – ' As usual Nell found that once she was asked to explain her uneasiness, she couldn't find the words that would pinpoint it. She saw again Juliet's expression when she'd talked about wanting another baby. She couldn't tell Alastair about that, and especially not now when one of his hands was already on her thigh and pushing up her tee-shirt.

When Nell and Alastair had first moved to Wharton, she'd promised herself she'd often be able to come up to London to art exhibitions. It was little more than an hour on the train and coming into Charing Cross was perfect for the major galleries. But it hadn't happened. There was never quite enough time in the school day to get there and back, and then she was offered the chance of teaching in Wharton's art department, which soon swallowed up more of her week than she'd expected.

She'd been lucky to get the job, she knew that. It wasn't as if she had an amazing career as an artist. She might have been promising once – they'd said so at art school – but Nell had ceased to believe in herself. She might be talented, but that wasn't enough. You had to be something more: you had to market yourself. She wasn't good at that either.

Plans for an exhibition at the beginning of next term of Common Room staff portraits painted by the Wharton art department had come at the right time. Portraits were beginning to interest her more than the landscapes on which she'd previously concentrated. Alastair encouraged her all the way; portraits were potentially lucrative and he was delighted with any success she had. Not that she'd attracted many commissions so far, but there might be some good local publicity when the exhibition was mounted. Clement Hunstrete always made a point of inviting the press whenever anything cultural took place at the school.

On this occasion, sixth formers studying art in the state schools in the town were taking part in a three day art marathon using Wharton's facilities and teaching staff. If there was cynicism in some quarters that these events were carefully staged to demonstrate that Wharton benefited the community and should therefore hang on to its charitable status, Nell hadn't listened to it. She loved the idea of having lots of teenagers enjoying themselves in the art department. Some of them would be girls from Rachel's school, and it would be fun to have a mixed group to teach.

'Go early and buy something gorgeous and ridiculously expensive to wear for our dinner,' Alastair had said, running a hand down the curve of her back. So now here she was, in a tiny boutique in Covent Garden, trying on the most beautiful dress she'd ever seen.

She stared at herself in the changing room mirror, sheathed in shimmering white silk painted with washed watercolour poppies. It was a young girl's dress, one to be worn at a May ball, or a summer party on the lawn where you danced barefoot. It was – she sought for the right word, and fell upon it – an *innocent* dress, one worn in the freshness of hope when all things were possible and the overgrown boy on whom you'd set your heart would surely ask you to dance when the slow and romantic song came on…

Nell recalled summers when she might have worn a dress like this, only she never had. She'd been at art college, floating through days shot through with the brightness of discovering London, drawing and painting all that crowded into her vision; nights crammed into student flats, cheap wine staining the floor, half-finished cans of beer littering every surface, the air blue with smoke. Nobody ever left; they went on discussing the meaning or meaninglessness of Life and Art and ended up sleeping on the floor.

It had all come to an end when she'd met Alastair because he wasn't a student but a teacher of politics at a sixth form college and more than ten years older than she was. She hadn't minded. Falling in love was what life was made for. But now she went to civilised Common Room drinks parties and rarely talked about anything that actually mattered.

She rose up on tiptoe, swivelled around and swayed her hips. The full skirt billowed and rustled with the secret promise of romance, the spider gauze silk lifted and caressed her skin. All at once she knew she was hungry for something.

I want to feel like a young girl again, to live with that intoxicating mix of silliness and fervent idealism, I want to be carefree and at the same time passionate. I want to feel tantalisingly, excitingly *alive*.

She remembered being in love – she'd called it that – and the fizzing of ecstasy and despair. A stream of boys whom she had flirted with, fallen for, parted from, sometimes apparently broken-hearted. Then Alastair.

The dress was too young for her. Nell told herself this, trying to sound firm, but knowing she was deliberately distancing herself from hearing it, as if the pronouncement came from a disapproving and tiresome aunt and could therefore be legitimately ignored.

'It's lovely on you, being so slim and all,' the teenaged sales assistant said, looking up from her leopard skin nails as Nell stepped out from the cramped cubicle to get a better view of herself.

'It's not mutton dressed as lamb?' asked Nell, hearing the aunt's hectoring tones.

'Sorry?' said the girl blankly, and it occurred to Nell she was too young to understand the expression and was probably vegetarian anyway.

'I meant I might be too old for white with poppies – '

The hard little face looked animated for a moment.

'Ooh, no. It's like for any age.'

Nell seesawed between longing for the dress and the aunt's dampening reminders that she might not have many opportunities for wearing it. Fashion editors always told you to buy clothes which went with the rest of your wardrobe. Co-ordination was all important and saved you from making expensive mistakes. Failure to take this into account was why seventy-five per cent of women – or was it ninety-five – bought things and never wore them. Nell had never in her life taken any of this advice. She liked her wardrobe to be happily haphazard. So did Alastair.

And today was one of her good days. Hair shiny, skin and eyes clear, arms and legs light and fluid. The perfect day on which to buy such a dress. If she didn't buy it – but she must. It was impossible not to.

'Thank you,' she said firmly. 'I'd like to have it, please.'

Even your extravagant husband didn't mean you to spend *quite* so much, was the aunt's parting shot, but fainter now, as if she knew she was losing the battle. There was even a peevish note, as if she had known from the beginning that this particular one wasn't worth fighting but she'd done so for the sake of duty and out of sheer habit. Nell carefully pulled off the dress and wriggled back into her jeans and jumper. She punched in her PIN without checking the amount. That way it would have less chance of nagging at her conscience.

It was still too early to go to the National Portrait Gallery to hear the lecture. Nell went into a cafe, bought herself a tuna sandwich and a latte, and settled herself on an empty bench in the winter sunshine, the carrier bag with its silky rope handle at her feet.

She closed her eyes and began to imagine herself wearing the dress, walking through a summer garden. She could feel the grass soft between her toes, the faint stain of green on the soles of her feet, the blue and violet shadows on the whiteness of the dress. People stood in clusters under dappled sunlight, blocks of impressionist broken colour, but there was one special person for whom this dress was being worn, and Nell flitted about the lawns searching for the face she wanted. The dress is for you, I bought it for you.

Then at that moment she saw him, a figure with his back to her leaning on a gate, a man lost in contemplation of the open fields and hills beyond the garden. She ran towards him, driven by blind instinct, the white dress scattered with scarlet poppies lit and floating in the sunshine. Just as she reached him, he turned round, and it was in this moment, as he smiled down at her, that she saw his face. It wasn't Alastair. It was Dr Auerbach.

Nell leapt to her feet, at once confused and angry with herself. She pulled out the dress, carefully folded in tissue paper, stuffed it into her shoulder bag alongside her sketchbook, and crumpled the shop's luxury carrier into the nearest bin. She would put the dress away and tell Alastair it wasn't suitable for the winter. By the spring she would have forgotten meaningless daydreams that came out of nowhere.

Assorted skinny-jeaned students and middle-aged ladies in comfortable shoes were pouring into a lecture room at the National Portrait Gallery. Juliet said women came to these events in the hope of meeting a soul mate. If so, they'd be disappointed, Nell decided, for the men she noticed appeared to have their minds focused exclusively on art history.

Nell had seen the lecture's title 'An Englishman and a lost Rembrandt come home' on the website listing gallery events.

Rembrandt had been her mother's favourite artist, but she would never have seen this particular picture. It had been unheard of by the general public before now and only just acquired by the National Portrait Gallery.

A scholarly man in a beautifully-cut pale grey suit began to speak reverently about the painting, which was mounted on a lectern beside him. It was very small, and showed the head of an old man with a beard, a hat casting shadows over his face. Thomas Daintree had been an English physician of great distinction who had followed his Royalist patron into exile in Holland after the execution of King Charles I in 1649. He hadn't lived to see the restoration of the monarchy in 1660; records showed that he'd died the previous year in Amsterdam, just a few months after Rembrandt had painted his portrait.

Nell could never remember afterwards whether the extraordinary conviction that Dr Auerbach was in some way connected with the painting came into her mind before or after she realised that the dark head in a row near the front was his. He turned his head slightly, and she began to examine what she could see of him, turned three quarters away from her. There was no mistaking the dark hair cut very short nor the harshly defined angles of jaw and cheekbone.

She might have got over her initial shyness with him, but the last visit to his consulting room was too recent for something that might have been embarrassment, only it wasn't, to have faded. Then there was that humiliating fantasy on the bench! Meeting him again would be awkward. She'd have to pretend not to see him.

'This painting is an example of what we call Holocaust art – art that was stolen from Jewish families during the Nazi era.' Nell jerked her thoughts back, and tried to listen to the rest of the lecture. 'Over the years there have been many claims to stolen art by descendents of victims. Often the paintings concerned have been bought and sold in good faith over the years following. Who does the work belong to in law? There are no easy answers.

'Thankfully, with the painting in front of you there are no more torturous moral dilemmas. Thomas Daintree's practice and written treatises led to considerable advances in seventeenth century medical science. Owing to the generosity of the owners, Rembrandt's portrait of him can now take its place in the National Portrait Gallery, alongside all those who have contributed so much to this country's life and history.'

Nell began to slide though the throng of people towards the exit, but then she saw that Dr Auerbach was leaving as well and they would almost certainly meet. She turned back. She would have another close look at the painting, now that the knot of older ladies clustered around it was unravelling.

She peered into Thomas Daintree's sombre eyes. They stared at something just beyond the viewer, brooding over the memories and griefs of old age, and even his own approaching death.

Someone came up and was standing behind her. She turned round in confusion.

'He makes me think of you, and I don't know why,' she burst out before she could stop herself. She felt her cheeks burn, forced herself to look into his face and then forgot everything in the kindness of Dr Auerbach's smile.

EIGHTEEN

It was a mistake of course. Lewis acknowledged this even as he turned to walk towards the front of the lecture room where Nell was standing.

Leave her alone. Only a fool goes near the danger he's already seen.

It was a surrender which made going back impossible and the rest of the afternoon inevitable. He kicked the voice of his conscience quiet and slammed the door on it. But he could still hear the whispered warning.

He'd set himself rules for his married and professional life, and had kept to them. Dr Lewis Auerbach: unavailable. That had always been the message, given out in unmistakable terms. To hold himself aloof had been his way of avoiding the pitfalls that awaited anyone in the so-called caring professions. It was all too easy for the line between patient and doctor to become blurred. He'd promised himself he would never lower his guard, never put one foot into that treacherous water. The discipline had served him well. It had finally become a habit.

Then, without warning, the world he knew had retreated, had become shadowy, unreal. This autumn he'd met Nell Garwood, and since then he looked at everything with sideways eyes, for her image was always there.

'What a relief nobody else among the audience had the same instinct,' he said as he stood beside Nell, the portrait in front of them. 'But knowing you as I do, I might have guessed that you might.'

'And I might have guessed that you too love Rembrandt, because you do, don't you? Is that why you came – no, it's more than that, isn't it, your connection with this painting? There's some mystery. I wish you'd tell me – tell me *everything*.'

She didn't mean it, he could see that, but she'd given him an invitation he was incapable of refusing and God knew he'd already been indiscreet enough.

'Yes,' he said. 'I don't think there's anyone else who paints with that level of psychological insight – revealing the inner conflict and vacillations between good and evil.'

'It's the *inside* of people's minds,' said Nell. 'Which you know about from your work, better than almost anyone.'

'There's a place here where we could have a cup of tea,' he said. 'If – '

She shook her head blushing.

'I *can't*. I mean, you don't know me, and I'm not – you mustn't waste your time on me – '

'You won't be wasting my time,' he said. 'But perhaps you're politely telling me you'd be wasting yours.'

This was unfair of him, and dishonourable too. He didn't care. She shot an enquiring glance into his face, working out how far he was teasing her.

'You're laughing at me – '

'Sorry.'

'Don't be. It's nice. And what I meant was, I'd love to. If you're sure – '

'Entirely certain.'

'Will you explain it all then about the Rembrandt? It's not boring for you?'

'Boring for *me*? I've been lecturing medical students all morning, and almost certainly boring *them*. I noticed several of them falling asleep. Please stop me if I do the same to you.'

'At UCL?'

He realised he must have looked surprised, for she hurriedly explained, 'I had an idea you lectured there occasionally, I must have read it somewhere.'

He tried to ignore the pleased feeling her words gave him. It could not, it *must* not, be anything to him that Nell remembered something about him. What he felt for her must always be starved, even though it had become the part of him that was most alive.

'You're giving me a very psychiatrist sort of look.'

'Which is?'

'Oh, you know, scrutinising but inscrutable.'

They started laughing at the same moment. All at once he knew he was happy.

'My husband wanted me to go shopping after the lecture,' she confided to him, as they went down to the cafe in the basement. 'But I've done enough already. Hearing about Thomas Daintree will be much more interesting.'

They queued for tea and cakes, with her taking some time to decide between the merits of an iced walnut cake or an almond sponge with an apricot filling.

'It's my birthday. At least that's my excuse. It's really because I never have much success in getting cakes to behave like the recipe says, so I make the most of them when I'm out to tea.'

'Happy birthday! I hope you're having a more exciting celebration later on?'

'Yes, thank you. I suppose I shouldn't be eating cake now, but I'm jolly well going to. We're having dinner in a French restaurant that's opened in a village near us.'

A small unreasoning shadow, a flicker of possessiveness. *Don't ask for any more details.* He led the way to an empty table and put down the tray. As she helped unload the plates and cups she smiled at him with the childlike candour he remembered from their last meeting.

'I'm so glad I didn't come with a friend to the lecture – I wouldn't have been able to have this wonderful time with you. I ought to have paid, though, as it's my birthday.'

'Don't be silly.'

'All right then. Actually I must just go to the loo.'

She reappeared after a few minutes. He saw she'd made no change to her appearance, not even brushed her hair, an omission that struck him as entirely consistent with what he knew of her and unlike other women. Then it struck him that she might behave very differently with other men. The idea was unpleasant to him, and worse was his own shame in knowing this was so.

'Please go on with the story.'

'You were right about my connection with Thomas Daintree.' Lewis pulled himself together. 'But he wasn't an ancestor. The painting once belonged to my great-grandfather who lived in Amsterdam before the second world war.'

'So it was your family – *you* – who gave it to the National Portrait Gallery? And you don't like it to be known?'

'No – I didn't want to be wheeled out to answer questions about my family at the lecture.'

'Go on – '

'My father remembered it on the wall of my great-grandparents' house in Amsterdam when he was a small boy before he came with my grandparents to England in 1933. Around twenty years ago, my father set up a search for it which was eventually successful, if you can call it success. I've never been sure. He died last year and thankfully my sister and I were in agreement that we didn't want to keep the painting for ourselves. She lives in America, but we decided it should come to a gallery in the UK.'

'Not go back to Holland?'

'We thought this was the right place,' said Lewis. 'Thomas Daintree served his fellow countrymen for most of his life and his portrait belongs here if anywhere. But it's not just that. Around fifty thousand or so Jews came to Britain during the thirties. My grandparents never forgot the debt they owed to this country.'

'What happened to your great-grandparents?' She looked at him with a painful expression of anxiety. 'I think I know what you're going to tell me.'

'Yes,' Lewis said. 'After the Germans invaded Holland in 1940 thousands of Jews were deported. Most of them were taken to Westerbork, the transit camp in the north-east of Holland. From there they were taken to the extermination camps of Auschwitz and Sobibor. Ninety-nine out of a hundred never came back.'

'And your great-grandparents were among them?'

'They were arrested in 1941 and all their possessions taken, the Rembrandt among them. The family were entirely wiped out. So there was just my grandparents and father left.'

'I suppose all psychiatrists – not only Jewish ones – would have been desperate to get out of Germany and Austria as well because of Hitler believing that everyone who was mentally ill or disabled should be killed.'

'In which many psychiatrists colluded, lest they lose their careers. Though there were some inspiring exceptions – Hans Gerhard Creutzfeldt among them. The interaction between political ideology and psychiatry is an almost unimaginable evil.'

'I was reading about your grandfather,' Nell said, and again he felt a rush of warmth and pleasure that she had been interested. In psychiatry, in his grandfather, in him? 'I was thinking of all the good he did. He couldn't do anything for all the thousands who died, but he did all he could for the living.'

For a moment Lewis imagined the old man sitting with him and Nell at the table. He would be leaning forward, his eyes bright and sharp, darting from face to face, listening, speculating, arguing, his English still heavily laced with a Dutch accent. Then he would fall silent, and spoons and forks would be moved swiftly around the cluttered table as if they were opposing armies in his mind, and he was marshalling them, rearranging his ideas in the light of what was being said.

'I was starting out at medical school when my grandfather died. He was in his nineties but he was still watching and searching, passionate to grasp what it means to be human. But I think the guilt at having got out in time and survived never left him.'

Guilt. Did a man's life always come back to this? He began to explain to Nell what his grandfather had worked for, how he'd striven to help some of the traumatised children who had lost everything. He was telling her too much, he knew that, but he couldn't stop. There was nobody else who listened to him with such self-forgetful ardour, nobody else to whom he spoke of these things without feeling that he was becoming a bore, an obsessive who couldn't let go of the past.

'The rest of his life was a sort of atonement?'

She'd propped her elbows on the table, her chin in her hands, questioning eyes fixed on him.

'An attempt at it. He continued to be haunted by theories about good and evil, which undoubtedly grew out of what he knew had happened to his own people. But I think he was driven in another way too. He'd been given an immense intellect and knew he must use it to its fullest extent. It was an offering up.'

'I heard a sermon recently about whoever's given much, much will be required, it's somewhere in the Bible. Don't you think it's alarming? The person preaching said it was one of the things – and there were quite a few others – he wished Christ had never said.'

'We must all find it so in one sense. If Christ *did* say it then I agree it's worth grappling with what he could have meant – and in what context. That sometimes helps. Are you a regular church-goer?'

'No – some of the ones I tried when I was a student were like a club where you had to obey the rules. Everyone used a particular language, and you were left out if you didn't have enough faith or the right kind of faith. Which I didn't. But I think I went to the wrong ones.'

'Ah yes, the jargon that makes a people feel they belong and excludes the outsider. It's easy enough to fall into – and probably impossible to steer clear of entirely.'

'More silence might help,' said Nell. 'But I suppose going to church is an opportunity to talk together to God. I mean if you don't go at all, you can end up somehow doing without him most of the time.'

'We can,' said Lewis, his heart unexpectedly heavy within him. 'It's easy enough to forget God altogether.'

'There are chapel services at Wharton I sometimes go to. I mostly love *those*. Do you? Go to church I mean – or a synagogue?'

She was flushing as if wondering whether she'd erred in asking him this, or was she remembering something – or someone?

'Occasionally to Southwark cathedral or somewhere with the same all-inclusive approach. Everyone welcome whatever their race, gender, class or sexuality. Like you, I don't like the idea of barriers being put up. I was brought up largely outside Judaism – my father did follow my grandfather in that he became a psychiatrist like him, but he rejected everything else about him. Including his Jewish heritage. Neither my sister nor

127

myself were taught to think of ourselves as Jewish or even to speak Dutch alongside English.'

'Didn't that hurt your grandfather, given what had happened to his family?'

'I grew up with the rows and arguments…I set myself against my father, just as he did against my grandfather. My father became caught up in the anti-psychiatry movement of the sixties and seventies. He left my mother and eventually took himself off to America.'

'Perhaps your father searching for the painting was a way of undoing some of his early rejection of being Jewish.'

'My sister wanted to believe that. Yes, it might have been part of his motive, a very small part. My father had a rough deal. Much more than I ever allowed myself to understand. My grandfather could certainly be pig-headed and obstinate in pursuing what he thought was the right course; ruthless too in his own way. The children of psychiatrists don't necessarily benefit.'

It was new to him to speak of his father without conscious resentment, and he was surprised at the easiness of it. Between Ursula and himself the subject of his relationship with his father was never raised. He could sense Nell holding back from asking the inevitable question and answered before she had time to form it.

'No, I've no children of my own.'

He kept his voice as expressionless as possible. He was good at doing that.

But why draw back now? It was already too late. He might hide this secret grief, as well as the greater one behind it, from other people, but he wouldn't be able to pretend with this woman. The sensitivity to the hurts of other people that was so much part of her must lead her instinctively to the sores inside him.

128

He rested for a long moment in the unselfconscious friendship she offered, watching as a tendril of glowing brown hair escaped and fell across her cheek. There was something quietly trustful in her gaze. He fought the desire to be entirely honest with her, to tell her everything that troubled him, knowing the burdens he dragged around with him would be safe in her forgiving sympathy.

He looked down at the cake crumbs on his plate to hide what he was thinking. It was another thing he was good at.

His colleagues, his secretary, above all his wife of seventeen years, they were all losing substance. They faded into a vague distance on the horizon, misty irrelevancies with which he was no longer connected. All powers of resistance left him. Nell alone was his whole life. To him she was reality, she was the one thing that connected him to meaning.

All around them people ate and drank and talked, but he was conscious only of the fullness of the present moment. *Something of the divine cuts vertically into the horizontal flow of time and makes it infinite* – words heard as a boy came back and for a dazzling instant spun light-filled into sense.

'Do you still have your mother?' Nell asked.

'I have. She lives up in Hampstead.'

His mother would like Nell. But they would never meet.

'And you – you told me at Brookner House there's just your mother-in-law?'

'You always remember things. My own mother died when I was seventeen. She brought me up by herself, my dad was an artist of sorts and not at all reliable according to my mother. I can hardly remember him, so I don't miss him.'

'It must have been very hard for you to lose your mother so young.'

'We lived in the middle of nowhere in Shropshire, just on the edge of Wales. She died suddenly, that is, I wasn't expecting it so soon. I'd just started at art college here in London. I wasn't there – at the end.'

Her voice stumbled over the last sentence and he saw how much she still suffered from the memory – and something more.

'The loss of a much-loved mother is a frightful thing for anyone,' he said. 'It can have lifelong effects when it happens in childhood, and you were only just past it. But you've come through it. I reckon your mother would be pretty proud of her daughter if she could see her now.'

'Thanks – '

He stared at her, not caring for anything beyond the simple fact of her beloved presence. She was there with him, no longer the tantalising figure who haunted his dreams, the object of forbidden fantasies. She was close enough to touch – if only he could.

'I haven't asked you about Rachel,' he said gently. 'But we'll talk next time. I'm afraid it's a bit of a trek to Brookner House for you.'

'You go past all those fields of sheep, so the drive's fine. You can't get anything more beautiful than sheep with the sun lighting up their backs, can you?' Her mouth lifted with the complicit smile that assured him of her unquestioning confidence in his understanding and agreement.

Did she, like him, have the time and date of Rachel's appointments always in her head? He looked into her face, transparent in its unpremeditated honesty. Of course she didn't. He almost hated himself for his duplicity.

'I must go,' said Nell.

'Yes. You must go.'

They left the gallery and he walked the short distance with her to Charing Cross, turning swiftly out of the station and cutting short her thanks for the tea and cakes. He began to walk aimlessly towards Westminster and the river, with no end in view and not knowing where he was going. He found himself at Tate Britain, and stared up at its windows without seeing them.

Abruptly he swung round and plunged back the way he'd come, conscious only of the craving to be where she had been, as if by inhabiting that space he could summon her back to him. Nell. He hadn't used her name to her, hadn't had the joy of looking into her eyes and saying the word out loud. He whispered it now, over and over, driven by an agony he could hardly understand. He reached Charing Cross and scanned the departures board. Wharton. There was a train leaving in a few minutes. He watched people piling through the ticket barriers and into the train. He started forward as if to join them. A whistle blew and the train pulled out of the platform.

'You're a fool,' his father had said.

'I'm still going to marry her,' he said. *Not such a fool as you, swallowing crackpot theories without knowing what they are. Do you have any idea of the damage you've done? Playing fast and loose with people's lives, pretending you have all the answers.*

'Boyfriend, girlfriend – fine. Keep it at that level. If you marry her you'll live to regret it. She's not up to you – not fit to be married to anyone, if you ask me.'

'I haven't.'

'You aren't even qualified yet. Twenty-two! You're still a boy, and she's just a child – worse than a child, a child who doesn't look like growing up. You need to ask why.'

'Being nearly killed in a car accident might put a delay on anyone's growing up.'

He kept his voice neutral because he could feel anger piling up. His father knew nothing, nothing. He hadn't made a good job of his own marriage, had he, walking out of the family home when Lewis was in his teens 'because it wasn't what he wanted'. So a man had to have what he wanted, did he, and go halfway round the world for it, and that was more important to him than staying around for his children?

He'd never learnt anything at all about wanting and needing, he was just a jobbing psychiatrist, cashing in on the credit Lewis's grandfather had brought to the name. His grandfather had been dead for nearly four years now, but Lewis would have listened to *him*, he'd done so all his life. From his earliest childhood he'd known he wanted to follow his grandfather – and to be as unlike his father as possible.

Why should he take any notice of what his father thought? Hadn't he sold out wholesale to the anti-psychiatry merchants? There had been some inspirational and visionary thinking then which looked to change the whole face of psychiatry, but like every revolution it had its fanatics and delusional methodology. His father had dabbled about with every new publication and crackpot practice and hadn't thought for himself, that had been the trouble all along. It was why he'd messed up his career, why he was still clueless about what he was actually doing, or meant to do, as a psychiatrist, where he stood in the whole psychiatry debate. Lewis wasn't going to listen to anyone who hadn't even made a decent stab at asking the right questions.

'Quite. But aren't you confusing love with pity?'

She'd been in a car crash. When he first saw her, she was lying motionless in a London hospital bed, her pale translucent skin and white-blonde hair ethereal against the softness of the pillow. She looked at him with huge frightened eyes, blue pools of opaque infinity. Victim's eyes. An innocent animal knowing the knife is about to strike might look like that, he thought.

Afterwards he wanted to save her, to protect her from everything that might hurt her. She was nothing like the girls surrounding him at medical school – clever-talking, hard-edged, elbows out.

'You don't know anything about either,' he said to his father.

'I was waiting for you when I was a little girl,' she said, weeks later and out of hospital, her softly warm Dublin accent adding a beguiling allure to her words. She hadn't yet allowed him to sleep with her, but he was patient. She was still frail; she needed time.

He pressed her body against his and stared down into her face. Her moods were like a fast-moving sky, blown from sweet dependence into a fizzing brilliance that dazzled his senses. She was endlessly, achingly beautiful. He spent his days wanting to hold her in his arms, to protect her from ever being hurt again.

It wasn't pity. He was training to be a doctor for goodness sake. He knew about keeping your distance. He also knew his love for this girl wouldn't go away, even if he was only twenty-two and years away from the psychiatrist he was set on becoming.

They were married within three months of their first meeting.

You're a fool. He was almost forty and he knew this now.

His father had lived long enough to become disillusioned with the ideas of the anti-psychiatry movement. He'd gone to America to find himself. It didn't look as though he'd done so. He'd died with disappointment in his face and Lewis couldn't forget it.

But he'd seen something Lewis hadn't. Some clue about the eighteen year old Ursula that he himself had missed. Or refused to see. His father had been right all along. It was hard to forgive.

There was no longer any denying the extent of Ursula's illness – and its likely eventual outcome. In sickness and in health. He'd made the promise. Not just to the girl he'd married, but also to himself.

You're a fool. Yes, I am a fool, he told himself. But what use is knowing it now? There's no way out.

If only there wasn't the temptation of seeing Nell every time she came with Rachel to Brookner House. Would it then be possible to keep his promise, to put Nell out of his heart and mind, to forget her altogether?

Hours later, Lewis caught the train home. As he put in his key to open the front door he could hear the muffled sounds of the piano being played. His wife was waiting for him.

He stood for a moment, against his will listening to the melody that played on his guilt. One of Mendelssohn's *Songs Without Words*. Each note was further pain.

He'd had today. Two hours with the woman he both passionately – and rationally – loved. He confessed it to himself at last.

He could not regret it – yet. But as he leant against the dresser which had once belonged to his grandfather, dry-mouthed and quietening his rapid heartbeat, he knew it had been a mistake.

NINETEEN

Nell threw a despairing glance at the car mirror. The man driving the van behind her was pushing right up close, to punish her for not breaking the speed limit. She pressed her foot on the accelerator. She hated these fast roads where you had to make split second decisions and assert your right to a place on the road.

She'd driven Rachel to Rosie's house hundreds of times and was used to wishing that Rosie lived in Wharton rather than the much busier Pavebridge half a dozen miles down the A road. Today she also wished Alastair had offered to take Rachel, who along with two other friends was going to stay the night with Rosie, before Hilary took all four girls to Gatwick in time for their flight very early the following morning.

Quite apart from feeling sick and tired all the time – not exactly surprising after having her mother-in-law to stay for a whole week at Christmas – it would have given her the afternoon to start thinking seriously about the Turner Room exhibition. Rachel still refusing to eat properly meant she hadn't been able to concentrate on anything other than worrying, but now with both children going away she must make use of the few clear days ahead.

Alastair taking Rachel would also have been a time when Rachel might have opened her mouth and said something. Car journeys were good for talking with children. They didn't have to look at you, and that helped when they wanted to say anything difficult. Rachel hadn't given any signs of wanting anything at all over Christmas except to get away from her and Alastair – and above all, Barbara. That was fair enough, Barbara being what she was – but still Nell clung to the idea that things might come right, if only everyone tried harder.

'You wouldn't like to take Rachel to Hilary's instead of me?'

'We agreed I'd go with Sebastian and Vail up to King's Cross for their train to Aviemore,' Alastair protested. 'And then I wouldn't mind having a few hours to myself in London. I'd like some recovery time from my mother.'

'So would I.'

But Nell didn't pursue it. Alastair was very good to Barbara. He might sigh behind her back, but the only face he showed her was that of a fond and considerate son. He did, Nell thought, love her; if he didn't, his mother couldn't have guessed.

'More to the point, Hilary's impossible to get away from. I'll get dragged in and kept talking for hours with the other mothers. Hearing about other people's Christmases is hardly entertaining – and ours was far more wonderful darling because of you.'

Beside her, Rachel fiddled with her mobile. Nell shot a sidelong glance at her. What she'd seen in Rachel's bedroom last night lay heavy in the air between them, a mother-daughter silence that Nell had once thought could never happen to them, simply because it had never happened with her own mother. But why must she always compare the relationships when it only made her unhappy?

She ought to have said much more, dealt with the situation as Hilary would have done. Then at least she'd *know* and Rachel would know that she knew. But instead she'd wavered and then shrunk from confrontation – as she always did – turning it into yet another incident that had to be locked up in silence.

'I don't need to pack yet,' Rachel had said, when Nell had

come into her bedroom with some newly-ironed clothes, some to be put away and others as possibles for the skiing trip.

'This top is pretty for the evenings – '

Nell placed the heap on a chest of drawers. Rachel, slouched on her bed in a sleeveless tee shirt, didn't move.

'I don't want any more stuff thanks.'

Nell pulled open a drawer to put things away. Lying partly hidden by knickers she could see a knife. The small, razor-sharp vegetable knife that belonged in the kitchen. She stared at it, her mind snapping back to the middle of last term. She'd wanted to slice tomatoes or peppers and she was rummaging in the kitchen drawer. The little knife she always used was missing. She'd bought another soon afterwards.

Rachel wasn't looking at her. Nell pushed the shirts into the drawer and shut it. Her body went ice-cold. She heard Dr Auerbach's voice asking her about self-harm. Since then she'd read about it on the internet. But she still hadn't made the connection.

For a second she knew an urge to turn round and scream at her daughter for all she was putting the family through. Count to bloody ten. Go *on*.

Giving way like this to her own terror wouldn't help Rachel. If you're older you've had longer to learn how to live. In a confrontation it's for you to go ninety per cent of the way to meet the other person. The kind of thing Eleanor might say.

She turned round, trying not to look too obviously at her daughter's bare arms.

'Darling – if you suddenly feel you don't want to go skiing, it doesn't matter. I know what it's like to change your mind about things – and I'd hate you to feel pushed into anything. It's not too late to back out – '

'What are you on about? So I'm not waiting by the front door – '

Rachel had taken the knife from the kitchen drawer. She

hadn't used it, there were no marks…but she'd wanted to, she'd thought about it enough to have kept it hidden all these weeks. Please God help me not to make everything worse.

Tread lightly. Eleanor again.

'All right, darling. I'll stop being a tiresome fusspot. Why don't you go and get your passport – it's in one of the desk drawers in our room.'

Rachel shot her a look that might have been indifference – or could have been contempt.

'Why are you reading that book by Dr Auerbach? I notice you don't leave it lying around where Dad might see it. And it's a crap title.'

'It's from the beginning of *Hamlet*,' Nell evaded the accusation. 'I'll miss you – '

'Will you?'

'We both will. You and Sebastian. Terribly. I have to keep cheering myself with thinking of you skiing. I've often felt bad that we've never had a family skiing holiday because I didn't like it the one time I tried. Dad used to ski a lot before he met me. You'll have a wonderful time.'

She longed to hug her daughter close, to tell her for the hundredth time she would do anything in the world to help her, to assure her she was loved as she was, to plead with her to be more open about what was troubling her. But another deeper instinct told her that just before going away from home for the first time, even though it was only for six days, wasn't the moment for forcing confidences that had been withheld for so many weeks already.

When she next took Rachel to Dr Auerbach she would tell him about it. As she thought of his solid and never-failing kindness she wanted to burst into tears of relief and gratitude that whatever happened she could always run to him and he would be there.

'Dad will probably collect you when you come back,' she said now, turning into Hilary's road and looking for a parking space she might have some hope of getting into.

Rachel threw her a hostile glance.

'Thanks for nothing.'

'Darling, have Dad or I done something wrong? Because if we have – '

'You really don't get it, do you?'

'Is this why you're angry with us – '

'You never *see* things. You don't want to know.'

Nell wanted to stretch out her hand to touch her but already she'd reached the end of the road without seeing a space that was big enough.

'I'm sorry,' she said, trying to be calm. 'I'll go round the block and try again. Darling, what is it? What don't I see?'

'You're always saying you're sorry. It doesn't mean anything if you don't change. People stop listening.'

'I'm listening now – '

Nell struggled to manoeuvre the car into a space, mounting the pavement twice as she tried to straighten the car before giving up. Rachel undid her seat belt and re-checked the screen on her mobile.

'You think you and Dad are so perfect together don't you? And bloody Gran twittering all through Christmas about broken families. Doesn't it occur to you to wonder why she kept on about it so much?'

'Gran can only do black and white thinking, we all know that, darling. But that's fundamentalism for you. We won't see her again until Easter. You don't have to take any notice.'

'I don't – but *you* should. Don't you realise that she's twigged what's going on?'

'Darling, we've never talked about you with her. I know how awful it is to have her saying she'll pray for you in that tiptoe voice.'

'The family that prays together stays together,' mimicked Rachel. 'Some hope. You still haven't a clue, have you?'

She put her hand on the car door as if to get out. Nell said quickly, 'Darling, I hate to feel I've made life harder for you – please tell me how I can put things right between us.'

'You're trying to have another baby, aren't you?' Rachel said fiercely. 'Is that why you don't want to know about anything else?'

Nell took a careful breath. She must give Rachel an answer. But what could she say? She hadn't been honest with Alastair.

'Don't bother lying to me. Why is there a pregnancy test in your room? You ought to hide things better if you don't want people to know. I saw it when I went to find my passport.'

'I'm sorry,' Nell spoke a little unsteadily. 'It's true there have been times when I've thought it would be nice to have a bigger family.'

'You'd better not. Or are you changing your mind because you know you're a rubbish mother? Or because of Dad? Because you've guessed what he's up to?'

'What are you talking about?'

Rachel fixed her eyes on the rows of parked cars. She said, as if her mother was being even more dense than usual, 'Can't you see? Dad's having an affair. That's what I meant about Gran. She can see it all right. But you don't. You never see anything. You're so fucking gullible.'

Nell sat very still, hearing only her own breathing. In the passenger seat, her daughter pressed keys on her mobile. Outside the car, other people were living their happy uncomplicated lives.

'Please don't say horrible untrue things like this.'

'There you go again. It's your fault – you let him get away with it.'

'How long have you been thinking this?'

Rachel didn't answer. Her mobile rang.

'The others are there already.' She opened the car door. 'I have to go now. Don't you dare come in with me. You've parked crooked.'

TWENTY

She'd done it again. Parked crooked. The back of the car was sticking out into the road, the wheels weren't straight. Nell climbed out and leant against the scratched paintwork.

She'd driven back to Wharton unseeing and unhearing, wrenching the car around mechanically, oblivious of everything except the urgent need for Juliet to tell her that Rachel was making everything up, that fantasies like this were common among teenagers, and in Rachel's case triggered by the paranoid thinking of the beginnings of anorexia.

Of course Alastair wasn't having an affair with anyone. The idea was ridiculous, impossible. The other wives in the Wharton Common Room might flirt with him and Alastair was always his easy-going self with all of them. Never by a single word or look had he given her cause for jealousy. Not even with Trevor's ex, who'd tried hard enough to get more than just his admiration.

Nell willed herself to hear Juliet's laughing reassurance in her head, just as she'd heard it so many times during the years of bringing up the children. They'd always shared worries, and Juliet had never failed to make them lessen, if not disappear. Juliet, despite the twitchiness which had spoilt things between them last term, would make everything all right. Who else could she turn to, if not the friend who'd been closest to her almost all of Rachel's life?

It didn't occur to Nell to ring Juliet's doorbell. That was kept for when she and Alastair came to supper, and then it was done jokingly as if they were acting a part for the evening, playing at being hostess and guests. On all other days over the summer Nell had skipped up the little paved path that led round to the back garden and the kitchen door, just as a child might, on a play date with her best friend, and Juliet would wave hello.

She ran past the familiar weeds and piled-up flowerpots and opened the gate into the garden. Light from the house flooded the dusky grass. Juliet never bothered to draw curtains. There she stood for a moment fighting the breaths which came and went, jerky and sharp, and looked through the kitchen window.

At first the room appeared to be empty. Then, at the far end, she saw Juliet. She wasn't waving. She was quite still, with her back towards Nell and she was being kissed by Alastair.

For one convulsive minute Nell stared, uncomprehending. It wasn't Alastair. Someone who looked like him. It was a mistake. Something berserk in her brain because of Rachel and what she'd said. Alastair was at this moment still in London, giving himself a break after seeing the boys off at King's Cross. Foyles, he'd said, I'll have a good browse and catch up with what's new in history and politics textbooks. She could hear his voice telling her he'd be home early evening, about the same time as her. Around six, you won't get away from Hilary's before that. But she had got away, and now it wasn't even five o'clock.

She hadn't believed Rachel. Rachel would say anything just now, she made things up. Nothing that she said could be relied on: what she ate, what Dr Auerbach said to her, what was making her behave the way she did. She said whatever came into her head. Nell had rushed round to Juliet's house not because she believed for one moment in Rachel's sudden flung-out accusation, but to reassure herself it was nonsense – not that

143

she needed any reassurance, but – and here Nell's thoughts fell into unfathomable confusion.

Now she stood quite still, staring at the intertwined bodies hardly understanding what she was seeing. Juliet's arched back, Alastair's wide shoulders bent over her. Hands buried into the dusky silk of Juliet's hair. Alastair's hands, which only this morning had held and caressed her in just that place. She put up a doubting hand to touch the back of her neck. The echoes of his touch slid across the skin and prickled into coldness. In a minute of white ice silence she could only hear her own shallow breaths, feel the clogged thumping in her chest.

Juliet was wearing a red shirt Nell had never seen before. A flaming, rich red. Burning shards of colour started to explode in Nell's head, fragmenting into dizzying, chaotic shapes. It wasn't her best friend Juliet who was embracing her husband but some other woman in alien clothes.

This isn't happening.

She must have made some movement. Alastair turned his head to the window. In one instant he thrust Juliet away from him, a swift sharp glance raking the dark outside. She saw him start. He'd seen her. For one terrible moment they stared at each other, Alastair silhouetted in the electric light of the kitchen. With a strangled gasp, Nell turned and fled back to the little side path, wrenching open the gate. As she reached the pavement, the front door was flung open and Alastair plunged towards her.

'Nell – for God's sake, let me explain – '

Not even to save Rachel or Sebastian could Nell have stopped running just then. Sick terror consumed every corner of consciousness. She had to get home, to throw up, to scream, to cry. But Alastair caught hold of her, pulling her towards him.

'Don't run from me like this. It was nothing, a moment of madness – you *must* understand – '

She was being swallowed up, shot at by poisoned arrows.

'Oh please God, no! You can't be – not you – '

'*No*! Nell, darling, come away – come home with me, I can explain everything – '

A group of youths appeared at the corner of the road. They might have been Wharton sixth formers who lived locally, Nell couldn't tell. None of them looked familiar in the distorting light of the streetlamps. Alastair froze and lowered his voice to a whisper.

'Please – we can't talk here.'

'I can't talk *anywhere*.'

'Just come away – '

Juliet's front door was still open and perhaps it was this that suddenly decided Nell.

'Let go of me – y*ou* go away!'

She twisted herself out of his grasp, and whirled away from him and into Juliet's house, slamming the door behind her.

The hall was empty. Nell ran straight for the cloakroom and was violently sick. Her whole body felt icy cold as she hung over the merciless white ceramic, waiting for the next wave of nausea to overcome her. At last her heaving stomach subsided. She flushed the loo and dragged herself upright, wiping her mouth with paper tissues.

'Nell?'

Juliet had crept out of the kitchen and stood silently in the hall near the cloakroom door watching her. The cloakroom where the two of them had jokingly complained about boys being unable to aim properly, how lavatories ought to be better designed, the yucky and unstoppable yellowing of the floor. All of this Nell remembered now with absurd irrelevance as she slowly washed her hands and splashed water over her face in the basin.

'I'm sorry.'

Juliet said this so quietly that Nell hardly heard her. But she knew immediately what it meant. Something of her ability to think and react came back to her, and also something of courage. She turned to look Juliet full in the face.

'Tell me it isn't true.'

But even as she said this she knew she was being a child, the child who skipped heedlessly up the garden path, refusing to acknowledge that the party was over, the present never arriving, the race lost. It *was* true. Juliet's voice and face said it all. No amount of toddler stamping of feet or shutting of eyes was going to make it go away.

An ungovernable rage flooded through her so that she wanted to strike at Juliet's face and hurt her and go on hurting her. For a second she gave in and lifted her hand as if to hit that enemy animal face, but then she saw Juliet flinch and step back. Anger and sadness swirled around her, fighting in a red fog.

'I don't believe this is happening. The friend I trusted most in the world, doing this to me – *now!*'

'Now?'

'You *knew* where I've just been, didn't you? Taking Rachel to Rosie's, that I wouldn't be back till much later, but I am, you see – and you've chosen this moment to – ' the words she wanted fell into chaos and out of reach. She pushed her hands back against the doorframe, shrinking away from Juliet.

'I was conveniently out of the way. So you grabbed your chance and – '

'You could look at it like that – '

'How else can I look at it? You *used* Rachel's illness, you chose this time to – '

It was the calculation of it, the cold-hearted deception, that was the worst of all, worse than Alastair kissing Juliet, worse than Juliet – but she was getting things the wrong way round, putting them in the wrong order, she always did.

'I didn't think of it like that.'

Nell stared at her in disbelief and found she couldn't speak. It wasn't a moment of madness. Rachel had said that Alastair – terror cut into her, a hot and cold knife. How long had it been going on? All this term while she'd been so preoccupied with Rachel? Her brain plunged wildly, back across the weeks. The summer holidays, the start of term? Or before Juliet had come to Wharton, when Juliet had been living in London?

'Do you really want me to tell you how it happened, how I came to – to do this?'

Nell gestured towards the kitchen and then wished she hadn't. Alastair had been in it just now. But he must have been all over the house. He may have been there for several hours – have come back from taking the boys to London and gone straight to Juliet, just as she was setting off to take Rachel to Rosie's house. The sofa in the sitting room, Juliet's bedroom with its white lace on the double bed – the stain was everywhere.

'I don't see how you can explain. How anyone could.'

Juliet pushed open the door into the kitchen. Nell went over to the window and stared out into the shadowy garden, half expecting to see her own ghost staring back at her from where she had stood a lifetime ago. Then she slowly drew the curtains across the window. Behind her, Juliet poured milk into a saucepan and frothed it up. At the sink Nell could see two wine glasses and a half empty bottle.

'You've got it wrong,' Juliet said. 'I haven't been having an affair.'

'Don't lie to me. I saw you from the garden.'

'It – it was the first time – '

'No it bloody wasn't,' Nell interrupted her. Rachel's tight little voice was going round and round in her head. *You never see anything, do you?*

'Alastair will say the same.'

The bitterness in Juliet's voice underlined what Nell knew

already. Obviously Juliet and Alastair would deny it, and expect her to roll over and give in. Scorching humiliation burnt through every vein. People thought she'd fall for anything, she was a soft touch, so gullible as to be actually deficient, just like her mother had been with her feckless father.

'You've been lying to me all this term haven't you?' Anger so violent that it frightened her took hold of Nell. 'Or is it longer than that? You took that money for the Wharton deposit in September, was that Alastair's payment to you?'

This wasn't her voice speaking, it was someone else's, a suddenly vicious woman lashing out like a cornered animal.

'You always had other men. As many as you wanted. All those stories during the summer about Ralphie and Guy and Jonathan – were they all just window dressing? Made up to put me off the scent?'

'It never entered your head, did it, that Alastair might find other women attractive? Or that I or anyone else might want him for ourselves? That someone like me might eventually be unable to go on holding off for your sake?'

'So you went on pretending to be my best friend,' said Nell, the words beating slowly and painfully in her head, 'but all the time it was him you wanted.'

'Is it so surprising? It's not exactly an unusual scenario you know. Husband and wife's best friend. It's practically a cliché. Why do you always have to shut your eyes to human nature?'

'So I should have expected it, should I? Or it's even my fault?'

'I didn't mean to fancy your husband, it just happened.'

'You had nothing to do with it. Couldn't help it even. Are you asking me to feel sorry for you?'

'Okay. You might see it like that. But I didn't. I tried to push him out of my head, to kid myself I could make other relationships take over. You don't believe me, but it's true. I did try. It didn't work.'

Juliet filled mugs and put them on the kitchen table, as if they were an offering alongside her explanation, demanding acceptance.

'I wonder how many times you've made cappuccinos for us like this,' Nell dashed her jumper sleeve across her face, 'and yet I never guessed what was in your head.'

'Oh Nell, it wasn't like that. We *were* friends, I wanted us to be always friends. You're the friend I've dreamed of all my life.'

'But you do this to me.'

'I wasn't doing it *to* you. You must understand that. I never ever for one moment wanted to hurt you. How could I, feeling as I do about you? You're *my* best friend, for God's sake.'

'I thought friendships were sacred.'

This was the wrong word. Nell despised herself for using it but she couldn't think of another. What was friendship after all, if it didn't involve sacrifice and loyalty over and above irrational desires and selfish urges?

She sat down at the table, where she'd sat so many times before, but she could only feel the coldness of her hands and a great painful tightness in her throat. She thrust the mug savagely away from her. Milk slurped on the waxed pine like bile and started dripping onto the floor.

'You never gave hurting *anyone* a thought! Trying to pretend you didn't mean it! What do you know about anything – about love or trust or – ' she fumbled for the words that wouldn't come.

'You're right. I don't know about these things – not like you do. It's one of the reasons why your friendship's meant so much to me. It's been almost the most precious thing in my life.'

A lump came unbidden into Nell's throat. Juliet had always come out with things like this. Quite unexpectedly, she gave more than you asked of her. An unexplained and prodigal sensitivity that had warmed Nell for twelve perfect years.

Memories crowded into her head. Juliet whisking her to the front of the queue for the ladies when she'd been six months pregnant and feeling she couldn't wait another second, Juliet rushing round to their London flat at two o'clock in the morning when Sebastian had been taken ill with what might have been meningitis and Alastair had been away, Juliet taking a giggling and besotted Rachel out for girlie treats.

A small, strange urge to forgive her friend flickered into life. If it had in truth just been today…

It died almost immediately. She knew it was the old childish longing for a Happy Families existence, for their lives to be put back by magic to the way they once were. She swallowed painfully, the tears pricking her eyes. She wasn't as infantile as that.

'So much to you? Not enough to stop you trying to take my husband away from me.'

'I haven't taken him from you. He's still your husband, not mine.'

'But not for much longer if you get your way.' She heard again her stupid, oh so stupid, voice telling Juliet how she was going to get pregnant and surprise Alastair. 'You thought Alastair wouldn't bring himself to leave me if I was having another child.'

'He married you when you got pregnant with Rachel, didn't he?'

'You're only saying that to hurt me. You know perfectly well it wasn't anything like that. Alastair didn't want to wait – I'd told him what my mother went through, never getting any commitment from my father and then being tossed aside like a used-up rag when he fancied painting some different scenery. Alastair didn't want to be like him.'

'He always did believe he's capable of being something more than he is – the grand gesture, the faithful husband.'

'Shut *up.*'

'Oh Nell, can't you see what it's like to be pulled both ways? I do really love Al you know.'

She was calling him Al. Why did this hurt so unbearably? *Nobody* called Alastair Al. He always said he didn't like it; it had been a familiar joke between them, to be used when she was teasing him.

'So you moved here to be near him – and to try and take him from me. You *lied* to me.'

Juliet picked up a spoon and trailed chocolate powder with painstaking deliberation across the surface of her cappuccino.

'I never lied to you. I never needed to.'

'Meaning?'

'Haven't I already told you that if you'd asked me yesterday if I'd been sleeping with your husband, the answer would have been no?'

You never see things. You don't want to know.

Did Juliet really expect to be believed? Contempt at Juliet's disingenuousness struggled with astonishment at her own idiocy.

One more question must be asked.

'Has he told you he loves you?'

Juliet met her gaze.

'Do you really think I would have let him touch me on any other basis?'

'Why not? It's what you always do with men. According to you.'

'Anyway, I'm not the first. Do you honestly think I am?'

Nell stared at her unseeingly.

'I don't believe you.'

'That's up to you.'

The telephone rang into the silence. Juliet ignored it. Then

151

the shriller ringtone of Juliet's mobile. Alastair calling to find out what was happening. Trying to talk to Juliet, not her.

Was he ringing up to find out if she'd bought the fairy tale about it being the first time they'd slept together? Had he put Juliet up to saying that? Yes, of course he had.

The agony and humiliation of this realisation was too much. She stumbled out of the kitchen into the darkness of the street.

TWENTY-ONE

There was no sign of Alastair.

He must have gone home. He'd be waiting for her there. What was she to say – or he to her? One click of the eye's camera and he'd turned into a stranger.

Terror flooded over her. She was absolutely alone. Everything familiar, safe and happy had been snatched away, and she was falling into a nightmare existence.

She couldn't go home. Not yet. She wanted to run and run, somewhere, anywhere. But she couldn't do that either. She crouched against a lamp post, shaking uncontrollably.

Martin. He would help her. Then with a desolate jolt she remembered. He was away visiting his parents in Coventry.

She'd lost her mother. Now she'd lost her best friend and her husband. It wasn't fair to tell Eleanor and expect her to keep it from Clement. There were others like Hilary, but they had families and busy lives. She couldn't land on their doorsteps in this state.

For one spinning minute she thought of Dr Auerbach. But he was a child psychiatrist. He didn't fix life for adults. And that was what she was, even if she didn't feel like one. She was going to have to *be* an adult now, not this snivelling baby who expected other people to pick her up and kiss everything better.

She began to walk slowly down Juliet's road, then through

the town. In the High Street she passed groups of girls dressed and scented for an evening out. She stopped to sit on one of the benches where homeless people slumped with their dogs during the day and pulled out their sleeping bags at night.

For unmeasured hours she stared in through misty windows of pubs and wine bars at the warmth, the bright lights, the noise and chatter. People were laughing, buying drinks, exchanging news. Last night she might have been one of them. Now they were from a different world.

It was beginning to rain. She left the bench and went further up the hill. Waitrose. The local theatre. A Freddie Mercury lookalike in a white vest singing *Who wants to live forever*. The magic shop where Juliet had bought Sebastian the tricks he'd wanted for his twelfth birthday present in September.

Lightening ripped across the sky, instantly followed by a crash of thunder and bursting clouds. In a few minutes she was drenched, her jersey and jeans clinging cold and clammy to her skin. She trailed back down the hill, hunching her shoulders against the wet. The church on the corner was shrouded in dark shadows. She'd never made the effort to go to it.

Oh God, get me home.

But God wouldn't be listening. You couldn't expect him to come to your rescue when you hadn't bothered with him because you were too busy having a good time and enjoying yourself.

Alastair was sitting at the kitchen table with a drink in his hand. He looked so normal that for a crazy moment Nell wondered if he was going to pretend nothing had happened. Even to wish that he would. It would after all be like him, and then she too could pretend.

Alastair jumped up, not quite looking at her.

'You're soaked!'

'Yes. Didn't you know? It's raining.'

She glanced at him, unable to think of anything to say, then turned away.

'Nell, wait, give me a chance to explain.'

'I'm too cold.'

'Just let me tell you I'm sorry, I didn't mean it.'

'I don't give a damn if you meant it or not!' Nell suddenly shouted. Every bit of her body was beginning to ache.

'I'll run you a hot bath.'

This too was familiar. Alastair was always quick to offer comfort. Not just to her, but to everyone. It was one of the things she loved about him. But Juliet had loved it as well, and now she didn't want him fussing over her, smirching her with attention that was too lightly given.

As she peeled off her wet clothes in the bedroom she caught sight of her body in the long mirror, her skin all pale and blotchy where her clothes had stuck to her, her hair straggling down her neck in ugly rats' tails.

'I'll bring you up a hot drink.'

'I don't *want* a hot drink.'

She locked the bathroom door to get rid of him and lay down in the water, pulling herself down the bath so she could submerge her face. Steam clouded the room, the warmth invaded her body and at last it felt as though it belonged to her again.

Coming back into their bedroom, Nell saw that Alastair had left her a mug of hot chocolate, and this small gesture made everything hurt worse than ever. Her body might crave it, but his making it for her after what he'd done almost choked her. As she thought of Juliet standing over the cooker boiling milk for the cappuccino she hadn't drunk she began to cry again, but in a drizzly worn-out way, as if she had no energy to feel anything, not even such misery as this.

Alastair crept into the room. He might have been Sebastian

after being found out in some childish misdemeanour, afraid of her crossness yet craving reassurance he was still loved.

'Do you love her?'

The words came out before she could stop them. They were pointless. If you looked at it one way, it made no difference whether Alastair thought he loved Juliet. It all came to the same thing in the end. He'd been unfaithful. Whatever Alastair chose to say now didn't matter.

'No – not love.'

'Then why?'

'I don't know.'

She'd been married to him for fourteen years. It was long enough for her to have learnt that he probably *didn't* know. He never did examine why he found himself in uncongenial situations, only how to get out of them.

'She was my best friend. If I wasn't enough for you, why did you have to pick on her?'

'Oh Nell, how can I give a reason? Because she *is* your best friend. Because you were preoccupied with Rachel. Because I thought she's like you – '

'She's not remotely like me. Or we wouldn't be having this conversation.'

He looked away from her and didn't speak.

'You told her you loved her, didn't you?'

'You know I love *you*. Can you still love me, after what I've done?'

His face held an expression with which she was familiar. It was the one he used when he was late, when he'd forgotten an appointment, when he'd given her the emerald ring. He simply wanted her to agree with him, for everything to be made smooth again. He'd always been able to make people do what he wanted. It was all part of the charm he used, yet was hardly aware that he used.

There was only one answer she could make. As she made it she knew it was the one he expected – and that he was cruel in asking her.

'What do you think?' she said, unable to bring herself to say the actual words. 'Even though I don't know how you could do this to me, to the children. To risk losing all we had for a moment's madness – is that what you called it outside her house? But it wasn't, was it, it's been going on for months – and before that there were others – '

'But it *was* – whatever you may think, I have *not* been cheating on you. Not before today, and never – Nell darling, don't look at me like that! – never with anyone else. You've always been everything to me.'

She didn't believe him any more than she'd believed Juliet.

'It's not about you – or the children. Only tell me what I can do to prove to you that I love you.'

'I won't make the obvious comment.'

'I don't want to lose you. I can't understand why it happened, giving in to an idiotic and completely unsought impulse like that. It was a split second of not knowing what I was doing – and then Juliet – '

'Yes, you did. You were going to be in London all day. You came back to be with her.'

'Nell, just tell me.'

It's too late to be told, she could have said, but where would that get her – or him? They must work this out together. She was beginning to realise that it was all going to be down to her. The thought almost crushed her.

What he had done had destroyed the image she'd had of him. It hadn't been real. She saw that now. But she'd believed in it.

'When your faith in someone is shattered, I don't see how you can recover it.'

'Some women couldn't, but you're different, Nell, you're better than other women,' he pleaded. 'It was all a mistake, never ever to be repeated. Let me make it up to you. Please, darling.'

She stared at him in disbelief. Did all affairs lead to these puerile flatteries, these childish bargainings?

'It's not something you can make up for. What are you proposing, that I carry on as if nothing has happened? With Juliet living just a walk away from us – ' she stifled an inward sob, remembering. 'Oh God, the car. I left it there. Outside Juliet's house.'

'I fetched it.'

So he'd gone back there.

'It's not just me – it's Rachel and Sebastian – '

'But darling, they'll never know. Unless you mean to tell them.'

I can't tell you that Rachel already knows it all, and today she told me. This is what you've done to the daughter you love so much.

'Do you imagine for one moment I'd burden them with it? Vail's Sebastian's greatest friend, and he's like another brother to Rachel. I wouldn't *think* of ruining things between them.'

'Sweetheart, let me take you away for a few days,' he said, apparently not noticing the bitterness in her voice. 'A break, just the two of us. Get right away from all this.'

He never did notice – unless it suited him. How could he even think that she could be won over by a holiday?

For a moment the insult kept her silent. She clenched her hands tightly together. Then she realised that this was Alastair, who believed that all difficulties could be removed with pleasant talking, with promises of a good time, with flattery. The thought came to her that Juliet had understood this, and used it, as she too had done, finding comfort in such accommodation.

'Rachel and Sebastian aren't back until after New Year. That gives us a clear five days. Please darling, say yes.'

'Sebastian's coming the day before her.'

'Four days then.'

'I've got the Turner Room exhibition to do. That was why we were so pleased about the children being away, remember? But no, you didn't remember, you were thinking about other things.'

'Can't you give me this chance to show that I'm sorry, more sorry than I've ever been about anything? Can't you believe me?'

She did. He *was* sorry, she could see it. But was he sorry because he found himself in a disagreeable situation – this would be so like Alastair after all – or sorry because he'd hurt her?

'I hate myself for making you unhappy,' he said, as though answering her unspoken question. 'I'll do anything you want. And I promise you it'll never happen again.'

She could feel her resistance giving way, as much from tiredness as conviction.

'There's no point in making promises like that. Not any more.'

How was it she was going to agree to go away with him when the idea of it appalled her? For she would agree, she knew that already. But she didn't want *him* to know it.

'I won't be able to get all the art work done.'

'There's still time afterwards, before term starts. I'll help, I'll do whatever I can for you.'

He might have been one of the fourth formers offering to mop up some spilt paint.

'A couple of days then,' she said. 'I wish I could con myself into thinking it will do any good. I can't fabricate belief like you do.'

Was there ever a wife so craven as she was, who gave up their pride with so little argument? Other women would have demanded details, dates, times. Even though such knowledge would be torture, they would insist on knowing. But she couldn't bear to even ask the questions.

You don't face things, Rachel had hurled at her. It was true. She didn't. Hadn't she refused to believe her mother was dying all those years ago?

'Amsterdam,' he said, stretching out his hand towards her. 'Is that where you'd like to go?'

Her day in London at the National Portrait Gallery came back to her. Drinking tea and eating iced walnut cake with Dr Auerbach. He'd told her about his great-grandparents going to a concentration camp. Stinging tears gathered in her eyes.

'No. Not there.'

'I want you to choose, darling. Anywhere you like.'

'I don't bloody *care*,' she finally snapped. 'I don't want to go anywhere. Especially with you. But I will.'

Was she going to have to sleep beside him? She jabbed the bed with her foot.

'And I'm not having you in here tonight.'

'I've already taken my things to the spare room.'

He shut the door quietly behind him and Nell looked again at the bed. She saw that not only were his pyjamas missing but also the hefty crime novel paperback he was currently in the middle of. She climbed under the double duvet and shivered until the early hours. At last and when she'd given up hope of it, she fell asleep.

TWENTY-TWO

Two days later Nell was standing at the window of a hotel in Rome. Their room was opulent with antique furniture and heavy embossed draperies. The bed, with its elaborately carved headboard, was covered with shiny dark red damask and piled with matching tasselled cushions. Nell averted her eyes from it and remained at the window.

In the piazza below, groups of Italian teenagers talked and laughed. Nell thought despairingly of Rachel and Sebastian. Both of them were with their friends, enjoying their first-ever go at skiing and would be sorry when it was over. For all this Nell was thankful – but still she couldn't stop herself longing for them with the fierce physical hunger she remembered from when they were small children.

All the time her brain churned its relentless treadmill. Why had Alastair turned to Juliet – what had she not done or been that had made him want something more? Over and over again, she found herself going back over the years of friendship with Juliet but everything had become confused, had lost its sharp focus. That had been from another life, she'd been another person, thoughtlessly and carelessly happy, not the Nell standing here desolate in this luxury hotel bedroom.

'You need a drink, darling,' Alastair said. He went over to a glass-topped table and took out a bottle from a silver ice-filled casket. 'It's the inevitable Prosecco, but I know you like it.'

Drinking fizzy Italian wine with a handsome man smiling into her eyes. It was like a clip from the romantic comedy she'd taken Rachel to see before Christmas. But what help was it to her?

After a few sips she began to feel nauseated, waves of disgust and loathing flooding over her like poison. How could you go on living when all you felt was such searing jealousy and hatred?

Her husband was standing a few feet away from her and this too was almost unbearable. She fought the impulse to snatch her bag and run from the room. In her imagination she saw herself making a dramatic bid for escape, as the heroine in the film had done, racing back to the airport, leaving Alastair behind in this claustrophobic hotel with its soft carpets and gilded mirrors which enclosed her like a prison.

From her bag flung onto the dressing table, her mobile phone beeped. A message. She put down her glass thankfully and checked the screen. It was a text from Rachel.

Sorry mum u r not rubbish i told rosie bt i think she nu skg gd i miss u Rachel x.

Tears gradually blurred the letters. A wave of hot love swept through her. If only Rachel would get better, she could bear it all. She stood quite still, staring unseeingly at the screen, sorting and steadying opposing thoughts.

'It's Rachel,' she said, keeping her face averted so Alastair wouldn't see it, her voice sounding light even to herself. 'No broken limbs so far and she's enjoying the skiing.'

'We'll all go together next year,' he promised. 'You don't have to ski if you don't want to. But it would be good to go as a family.'

This was the man who had quibbled over spending the

money on taking Rachel to Dr Auerbach and who was spending goodness knows how many euros on this trip to Rome. The man who'd insisted they couldn't afford a third child.

Her hand tightened over her mobile. *Alastair has never denied himself anything and he isn't about to start now. He'll go on accepting whatever falls into his hands, not questioning the cost to the people he loves – or to himself.*

She'd fallen in love with the man she'd wanted him to be, and not the man he was. She'd seen the surface kindness and good humour, and mistaken it for a deeper goodness. But worse than this was her continuing and cowardly deception of herself as well as him, for she'd gone on pretending he was other than he was, and all because she couldn't bear to admit to herself that she'd blundered in the most important decision of her life.

She'd given her love to a false god.

Hadn't her mother done the same?

'Let me show you how much I love you.'

Alastair came up to her, as if to put his arms around her. Nell snapped off her mobile.

'Wait – '

She went into the bathroom, closed the door and leant against it. She'd stuffed her diaphragm, not used since September, into her washing bag, sick with fear that it might be already too late. Her period was overdue. What if it didn't come? Even thinking about the possibility of being pregnant brought on the restless nausea which hadn't left her since she'd been sick in Juliet's cloakroom. She'd wanted a baby and hadn't looked beyond her own wanting. In spite of every warning that might have stopped her, she'd gone on taking no notice.

For hadn't she, at some subconscious level, known that something was wrong between her and Alastair? Somewhere, deep inside her, had been an uneasiness, a faint whisper that something was unreal, there was something she wasn't noticing, wasn't asking. Last summer term when she and Alastair had rowed …the summer holidays when he'd played so much tennis.

Juliet moving to Wharton had blinded her. She'd seen everything as she'd wanted to see it, through the one lens of her own choosing. And then there had been Rachel suddenly hating everyone, and after that she'd been floundering, unable to make sense of what was staring her in the face.

The day she'd looked at the bank statement, Hilary's phone call, Dr Auerbach's guarded face – all these things ought to have made her pause.

But she hadn't. She'd ignored them all.

Now she might be getting what she'd thought she wanted.

A random memory came into her head of Rachel aged seven being made to stand outside the school staff room for some nameless crime. 'You're being punished, so *look* as if you're being punished,' the head teacher had reprimanded her, and afterwards she and Alastair had laughed at how ridiculous it was.

She was being punished all right for deceiving Alastair – did she look as if she was?

In the mirrored wall, she examined her pinched and hollow-eyed face, just as she'd done the day she'd crept into Alastair's study. Once Alastair would have held her in front of a mirror like this, caressing her body and she would have responded with delight and gratitude for the pleasure he gave to her. She shut her mind to the picture and made her preparations, all the time trying to shut off consciousness of what she was going to do when she reopened the door.

This horrible room, redolent of bought sex, where rich men leered and women sold themselves, where husbands used clichés like this to gullible mistresses. And wives were gullible too, for even now her husband was sliding his hands around her waist and murmuring endearments into her neck and she was going to have to endure it.

'Not now – not yet – '

'Please – '

He put his hands behind her neck and tilted up her face so that his lips met hers, and guided her towards the bed.

'Kiss me,' he said, 'to show that all is forgiven.'

He's said this before.

A memory of white roses, sterile and scentless in cold Cellophane. A brief vision of the long years ahead when he would be saying the same thing and she would have to listen, knowing the falsity of it all.

Why should that first kiss be more invasive, more abhorrent than what followed? That too was repugnant for her, though Alastair's touch was as gentle and considerate as it had ever been. She lay there not resisting, but dry and shrivelled, dead to all feeling except that of distaste to what was happening to her body.

Afterwards she lay quite still, watching with wide open eyes the chandelier over her head. She was in Juliet's garden again, staring in at her friend wrapped in Alastair's arms. Upstairs was Juliet's unmade bed, the rumpled sheet pregnant with the smell of sweat and passion. In the kitchen were the glasses of wine they'd been drinking, put down unfinished while they stopped to push tongues down each other's throats.

Would it become easier after this first time, would she learn to pretend – as Alastair evidently could – that their love-making could resume unmarred? She might determine – she *had* determined – that she would do all she could to wipe Alastair's infidelity out of her head. She might be having his child. But all the time she knew her forgiveness had come to Alastair too easily.

It wasn't forgiveness. It was just a fake – artifice made of cracking plastic.

She swivelled her eyes to the still half-filled glass of

165

Prosecco on the bedside table. She hadn't been able to finish drinking it. It might have helped her – made it easier to distance her essential self from Alastair's possession of her, blunt the outrage at being in some way degraded as he lay on top of her.

If submitting to his caresses was like this! She shuddered inwardly. She couldn't go on doing it.

But she must.

She'd agreed to come here to Rome to mend their marriage, had shovelled the hurt and pride into a boxed-up space in her head. She was submitting to a cliché she couldn't believe in – and that meant she was agreeing to what happened both in and out of the bedroom.

TWENTY-THREE

'I don't want to talk about – you know,' said Rachel. 'At least only enough to say I meant what I texted you, Mum. I'm sorry about what I said. And other stuff.'

'Never mind what you said, darling. There's something I didn't tell you about, and I ought to have done. I saw you had a knife among your clothes. You know what I thought then, don't you?'

'I'm not doing – what you think I'm doing.'

'You took the knife – '

'I *had* to – it made me feel *safe* – '

'Darling, you're always safe. If only I could help you see that.'

'Dr Auerbach – '

'Does he know? About the knife?'

'Why are you asking that?'

Rachel had come home with a defensive face. Nell, after one look at her, knew that however hard the last few days had been, something still harder lay ahead of her. She must convince Rachel, aged thirteen and with only the haziest grasp of the complexity of adult mores, that she must try and put what her father had done out of her head and into the past.

Alastair and Juliet might have denied that their affair had been going on since the summer, but Nell knew better. Rachel had learnt of it. To probe a thirteen-year-old child for details about her father's unfaithfulness was unthinkable. Nell couldn't bring herself to put Rachel through it. She might never know exactly what Rachel had heard or seen, and she would certainly never ask.

What people called moving on – another clichéd expression Nell hated, but was going to find herself using – would ask a lot of them both. Nell saw clearly that it couldn't be attempted without a fundamental shift in their relationship. They must be in each other's confidence, almost as equals, if the thing was to be done.

'Darling, it might be easier to say anything you want to now. Sebastian's with Vail getting stuff for school and Dad's out until later at a department meeting – '

'Seb doesn't know,' said Rachel quickly. 'Nor Vail.'

'What you said in the car about Dad – I hate to think of you having to bear all that by yourself. But I'm glad you felt able to tell me about it in the end.'

She'd repeated the words Dr Auerbach had used. Wasn't he a man to whom one could say anything, in spite of – or was it because of? – the way he shrouded his expression into that curious blend of concern and detachment?

They were once more in Rachel's bedroom, Hilary having delivered Rachel home with an unquestioning thoughtfulness for which Nell was grateful. On the floor lay Rachel's half-opened bag, dirty washing spilling out, but that could wait until later.

Rachel knelt and fiddled with the broken zip.

'It's true then.'

'There's been something, yes. But it's over.'

'It was when you went away on the art trip. I thought I heard – but I wasn't certain.'

'I'm so terribly sorry, darling. For everything.'

Rachel turned her face towards her, her eyes filling with tears.

'Oh Mum, I hurt you, I meant you never to know.'

'I understand all that – '

'I was angry with you for not seeing. A bit of me *did* want you to find out. Then I saw the pregnancy test. I *had* to say something then because if Dad was planning to leave – it was like I was in a trap, and whatever I did was awful.'

Nell's hand moved as if to touch her stomach. The sick fear she was already pregnant lay coiled, a cold snake waiting to strike.

'You did the right thing darling. You can be quite certain I'll never tell anyone about it. Not Dad, not Sebastian. Your text – when I got it in Rome – I can't explain what it meant to me.'

Nell reached down to stroke her daughter's hair and realised that for the first time in months Rachel didn't jerk her head away.

'You've been amazingly brave about it all, far more than I would have been at your age. I'm so proud of you. Will you believe me when I tell you that Dad and I have talked things through and got things straightened out between us?'

'Things?'

'Sorry, darling, I was being feeble. Hiding behind words. I meant about Juliet. And Dad.'

There was a silence. Rachel said in a small voice, 'They were having an affair.'

'Not a serious one. But these things happen. Grown ups acting senselessly or without thinking properly and hurting the people they love. Often when they've been drinking – and afterwards they wish they hadn't. It's like that with Dad.'

'*Does* he wish he hadn't?'

'Absolutely.' Nell realised she was struggling to sound convincing. 'He's promised me it was all a silly mistake. On both sides. It's in the past now, and we're going to pull together to put it behind us. Can you do that?'

'Can you?'

'I'm trying to.'

'You're talking like someone out of a yuck magazine.'

'I know. I can hear myself.'

Rachel gave her a sideways look.

'I did tell someone. I wasn't going to, but I did in the end. I told Dr Auerbach, but only if he wouldn't tell you. He said he wouldn't. I knew he'd keep his promise.'

A picture came into Nell's head of the inscrutable expression Dr Auerbach wore when he was at Brookner House. He must always be filing away small impressions, clues, throwaway remarks, but nothing of this ever showed on his face. That remained impassive, dispassionate, even a little distant. He would remember everything, but reveal nothing.

'Yes, he always would.'

'Do you mind, him knowing, I mean?'

'Why should I?' The lightness of tone came easier than she expected. 'It's good you could be open with him. He at any rate didn't fail you as I've done. I ought to have realised, spotted what was happening. Do you think this is what's really been the trouble – why you've not been eating?'

'Dr Auerbach said it was. But I think he knew already.'

Nell went still.

'Knew – ?'

'Or like guessed – that it wasn't really about food. When I talked to him he made me see that things were okay. Or could be, anyway. That I didn't have to do stuff – '

Something that might have been shame ran over Nell as she heard this. She wanted to ask more, but that would be unfair. Rachel's sessions with Dr Auerbach were for her alone, and she must never comment, never criticise, never interfere.

Dr Auerbach must have been thinking about all this when she'd met him in the National Portrait Gallery on her birthday.

All that had happened then, the way he'd looked at her, the gentleness of his voice, came back to her in a suddenly altered and unsettling light.

She'd need time by herself to go over it before she could understand how this made her feel.

And yet even as these thoughts were running through her head, she was telling herself that none of it mattered, beside the one important thing which was that Rachel had found the help she needed. She made an effort and said, 'I should think he'd understand anything and everything.'

He'd told her that he had no children. He'd turned it off lightly as if it wasn't the grief to him that it must be; he was a man who would be the kindest and wisest of fathers. She remembered feeling ashamed of her own greediness and a barely-acknowledged and preposterous longing to wipe away something she thought she saw in his eyes.

'I don't think I need to go and see him again though.' Rachel's voice sounded deliberately casual. 'I'm fine, okay?'

'But Rachel – '

'I've made up my mind.' Rachel looked away, twisting her hair. 'Me and Rosie, we think it's better this way. We've decided.'

Nell knew she ought to feel nothing but relief at hearing this. Instead she was aware of alarm and something else she couldn't understand. She told herself she'd come to rely on Dr Auerbach as the only person who could help Rachel. He was a professional who knew what he was doing and was paid to do it. With him looking out for Rachel she'd known nothing awful could happen. Yet if Rachel didn't need him it was obviously absurd to go on wasting time and money trailing over to appointments. Dr Auerbach would be only too thankful to have Rachel off his hands.

She ought to be thankful too.

'All right, I'll cancel. You can always change your mind, you only have to say.'

'Yes, but I won't.'

It wasn't surprising Rachel was turning instead to a friend of her own age, and there was certainly nothing Nell could do about it. And Rosie was a sensible girl…

'You know darling, things aren't always as easy for grown ups as we pretend. I mean, we are every now and then tempted to behave very badly. You mustn't blame Dad too much.'

'I can blame Juliet,' said Rachel. 'I hate her. How can friends do things like that to each other?'

'I don't know,' said Nell, once more on the edge of tears. 'Or why people give in to temptation without thinking what it means. Even the best of them.'

She saw again the infinite kindness of Dr Auerbach's smile. But was that too only an illusion? With a struggle she thrust the image away.

'You know how Dad would do anything for you and Sebastian. He just wasn't connecting.'

'That's what Rosie says. We like talked it over in France. She said loads of the mums at school think he's really fit, and it wasn't such a big deal. I mean, people are always having affairs aren't they? She said they can't all split up over them.'

If Rosie's attitude struck Nell as verging on cynicism, it was at least eminently practical. When after all did tolerance – which Nell now thought of as the only, if tentative, substitute for the forgiveness which wasn't yet possible – become weakness? Or was it that some people expected more than others of their husbands or wives, possibly too much?

'That could be a good way of looking at it.' Nell abandoned the rush of new ideas crowding in on her as too complicated to grapple with until later. She gave Rachel a hug. 'If we're going to get over it, and we are, aren't we, the two of us?'

'I don't know,' said Rachel, her face hardening. 'There's Dad. Three of us. And Juliet. That's four.'

'Yes,' Nell said slowly. 'There's Juliet.'

She and Alastair had come back from Rome, Nell with dumb relief and Alastair wary. Neither of them admitted what had become more obvious with each hour, that the time away had been a failure. She'd known before she went that it would be. Alastair might pretend to himself – and to her – that infidelity in marriage could be sugared over as if they were teenagers having a tiff. It couldn't.

Nell still hadn't seen Juliet. The dread of facing her dug into her brain like a malignant fungus. She ought to be dealing with it, fighting the enemy, battling to save her marriage, as women's magazines inevitably put it. But she didn't have any energy. Was Alastair in contact with her? Nell refused to ask, to watch for the signs, turning her back with what ought to have been adult dignity but transmuted into childish sulkiness. She wouldn't humiliate herself, even though the ugly question corrupted every thought and speech.

A moment of madness, Alastair had called it. But it hadn't been that for Juliet. She'd said, quite openly, that she loved him. She wouldn't give him up as easily as Alastair chose to think.

TWENTY-FOUR

The Wharton term started. Sebastian and Rachel went back to their schools and to all outward appearances life went on as before. Alastair was the same as he'd always been – easy in his manner to everyone and openly affectionate to those closest to him. As she watched him, Nell asked herself if this was how too many couples lived. Smooth faces stretched over the tensions and indecision within: is that what happened to all marriages when the shine was knocked off? Shame and loneliness, they ran alongside each other all right.

She didn't dare look into the future. At any moment she might meet Juliet, or Juliet might ring her. Before long Sebastian would notice something. Then it came to her he might already have done so, and be suffering silently, imagining what it might mean and too afraid to ask. He'd always been a child who hated anyone to be cross with him, who hid from the dark.

She ought to do something positive, confront Juliet, deal with things, like another woman, a woman with more self-respect, would have done. But she did none of these things. She only asked to get through each day.

She *did* get through the days. One thing made this possible, and it was a big thing. Rachel was trying, really trying. Not speaking much – at least not at family mealtimes – but no longer refusing to eat. Nell was so strung up she hardly dared to believe it. It was as though just when God was heaping another sorrow onto you which looked like crushing you altogether, he got round to doing something about lifting a different one away.

It didn't enter her head to talk with Alastair about the change. If fear and an overwhelming sense of betrayal lay at the root of Rachel's unhappiness, then Alastair must take most of the blame. But he would never see it like that, Nell understood this at last. And what use was blame when it came down to it? What good would it do to any of them in the day-to-day rebuilding of family trust?

She hadn't missed having a father. She didn't even know if he was still alive, and had never cared to find out. He'd never bothered with her, and he'd dropped her mother when the fancy took him. He might have dressed it up as pursuing artistic freedom and fulfilling his creative gifts but Nell knew better. An original artist who needed to be shielded from the daily grind of earning a living? No, just a lazy con man who had taken advantage of her mother's misplaced idealism.

She'd dreamed of a perfect father for her children. Alastair had been almost that. On one level he'd been everything that a manual for family life might have prescribed. But the eggshell sheen of a sweet temper had all the time covered a self-indulgence that couldn't say no, even it meant risking the happiness of their children.

Setting up the exhibition in the Turner Room in the few days before term started had kept her busy, even if her mind was hardly on the work. Nearly forty portraits of members of the Common Room lined the walls, sixteen of them hers.

'Why are none of them life studies?' Oliver Benson demanded, sauntering into the first art lesson of the term. 'It'd make for a more entertaining show.'

'I couldn't get anyone to pose,' said Nell unthinkingly.

'Not even your husband? The one you've done of him is

surface stuff. I was thinking of the publicity some nude pictures would attract. The Hun likes a bit of that doesn't he? Publicity, not the other thing, Mrs Garwood, do keep up.'

Getting the lower sixth into the Turner Room with an idea of encouraging them to look critically at work by those teaching them had been Trevor Faversham's idea. It was one of his less happy ones. Nell could only be glad he couldn't hear some of the comments being made by teenagers blithely oblivious to the offence their casual mockery might give.

She followed Oliver's disparaging gaze at Trevor Faversham's modernistic representation of Wharton's headmaster. It had to be admitted that Clement Hunstrete, whose artistic tastes were limited to the painstaking and gleaming perfectionism of medieval and early Renaissance masters, had displayed a lack of gratification at the result.

'If only Trevor had an ounce of tact!' mourned Eleanor when she'd seen the finished painting at the end of last term.

'I did try and suggest that something more in the grand manner would go down better.' Nell had listened to Clement's grumbles. 'But Trevor went all huffy and read me a lecture about artistic integrity.'

'Arty people are *always* tiresome,' said Eleanor. 'Though you never are, so it's not a fail-safe rule. Perhaps it's just men.' She sighed, as if thinking of something else.

Looking at the rest of the paintings in the exhibition, Nell couldn't help seeing that her own work created the most impact, and in spite of everything to make her miserable she was proud of what she'd achieved. Her portrait of Martin was the best she thought, but there were others she was pleased with, including one of Jim North, which Sue had offered to buy for a much higher price than Nell had hesitantly suggested.

'You've made him look like the original sneak,' commented

Oliver, 'like a super-smart rat who's thinking, you can't con me, so don't shit yourself trying.'

'You mean I've brought out his penetrating intelligence at spotting who's not doing what they ought to be,' said Nell, smiling in spite of herself. 'Which in your case at this moment is going back over that drawing and correcting wherever you haven't made the effort to look properly. You do a very nice line in caricature, but this particular piece of work isn't the place for it, and my portrait of Mr North wasn't either.'

All the time she wondered at herself, that she could go on talking to the boys and organising the art lessons as though nothing had happened. She was grateful for their normality, for their youthful self-centredness mixed with casual and sometimes surprising thoughtfulness.

Even Oliver Benson's irreverence and impudence helped. Oliver might be slippery and far too familiar, but he combined this with so much wit and bittersweet camaraderie that it was impossible not to become attached to him. She watched him screw up his face in a mocking grimace; for a painful instant he could have been Juliet.

Involuntarily, she turned to her painting of Alastair, done over the summer, holding a tennis racquet, its rapid brushstrokes and sketchy brilliance of primary colour conveying an untroubled happiness. She looked at it in disbelief. How could she have missed what lay behind the pose? She'd been deceived by a surface charm of manner, she'd invested the last fourteen years of her life in it. There it all was, captured on canvas, a lie.

If only she could have left it out of the exhibition! But that would have provoked questions from too many people. Everyone thought they were a devoted couple. They must go on thinking that.

In the second week of term, the Wharton art festival started, and girls from the local school poured into the art department, darting speculative glances with smokily made up eyes at the more attractive boys. Nell threw herself into the work of getting all the teenagers absorbed in the projects she and Trevor Faversham had prepared for them, and for three hectic days had no time to think about anything else at all.

On the Saturday she realised her period still hadn't come. She'd have to tell Alastair soon. Her mind see-sawed between pictures of the future, all of them frightening.

The weather had turned bitter, with grey, overhung skies. Cold enough for snow. Nell shivered. Tomorrow – she'd tell him then. She gave the children an early supper and left them to get on with their homework – or in other words to watch television.

She looked at her watch. In less than half an hour she had to go to the reception in the Turner Room being held to celebrate the portrait exhibition and the success of the joint art project, with the additional agenda of raising money for the new sculpture studio. There would be hundreds of people coming in and walking around admiring, or more likely criticising, the work on display. Nell couldn't imagine why any of them would be putting their hands in their pockets as Clement Hunstrete fondly imagined – why on earth should they, given that the school facilities were already more than state schools could dream of – but she'd have to stand about looking professional, poised to explain and discuss the art department's teaching methods to inquiring potential future parents. She dreaded she'd be unable to get to the end of a coherent sentence.

She changed into a clean skirt and silver grey polo-necked jersey. Still twenty minutes left. She brushed her hair very thoroughly. She felt a little sick.

Go on, get on and use it. Then you'll know for certain.

Almost unconsciously, she reached for the sweet pea painted china box on the dressing table. It had belonged to her mother and was spilling over with odd earrings, tangled beads and bracelets. At the bottom, like a green daisy, was the emerald ring. She touched each point of the crisply curving petals encased in white gold, unsure of what she was thinking. She slid the ring onto her finger.

She rummaged in a chest of drawers for the hated pregnancy test she'd bought all those weeks ago. Alastair was safely out of the way organising the junior debating society, and had told her he'd meet her in the Turner Room when he'd finished. She had time.

Her hand hovered over the box and began to pick at the wrapping. She hadn't bothered doing one with Rachel and Sebastian. She'd known already.

She tried to read the instructions, but found herself going back to the beginning, realising she hadn't taken in a single word. She began again for the fourth time. Step one.

She shut her eyes. *I know what the answer is already. I don't need this.*

Her mobile rang. She leapt to her feet and stuffed the wretched package back into the drawer.

It was Juliet. Her voice sounded muffled, cautious. Nell froze, then sat down again on the bed.

'I'm just outside. Can I come in? I need to talk – '

She couldn't go on hiding now. She closed the drawer very quietly and went downstairs, saying nothing, still holding her phone. As she opened the door she saw Juliet's face, drained and squeezed into colourlessness.

'Nell – please let me talk to you – '

Nell looked at her without focusing, blank with despairing tiredness.

'There's nothing you can say now. After what you've done. We must just get on with it.'

'Get on with it? Is that what you call it? Nell, you're my friend, for God's sake!'

'You *were* my friend,' said Nell as steadily as she could. 'But you spoilt all that. So now we need to have time away from each other, not see each other at all. So go away.'

'Before I do, there's something I have to tell you. Something you have to know.'

Panic swam over Nell.

'There isn't anything you can tell me that would help either of us. And I've got to go out now. ' She clutched hopelessly at the door. Juliet didn't move.

'I ought to have said ask,' said Juliet. 'Because that's what I'm going to do. What I've been screwing myself up to do for – for too long. I'm asking you to leave Alastair.'

For what might have been a minute Nell was unable to speak. She stared into the brilliant blue of Juliet's eyes, and took a backward step into the hall.

'You've got a bloody nerve,' she said. Then she remembered the children, and knowing only that they mustn't hear anything, came quickly out of the house. She shut the front door, shoving Juliet in front of her.

'I don't want you in my house,' she said, rushing into the road towards the school. 'And I've got to go this very minute. You always did have perfect timing. You knew Alastair wasn't in, didn't you?'

'No,' said Juliet very quietly. 'Al hasn't spoken to me since – that's why I'm here. Because I can't bear it any longer. You're my friend – but I *need* Al.'

'Nobody *needs* someone else's husband.'

There was a silence.

'You know nothing about it,' said Juliet. 'Be thankful for that.'

'If Alastair wanted to leave me,' Nell walked on even faster, 'he could. Nobody's stopping him.'

'It's the children – he's afraid of losing the children. And you've forgiven him – so how can he leave?'

'Get away from me,' said Nell, shivering. The bitter cold was hurting her throat and she'd come out without a coat. She turned into the school entrance gates. Surely Juliet wouldn't pursue her any further.

'Not until you hear me out.' Juliet tried to catch hold of Nell's arm. 'You don't belong with Alastair – you never have. Can't you see that? You don't think the same way.'

'And you do?' interrupted Nell brutally. 'Or so you've persuaded yourself – and that makes everything all right.'

'I love him more than you do.'

'You don't come into it. Do you honestly think I'd leave him, or that he'd leave me?'

'I wouldn't be humiliating myself now if I didn't – '

They'd reached the end of the cloisters built along one side of the quad. Nell pushed open a heavy oak door, and then stopped to bar the way.

'Don't go on with this,' she said. 'For both our sakes. You see, it's all too late. I'm pregnant.'

Juliet stared at her.

'You can't be.'

'What would you know about it?' said Nell, as nastily as she could. The daisy ring twisted, too loose for her frozen hands.

'That you aren't pregnant. Isn't that enough?'

Ahead of them in the stone-flagged hall leading to the Turner Room Nell could see Alastair coming towards them.

'Nell! For God's sake, what the hell is going on? People are starting to arrive – '

'You'd better tell him what you've just told me,' said Juliet.

Nell said slowly, 'I've just announced that I'm expecting your child.'

'And I've suggested that it's hardly possible,' said Juliet in a light cruel voice that Nell had never heard before. 'You made sure of that, didn't you Alastair?'

Alastair glanced from one to the other, retreating from involvement.

'Juliet, not now. This is between Nell and myself.'

'It wasn't fair to deceive her,' said Juliet. 'I said so at the time.'

In the distance Nell could hear boys' voices, cars pulling into the parking area, snatches of a radio being played.

'Deceive me about what? Is there anything left?'

'Your husband had a vasectomy on the quiet last summer term, after I told him I would be moving to Wharton. Around exam time when he had a reason to be tired and keep his distance. You never cottoned on, did you?'

There was something so unbelievably sordid in this revelation that Nell recoiled as if stung. Alastair couldn't have done this, he couldn't have sunk this low.

'Alastair?'

She hardly needed to look at his face. His silence told her that everything Juliet said was true. She said chokingly, 'You did this, without a word to me? For God's sake, I'm your *wife* – '

'Do you imagine I could bring myself to ask you? Or that you'd have agreed to it?'

'But *why?* I'd have understood if only you'd said – Alastair, you could have told me!'

'Would you? You couldn't have begun to.'

'So it was all planned between the two of you, and you fobbed me off with a ring.' Nell gripped her hands together, golden petals digging painfully into flesh. 'While all the time I – ' she stopped as something else sank in. She looked sharply at Juliet and knew immediately that for an as yet unknown reason Juliet had never said anything to Alastair about how she had tried to get herself pregnant.

'He said he would break with me altogether if I ever gave him away,' said Juliet.

She could see through him now. It had been the easy option

for him. He'd always walked in the sun, it wasn't in him to do otherwise. He'd have probably told her sooner or later, when the right moment came.

'Three children were enough, you said.' Juliet fixed her blue gaze on Alastair. 'This was your only way of making sure that I – or anyone else for that matter – didn't get pregnant and land you with being the father of another child.'

Three children. Vail. From a long way off, Nell heard a voice that wasn't her own.

'It isn't true.'

'Alastair? Aren't you the father of my son?'

Hard and painful breaths came and went. Hatred and jealousy, pity and revulsion fought without meaning or understanding.

'Just tell me the truth.'

His eyes had gone opaque. She knew that look. He put it on when he was disengaging himself. All at once she felt sick and cold with fear, for it could mean only one thing.

'I can't believe it.'

But she did.

'Vail is your child.' Nell dragged out the words. 'And I never even suspected.'

She stared at her husband as if seeing him for the first time. 'All those years. You must have started your affair soon after you first met her at that hateful theatre. When I was expecting Sebastian.'

What kind of man would start sleeping with another woman when his wife was about to have their second child? The man she'd chosen. He might have told her countless times he would never stop loving her, but that love hadn't counted for much. She hadn't been enough for him even in those early days. She'd thought he was as happy as she was, but she'd got that wrong too. He'd only been married to her for a year and a half when he'd found someone he wanted more.

'He thought he couldn't leave you then,' said Juliet. 'I didn't ask him to. But then when I had Vail – '

'You got pregnant on purpose, don't bloody deny it. All those lies you told us about Newland. And what about Vail, where is he in all this? Did you ever think about him?'

'It *was* a mistake – ' Juliet said quietly, but Nell kept her eyes fixed on Alastair's face.

'The material side, isn't that all you cared about? You looking after our money with no online banking so I wouldn't spot any payments from the account. I played into your hands, didn't I?'

'I can't expect you to understand,' Alastair said, his gaze shifting around the space between them, 'or even believe me. I meant to do the right thing, what looked like the right thing at the time.'

'The right thing for *you*!' Nell burst out passionately. This was the man she'd lived with and loved without apparently knowing him – together with the false friend playing her last card.

'It *wasn't* the right thing! Not for me, not for *any* of the children. You didn't care, did you, either of you, about how many lives you ruined, you don't have it in you to care – '

Hatred of Juliet, of Alastair, of her own blind stupidity, spilled over into unreasoning rage. She whirled round and ran into the Turner Room, oblivious to a scattering of early guests and the sixth form art students arranging wine glasses on a long white-clothed table at the far end of the room.

Halfway down one wall was her painting of Alastair, bronzed from the summer, smooth brown hair glinting, a smile just touching his lips. It was a smile she knew well. Now she knew what it meant. She slammed her fist into the painted face, buckling the bright surface and tearing the canvas with the sharp edges of the daisy ring. From behind her she heard Juliet cry out and Alastair swear.

'If you want a shit who can't love anyone except himself, then you can have fucking well have him – ' It was childish enough and Nell hardly knew what she was screaming, seizing only on what tumbled into her mouth. 'I wish I'd never *met* either of you!'

With one savage thrust, she wrenched the picture off the wall. There was a crash, and then a moment of appalled silence.

TWENTY-FIVE

Afterwards, Nell could hardly remember the few minutes that followed. There was a confusion of exclamations, a boy laughing, the slam of a door. Alastair tried to pull her away, but she fought him off. Through the red mist swirling around her, she saw startled faces, and someone, it might have been Oliver Benson, knocked a bottle of wine off the table.

Then there was Martin's voice. She turned to it like a child. He was the only person she could trust. He took her back to his flat, poured her out a drink, and when she didn't want that, he made hot chocolate for them both.

'Don't say anything,' said Martin, 'unless you want to. There can be too much talking.'

He was studying her with a troubled face, as if he didn't know what to say. A woman would have asked questions, demanded details, expressed opinions. Nell thought of Hilary, vociferous and busily kind, and was grateful for Martin's silence. He must have come into the Turner Room just as the painting had crashed to the floor. He couldn't know what the row was all about, and because he was Martin, he wouldn't ask. She sipped her hot chocolate, hardly knowing what she was doing.

'I'd better go home,' she whispered. 'I can't take it in. What it all means. I don't know where Alastair is – and I don't want the children to hear about anything before – '

'I don't suppose anybody from outside the school saw anything. There was only a handful of people in the room as I came in. They won't have grasped what it was about. Otherwise it was just boys, the sixth formers who'd volunteered to help with serving drinks.' Martin's face tightened. 'But I'll walk back home with you now. The reception will be in full swing and nobody will miss you.'

'I shouldn't have done it – '

'Righteous anger…there's a place for it. We may take ourselves to task about other kinds – '

A knock at the door made Nell jump up.

'I'm sorry, Martin. This isn't fair on you. I shouldn't be here. It'll be Alastair – '

Eleanor Hunstrete hovered in the doorway, flecks of snow littering her untidy hair.

'Such a nuisance,' she said, looking distractedly at Martin. 'Half the people who ought to be there and giving us money for the sculpture studio will use it as an excuse not to turn up.'

'I'm so dreadfully sorry.' Nell hung her head. 'It was a disgraceful way to behave. Something awful got into me.'

'It's not your fault. The weather forecast girl, the one with arms like those plastic straws with a bendy middle, warned this morning that a blizzard was on the way, so even Clement can't complain. Though I'm quite sure he will. Men always have to blame someone or something.' Eleanor sighed, shaking melting snow from her shoes onto Martin's carpet.

Astonishment and gratitude flooded over Nell. Everything else might be disintegrating all around her, but the headmaster's wife would be unchanged. Her imagination rocked wildly to Eleanor watching breakfast television in a fleecy dressing gown, a cup of tea going cold beside her.

'I meant about what I did. In the Turner Room. I can't

explain it, but I – and now there'll be a dreadful scandal with people saying things – '

'You fainted and accidentally damaged one of your paintings so it's had to be removed for repair,' said Eleanor with unusual firmness.

'Nobody's going to believe that – '

'Why not? Fainting used to be fashionable. When I was at school with your mother, girls were *always* doing it, usually to get out of morning assembly. We decided a stroke would have sounded unconvincing, as they usually happen to someone older.'

Nell couldn't think of anything to say in answer to this. Martin too was silent, indicating these discretionary measures were not his responsibility.

'Sue asked me to come and tell you. It'll be the official line given out by Jim – and Clement too – and that's all that counts. You'll see.'

'You ought to be angry, I've ruined the evening – there's no excuse – '

'You can tell me the whole story another time. These things happen…' Eleanor looked puzzled for a moment, as if forgetting the reason for them. Her voice trailed away. 'Alastair's gone somewhere – but I expect he's waiting for you at home.'

'Some of the boys saw – '

'Sue will tell you boys are like servants in former times, there's no keeping anything from them, so there's little point in trying. She ought to have been a government minister, think how good she'd have been compared with the one who looked like a hamster. Or was it a guinea pig? Martin, are you seeing Nell home? I must get back to the Turner Room. Some of the people look rather dreary, but I'd better go and be dutiful.'

After Eleanor had gone, Nell looked fearfully at Martin.

'What am I going to do?'

'You're going to go home,' said Martin, regarding her steadily, 'and find in yourself the courage I know you have, but haven't much needed until now. We have to go on reminding ourselves mistakes don't matter much – if we can learn from them something we can't learn any other way. But there's no putting it off.' He thrust an ancient grey coat at her. 'Here, put this on, the snow's most likely getting heavier.'

They walked in silence down the stairs and out into the quad. Nell pulled the coat tight around her. White flakes were drifting thickly from a dark sky.

Martin left her at her front door, just resting his hand on her shoulder with the lightest and briefest of touches. For a fleeting moment, she longed to beg him to say a prayer for her, but in the next told herself he would do so without being asked. She watched his retreating back disappear into the shadows, then let herself into the house.

The sitting room door was closed. Standing in the hall, she could hear the theme music from one of the endless television soaps beloved by Rachel and Sebastian. She imagined them sprawled on the sofa, the remote control between them, the volume turned up high. She tried to ask God to help her, a senseless prayer that dried up and evaporated into nothingness.

Panic swept over her as she tried to think what to do. Where was Alastair? Had he come home and told the children something of what had happened – no, he wouldn't have done that. He never did anything that might lead to unpleasantness. He would have gone with Juliet. Not because he wanted to, but because Juliet would have made it impossible for him to do otherwise.

To throw Alastair out so that he had no choice left to him. That was what Juliet wanted her to do. She was falling into the trap Juliet had set, but it was too late to care. Nell saw all this at last in its stark simplicity. It was like finally being told by the doctor exactly which deadly disease you were going to die from.

I can't be pregnant! It washed over her like morning light flooding into a room when the curtains are drawn. She drew a long, even breath. Tension drained out of every part of her body. If Alastair had had a vasectomy, there couldn't be a baby. Slowly, thankfully, she placed her hands across her stomach.

She'd struggled to put Alastair's affair behind her – and had altogether failed. Now it was as if windscreen wipers had switched on in her mind, clearing away the fog which had obscured it, cleaning it of dirt. The clogging fear that a baby might be growing inside her was gone. She was free to think and act for herself, and not for an unborn child.

She'd tried, and she believed in her heart he'd tried too, but always with a sense of futility, a battle already lost. She saw herself lying on the bed in Rome, inert and defeated after Alastair's lovemaking. It was never going to work, not because such reconciliations weren't possible, but because of the people they were. Or – and here Nell struggled to be just – because of her. Love for the person you were married to, it had to be all or nothing.

She couldn't go on living with Alastair knowing what she now knew. Whatever was happening between him and Juliet at this moment, however much he might be vacillating – and Nell could be sure he was – she must throw him out, and she must do this immediately. She must tell him to go, or that she would go, with the children. This evening marked the end of a game Nell no longer wanted to play; broke and landing on Mayfair at last almost with a sense of relief that the throw of the dice was no longer to be dreaded.

Juliet had won. Nell could see this quite clearly. Was Juliet happy at this moment? She might be triumphant, have got what she wanted, but how soon would she begin to feel she'd paid too high a price for it? Would Juliet, in the years to come, look back with something more than regret?

Nell lifted her hands away from her stomach and glanced at the closed sitting room door. The lump in her chest kicked painfully, shooting out needles of sharp frosted misery. How was she going to break this to the children, how could they be shielded from the devastating hurt of Alastair and Juliet's betrayal?

Worst of all, there was Vail – the child she'd loved as the son of her best friend. How would he, brought up to believe one story about his background, be able to accept the truth? He might be confident and clever, but surely neither of these qualities would be enough. A profound anger, more bitter than that which had overtaken her in the Turner Room, began to burn inside her as she thought of all that Vail must suffer because of what Alastair and Juliet had done.

Very quietly, she opened the front door again and crept out into the street. She walked quickly, swathed in Martin's coat, swirling flakes of snow coming to rest on her bent head, the cold air a knife in her throat and ears. Outside Juliet's house, she stopped for a moment fighting for breath, looking up at the windows. All the curtains were drawn. For a moment she thought she saw a shaft of golden light as if a curtain had been moved, but then there was darkness again.

'Mum?'

Two children emerged from the path at the side of the house.

'Rachel – Sebastian! What are you doing here – I thought you were at home!'

Sebastian flung himself at her. 'Vail texted me – he said to come – so we did – but we were watching for you so you wouldn't – Mum, it isn't true, is it? Dad and Auntie Juliet? And that Dad – that Vail is – ?'

191

'Yes,' said Nell very quietly, her eyes at that moment catching sight of a third figure hesitating in the darkness behind the other two. 'It *is* true. Vail is your half-brother.'

For one horrifying instant she was gripped by a base compulsion to say something infinitely cruel to Juliet's child. She closed her lips tight shut. The impulse faded almost immediately, leaving behind it shock and repulsion. This was the human heart, in all its unimaginable evil.

From somewhere unknown, strength and courage came. She raised her voice.

'And will *always* be totally loved by us all.' She reached out her arms as if to draw him to her, sensing rather than seeing his expression of fear and doubt. For a few seconds he stood quite still, and then with a clumsiness uncharacteristic of him he came towards her in a little rush to be hugged.

She felt his cheek wet against hers. He'd been crying. She put her arms around all three children, feeling she'd been saved from an unfathomed and terrifying darkness.

'Where's Dad?'

'He's inside with Juliet.'

Nell could tell nothing from Rachel's expressionless voice. She tried to think clearly, the wet of Vail's tears stinging cold salt on her face. She was going to do something so difficult, so unlike herself, that every inch of her wanted to resist and run away.

But she'd run away for too long already.

'We're a family,' she said, trying to keep the shakiness out of her voice. 'So we're going to sort things out as a family, because we belong together. I'm going to go and talk things over with Dad, and your mum Vail, and between us all we can make things better than they are at the moment.'

She released herself as gently as she could and moved as if to go in the front door, but Vail clung to her.

'Do you hate my mum?'

Again she pulled him to her.

'We've made mistakes, made wrong choices, done selfish things. We need to have time to ourselves now to talk things over. There's something very important to sort out. That's between us grown ups. Then I'd like the three of you to come in and we can go over it together, as a family. But I think that underneath everything your mother and I will always care about each other. Love can't just go away – '

That would have to do. Trite words. She could only hope Vail wouldn't see the glaring inconsistency at the heart of them.

Inside the house was quiet. Nell pushed open the sitting room door, gesturing to the children to wait in the kitchen. Alastair was standing propped against the mantelpiece, his face wiped of its patina of shiny living.

'Where's Juliet?'

'Upstairs. Putting on her coat. We were just going to bring the children back – oh God, Nell, there's nothing I can say is there?'

'Not much,' said Nell, as Juliet came into the room. She'd put on a scarlet jacket and scarf Nell had never seen before, as vivid as the shirt she'd worn last month. Juliet was flaunting her success.

Hatred and jealousy and grief: all these piled into Nell like a great sea wave knocking out every sense and breath. To say anything at all was impossible, she couldn't find the words. She stood there dumb and heavy, with a great stone in her chest.

Then she remembered the three children huddled in the kitchen. She must fight for them as well as herself. She must pretend she was strong, a woman who was in control of her own emotions and decisions. She must do all this, and go on doing it because if she didn't – but that was too frightful to imagine.

'I've brought the children into the kitchen. I found them outside. Before they come in here, there's something I want to say first to you, Alastair. I won't live with you any more. So you can get out.'

She'd said it. The next bit came easier.

'You weren't able to choose between us – no, you wanted to have both of us. You took everything that was offered to you. So I'm making the decision for you. I'm leaving you – or I'm insisting you leave me. Not this minute if it's not convenient' – acid shrivelled the words into spikes – 'but just as soon as you can pack up your bags.'

'I did love you Nell. I do love you still.'

Looking at his stricken face, she realised he was speaking the truth. For men like him it was all too easy to love two – or perhaps several – women at once. It was simply the way he was. Juliet had seen it and she hadn't.

'Yes,' she said, 'I think you do. But that isn't enough for me. Another woman might put up with it. I can't.'

'Half a loaf is better than no bread,' said Juliet with a twisted smile. 'I've been testing out the truth of that for years.'

'Alastair will live with you now, Juliet. You won't have to share him any more. But I think you owe it to me to explain, how you could, how anyone could – and for all these years – ' she choked and couldn't go on. She'd been made a fool of by her husband and best friend. They'd held her in contempt and exploited her.

'I *can't* explain.' For a moment Nell wondered if Juliet's blue eyes were filling with tears. 'I only know I've loved Alastair ever since I first saw him.'

'When you knew he was a married man. Introduced to you by his wife. You set out to take what belonged to someone else as if nothing else mattered. Though it's taken you long enough to get your own way. Not like you.'

'I told myself he belonged to me.' Juliet looked at her with quiet desperation, and now Nell could see Juliet was indeed holding back tears, Juliet who never cried. 'I did see Al first. And I loved him. Before he met and married you.'

Nell turned her gaze to her husband, knowing he wouldn't help her, and yet hardly believing he would allow Juliet to lie like this.

'I met him at a party,' continued Juliet. 'He'd gatecrashed it and was drunk. We went back to the flat I was living in then. To him it was a one night stand. Afterwards I waited for him to phone me, to come round. He never did. I knew nothing about him or how to find him – just his first name. I couldn't stop thinking about him. It turned into an obsession – and if you don't understand that, then you don't know much about love.'

'It did happen like that,' Alastair said. 'But I swear to you Nell I remembered almost nothing of that evening. Just after it I met you. You know the rest.'

'So when you spoke to me in the queue at the theatre and played that trick on everyone – '

'I didn't know at first,' said Juliet quickly. 'I hadn't seen either of you before that moment. Then you said the name of your husband. It might not have been the same Alastair but I couldn't stop myself. I even told myself that if it was him, seeing him again might change the way I felt, and so it was all right.'

'You *wanted* to think that.'

'After that I – oh Nell, you don't know what it's like to fall in love, totally and hopelessly, so that nothing else matters.'

'Obviously not.'

'Soon after that evening we started to see each other. I couldn't help myself. I *loved* him. But Nell, I really did love you too. That was what made it so hard for us both.'

A memory from that summer swung into Nell's head. Alastair playing tennis against Juliet in one of the London parks, herself in late pregnancy lying on the grass watching them, Rachel fractious in a buggy at her side. She remembered the heat and snatched echoes of broken speech, of laughter, her own endless sleepiness and heavy swollen body. Juliet had once been a junior county player, but she still couldn't get a game off Alastair and this had been a cause of hilarity for them all. Was that why she hadn't seen what was happening in front of her?

'I never in a million years meant to get pregnant,' Juliet went on, repeating what she'd said before with even less conviction. 'Alastair knows I didn't. It was a mistake, just as I've always said.'

'I want to go home,' Nell said, suddenly childish. Oh God, she wanted her mother. 'Now, with Rachel and Sebastian. But first we have to explain all this to the three of them, don't we? So they understand something of what's going to happen. And don't ever kid yourselves' – she hurled at them both – 'you'll be happy together. Because you won't be.'

TWENTY-SIX

Clement Hunstrete had occupied the position of headmaster of Wharton school for more than twelve years, but he'd never entirely succeeded in looking the part.

He'd been appointed for his sound, even brilliant, scholarship, the previous headmaster having spent too much time on the touchline. The governors, becoming agitated that Wharton was acquiring a reputation as first and foremost a rugby school, were anxious to redress the balance that had been lost. Clement, a fellow of Peterhouse, Cambridge and the distinguished contributor to learned historical journals, was selected to re-establish the ethos of academic excellence.

The governors had seen the success of their choice. Even his detractors – and there were many among the brawnier of the Wharton Old Boys – couldn't deny that Clement Hunstrete's tenure had witnessed a steady climb in the league tables and a multiplying in the number of boys gaining Oxbridge places.

His wife, with the outspokenness which made her quite unsuited to her exalted station, had once told him he looked like an amiable badger. In his gloomier moments her words came back to him. Eleanor had a habit of noticing people's resemblance to animals, but a more tactful woman would have stopped short of including her own husband.

Clement derived some comfort from reflecting that a

badger, particularly an amiable one – for Eleanor had stressed the accompanying adjective – was preferable to a water rat. This had been her choice for Jim North. When he'd expostulated in the mildest manner that Jim was his much-valued deputy, she'd assured him that having been brought up on *Tales of the Riverbank* she was very fond of water rats!

Looking across at Jim now, Clement began to study his physiognomy more closely. Was it those quick seeing eyes or the tendency of his mouth to twitch with energetic speech? He certainly gave an impression of being constantly on the alert, and wasn't this a characteristic of all rodents? Perhaps that was what Eleanor had meant. Illustrations from his boyhood favourite *The Wind in the Willows* crept into his mind. When this wretched business was over he must remember to ask Eleanor if they had a copy somewhere around the house.

Certainly Jim appeared especially perspicacious this morning. When Clement had first taken over as headmaster, he'd leant on Jim's expertise and wisdom at every turn, and Jim had never showed him anything other than respectful loyalty and good-humoured comradeship. To every department Jim was an institution, for he'd been at Wharton longer than any other member of staff. Even the bursar, that wet-blanket scourge of the school, was deferential to Jim and was never heard to contradict him.

Above all, Jim knew what undercurrents were making waves among the boys. He had an uncanny ability to know what was going on at any one level in the school. He could scent out trouble like a bloodhound and knew the culprits by instinct.

That was what deputy heads were obliged to do these days – cover the ground like a ruthless compliance officer in a company. They had to do the dirty jobs, the discipline. Headmasters like himself were too busy oiling the public relations aspect which was becoming more of a stranglehold every year. That was modern life for you; form over content all the time, but you had to go along with it.

When things went wrong, Jim was a first class ally. Sue too. She might be built like a cruise ship with upholstery to match, but she was full of staunch common sense and could be relied on to quell any destructive gossip among the younger Common Room wives.

At times like this, even his wife Eleanor had something to contribute. He eyed the coffee tray with its cafetière and bone china cups with approval, forgetting it was in fact his secretary Meredith who was responsible.

'It's too bad,' Clement said, switching his mind back to the reason the four of them were sitting in the headmaster's office overlooking the quad on Monday morning. 'Whispers in the Common Room are one thing. They're part of the air we breathe. But episodes like that on Saturday night and then this degrading lark this morning do a great deal of damage. The school can't afford it.'

He knew he sounded querulous. Headmasters shouldn't allow themselves to get upset over trifles. He'd spent most of the night – bother it, the last *two* nights! – telling himself that the Turner Room business didn't boil down to much more, yet he was still unable to resume the manner of an infallible elder statesman, trusted by all those who looked to him for their welfare and security.

It was because it concerned Nell. These things should happen to other young wives, the brazen ones who flirted with the bachelor staff and plagued the bursar about the state of their houses. His sense of chivalry was offended: women like Nell were emblematic of ideal womanhood! They should be protected and cherished by men who were worthy of them.

He allowed his mind to flit into imagining her as a medieval maiden and he was jousting, wearing her favours…the daydream ended when he remembered he was not a knight in the fourteenth century but a hard-pressed headmaster in the twenty-first and his wife was offering him a jam sandwich cream.

Nell was a favourite with his wife; Eleanor had been at school with Nell's mother, so naturally it was all right for him to have a slight fondness for her himself. That was how Clement put it, and if anyone else had suggested that his soft spot for a female more than twenty years younger than himself was anything less than above board he would have been indignant.

'We might have brushed through it perfectly satisfactorily.' Sue grasped the cafetière with a capable hand and poured out coffee for them all. 'People have learnt not to believe what they're told, but when they find the status quo unchanged, they get bored with asking questions. However, if Nell is now refusing to live with Alastair it's quite clear that the talk isn't going to die away so easily.'

'Why must these charming men turn out to be dirty dishes?' mused Eleanor. 'It's very unfair just when you've got fond of them. Like in those television dramas where one's favourite actor turns out to be the villain. Things ought to be arranged better – wickedness should show in people's faces.'

'Did Nell tell you she was determined to throw Alastair out?' Jim said, possibly not feeling equal to carrying on this interesting train of thought. 'I suppose in the heat of the moment it didn't occur to her that they're living in a school house, given to them because of Alastair's position as head of the politics department?'

'Oh Jim! As if that matters! Surely the school can sort out such minor details. Alastair's already moved into Juliet's house. I rang Nell last night. We didn't hear anything from them all day on Sunday, and I dreaded they were having terrible scenes in the way people do. But Clement told me not to meddle. Nell was in floods of tears. They've arranged matters between them she says, and will do everything quietly.'

'A good intention in theory, but impossible to carry out now,' interrupted Clement. 'Not after what happened this morning. Now we're settled you'd better let me fill you in. It's all very irksome.'

He took several sips of his coffee in the manner of one brooding over his wrongs. First he and Eleanor had arrived at the art reception in the Turner Room to be told that one of the exhibits had crashed off the wall just before the visitors arrived. It was badly damaged and had been quickly removed. For a moment he'd suspected one of those sixth formers who were hanging around, ostensibly to help with pouring drinks and make a good impression. All part of showing that Wharton boys could be civilised. Well, it sometimes worked.

Was it his own portrait that had fallen? It wouldn't have been much of a loss, though he'd have had that fellow Faversham making a meal over it. Artists had a nasty habit of being precious about their work, even if it was a collection of garish daubs that a four-year-old would be ashamed of.

On enquiring, he found it was Nell Garwood's painting of her husband Alastair. There was something mysterious about all this, and Nell wasn't even there. Apparently she'd fainted. Probably pregnant. That would be a bore, she'd have to go on maternity leave and he'd be pushed to find another art teacher half as good or as popular with the boys.

By the end of the evening though, he'd learnt the full story. Nell wasn't expecting a baby, but had just found out Alastair wasn't quite the pattern card she'd evidently thought him. A nasty moment for any woman. Not that anyone less innocent than Nell wouldn't have put two and two together long ago. A good-looking chap like Alastair – well! Nell wasn't the type to fight back either, didn't have claws like that glossy friend of hers.

Eleanor had been unusually upset, and after consultation with Sue had disappeared briefly, ostensibly to check Nell was all right. Needless to say Alastair Garwood had made himself scarce. Clement wasn't looking forward to the conversation he'd be obliged to have with *him*.

All that had been as nothing compared with what greeted him as he hurried to chapel this morning. He'd cut it fine. After sleepless nights worrying, not to mention indigestion, who could blame him? It hadn't snowed again overnight but he still found himself crunching his way through rock hard frozen footprints. The ground staff hadn't done their job properly. He made a mental note to have a word with the bursar.

The boys had churned up the snow across the quad, creating swathes and heaps of dirtied whiteness. Snowball fights. His mind drifted, switching with relief to his favourite medieval Book of Hours with its illustrations of the seasons in jewel-rich colours. Just so long as nobody threw a snowball anywhere near him, he thought he rather approved of boys engaging in such a traditional and historic pastime.

At the far end of the quad just outside the chapel doors he came across a crowd of boys swarming around a giant snow structure. One quick glance told him what it represented. Crudity was endemic to adolescent boys and had long since ceased to create any surprise, other than a faint wonder at the predictability of their preoccupations. In all his years at Wharton they had remained the same.

Snow as thick as this invariably led to erotic structures appearing overnight, usually in the quad. Often they were penises, like this present creation, but he recalled other bodily parts, more or less biologically accurate. This particular sculpture stood over five feet tall, and he found himself almost lost in admiration at the skill involved in its construction. It would have to be knocked down, that was plain enough, given its proximity to the chapel, but part of him regretted the necessity. Why hadn't they had the sense to build it somewhere less public?

A large piece of white card was stuck into the tip. Clement found himself wincing. It was poking out in a singularly unpleasant and suggestive manner. He stopped to inspect it. It was a caricature of a woman drawn with thick black marker, performing what Clement believed the newspapers referred to as a sexual act on her partner. The woman was Nell's friend Juliet, complete with pornographic embellishments, and although the ink was a little smudged the man was unmistakably Alastair Garwood.

What was he supposed to do now? Where the hell was Jim? The thing was thoroughly offensive. Gingerly he reached over and plucked the card from its slot. He folded it hastily into quarters and pushed it into his pocket under his gown, regretting the inevitable loss of his dignity and uncomfortably aware of smirking boys melting away through the chapel doors.

Something would have to be said. He began to compose an austerely worded request that he expected those boys who had seen fit to erect snow structures in the proximity of the chapel to remove them without loss of time. He was just rephrasing this to his satisfaction – it having occurred to him that erect was a verb best avoided – when Martin Darrow hurried past him.

It was unusual for the chaplain to be late. Even as this thought crossed his mind it occurred to him that it would probably be a good thing if Martin didn't learn about what had adorned the edifice so close to the chapel doors. Martin was not prudish exactly, but there was a certain puritanism about him, a self-appointed guard against the relentless smuttiness that made up life in public schools and no doubt everywhere else.

Then there was the Nell connection. She'd done a portrait of Martin, hadn't she? Not that Martin would have any thoughts of the wrong kind in that direction. Or in any other. He was too stiff-necked for that – uncompromising! Clement wasn't at all sure how he'd react to Nell's husband being the subject of coarse jokes.

As for the chapel service which followed, he'd spent the time running his eyes over the packed pews to see which boys were looking more than usually pleased with themselves. He hadn't got anywhere on that one.

He still felt aggrieved now. He'd better help himself to some more coffee. Without thinking he dropped in two lumps of sugar, forgetting that he never took it.

'Snow *always* causes trouble,' commented Eleanor when Clement had related the whole and displayed the offending drawing. 'One feels this might not have happened but for that. It changes all the rules. Only think of *Dr Zhivago.*'

'Given that there's no doubt the woman in this unsavoury piece of artistry' – Jim grimaced at it with distaste – 'is meant to represent Alastair's mistress, we can be reasonably certain the perpetrators were the boys who were in the Turner Room. Sixth formers studying art. They probably heard what went on and thought the opportunity too good to miss. Shouldn't be difficult to narrow it down – though I've a shrewd idea I already know who drew this.'

'You have to admit it shows a great deal of talent,' said Eleanor, eyeing the drawing with curiosity. 'I've always been amazed how cartoonists achieve perfect likenesses with just a few simple lines. I think Nell told me it was something to do with picking out prominent features and exaggerating them. Whoever drew this has certainly done *that.*'

Clement stirred uneasily. It was never any use trying to curb his wife.

'Nell would know immediately who'd drawn this – it must be one of the most promising boys,' continued Eleanor. 'But let's hope she never hears about it, she'd be terribly hurt.'

'Thankfully we don't require Nell to identify the artist,' said Jim, his tone more dry than usual. 'Ten to one the boys concerned guess that our hands are pretty well tied, given that Alastair's little affair has probably been long known to them. They've got an over-keen eye for misdemeanours among their mentors.' He gave Clement a thoughtful look. 'Would you like me to follow this up? We've got a scandal on our hands already after Saturday's debacle. This will only add to it. No doubt parents dropping off day boys were given a guided tour.'

'Any minute now we'll get a call from that nincompoop reporter at the Wharton Chronicle wanting a comment,' said Clement gloomily.

'Meredith will deal with all that for you, like she always does,' Eleanor soothed him. 'But aren't you exaggerating rather?' She put her coffee cup back onto the tray and got to her feet. 'I think I must go and see Nell and find out how she really is – and anyway I expect you and Jim are longing to discuss matters between yourselves. Shall Sue and I abandon you, now we've supplied you with the feminine angle?'

TWENTY-SEVEN

Left to themselves, the two men exchanged glances.

'We've trouble on a number of fronts,' said Jim. He counted on his fingers. 'Having the head of a department – albeit only the politics one – move out to live with his mistress in the town after a screaming match in public doesn't reflect much credit on the school. If we shrug our shoulders over that we're still left with the fact that Nell is living in one of the best of the school houses which will lead to questions being asked. You know what junior members of the Common Room are like if they feel someone else is getting better accommodation than they are.'

'The grasping modern generation,' said Clement, reaching for the cafetière. 'Schoolmasters are not what they once were. More coffee?'

'We finished it. We might consider going down the sabbatical route.'

'Send Garwood off on a fortuitously timed break and see how things pan out? Time for reconnaissance and all that?'

'It's been done before. Or even a temporary exchange with another school. Pity we can't do it immediately.'

'Have to be for next term. And what about the A level set? We'll have the parents up in arms at the lack of continuity.'

'It's nothing but revision in the Trinity term anyway with

206

the exam timetable starting in May. Delivering pre-exam master classes, that's the line to take.'

Clement shot him a grateful look. Jim could always be counted on for a balanced view – by which Clement meant reassurance. Indignant and emotional parents were almost as unpleasant to deal with as the local newspaper.

'Old Claverton-Hobbs owes me a favour. Remember how we relieved him of Ian Birt?'

'Ian might be an oddball – as chemists so often are – but he isn't a cad,' objected Jim. 'Not that Alastair is either, to be fair. It's merely the modern idea that undiluted happiness should be our default state. Anything less and we need another partner. Or a prescription from the doctor.'

'Exactly. Contradicting everything that should rule the life of a gentleman. The Common Room is becoming like one of those offices you hear about. The only people we can be sure aren't up to something boils down to the two of us.' Clement glanced down at his empty cup realising too late there was something like regret in his voice.

'Well, it's worth a shot.' Jim frowned at his fingers. 'If you think Claverton-Hobbs will rally. We did a fair amount of wheeling and dealing with them over last summer's Common Entrance borderline passes, didn't we? A London school too, that works in our favour. Any further away and we'd never get Alastair to jump at it. London's just near and far enough.'

'We get the breathing space, and Alastair may decide he'd like to stay there.'

'It still leaves us with what we do for Nell. Not just Nell either. Isn't the son – Sebastian – due to come here in a year or two?'

Confused memories of Martin as Saint Sebastian and Nell embracing him floated into Clement's head. Was this his moment for being a gallant knight?

'I'm not convinced Nell isn't worth more than her husband to the school,' he said carefully. 'Why don't we offer her a full-time position, the art department's overstretched as it is. That way Sebastian would be entitled to the full reduction in fees without any quibbles.'

'Look to get rid of Alastair on a more permanent basis then? Why not? It would have the useful advantage of avoiding the question of this other boy – if indeed the girlfriend is telling the truth and Alastair is the father?'

'It appears to be established that he is. Meredith's informed me he's already on the list for a place.'

'If Alastair stays here, the boy would on the face of it be entitled to the same fee reduction given to all sons of full-time staff. No harm in that, but it could be setting a precedent. We're having to give out bursaries non-stop anyway to keep the government happy. We don't want staff to start thinking they can get concessions for all their relations, however undesirable. It's a small matter but it's something to bear in mind. Might lead to complications.'

Clement traced an area of pattern on the Persian rug with his foot while he pondered this possibility. He disliked complications, especially when it meant confrontations with the bursar who he sometimes felt got the better of him simply because he could add up.

'You're saying that if Alastair was fixed up elsewhere, they'd presumably send the boy there, the fee reduction scheme being pretty standard. I agree it would certainly make life easier this end.'

'Better not commit ourselves to Nell just yet. See how things pan out. Might not want to stay here given what's happened. Let's content ourselves with reassuring her that she can stay in the house for the rest of the school year, and make any job offers next term if we're still inclined. That would be a sensible compromise.'

The thoughtful silence which followed was broken by a knock on the door. Meredith put her head round.

'Martin Darrow's here, headmaster. Shall I make more coffee?'

Before Clement could do more than shoot Jim a look of alarm and Meredith a reluctant assent, the chaplain had pushed into the room.

'I ought to apologise,' he said, his voice shaking with suppressed anger. 'Though why should I? I've never interfered with discipline, that's not what I'm here for. But I'm interfering now. I want that boy exposed. Shown up for what he is, thrown out, given the punishment he deserves.'

'That boy?' Jim leant forward. Clement noticed his nose twitched like a rat's. Eleanor wasn't so far off the mark. 'You're talking about Oliver Benson.'

'Of course I'm talking about him! What other boy has it in him to do what he's done?'

'Dozens, I imagine,' said Jim drily. 'Get boys together and they can behave like animals. Still, I'd already identified Benson as one of those behind this particular prank.'

'Prank! Is that what you call such a piece of deliberate cruelty?'

'You mean they concentrated their efforts bang outside the chapel? You may be taking that too personally,' Clement said, trying to be helpful. 'I imagine it was chosen as a convenient spot, being in the darkest corner of the quad, where they wouldn't be easily noticed. They must have built it very late last night.'

Martin brushed this aside with savage impatience.

'I'm not interested in that! I'm talking about the insult he put on top of it. That obscene drawing. You thought I hadn't seen it, didn't you, when I walked behind you this morning? Well I had, an hour earlier when I went into the chapel – '

Clement, watching the chaplain's face, puzzled over why he'd been unable to complete the sentence. Didn't they all accept that he regularly took himself off into the chapel to pray for the boys, the school, the Common Room and heaven knew what else? Martin never talked about his habits, nor pushed them on anyone else except by example, but he was recognised as a man of quiet and persistent prayer. There was something happening here Clement couldn't get hold of. It made him feel very uneasy. Thank God he had Jim with him.

'I'm very sorry, old chap,' he said, wishing he didn't sound so feeble. 'Come at a bad time too.'

'A bad time?' Martin stared at him. 'Perceptive of you. I can't stay now, I've got a class. I've said what I came to say, and I expect you to act on it.'

The door shut too loudly behind him, only to be opened a minute later by Meredith.

'I expect you still require this.' She plonked a fresh tray of coffee down on the walnut table, rattling the cups in their saucers. Clement, unnerved by the singular demeanour of the chaplain, noticed that she too appeared distraught. What was going on? He wasn't sure if he wanted any more coffee after all. It might be bad for his heart.

'What was all that about?'

Jim raised an eyebrow.

'The hitherto mild-mannered chaplain bursts in here breathing fire and slaughter – what do we make of it? Not that I'm unsympathetic. Very unpleasant business. Got him on the raw, that's clear enough, so he's making a fuss.'

'That's one way of putting it.'

'Why didn't he remove the drawing when he first saw it? It was the obvious thing to do. That way a lot less people would have seen it.'

'I'm beginning to think that people rarely do the obvious

thing,' said Clement petulantly. 'You're surely not suggesting he *wanted* it to be seen by everyone as they came into chapel?'

'It's one solution.' Jim sounded dissatisfied. 'Still, not like him to take his anger – however righteous – to such lengths as this. At least, I've never known him do so before.'

'Was it righteous anger?' Clement doubted. 'The man looked demented. Extraordinary. He's preached hard-hitting sermons enough in his time, but I've never known him cross the line into discourtesy before.'

'He wasn't himself, certainly. The explanation could doubtless be ferreted out.'

'Well, we'd better pacify him and take a tough line with Benson and his partners in crime, though really I don't see – ! You're sure it *is* Benson?'

'No question about it. He's already made a name for himself in the lower sixth as a spot-on caricaturist. I've been privileged to see some examples. Taken on the role of the year's joker – and knows how to home in on weakness. Pity he's taken to using his talents in this destructive manner.'

Clement grunted.

'A heavy talk for all of them and a rustication warning for Benson if he steps out of line again, would that do? But it's going thoroughly over the top. As well as being an infernal nuisance – the last thing I want just now is a confrontation with Benson Senior. Or anyone else senior. Parents get more exacting every day – drop them a hint that their son is anything less than a pleasure to teach and they're up in arms. Anything more draconian and they're consulting their solicitor.'

'I'll pull in those responsible later today, and in the meantime get a couple of prefects to knock the thing down. They won't relish the task but a prefect's life can't be all privileges.'

'And neither can a headmaster's or his deputy's, one concludes.' Clement glanced at the clock on the mantelpiece with its gilded putti supporting the face. Something about their complacently cherubic features had always annoyed him. Not even eleven yet. It had already been a very long and tiring day, and it wasn't likely to get any better.

'Something has just occurred to me,' he said irritably. 'Wishing Alastair on to another school is all very well, but who's going to run the tennis next term?'

He got to his feet and went over to the window. A dull grey blanket covered the sky. More damned snow on the way.

TWENTY-EIGHT

Eleanor, calling in on Nell later that morning, found the house empty. Nell must be teaching.

She trudged around the playing fields while Petrarch snuffled at drifts of snow, pondering over whether she should be trying to persuade Nell to try again with Alastair. It could already be too late. Clement – being Clement – would reiterate that she shouldn't interfere. Like most men he had an over-developed instinct for self-preservation when threatened with emotional and embarrassing conversations.

Alastair had always appeared to be such a model husband! It was hard to believe he could change into a monster who would betray Nell like this, and even more that Juliet's son was indeed Alastair's child. What very complicated lives people led.

As she was returning to the house, her feet numb inside her boots, Sue's astringent comments came back to her. Should one even *expect* a man who was so universally charming to everyone to confine his attentions to one woman? Or to put it another way, could other women be trusted to leave him alone?

'He's hardly one of your literary seducers.'

In times of crisis Sue could always be relied on to give an opinion, and in a manner which conveyed to her listeners that anyone offering a different one might as well save themselves the trouble. Having come back from her usual strenuous day in the courts as a magistrate, in the local prison seeing to prisoners' welfare, or chairing a charity committee, she sat down in the kitchen of the headmaster's house while Eleanor hunted for the sherry.

'I'd put it away with the custard powder when I was making trifle last week,' she apologised, emerging from the larder with the bottle and pouring them both lavish glassfuls.

'Alastair's just one of those men with too much going for them – they never *need* to be honourable or faithful. They get used to getting what they want without trying and naturally they take advantage of it. It's the same with pretty girls. They're always going to be admired and spoiled, so why should they learn self-discipline?'

'Aren't you being rather superficial? Censorious, too. It's how a girl reacts to her prettiness that counts. She might think nothing of it.'

'She's much more likely to think and make a great deal of it. To the detriment of her character.'

'Anyway, you can't accuse Nell of self-consciousness in that direction. She can be what used to be called plain, though at other times she's well, *unusual.* That's more interesting and has better keeping qualities than common or garden prettiness, I always think.'

'It's certainly how any woman who isn't beautiful in the obvious sense can console herself,' said Sue, with a slight touch of sarcasm. 'Mothers of ugly daughters have always clutched at it, in the same breath as protesting that looks don't matter, which nobody but a fool believes for a second.'

'Another thing I can't understand is why Nell should have misread Alastair so completely. Aren't portraitists meant to be perceptive about people's inner lives? The one she did of Jim for the exhibition is disconcertingly like him. If Alastair has been two-timing Nell all this while, it's strange she didn't see it.'

'She may have unconsciously turned her eyes away, as so many of us do. You knew her mother when you were at school, didn't you? Is there much resemblance?'

'She was one of those girls who always wanted to believe in something or someone bigger than themselves – not reckless exactly, just what people call misguided, though really it seems a little unfair…she dropped out after O levels and I lost contact with her. I'm always rather sad about that. Nell says her mother told her she was named after someone she'd looked up to when she was young…of course there's no reason to suppose it was me, Nell just likes to think so. But I wasn't surprised when Nell told me her father had disappeared off the scene when she was a small child. You know the saying about being born to trouble as the sparks fly upward? Her mother was like that. She almost *invited* it.'

'Not like her daughter then. I'd have said Nell's too anxious about giving offence. It would be better for her – and the men in her life – if she wasn't. She should get a grip and stand up for herself and to any man who messes her about.'

'We must make sure she doesn't fall victim to Trevor Faversham. That would be too awful. Fiction is full of idealistic women sacrificing themselves to men – think of Dorothea believing in Casaubon. *Middlemarch*, you know.'

'I never had any patience with Dorothea. Short-sighted enough to choose a dry old pedant and then a dilettante intellectual. She ought to have gone for that doctor if he hadn't been equally obtuse and married a fribble,' said Sue, apparently regretting that characters in novels were beyond her jurisdiction.

'I always feel sorry for Casaubon,' remarked Eleanor. 'To find out you've tied yourself to someone who you come to feel is judging you, to see the disillusion and pity in their eyes must be a never-ending punishment. It's difficult to see how Alastair could have stayed with Nell even if she'd agreed to it. Living up to being forgiven must be very uncomfortable.'

'Now you'll be feeling sorry for Alastair. People make their own bed to lie on. He's like a child who thinks he can have things both ways. None of us can. For long.'

'Fatally self-indulgent then, rather than what Clement would call a bounder?'

'He's lost a very good wife through his own weakness and inability to say no. Attractive married men are always going to be surrounded by women making overtures to them, since women have no qualms about going after any man they fancy. What a disgusting word that is. As if we were talking about a cake.'

'French Fancies,' murmured Eleanor. 'Clement was grumbling yesterday I'd forgotten to buy any for tea.'

'Even when it's the husband of a best friend. There's no excuse. People don't *have* to give way to their passions. They can actually walk away. They just don't want to.'

'I think I'd always be afraid of being punished.' Eleanor took a reassuring sip of sherry. 'Either in this world or the next.'

'Nonsense! You've got a conscience and would listen to it. That's the difference.'

'Conscience doesn't appear to have come into it with Alastair and Juliet, that's for sure. But there is one thing: he chose Nell in the first place. That says something about him. And he married her when she was pregnant with Rachel. He did the right thing there.'

'Oh Eleanor! As if their generation care about that!'

'No, a pity. I was trying to think of him as *initially* honourable. Still, I think he really loved her.'

'In his way.' Sue's voice was tart.

'You mean he didn't love all of her, the whole Nell, because he can't see the depth of her. I wonder if he does of anyone?'

'A typical man, then. Is this Juliet the femme fatale of popular fiction?'

216

'The siren who lures unsuspecting men to their doom? She didn't *strike* me like that when I met her once or twice with Nell over the summer. Nor was she disagreeably attention-seeking in spite of having the sort of looks men don't seem able to resist. She was just very *alive*. I don't think she looked up for it.' Eleanor ended this speech on a doubtful note, unsure of this last expression.

'Picking up on that kind of thing is rather outside your experience.' Sue finished her sherry and got up with the purposeful air of someone ready for the next round of good works. 'And from what you say, Juliet will be more than a match for him. They may do very well together.'

But Eleanor had stopped listening. Her eye had strayed to the spine of one of Clement's heavyweight art books on the Northern Renaissance which had overflowed from the sitting room and were now piled onto the top of the kitchen dresser. It showed a young girl with high pointed breasts, milky white skin and veiled provocative eyes. She reminded Eleanor of Tom's first girlfriend. The one she'd met for the first time at nine o'clock in the morning tripping down the stairs while seventeen-year-old Tom trailed behind her in his boxer shorts.

'There are times when I wish sex had never been invented. When you think about it rationally, it causes nothing but trouble.'

TWENTY-NINE

The warning bell had gone, but still the line of women waited, some with despairing sighs and tightening lips, others with the stoic good humour of those who have been too well brought up to complain. Among them was Nell, heavy with her second pregnancy, hating her pelvic floor, and wishing she was anywhere but in this shuffling queue for the ladies' lavatories.

'This is more entertaining than the play, but is that any consolation?'

Nell turned. The girl behind her looked around her own age. She had dark hair falling over slanting blue eyes and a mouth twisted into a conspiratorial mock grimace.

'Not much,' Nell agreed. 'Because there's hours and *hours* more. And my mother-in-law gave us the tickets so we can't just walk out.'

'I would if *I* had a mother-in-law like that! The old meanie. If she isn't with you, how can she ever know?'

'No – but you'd still feel ungrateful – you know how it is – ' Nell faltered, and then found herself smiling. It *was* ridiculous to care about Buttery Barbara.

'Today, and only today, I might. I'm here with one of those very good and earnest men who try too hard to do the right thing.' The girl flicked her fringe out of her eyes and began to laugh. 'Actually he was once my university tutor. I haven't the heart to disillusion him. Yet.'

'And Alastair – that's my husband – keeps peering at his watch and fidgeting. I've already caught a few glares from the people around us.'

'They should be too busy trying to glean anything enjoyable or meaningful from such a dire production to notice. Why don't the four of us meet up for drinks in the second interval? You'd like Newland, he's a one-off and intriguing, in spite of his taste for dramatic angst dragging on till midnight. Here, anyone pregnant should jump the queue, come on, I'll show you.'

Nell, still dizzy with love for her husband of less than two years and on good days the whole world besides, stared at the beautiful, wilful face offering friendship – and seized it.

'I'm Nell – '

'And I'm Juliet – '

But even as they spoke Juliet's eyes grew into huge devouring balls and her stomach swelled monstrously and Nell was running from the theatre before the baby came and yet she couldn't move because her body was suddenly heavy and heaving with labour pains.

Nell woke screaming. Cramps gripped her stomach. She reached into her knicker drawer to rummage for the painkiller tablets she'd hidden there after Dr Auerbach had asked her that question about Rachel and suicide, and swallowed two with a glass of water.

The pain was blessedly familiar. She'd never been really late like this before. She heaved herself out of bed and went into the bathroom.

All three children had cried when she and Alastair had told them that they were separating and that Alastair would be moving in to live with Juliet. *We'll all be happier in the end even if it's difficult at first.* Such insultingly inadequate words, but she'd said them.

Neither Rachel nor Sebastian had asked any questions, and had stopped crying only to stare stony-faced at the three adults. Vail opened his mouth to ask if he would be made to change his surname. Nell guessed he was pouncing on a detail because the whole picture was too overwhelming for him to take in. Now it must be up to Juliet and Alastair to comfort him.

Much later, she and Alastair had brought Rachel and Sebastian home. The one big decision had been taken; details too painful to face just yet must be worked out along the long desolate road ahead of her. Alastair would live with Juliet: that was enough to be going on with. The futility of thinking any further than the next few weeks was obvious to both of them. After that – Nell's mind whirled sickeningly around divorce laws about which she knew nothing – but she couldn't face thinking about it yet.

She got back into bed and shut her eyes. If only she could escape back into sleep. Voices and faces thrust themselves at her. The blue of Juliet's eyes. *Alastair's had a vasectomy.* The mask that was Alastair's face. *You can't deny it, can you Al?* Martin's coat around her shoulders.

Had she made a dreadful mistake telling Alastair to leave? Shouldn't she, for the sake of her children, struggle to remake her marriage? This was what children wanted wasn't it, to have their parents together. Couldn't she make another effort and carry on in spite of everything?

I do love you still. Alastair had said that. In front of Juliet. Wasn't it enough to be going on with, couldn't they make a go of it with that? *Half a loaf is better than no bread.*

There was a sound at the door and Sebastian crept into the room. She saw he had violet rings around his eyes as if he hadn't slept. He looked at her, a mute question in his eyes.

'Dad's in the spare room, darling. D'you want to climb in beside me? It's terribly early still.'

'You said you didn't love Dad any more.' Sebastian didn't look at her, but stood awkwardly, twisting the hem of his pyjama top.

She hadn't said she didn't love Alastair. But Sebastian thinking she had, told her what she knew already. People didn't hear what you said. Or what you meant to say. She saw the blotchy whiteness of his face, the bare foot kicking forlornly at the carpet. How honest should one be with a twelve-year-old?

'People change, darling and want different things. I wish it hadn't happened, but it has. Just as it does to lots and lots of families.'

'But why is it happening to us? What have we done wrong?'

'I don't know. Nothing. You and Rachel – don't think for one moment you've *ever* done anything wrong.'

'Mum?'

It was Rachel. She came in, shut the door and then leant against it, watching Nell and Sebastian with a mixture of defiance and shame in her green-grey eyes.

'I heard you talking. Mum, I know what you're going to do next, you think you'll send me back to Dr Auerbach, in case I go what you call down again. Well, you've got another think coming. In fact, I bet you never cancelled whenever it was I was next meant to be going.'

Oh God, she hadn't telephoned Dr Auerbach's secretary. She'd meant to when Rachel had said on the day she came back from skiing that she didn't need to go to Brookner House any more. She hadn't done so. Rachel might change her mind and the next appointment wasn't until after the art exhibition…these had seemed good reasons to put off a call she didn't want to make. From the adjoining bathroom came the relentless drip of the cold tap that wouldn't turn off properly. It needed fixing, and she hadn't got round to getting that done either.

'I don't *want* you and Dad to get divorced, I don't want

221

everything changing like this and everyone fighting and saying awful things to each other.' Sebastian wiped his nose with his pyjama sleeve, not looking at her.

No, and I didn't want my mother to die when I was seventeen, Nell thought with a silent inward sob. There was never ever any protection from the randomness of life, no escape from the terror of what might strike without warning. Having parents divorcing was little enough compared to the wretchedness endured by so many children all over the world, but it was real and terrible when it happened to you.

'It won't be like it is with some families,' she said. 'Because Dad and I will make sure it won't be. That's a promise.'

Rachel's eyes showered contempt over her.

'Mum, all that stuff last night about it being better that people were honest and how everyone would be happier in the end – why do grown ups have to come out with all that crap? You don't believe in it yourself.'

'I suppose because it's what I want to think, and saying it gives me hope that it will be true in the end.'

'But you hate Dad so much you can't stand to live with him any more, and that means you hate us too.'

'Oh Rachel,' Nell said, feeling the tears smarting. 'Nothing like this stops me loving you and Sebastian.'

'But you don't. You hate us because you hate Dad, it's obvious you do. Aren't we part of him?'

'It's a different sort of love. You must know how completely I love the two of you. And I don't hate Dad, how could I?'

'Because he treats people like shit. Thinking he can get away with stuff, just because he always has with you.'

'He hasn't.' Nell struggled for coherence. 'It's never felt like that. We've always loved each other and been happy together until now.'

'So why didn't you fight – why d'you let Juliet walk all over you? Going on about us being a family – that's a joke – and then not even trying to get Dad back.'

'I did try, but I couldn't do it.' Nell remembered that Juliet had used much the same words. Again Nell saw her, wearing the red shirt, pouring out cappuccinos for the two of them. Could you honestly measure how much you tried, or even be sure that you had? Nell didn't know.

'Oh yes? Then what are you crying about? I should have thought it was a bit late for that.'

'Just remember that Dad will always love his children more than anyone else in the world, the same as I do.'

'Don't give me that crap. If Dad loved us more than Juliet he wouldn't be doing this to us. Parents always have this idea they can get away with spouting all this bullshit about loving their children best. Do they think we're stupid or what?'

THIRTY

I stole my mum's boyfriend, and discovered he's a woman! My eleven-year-old gave birth down the toilet! Why I ran away from five different husbands!

Nell, slumped in the train, looked dazedly at the headings emblazoned on the cover of the magazine opposite her.

Compared with these stories – Nell glanced apprehensively around the carriage to check what other lurid tales might be on offer – her own drama was petty, a small thing of no entertainment value. But these women who so recklessly exposed what had happened to them in the true life sections of the women's weeklies were only a few stops down the line from where she was. For everything that had happened since the day she'd discovered Juliet in Alastair's arms showed how easy it was for your life to slide into chaos. Nor could anyone guess how atrociously you would behave.

Sap green trees and fields fresh with springing grass flashed past the windows, for it was now late May, and Nell – who ought to have gone to the preview day but it had clashed with Rachel's fourteenth birthday – was on her way to London to see the exhibition of the Royal Society of Portrait Painters in the Mall Galleries. Her painting of Martin had not only been selected – and this to Nell was unexpected enough – but also awarded a major national prize for portraiture.

Among all the baffled sadness which clung like a disabling

fog over her days Nell hardly remembered submitting the portrait in the first place, but Eleanor had insisted. 'It's time you started believing in yourself as a serious painter,' she'd said back in February, sounding unusually purposeful, as though she'd been pummelled into it by Sue North.

Where would she have been without Eleanor, who never by the slightest hint suggested she had anything more important to do than offer the eccentric comfort that was peculiarly her own? 'I'll do my best to fit you into my busy schedule, but do try and be positive' – it was a tone of voice that in her soreness Nell imagined she heard all around her. But never from Eleanor.

Eeanor's encouragement hadn't stopped there. Last night Clement Hunstrete had taken her out to supper. Nell knew the headmaster made a point of taking senior members of the Common Room out individually during the year, but not someone insignificant like her.

'Enjoy your meal.'

'That fellow Faversham making an ass of himself?' Clement shot at her, eyeing the retreating waitress with suspicion before inspecting the food in front of him.

Surely he couldn't know Trevor had insisted on taking her out the previous week? Nell shuddered at the humiliating memory. *Now that you're lonely like me, we could comfort each other, couldn't we?* What had she done to make him think she would welcome his repulsive advances, didn't he have any insight at all? Trevor had actually thought she wanted him to – Nell's face burned as she recalled it. Trevor had looked disbelieving when she'd slapped him down hard, and he'd sulked ever since.

Trevor, don't ever speak to me of this again.

He hadn't – but their old working relationship was spoilt. She began to think about leaving Wharton altogether, it wasn't too late to give in her notice for the end of term. But she might not get another job so easily and she couldn't afford not to be earning even for a short time.

'No – not at all – '

'Everything all right?' The waitress reappeared with a trained smile.

'It would be if we were allowed to get on with eating it without being interrupted,' Clement said testily. 'Nothing but nincompoops, these restaurant managers, thinking they have to perform like monkeys. Where was I? Ah yes, the art department. What with the success of the schools project, we think some expansion could be useful. With your husband in London now, we'd like to offer you a full-time teaching post starting in September.'

He took a mouthful of his grilled turbot and launched into the proposition, not quite looking her in the eye. Time the art department grew to meet demand, give you security, excellent solution to a tricky problem – these explanations were jumbled together like the seafood risotto she was eating.

'The governors want to commission a painting illustrating the quad buildings with the chapel as a focus point,' Clement hurried on. 'Something in the grand monumental style, you know, suggesting the history and timeless values of the school, to be hung in my office. An outstanding work of art to impress visitors and prospective parents. With you as the artist,' he added hopefully.

It all sounded unlikely. Nell guessed the idea had been Eleanor's. Wouldn't the governors prefer a more prestigious artist, or even the head of the art department, instead of the part-time art teacher whose architectural drawing was undeniably haphazard?

'Thank you for your faith in me,' she said slowly, touched by his sheepish expression – in her old life she'd have longed to seize hold of some paper and draw it! – 'I'd like to take on the painting. But not the full-time job.' She paused, trying to find words for the contradictory equations fighting each other in her head since the Easter holidays. 'You're offering me a lifeline, just like when you said to stay in the house when Alastair left. I know why you've thought of it. It's because of Sebastian, isn't it? But I'm not sure if he wants to go to Wharton any more.'

'My dear girl, you don't know what you're saying – '

'And I want him to be free to choose. Not feel under pressure to please me or Alastair.'

She saw he looked disappointed. He was far too much of a gentleman to coerce her.

'I'm sorry, I must sound so ungrateful. But I need to start making my own way, not be looked after by other people.'

Now, crossing into Trafalgar Square on her way to the Mall Galleries, Nell fought the urge to turn round and jump straight back onto a train to Wharton. Heavy grey clouds were massing across a sky which had started out too bright too early. It was going to rain, and she was wearing the wrong clothes.

What good would it do, going out for the day like this? Even the train fare was a waste of money when she was counting every penny. She'd been a fool to turn down the offer of a full-time job at Wharton. It would have given her and the children a measure of financial security, even at the price of freedom. But what kind of freedom would she have, with the prospect of crippling debt getting nearer each week?

They'd never had any savings, she and Alastair, their flat in London had been rented, and they'd always spent all they earned. Alastair would obviously pay as much as he could afford towards the care of the children, she could trust him for that she knew. But it wasn't going to be enough, because she was going to have to find herself somewhere for the three of them to live. Renting even the smallest house was going to gobble up everything she had. How were they going to survive? The idea that she would ever make it as an artist was stupid fantasy. It was running away. She was *always* running away. She'd run away from her mother dying.

Four and a half months of waking in the night, of lying in the half empty bed unable to sleep; hating Alastair, hating Juliet, hating herself for making such a wreckage of her own life, her children's lives. Hours when she found herself imagining the deception that had been running down the years, fury and shame and jealousy taking turns to visit in the darkness. Days when she'd gone to the lawyers to set in motion the whole sordid and saddening business of divorce, sick at heart at what she was doing but knowing only that there was no other way except through it.

In April, during the Easter holidays, Alastair and Juliet had left Wharton and moved into Juliet's mews house near Paddington.

'I thought she'd let it out,' said Nell bitterly and pointlessly. 'That was thick of me, wasn't it? She was hedging her bets all the time.'

There was now almost nothing left of Alastair at Wharton. He took with him only his personal possessions; it occurred to Nell for the first time how few he had. He was a man who lived lightly. None of the furniture went to London. Not even the leather armchair. Nell gave it to Tom Hunstrete for his room at Oxford.

'Why doesn't bloody Gran keep her mouth shut?' demanded Rachel, after yet another phone call from Alastair's mother, assuring Nell that if only she would come to Barbara's house church she could have hands laid on her and be healed from whatever was blocking her refusal to forgive Alastair.

'Because she hides away among fundamentalist and judgmental bigots who think they're right and everyone else is wrong,' said Nell, driven into plain-speaking. 'But I promise you she's not coming to stay here again – *ever*.'

'She went on at me in a really annoying way about being chosen by the Lord to lead people to him.' Sebastian made a scornful face. 'A rubbish choice if you ask me. You'd think God could do better than that.'

There was no disputing this.

'If only your mother hadn't died. Then me and Sebastian would have a proper granny, not like know-all Buttery Barbara.'

'You shouldn't call her that.' Nell's protest was half-hearted. Not to see her patronising mother-in-law was the one consolation on offer at present. In fact it would be a great help if she dropped dead of a heart attack. The fantasy flitted pleasurably across her mind.

'Why not? You do. And anyway it suits her. People shouldn't bore on to other people about what God says to them. It's boasting. They should let people find God in their *own* way.' Her daughter gave her an unexpected hug. 'Thanks for saying we don't have to see her if we don't want to.'

This wasn't exactly what she'd said, but it hardly mattered. Nell had already learnt there was nothing to be gained by continuing the pretence with the children that her mother-in-law was anything other than hard work of the more disagreeable kind.

Contrary to all Nell's expectations the children were already adapting to what had happened and thinking for themselves. Rachel might still treat both her and Alastair with reserve and sometimes painful criticism, but she was throwing herself into a teenage world of friends, boys and secrets, with no further signs of a return to the eating disorder of last winter. Nell breathed a prayer of thankfulness. Rachel and Sebastian, and Vail too, had more courage and resilience than she had.

But how had it all happened? Why had she *allowed* it to happen? Why hadn't she fought to keep him, learnt to get over stuff as other women did? These unanswerable questions played obsessively in her mind, a worn-out recording she couldn't switch off.

'I *can't* forgive that,' she'd said, low-voiced, to Martin. 'If it had been only an affair – I don't know. But his not telling me about Vail is like a poisoned shadow spreading back into everything we did together.'

If she had, Alastair might be with her now, happy and celebrating her success. She was beginning to understand that the loss of his friendship would in the end hurt worst of all. He'd been her closest friend as well as the man who shared her bed. She'd lost the companion of sunshine years, who'd always looked happy when he was with her, who'd teased her when she forgot things in the oven and praised her useless cooking, who'd only laughed when she'd written off the car in a multi-storey car park.

But she had the children. They were the all-consuming constants in an existence which continued to feel unreal. Alastair's new life in London etched itself into her mind with sharper focus. He was teaching at a leading private school while Vail had returned to his old prep school. Vail had been relieved, as if needing the security of the children he'd grown up with, as an escape from the changes at home.

'I've been moved into the scholarship class,' he told her at their last phone call. His voice, which had been high and strained after he'd first left Wharton, sounded confident. He too was adjusting to his altered world.

'Darling – I *am* proud of you. But I always am anyway, not just for doing so well at school.'

Why couldn't she be like the children? She tried to block out the images that crowded into her head: Juliet laughing as she cooked supper in the tiny kitchen, Alastair throwing Juliet's collection of glowing embroidered cushions onto the floor from the giant sofa, the two of them meeting Rachel and Sebastian off the train at Charing Cross on Saturdays.

And she had Martin – or some of him. Nell was beginning to grasp that Martin could only give so much. Something was happening to him, something was going badly wrong. She thought she understood some part of it, and was thankful her mother-in-law had never come across him. At other times she told herself she was mistaken. But his withdrawal into himself meant she hadn't talked to him – not properly – since the night he'd taken her to his flat and given her his old coat to wear.

As she thought of Martin and the disquieting look at the back of his eyes she wanted to begin crying again, and it felt as though she'd done nothing but cry for weeks and weeks until there must be no tears left. Instead she made herself go on walking, one foot in front of another, as if she was doing some military training exercise. Left, right, left, right – she'd never been any good at remembering which was which. Perhaps today would finally din it into her head, which was feeling like her stomach, too full and too empty all at the same time.

'Can I ask you a question?'

It was a young man with designer stubble and a clipboard. He was also standing too close. Nell blenched and took a step backwards from last night's chillies.

'Please don't. I'm not into beauty products and all that stuff. And I haven't got any money.'

'Are you someone who cares nothing about the suffering of others?'

Not the usual *can-I-talk-to-you-about-your-hair*, then. Just now Nell felt she didn't care about anyone's suffering more than her own. Why did these people pick on her? Because they always, always did. She made as if to sidestep past, but the young man took another lunge towards her.

'No,' said Nell. 'I mean yes. I'm in a hurry.'

'I won't keep you more than one minute,' said the man, who had clearly heard the same excuse too many times. He launched into a sea of facts and figures about squirrels and foxes and badgers, none of which Nell would have grasped, even if she'd been capable of listening. All around her people streamed past, enviably oblivious and uncaring of the iniquities inflicted upon the animal kingdom.

'You mustn't waste any more time on me – ' Nell tried to shrink away from him, but he waved his clipboard at her almost threateningly.

'Do you want to have it on your conscience that you've turned your back on what's going on in our countryside? By contributing a minimum of twenty pounds you'll have helped to crush the selfish pursuits of human beings whose only pleasure is to hunt down innocent creatures. Walk away and you'll be guilty.'

'Actually,' exploded Nell, finally losing her temper, 'I love hunting! At least, I've never done it, but I don't see what business it is of yours to interfere. And it certainly isn't mine.' She swung off past Nelson's Column, high on anger and the relief of escape, but the young man pursued her across the lights, yelling insults while passers-by stared.

I am a selfish bitch and thoughtless middle class cow who cares nothing for the suffering of others, Nell repeated as she arrived at the entrance of the Mall Galleries, the man's abusive shouts still echoing in her ears. He could be right. She hung her head.

A collection of middle-aged men and women were being escorted round the exhibition by an enthusiastic art teacher. It must be an adult education class on an outing. Nell edged nearer. You could learn a lot from people's comments. Sure enough, intrusive backgrounds, poor tonal work and misuse of colour were being discovered with a good deal of hilarity and satisfaction.

Unexpectedly Nell found she was smiling. There were some

232

extraordinary and wonderful portraits here by artists known and admired all over the world, but these people were enjoying themselves and this was what mattered.

'Now I want you all to make some drawings from portraits that interest you.' The teacher threw an encouraging glance at Nell. 'We shall discuss your findings in the class next week.'

Nell watched as sketchbooks and pencils were hauled out of bags, disappointed to realise she'd arrived too late to hear what the class had to say about her portrait of Martin. She repressed a sudden urge to join in with this pleasant group. These last months she'd lost her old habit of making quick sketches of everything around her. She couldn't concentrate, or find joy in anything beautiful or interesting. But today she had her sketchbook with her, ready for some drawings in the National Gallery after she'd finished here. As she retreated, she spotted two of the jollier ladies sidling away towards the counter displaying coffee and a selection of delicious-looking cakes.

Martin gazed out at her from the canvas, his ascetic paleness and luminous speaking eyes telling their own story. She stood in front of her work, not really seeing it. Instead she remembered all that had happened to her since she'd put on the first few tentative brush strokes of Martin's portrait. She'd been happily married, complacent even, wanting another child. Now she was on the way to being divorced. Would she ever know if she'd done the right thing for the children, for herself, and even for Alastair?

'You couldn't have done otherwise.'

Martin had said it. She searched the eyes that she'd worked and re-worked in an effort to get something approaching the truth – or the truth as far as she could interpret it in paint. They looked at her with an expression encompassing his acceptance of the human frailty around him. This was Martin: what he gave to other people, but not to himself.

Real, disinterested goodness in men. Once, a long time ago,

she'd thought she'd found it in Alastair. The dust from the final smashing of her idol now spread to other men. Jim North, Trevor Faversham, even Clement Hunstrete; were they all in essence the same underneath? Was unselfish kindness confined to men like Martin?

For some reason she started thinking of Dr Auerbach and found herself comparing the two men, or perhaps the three, for Alastair was always there in the forefront of her mind, obscuring her vision and confusing her understanding whenever she thought about anything at all. Alastair in whom she'd believed so passionately and whose open-handed warmth she'd mistaken for something else. But it wasn't fair to compare Dr Auerbach with other men. She hardly knew him. He was just the man who'd done so much for her daughter. A man sitting behind a desk.

But then there had been the time when she'd had tea with him on her birthday in the National Portrait Gallery cafe. He'd told her about his family and in an abandoned moment she'd been on the point of telling him the truth about her mother, the manner of her dying, which not even Eleanor knew really, just Alastair and Juliet, she wasn't going to tell the children until they were older.

It was all part of his training as a psychiatrist of course – getting people to reveal secrets. So that time with him was in a way an automatic response, which might be made to anyone and everyone. He did good things, yes, there must be hundreds of children and parents he'd helped. But that wasn't the same as *being* a good person. He was just pursuing his career.

She remembered the photograph in the consulting room. Maybe he was unfaithful to that beautiful wife. For some reason the suggestion was a painful and unpleasant one and so she abandoned it, her thoughts skidding into confusion.

'Wouldn't mind a bit of him.'

A bunch of schoolgirls giggled their way past. Nell sighed. Was that all her portrait conveyed of Martin? If so, it was a failure and shouldn't have won a prize. But then hadn't Rachel, who knew Martin, said much the same? Was sexual gratification really everyone's foremost preoccupation, and sometimes their only one? Was it healthier in the end to be honest about, and even act upon, these urges?

Nell was still struggling with these ideas an hour later as she stood in the pouring rain and pressed the keys for her PIN into a cash machine in the Strand. She retrieved her card, pushed it back into her purse and turned away without thinking.

'Hey, don't forget your cash – '

Her cash! Nell wheeled round, aghast. She snatched at the fifty pounds sticking out of the slot and turned to look gratefully at the man behind her who'd spoken.

'I'm so thankful to you – I can't think how I – '

She faltered. The man under his umbrella looked exactly like – no, he definitely was – Dr Auerbach. But even as this flashed though her head, she realised his smile was entirely impersonal. He didn't recognise her.

It wasn't surprising. Soaked rats' tails were plastered across her face. She bent her head, stammered something unintelligible and raced away from him down the pavement clutching the money in one hand and her bag in the other.

He didn't know it was me.

She stopped to thrust the hated notes into her purse, and found she was shaking. It would be safer to push the purse right into the bottom of her bag. She was beginning to feel that anything might happen to her now – pickpockets would target her, she'd cross on a red light, get on the wrong train.

Even if he did remember me, why should I care what he thinks?

'Mrs Garwood, are you all right?'

She knew that voice. Clipped, to the point. Nell turned

round, and saw Dr Auerbach behind her, breathing quickly as if he'd hurried after her.

'Yes,' she managed to say. 'Yes, I'm quite all right, thank you.'

He thrust the umbrella over her, examining her face, his own impossible to read.

'I do it all the time.'

'Do you?'

'It's the brain-paralysing after-effects of the fear of forgetting your number. Especially bad when there's a queue of people behind you.'

Hot colour burned in her cheeks.

'I didn't think you knew who I was.'

'Of course I knew who you were.'

'I mean, it must be difficult enough to keep all the people you look after in your head – I don't think hard-pressed consultants should be expected to remember the mothers of their patients – clients, that is,' she amended, remembering the term his secretary had used.

He said nothing for a moment, but stood observing her, frowning slightly, rain dripping off his jacket.

'Do you have time to have a chat, or are you rushing off to meet someone? Can I give you some lunch?'

Not pickpockets, nor crossing on a red light, not even the wrong train. Instead, an hour talking with the man who would be able to help and understand, and to whom she could say anything at all, because he was a psychiatrist and therefore unshockable. And it wouldn't be disloyal or indiscreet but totally safe. It was as if an angel had appeared, sent from heaven to rescue her. Nell felt a wave of such surprise and gratitude that she almost, but not quite, forgot everything but the immediate prospect before her.

'You must be too busy – ' she began feebly, but he interrupted her.

'I've been working all morning just near here.' He pointed back along the Strand. 'Something else I was due to attend has just been cancelled, and so I've finished for the day quite unexpectedly. I was about to go and get something to eat. Please come.'

Still she hesitated. It was wrong to take up his time – time he wouldn't be paid for – and who was she to expect it? There were other people, needier than her. He ought to be with them.

'It's coming up to your half-year birthday after all,' he said. 'Isn't that a good enough reason?'

The memory of sitting drinking tea with him at the National Portrait Gallery swam in front of her. Tears pricked at her eyes.

'Nell, please say yes.'

Was it the use of her name that broke into her defences? She looked up into his face and once again lost herself in the extraordinary tenderness of his smile.

'Thank you,' she heard herself say. 'I should like that more than – more than – *anything.*'

THIRTY-ONE

Nell. He'd said her name. *Nell.*

As he walked beside her, shielding her from the rain, he whispered the sound over and over in his head, conscious only of the ache of his love for her. Almost six months since he'd seen her. Lightless days of restless longing.

'It's late-ish for lunch,' he said as they sat down at a white-clothed table in a tiny Italian restaurant in Covent Garden. 'But the service is quick here, and the food is good. Give you some energy if you want to go to the shops afterwards,' he ended lightly, but not really meaning it, for she'd never impressed him as a woman interested in shopping, and was today carrying only an embroidered cloth bag with a sketchbook sticking out of it.

He thought of the paint-stained jeans she usually wore when she brought Rachel to see him at the clinic. She was wearing tidier clothes today, but evidently hadn't taken care to dress up to come to London. She hadn't done that even when it was her birthday. Her hair, dark and shiny with rainwater, and much longer than he remembered, was dripping onto a faded green cardigan and a cotton skirt which he'd already noticed was hanging off her. She'd lost too much weight.

A painting he'd seen in Tate Britain came into his mind, a Gwen John study of a young girl, *The Convalescent*, it was called.

A portrait full of intense emotion, yet so quietly expressed you might walk past it and miss its extraordinary depth…

'Mrs Garwood telephoned to cancel her daughter's appointments for the foreseeable future,' his secretary had told him in the middle of January.

He'd stared blankly at Dilys and asked her to repeat the message.

'Did she give a reason? Why didn't you put her through to me?'

'She didn't ask to speak to you.' His secretary bristled. 'Not directly, so naturally I didn't trouble you.'

An overwhelming urge to contact Nell pressed upon him like a weeping sore. He knew better. Psychiatrists didn't cross the line. He could write a polite note expressing regret and offering to be of service at any time in the future, but any more than this was unprofessional and unethical.

He hadn't done so – and then there had come a brief letter, to his eyes stiffly written, in which she thanked him for all he'd done for Rachel, who was so much better that she no longer needed further help.

Didn't this sudden cessation of Rachel's appointments offer him the escape his conscience demanded of him? He'd known only that it sent him down a lonely dead-end of despair. Once he'd thought he could control the path he'd determined on. Now he didn't trust himself.

Looking at Nell across the table from him, flushed with damp and shyness, his heart filled with joy at the closeness of her. He imagined putting his arms around her and feeling her slim body pressed against his, her heart beating against his own. Instead he said, 'I hope you're as hungry as I am. Let's have something warm and comforting.'

It was as she bent her head to study the menu – or to avoid his scrutiny – that he saw her hands. They were as he remembered, square and strong with short unvarnished nails – but there was no wedding ring.

His heart missed a beat. Questions crowded into his head. He uttered none of them. He drew her attention to the menu, taking care to maintain the formal courtesy he used on all public occasions, and they ordered *pollo con zucchini* and a bottle of *Pinot Grigio*. He was not a man to whom small talk came easily, but he guessed she wanted time to feel once more at ease with him, and murmured neutral remarks that required no particular answer.

'I haven't ever said thank you properly for all you did for Rachel,' she interrupted. 'I've wanted to, but – '

'You *did* thank me. In your letter. Are you both all right?' He was stammering, feeling his way until he knew how much of what Rachel had told him had been repeated to her mother. No wedding ring. He looked at Nell's thin face. She'd been having a hard time. Frustration at his own helplessness to do anything for her surfaced, only to be quelled as he reminded himself that even if he was still seeing Rachel, there was little he could do for Nell.

'Don't answer that if you don't want to,' he added gently. 'Tell me first what you're doing in London.'

'It's all right – and Rachel's doing pretty well. She and Sebastian are with my husband just now. As for me, well, I do a bit of painting of my own – as well as teaching art, I mean – so partly I've come up to look at some architectural sketches in the National Gallery. I need some inspiration for a commission I've been given. Buildings aren't exactly my kind of thing, I'm useless at getting perspective correct.'

'Aren't paintings often more expressive when it's not? Like van Gogh's crooked walls and rooftops. What's the other part?'

'I've got a painting in a gallery near here – '

'A private gallery? Is it for sale?'

'It's in the Mall Galleries. They have exhibitions all the time – at the moment it's portraits.'

He noted she said this with some reluctance, and concluded that it must be an honour to have work accepted.

'Is it of one of the family?'

'No. It's of the chaplain at Wharton. I painted it last year before I brought Rachel to Brookner House.'

'You know him well?'

'Yes – no. I only really got to know him when he was sitting for the portrait. He's – he's a very unusual man. Almost a perfect man.'

It was the flush of consciousness he perceived in her face rather than the words themselves which caused Lewis to feel angry with himself. If she couldn't be his, what did it matter what praise she gave another man? He thought of the husband who'd betrayed her with her best friend. Had she turned to this chaplain for consolation and fallen in love with him?

'He has an obsession with jigsaws,' Nell continued, 'of paintings from art history – he was doing Pieter Brueghel's one of Icarus falling into the water and nobody noticing.'

'*About suffering they were never wrong, the Old Masters,*' quoted Lewis, remembering the poem.

'Yes – and it *is* like that, isn't it? People enduring all kinds of unspoken unhappiness and we're just opening a window or just walking dully along, or however it goes. Auden understood it just like Brueghel did, and Martin too.'

'Martin?'

'Martin Darrow, the chaplain, I mean.'

She blushed as she said the name, adding to Lewis's disquiet.

'I'm glad,' he said, trying to keep his voice as objective as possible, but fearing he sounded constrained, 'you've had someone so – so *perfect* to whom you could talk.'

'It's worse for children,' she said, avoiding the question underlying his words. 'There's so much of it secret, endured silently, ignored by hurrying adults. It makes me ashamed to think how often I've missed hidden miseries or somehow rushed at them with a clumsiness that made things worse.'

'You even thinking like this means you won't have missed much.'

'I got everything wrong with Rachel. She told you things she felt she couldn't tell me.'

'It's what I'm here for. But there's always that space between human beings.' A rush of sadness, of grief, suddenly hit him, and he continued almost with despair, 'We can't ever wholly understand even the people we love best.'

'I'm getting divorced.' She dashed at the words, a finger running across the base of her wine glass. 'My husband, he was having an affair with my best friend almost all of our marriage. I still can't quite believe it, like people are said not to believe it when they're told they're going to die, when they don't feel ill. Because it was all so sudden. Or so it felt like at the time, although when I look back – '

Again he heard Rachel's young voice breaking over the words, and saw her defeated eyes full of unshed tears and misunderstood anger.

'Dr Auerbach, Rachel told you, didn't she?'

'A little.'

'It had been going on all the time,' Nell said haltingly, 'and I never guessed. When I first knew, I thought I could put it all behind us. I *pretended* to think that. Then I found out Juliet's boy is Alastair's and last summer he'd – I couldn't go on living with him after knowing that.'

God in heaven. An unacknowledged son aged what, eleven, twelve? He was shocked at what Nell must have suffered and asked himself what sort of man could betray this girl, could even want to *look* at anyone else. If she were his – he thrust the thought away from him.

'Before it all happened, there were things about Alastair that I didn't – but I blanked them because I couldn't face admitting them to myself. We'd got married in such a rush, Alastair said he wanted to make up to me for what my mother had gone through with my dad – not that she cared either way about having a ring on her finger. It was as if Juliet understood it all without ever saying anything. She knew how I felt about my mother too – more even than Alastair really. She wasn't just a friend, she was – ' she stopped, and then said with a kind of childish resentment, 'People aren't always what you think.'

'Nobody ever is – and some of them can't be.'

'*You* are.'

He must put himself behind the desk in a consulting room. The story she was telling him happened everywhere all the time. Two women who are best friends falling in love with the same man and then fighting over him. It was depressingly predictable.

But as he went on listening he began to think Nell was no longer in love with the husband she was now divorcing, that she may never have loved him as completely as she might in the future love someone else.

She must have been still in her teens when she'd met him, without the mother she'd been so close to. She hadn't had a father figure in her life. A charming man ten years older and likely to have girlfriends coming out his ears but choosing her – he could guess at the perplexity and misgiving that must have set in when her over-idealistic view of the man she'd given herself to inevitably began to lose its conviction.

She would have taken it badly. He'd already perceived a predisposition to a certain innate anxiety, a tendency to blame herself because this offered an escape from something else that frightened her more. Natures like hers, ardent, seeking to worship, were all too prone to make disastrous miscalculations, and perhaps this was what Nell had done.

'You're thinking you'll never be happy again,' he said, watching her face. 'But you will.'

'When my mother died, I thought I never would be. I'd told myself she was getting better, that she was going to be all right. I was all set to start at art college here in London – I *wanted* to think it. So I went. That's what I regret so much – because three weeks later she was dead. I'll always go on and on wishing I hadn't gone, delayed my place by a year – '

'Your mother in her illness may have seen things differently and been glad you went.'

'Yes, I think she did. I know that ought to make it better but it doesn't. I still mind terribly that I wasn't there for her when it happened.'

She fell silent as if making up her mind about something. He poured the last of the wine into her glass and then his own.

'You see, it wasn't illness in the usual sense like cancer. She did a lot of drugs when she was with my dad. He was into it big-time, he introduced her to them. She went on taking things on and off through all my childhood. It's what she died of. Oh God, I'm telling you all this stuff I don't tell anyone else, is it all right?'

'What do you think?'

'That I don't need to ask the question. I'm proud of my mother and we were always everything to each other, don't think I had an unhappy childhood. I didn't. She had such a foul time with my dad walking out on her, though she always said he couldn't help the way he was, and she'd created enough hassle for other people in the past.'

'Did you go along with that?'

'Some of it. But I did want a different life for my own children. I hate how I've broken up the family when I might

244

have held it all together, and got over it. As well as hating myself for being so stupid as not to have *noticed* what was going on. You see, Juliet wasn't the only one. There were others, I don't know exactly, I couldn't bear to find out. My whole marriage was a sham and on top of that I was a coward.'

'You made a mistake. Nothing more.'

'Alastair's doing everything to be generous to me now – to do with the divorce settlement and so on – we've hardly needed the lawyers. That helps. But I'm all knotted up and bitter inside – as well as feeling scared stiff of the future and so tired that I can't even think straight.'

'I should have said you're coping extraordinarily well, just as I would have expected. As for all the anger and fear, I've an idea we shouldn't feel obliged to get over things according to other people's timetables.'

'People keep badgering me about going for counselling – I'd simply hate that – and I can't bear any of these self-help books either, everything like that just makes me angrier than ever.'

'I should think they might.' Lewis smiled faintly, watching her thick straight eyebrows draw together in a frown. 'We can't switch on forgiveness. It's likely to come in time, probably slowly, by unexpected routes, in unlooked for ways. When that happens you *will* forgive him – and yourself as well. But there's no hurry – and no need to be hard on yourself while you wait.'

She lifted her eyes fleetingly to meet his.

'I think you must be the kindest and – and *goodest* man I've ever met.'

'Lewis!'

It was a fellow psychiatrist who was greeting him, appearing at their table with the disconcerting suddenness of a magician. It flashed through Lewis's mind that this was how Dermot Fitzgibbon always entered his consciousness. He must have been

245

lunching in the far corner of the restaurant and Lewis hadn't seen him. With an effort, he forced himself to let no displeasure cross his face. No way would Dermot go away until he learnt who Nell was.

'I'm afraid this is an old sparring partner of mine. Nell, let me to introduce you to Dr Dermot Fitzgibbon. Dermot, this is Nell Garwood.'

Lewis took in Dermot's quick scrutiny of Nell and cursed himself for bringing Nell to this restaurant. He ought to have remembered Dermot might be here for it was the nearest to the *Steep Stairs* centre where they'd both been working that morning.

'So this was why you disappeared so promptly at lunchtime.' Dermot was laughing at him. 'Well, you do more than your share, far more.' He turned to Nell, his Irish accent exaggerated. 'Don't you be telling me Lewis has been trying to rope you in as well. These kids at the centre are becoming an obsession with him, and there's no changing him when he's an idea fixed in his head. You should make your getaway while you can. Do you know what he's up to now?'

Nell had half stood up to shake hands. She said, smiling, 'No – but I'd *like* to know. I love hearing about other people's work – especially when it's the kind that changes things for people.'

'Then I'll leave Lewis to explain everything to you himself. I've a feeling he'd prefer it that way. Though he won't be telling you the whole story, I'm thinking.'

'It's a small project set up to help street teenagers with mental health problems – ones who for various reasons would otherwise fall through the net,' said Lewis quickly. 'Dermot and I are among a group of child psychiatrists and psychologists – together with art and music therapists – who contribute some time to it.'

'And not just their time,' said Dermot with a quizzical glance

246

at Lewis. 'The money has to come from somewhere so it's a piece of good luck that some are willing to contribute more than others.'

Lewis knew he looked annoyed, but was unable to hide it. It had been agreed from the first setting up of the scheme that nobody should speak of the amount individuals contributed to the running costs. There was no way anyone except the accountants could know the sums involved. If he, with no children of his own, and earning more than he needed, chose to give as much as he could for something he felt so passionately about, then what credit was it to him? The image of the rich Pharisee came before him. God forbid he should ever fall into that trap. For a moment he felt smirched by Dermot's words, before realising Nell wouldn't have caught on to his meaning.

The expression on Dermot's face was as always, half-ironic and half-knowing, but Lewis had learnt over the years how to deal with him. Dermot was both volatile and disruptive, but these traits ran with his personality; Lewis had never known him to be deliberately malicious. He might speculate, but he would – at least in front of Nell – keep any of his more sordid conclusions to himself.

'So he's a psychiatrist as well?' Nell asked, when Dermot had gone. 'He's not at all like you. But he must be a good man if he works with you at this centre.'

'He started out as a GP,' said Lewis, 'but then retrained in psychiatry. He's one of those mavericks who can sometimes pull tricks out of the bag with hard cases, a very gifted man with some interesting ideas of his own. That's not always popular with the authorities, but psychiatry like any other discipline needs original thinking or we drown in the ruling viewpoint. We've had a good many discussions over the years about what's happening – and going to happen – to psychiatry.'

Lewis didn't add that Dermot was both an alcoholic and a

former drug-user, guessing that the signs, so obvious to him, would not be evident to Nell. At the same time he pushed further back into his consciousness the suspicion that Dermot had been forced to give up his earlier career in medicine on being given a positive diagnosis of HIV.

He was almost certain that this too wouldn't occur to Nell. Loyalty demanded his absolute discretion and over the years it had never slipped so much as by a glance or a word. He and Dermot had been at medical school together; even more important, Dermot's family lived near Ursula's in Dublin.

Dermot, though himself unstable and ambiguous in all directions, belonged to the days of Lewis's innocence. A lifetime ago. He'd known himself then – or thought he had. But how could anyone know anything of themselves before they had lived and suffered alongside everyone else?

Suddenly he wanted to get out of this room where Dermot Fitzgibbon had been watching him.

'It's stopped raining. Do you have to go somewhere now?' he asked abruptly. 'Look out of the window, there are no more umbrellas. Shall we go to St James's Park?'

'If you promise to tell me more about this children's work – '

'And you promise to tell me more about yourself – and your mother – and Rachel – '

She lifted her grey eyes to meet his urgent entreaty as sun and bright colours shone through the spattered glass windows.

*

She said she didn't want him to walk back with her to the National Gallery where she was going to look at some architectural drawings, but would leave him by Admiralty Arch. He thought he would remember the hour he had with her strolling through the shimmering greenness of the park until the day he died. They'd been like two children, with no shadow of constraint spoiling their togetherness. They'd wandered about, hardly knowing where they were going, and they'd bought ice creams and watched the ducks and through it all he was drunk with the fierce joy of their being together.

'I can't believe I've had such a day as this has been,' she said as she was leaving him. 'I don't know how to say thank you.'

Did she sense that all he wanted to do at that moment was to pull her into his arms and press his lips to hers? Did he, in the fierceness of his hunger for her, make some involuntary movement towards her? Was that why her face changed so suddenly, why she turned away quickly and ran from him, across the lights and back past the lions of Trafalgar Square?

He stood watching her disappearing figure, his joy evaporating into a desolation which instantly grew hydra heads of irrational terrors. Was she running away from him or towards somebody else?

The Mall Galleries would still be open. He wanted – he needed – to see the portrait Nell had painted of Martin Darrow. Because it was possible she was in love with the chaplain of Wharton school. She'd spoken of him as a confidante, as a trusted friend, as almost perfect. They would have been closeted together while she was painting his likeness, with all the intimacy that would have brought. Artists and models, it was a common enough story, though it was usually the male artist seducing or seduced by the female sitter.

A picture of Martin Darrow as one of those self-assured evangelical smooth talkers who taught and wielded what they saw as God-given authority of men over women began to take shape in his imagination. He could see how Nell, betrayed by one man, might become entrapped by another. Her innocence would attract a man who liked to control others, but would in the end be crushed altogether. He recognised the knot inside him as jealousy and hated himself.

He saw again the sudden expression of alarm in her face as she bolted from him. He'd betrayed her trust with that small movement towards her. She'd seen the yearning in his eyes and all at once realised he wasn't the kindly psychiatrist she could trust with her secrets, but a man with selfish desires. If he'd hurt her like this – made her life harder! If he had, he must give her up altogether. Yet he knew he could not.

Outside the gallery shafts of late afternoon sun from a washed blue sky streamed through the leaves of the plane trees, spangling the ground in gold-dappled radiance. Lewis hurried through the doors. To stand in front of the picture she'd painted; it was the closest he could come to her now.

It was a remarkable painting. Even he, with nothing more than average knowledge of artistic technique, could tell. For a moment he was knocked off balance, moved by some emotion he couldn't explain to himself. Nell, whom he loved so passionately, and so entirely without hope, had created this work of art.

He stood in front of the massive canvas as though in worship. The paint was applied in clearly defined and pure colours, as if expressing the transparency of the character of the sitter. Lewis examined the face carefully, noticing the clean planes, the classical moulding of brow and nose. It was a beautiful face, but there was nothing of the consciousness, of the arrogance of physical grace. The possessor of such loveliness must be aware of its powers of seduction, of its entitlement to earthly reward. Yet this man made no claims.

It was above all a suffering face. Why had Nell chosen to bring out this so unequivocally? He remembered the tears she'd shed in his consulting room, tears for the griefs and unhappinesses of the unknown and unseen people around her. Was Martin the object of her compassion or an as yet unconscious love, which given her nature must surely develop from it? What kind of man was this Martin Darrow, the chaplain at Wharton school?

Walking back across Trafalgar Square, he switched his mobile on and ran through his voicemail messages, deleting them as he listened. Then he heard Nell's voice, a little diffident.

It's Nell. I hope you don't mind me using this number you once gave me. It's to say thank you for everything you did for me today, every minute of it. I hope I didn't make you late for other stuff and thank you – the message tailed off into silence. Lewis clutched the phone tightly, leant against a corner wall and immediately pressed to repeat the message. Again he heard her stumbling words, soft against the hammer of his own breathing. Without giving himself time to think, he pressed reply. It went straight to voicemail and he heard himself say, *when can I see you again?*

THIRTY-TWO

'Why is it I can never make a telephone call in my own house?'

Clement Hunstrete came out of his study ready to be annoyed with someone or anyone, for his new shoes were hurting and he required sympathy.

He trod heavily into the kitchen where his wife was emptying the dishwasher and making tea at the same time. His younger son George sat sprawled at the table apparently absorbed in *The Sun*, his long jean-clad legs draped over the neighbouring chair. It was an attitude Clement had no doubt was exactly calculated for maximum parental irritation. Eleanor ought not to put up with it.

'Is that vest you're wearing appropriate clothing for your mother's kitchen?'

'Oh, she doesn't mind, do you Mum?'

'That's not the point. And don't push it onto your mother.'

'You need to chill out,' said George, shifting his feet off the chair but not bothering to look up from the match scores. 'What's all the grouch about anyway?'

'It's not often I make a request of my family,' Clement eyed George with disfavour, 'but I should like to recover the use of the telephone. Tom appears to have appropriated it for his personal use. I may be regarded as the least important person in this house, but that much consideration I *am* entitled to.'

'Yes, dear.' Eleanor closed the dishwasher and straightened up. 'He does usually use his mobile. And he's going back to Oxford tomorrow. I thought you said you had to be with the bursar this afternoon about the new pitches for the first fifteen. Or is it the first eleven?'

'So I have been until now. It may be half term but I still have to work. I've just tried to make an important call. It would appear I can't even do that.'

'It's not Tom's fault, someone's nicked his mobile.'

'More expense.' Clement leant against the Aga, in his year-round favourite position, warming his bottom. 'No doubt I shall be asked to foot the bill for another one.'

'Oh, it'll turn up under a girl's bed somewhere,' his son reassured him. 'Keep your wig on. Here Dad, you can use my iPhone if you like.'

'No thank you. I have no desire to have to make calls on an uncomfortable and unnecessary gadget when there's a perfectly good house telephone, if only my family would allow me the use of it occasionally. Some of you seem to forget this is the headmaster's house.' He remembered another grievance and frowned at Eleanor. 'And you were on the line *ad infinitum* to Sue before lunch. Has something of vital significance taken place?'

'Women don't need *that*,' said Eleanor, as she poured boiling water into the teapot.

'It's a mystery to me how you can talk to her for hours on end and then never remember anything she actually said. Didn't she have any news?'

'Only Trevor Faversham asking her if she knew any more about Nell's plans, and what was the school doing to help.'

'That stick-in-the-mud. It's not for him to poke his nose in. I can't believe Nell would give him the time of day.'

'Yes, but have you and Jim said anything to her as to plans for next year? Don't forget she must be worrying about Sebastian as well.'

Clement avoided his wife's eye. He was uneasily aware of murmurings that he'd dithered over Alastair Garwood. As if anyone else could have managed any better! At least he'd got the chap fixed up in a top London school apparently delighted to have him, and the young graduate who'd replaced him was presentable enough, if you shut your ears to the Birmingham accent. Now Eleanor was going to get at him over Alastair's abandoned wife! He had a sudden urge to surprise her by letting her know he wasn't the slow-top she took him for.

'We went into all that last term, and it took some delicate manoeuvring.' Clement reflected bitterly that everything in a tightly-knit community like Wharton always did. It was only by some miracle the local newspaper hadn't caught on and published a nasty little story following the art exhibition debacle. 'I informed her last night that we've decided to offer her a full-time position in the art department as from September. She turned it down, said something about thinking for herself.'

'It might have come as too much of a shock to her.' His wife smiled placidly at him as she poured out cups of tea. 'Give her a few days to mull it over. You'll have got a good dinner anyway by taking her out, better than the leftover cottage pie we had here.'

It was typical of Eleanor to take this prosaic line. Pushing him into things and offering spurious concerns for his digestion! Just when he wanted to think of the evening he'd spent with Nell as having a touch of romance about it. Women were extraordinarily insensitive at times. It was almost as if she saw him as incapable of being a man, of having red blood in his veins.

That's what it is, he decided, warming to this self-portrait of a man capable of grand passion for a beautiful young woman. A late-flowering and touching romance – it would be the delightful secret life which he was sure he needed.

It wasn't as if he would be hurting anybody. Eleanor probably wouldn't even notice. If he became pale or went off his food as the great chivalric lovers had done in the middle ages, he could imagine her absentmindedly offering him some Andrews Liver Salts and then settling down to read her favourite Anthony Trollope or waltzing off to walk the dog. His eye fell on Petrarch stretched out by the Aga next to his feet. I'm only fifty-eight, he remembered indignantly, and already she's treating me like the family retriever!

'You did tell her as well about the governing body commission? Such a pity they want buildings. Nell's real gift is for portraits and landscapes.'

'Of course I did!' A thought occurred to him. 'She sounded nervous about it. Perhaps I should have another word with her about it today. No time like the present.'

'That's a good idea. But won't you drink your tea first? I'm afraid Petrarch stole the rest of the gingerbread.'

Tea without any cake! What would she say next!

'And why are you reading that rag?' Clement glared at George, poring over *The Sun*. 'How is it that I work round the clock to pay for my sons' education and all they can find to do is read the gutter press?'

'It's my gap year. Haven't I been slaving away building water drains in Africa? Anyway, it's a very entertaining newspaper,' protested George, turning over pages in an exaggeratedly laid-back manner. '*The Sun* isn't just for chavs, you know.'

'At your age you should be reading a quality newspaper, so that you can make an intelligent contribution in conversation. Even if you're determined to be a cultural philistine you could at least take an interest in politics.'

'Didn't do Greasebag Garwood any favours, did it? He was

into page three stuff big-time, but you're such an innocent you never know anything about anything.'

There was no answering this. Clement searched around the worktop, and picked up a packet of biscuits. Not his favourite Fig Rolls, but they would do.

'I only know that the British packaging industry is making life quite intolerable. How am I supposed to get inside this damned thing?'

'There's a tab somewhere you're meant to tear.'

His wife was regarding him with the patient expression she adopted for carol concerts, the dentist's waiting room, and now, Clement told himself peevishly, for him.

'Where? I can't see it.' Clement wrenched at the wrapping and a stream of Bourbon Creams hurtled onto the floor.

'Now look what you've made me do!'

Petrarch got onto his legs in a leisurely fashion and proceeded to devour the fragments, before sniffing appreciatively at his benefactor.

'Do drink your tea before you go,' said Eleanor, offering him his cup.

Clement brushed it impatiently aside. He *would* go and see Nell just as soon as he'd changed his shirt. Shutting the kitchen door with just the right amount of firmness to show he meant business but was above slamming it, he stomped up the stairs. In the bedroom he selected what he thought was an artistic shirt, a purple and yellow check bought when he'd been at a loose end in Gatwick airport. It ought to appeal to a woman who had studied Fine Art, and it would prove he had an eye for colour.

Checking his appearance in the mirror, he decided it was reasonably satisfactory, so long as you didn't compare him with anyone too much younger. He still had his hair – well, some of it – and surely the grey lent a distinguished air? He didn't pretend to resemble the hero in a costume drama like Alastair, but good looks weren't everything. What women wanted was someone masterful who could take care of them, and make their decisions for them.

The vision of himself in this role was altogether delightful. He was able to forget that he'd spent the last twenty years of his life avoiding making any family decisions, or indeed doing anything much for himself at all. The strong silent man whom women admired, that was what he was underneath, he told himself, enjoying this new sensation very much.

He got his favourite holiday tweed jacket out of the wardrobe and then went to the bathroom used by his sons to slap on some of George's aftershave. Too lavishly, perhaps. He sniffed anxiously. It did have rather a strong smell. Perhaps he'd overdone it. He splashed his face with cold water and rubbed it dry with a bath towel, forgetting to replace the lid on the bottle.

Going back into the bedroom, he picked up his packet of liquorice allsorts lying on the dressing table. But there were only the aniseed ones left. Eleanor knows I don't like those, he thought crossly. She ought to have bought me some more. Did all wives neglect their husbands like this? Really, the things men had to put up with! He crumpled up the packet with an angry movement and threw it on the floor. He would leave it there for Eleanor to pick up.

Just as he was turning the corner of the road where Nell lived, it occurred to Clement that he ought to arrive with something. A box of chocolates? Women had a thing about chocolate.

But he might choose a variety which had all sorts of connotations he would be unaware of, an on-going gag or soap opera storyline which would make him look ridiculous. That was the trouble with not watching television. You missed the advertisements and so you didn't catch on to these innuendos. Tom or George would be able to enlighten him, in fact this was something sons ought to be doing for their fathers. He must make a point of asking one of them. One of their greatest amusements was his ignorance about all things modern and here was a chance to indulge them.

Flowers. Yes, that would be better. Nell looked so much like a flower herself, thought Clement with a gush of sentiment, that she should surely appreciate being brought flowers now that she had no husband to give them to her. He began to imagine her standing in the doorway, her slim figure holding a scented bouquet, her face buried in the blooms, before lifting luminous and tear-stained eyes to his.

He hovered on the pavement relishing the picture. He would buy Nell some white lilies, or should it be roses? Eleanor was fond of sweet peas he believed, but could you get them at this time of year? It was only May and they might not be ready yet. Some vague notion of flowers being flown in from all over the world came into his head, but his knowledge of botany was limited and the question was beyond him. And now that he came to think of it, he couldn't remember if Eleanor had said she liked sweet peas or whether she'd been talking about someone else. It was safer to avoid them altogether.

Roses would undoubtedly be best, and had the added advantage of having a certain poetic and historical quality about them. They expressed the emotions he was sure were now sweeping over him. *If love were what the rose is, and I were like the leaf* he began to quote to himself, but the rest of Swinburne's lines eluded him. He needed Eleanor with her encyclopaedic knowledge of English Literature, but that would involve him in awkward explanations. Nor could he quite imagine himself carrying off saying the lines with the mixture of spontaneity and fervour the occasion required. He hoped Nell was not the kind of woman who would expect too much in the way of poetry.

'Hello, Clement! You're looking very furtive. What an interesting shirt you're wearing! Are you off somewhere exciting?'

It was typical of Sue that she should appear at just this moment, another bossy middle-aged woman intent on interfering with a man's perfectly harmless and ordinary plans for spending his time. And the way she phrased her comment, as though it was out of the question he was *really* doing anything exciting. She and Eleanor turned everything into a joke. Well, he would show them he was not to be laughed at. They should learn that he was not going to sit placidly and uncomplainingly in the jelly mould they'd made for him.

'I'm going into the town,' he said shortly. 'It's one of the great blessings of half-term and holidays that I can have some private life.' Surely she would take herself off now?

'Don't we all feel the same? It's such a joy not to see boys everywhere you look. Well, come July and we'll have eight weeks of peace. Shall we stroll along together? I'm only going as far as the newsagent. Jim's *Church Times* hasn't been delivered again.'

Clement sighed. It was extraordinary how insensitive women could be. They might all be conspiring to make life difficult. Blunted social antennae summed it up; this was hardly the moment for cosy talk about domestic details.

'That would be very pleasant,' he said, reminding himself that Sue and Jim were old friends. If only she wouldn't keep peering at him in this speculative way! 'I'm actually on my way to get some flowers for Eleanor.'

That would cover him if anyone caught sight of him walking back with a bouquet. In fact he'd better buy two bouquets to be on the safe side. A big one for Nell, and a smaller one for Eleanor, or should they be the same size? That might be less complicated. Yes, two matching bouquets would be a great deal easier to manage. No doubt this was how men who regularly deceived their wives arranged things. It was clever of him to have hit on this so soon. He walked jauntily by Sue's side, feeling pleased with himself.

'How very nice. Is it to mark something special?'

Was he going to have to invent a reason for giving Eleanor flowers? wondered Clement resentfully. But what could it be? Not her birthday, Sue would certainly know it wasn't. Women had a remarkable capacity for knowing the dates of everyone's birthdays; even Eleanor, who forgot most things, always sent cards to a tribe of godchildren and distant relatives they never saw from one year to the next. Their wedding anniversary? Again too risky, especially as he couldn't quite remember the date himself. June, he thought, a picture of sun-baked grass in a churchyard coming into his head, or had it been July?

'Nothing in particular,' he came up with, trying not to sound sheepish. 'I thought it should be a surprise.' That was better. Sue was looking at him appreciatively. He congratulated himself. An impulsive, sentimental man who buys his wife presents to demonstrate his love, that's what I am, he thought complacently, temporarily forgetting that it had been Nell who was to be the recipient.

'Jim never buys me surprise flowers,' said Sue. 'Eleanor will be thrilled.'

Will I have to buy a third bouquet now, to keep her happy, thought Clement almost desperately. Or had there been a hint of sarcasm in her tone? Naturally he was perfectly able to deal with any obstacles that came in his way, but he was starting to feel harassed. He quickened his step and hoped he would not bump into anyone else he knew.

The age of chivalry, he ought to have lived then. Indulging an idealised love for an unattainable woman, a knight riding forth rescuing damsels in distress…Pre-Raphaelite paintings of medieval maidens with rippling hair and startled eyes drifted across his mind. He went off into a happy dream, allowing Sue's remarks to float over him.

'Well, I'll leave you to choose Eleanor's flowers,' he heard her saying as she stopped outside the newsagent. 'That won't be difficult – though I did read in *The Daily Telegraph* recently that most men haven't a clue which are their wives' favourites.'

As Clement pushed open the door of the town's most expensive florist, it crossed his mind that he could hardly arrive at Nell's door carrying *two* bouquets of flowers. He would have to go home first, and then he would get embroiled in questions from Eleanor, or even worse, Tom and George. He was beginning to see that playing the role of the strong silent man was not without its pitfalls.

Perhaps the whole thing was going to be too complicated. But now he'd committed himself to getting flowers for Eleanor. Bother everything, it was too bad of Sue to have forced him into this position. He looked around at the buckets of colour feeling aggrieved, and dug into his pocket. When he found only a two pound coin, he realised he'd forgotten to transfer his wallet when he'd changed his jacket. He certainly couldn't buy any flowers now. Providence was giving him a way out of his difficulties.

Nell's flowers would have to wait for a more auspicious occasion. Of course he could still drop by and offer to be a shoulder to cry on. On second thoughts, he decided he was rather tired and would prefer to have tea at home.

As he backed out of the flower shop it occurred to him he might as well spend the two pound coin. He would stop off at the newsagent on the way back and fortify himself with some liquorice allsorts.

THIRTY-THREE

When Lewis first heard the news on the car radio it didn't register with him as it ought to have done.

It was the morning after he'd seen Nell in London and he was driving to Brookner House. Already his mind was already disturbed on too many different levels. He'd left Ursula in a state of mind that he knew from experience heralded a slide over into deeper psychosis. At such times her mood would cycle rapidly, lurching into the hallucinations and delusions which marked the acute episodes of her illness. These were becoming more frequent and more severe, despite the regime of antipsychotic drugs aimed at keeping her mood stable. He had once dreamed of a miracle recovery. He could hardly remember when that hope had finally died.

'I should have been killed in the car smash so you'd never have met me.'

Last night, staring into his face, the old accusation, all emotion flattened. It was now a vain repetition, divested of any connection to meaning.

'We met and we married,' he said, taking her into his arms. 'We made a promise. It means we shall always belong to each other – and it means I shall never stop loving you and being glad of your love for me.'

But she was becoming deaf to all the reassurance he could give her. A storm was about to break.

He woke in the early hours, gripped by panic new to him. If it should chance that he was right in his forebodings would he be able to see her through it? They'd lived through these times together before now and survived, but his heart was heavy within him. He recalled the last time, the botched suicide attempt, the weeks in hospital, his growing anguish at his inability to save her from this illness which was destroying her mind with such implacable cruelty.

That had been nearly two years ago. The prognosis given then by the psychiatrist leading the mental health team caring for her had been bleak. With the intervals between grave psychosis becoming less, she was unlikely to be among the minority who recover completely, or whose symptoms can be sufficiently managed as to lead a normal life.

And Nell. He counted the hours since he watched her run from him across Trafalgar Square. Hours when he'd checked and re-checked his mobile. There had been no message.

Love, desire, guilt; all these mixed with horror at what he'd brought himself to, and made him unable to think clearly. In sickness and in health. It might have been in the blind ignorance of youth, but he'd made that promise to Ursula. What sort of man was he to long for another woman when his own wife was so pitiably dependent on him?

How arrogant he'd been, thinking he could keep his life in compartments. Yet after a fashion, he'd succeeded. He'd seen off the transient sexual temptations that had offered themselves, he'd sought and found solace in believing in the value of his work. All this he had done.

Until Nell. He pictured her face as he'd first seen it in his consulting room, serious grey eyes filling with tears, winter-earth hair falling across flushed cheeks. In that fatal hour he'd taken a wrong turn which was bringing him both indescribable joy and grief.

What had it led to, this silencing of the conscience which scratched at his peace each night as he lay beside his wife? He relived the moment by Admiralty Arch – and the message he'd left on her mobile phone. These actions had crossed the lines of honour, of principle, but his conscience whispered that he had in truth done so long before.

There wasn't going to be a message from Nell. There must never be one. There was no other safeguard.

His father's voice again, insistent across the years that had gone: *You're a fool.* Yet even now, as he confronted the black tunnel before him, he couldn't imagine how he could live without the ideal of Nell in his head.

'Terrible isn't it, that boy murdering his family like that? The telly was full of it late last night, blaming the mental health services. As if they can prevent these things, any more than the police can stop all these London knife crimes.'

His secretary was handing him a cup of coffee as she spoke. With an effort Lewis remembered the drive to Brookner House. The radio, something horrific, that he hadn't taken in. He said automatically, 'I didn't watch any television last night, just caught a few words on the radio coming here. Did you say it happened in London?'

'Peckham. Fifteen he was, ran amok with a knife and killed his parents and younger sister before throwing himself in front of a train. There's only one thing to be thankful for, I said to myself, he wasn't one of yours.'

Dilys looked at him expectantly.

'And Dr Dermot Fitzgibbon rang just now, could you call him urgently.'

Dilys didn't ask, as she might have done, whether this was connected to the news of the tragedy. Lewis said nothing further. He felt almost certain that Dermot was involved, that the boy was under his care. A boy attending *Steep Stairs*? An icy shiver ran through him. The fear that a patient might commit suicide was part of a psychiatrist's working day and must be lived with; violence on this scale was the stuff that stalked his worst nightmares.

With a heavy heart he went into his consulting room to prepare for the day's appointments.

But first of all he must telephone Dermot.

*

Nell took her mobile phone out of her pocket and stared at the screen. *Listen to voice messages.* What was happening to her? She couldn't help it. Her fingers pressed the key. *When can I see you again?*

She saw again the extraordinary tenderness at the back of his eyes as he'd listened to her. She pressed the key again. How many times had she replayed these precious words since yesterday?

It was deliberate walking into temptation, she knew that. Dr Auerbach was married. Married to the beautiful woman in the photograph. The woman he never spoke of, not even indirectly. This wasn't strange, for she'd seen from the first that he was a man with deep areas of reserve, and instinct told her that he loved his wife. Self-disgust swept over her, just as it had done as she was saying goodbye to him yesterday, so that she'd run from him and the spurt of fierce, naked desire he must surely read in her face.

She must *not* get dependent on him. Hadn't she read an article only last week about American women falling in love with their shrinks or else their personal trainers? This wasn't the same, it couldn't be. It was only that gratitude for his goodness and kindness made her want to kneel at his feet, to almost worship him.

Lewis – but she must think of him only as Dr Auerbach – had given her his time yesterday because he cared about her being unhappy, just as he would for anyone who came across his path. His message on her mobile was part of this: letting her know she could turn to him at any time, that he was there for her, the same as he'd been for Rachel.

She wouldn't reply. Or not yet. Doing so immediately would be demanding too much, taking something – it would be, and she fought hard against accepting this – it would be *wrong*.

*

Martin walked along the corridor of the sixth form centre building, reading the labels on the doors. On either side were study bedrooms, little more than cupboards with just space for a bed and a desk for those sixth form boys not living in boarding houses.

Oliver Benson. He stopped and stared at the name, his throat tightening, his mouth going dry and hard.

If only they had a chaplain like you at Rachel's school! Nell, in the Autumn, collecting the portrait from his room. She wouldn't say that now.

The day before half term he'd walked past Nell talking to Oliver by the door of the art studios. He'd been unable to control the sudden fury that swept over him. Nell had stared at him, struggling with some emotion he couldn't fathom, as though she was seeing something that made her afraid.

He was destroying the work of his life and yet he couldn't change. It wasn't possible to contain this desire to hurt Oliver and yet to be as he ought to be to the rest of the Wharton community, the two things couldn't be separated. He was cheating the boys, failing to give anything of good to them. His hatred for Piers and Oliver Benson was eating him up, an invasive cancer, rampant and aggressive; here he was, hanging around the school in half term week sniffing after old prey when he ought to be in Coventry, spending time with the mum and dad whose faces would fill with simple joy whenever he visited.

At this rate he was going to have to leave Wharton, the place that had shaped his life. He'd have to leave Nell. Not that she needed him as she once might have done. He wasn't doing anything for her anyway.

He'd turned away from Nell this term, knowing himself to be unfit for such a one as she was. Nell who never asked anything, but looked at him as if she understood it all. He could have confided everything that was crushing him, but his pride and shame had kept him silent. He'd hugged his dirty secret and his thirst for revenge to himself all year. That was how it had to be.

And yet she knows it all, he told himself. She's seen the man underneath the perfect chaplain I've schooled myself to be in the struggle to atone. She knows it all, and she doesn't turn away.

Without meaning to, his hand moved towards the handle as if to open the door of Oliver Benson's room, but at the same instant Jim North came out of the one next to it.

Martin froze. How was he to explain why he was wandering around the sixth form study bedrooms in the middle of half term? But to his surprise the deputy head was evidently too preoccupied with his own business to wonder about anybody else's. He nodded at Martin and shrugged his shoulders.

'The usual half term check for illicit substances. A pretty thankless task. It never ceases to amaze me the way boys leave so many clues behind them. We're not quite so disingenuous or ignorant about drugs as they like to think.'

Before he could stop himself, Martin glanced at Oliver Benson's door. Jim made an expressive face.

'Yes, that could be a likely one. A slippery customer on the surface, though it might just be the image he likes to put about.'

'Not only the surface.'

'Oh?'

Martin began to edge away, unable to keep the bleakness out of his face.

'I knew his father.'

*

It was just before eleven when the first journalist rang.

'Dr Auerbach, Craig Parker was known to be a paranoid schizophrenic and yet within days of seeing his psychiatrist Dr Dermot Fitzgibbon, he murders his parents and baby sister. Today's *Daily Mail* describes you this morning as the country's leading expert on schizophrenia, so can you explain how a psychiatrist could have missed the warning signs?'

'First of all, I am not the country's leading expert,' snapped Lewis. 'But if I were, the *Daily Mail* wouldn't know it. As to what you call warning signs, why can't you understand that psychiatry – any more than anything else – can never be all-knowing? Human behaviour can never be one hundred per cent predicted. You might as well cry for the moon as to demand total certainty in this world. It can never exist. This means there will be on rare occasions tragedies like this, which no psychiatrist, however skilled, can foresee or prevent.'

'So in your opinion Dr Fitzgibbon cannot be blamed for the deaths of three innocent people?'

'You heard what I just said.'

'It's alleged that Dr Fitzgibbon is a friend of yours and closely associated with you. Does his style of working mirror your own?'

Lewis put down the telephone. Already he could see that

the knives would be out, not just for Dermot, but for the whole profession of psychiatry. He glanced at his watch, thankful for a cancellation which was giving him some breathing space. He switched on his computer. He'd better see what else the national dailies were saying.

Twenty minutes later he got up and stared out of the window. Every paper had majored on the story. *The Guardian, The Times, the Independent* and *The Daily Telegraph* had gone further with articles detailing the growing failures of the mental health services. The unacceptable number of people killed each year by maniacs let loose into the community was largely due to the arrogant incompetence of psychiatrists and psychologists who spent more time quarrelling over methodology than they did protecting the public. Add this to the spiralling rate of mental illness, the chronic shortage of beds in secure units, escalating teenage suicide in young offender institutions and the dearth of talent among medical students choosing to specialise in psychiatry.

All these were packed into tirades from both ends of the political spectrum but unashamedly designed to whip up public alarm.

As well they might. The mental health services had long been chronically underfunded. Mental health was the poor relation of the NHS – and would remain so, until Britain woke up to the need to do something about it. Craig Parker, as the papers claimed, had in truth been let down by the system, which failed so disastrously to bridge the gap between children's and adults' services. With one person in four likely to have mental health problems at some point in their lives it was about time the government grasped the nettle.

But it wouldn't. It would drag its feet because this wasn't a vote winner, nobody wanted to know about brain sickness, to face up to the extent of it amongst human beings. Mental health was too nebulous, too subjective compared with physical illness; it couldn't be measured so easily, clear targets couldn't be set, success couldn't be demonstrated so unequivocally and attractively.

There would have to be many more tragedies like this for anything to be done. People needed to be more afraid.

And if they were? Lewis learnt what this meant over the following days.

An avalanche of telephone calls piled in from journalists of all kinds wanting a comment from him. He was the author of *Who's There?* the ground-breaking book on childhood psychosis. He was the grandson of Jacob Auerbach, famous for his pioneering work of rehabilitation amongst Jewish refugee children. And there was his father too, a psychiatrist of note during the anti-psychiatry debate of the late sixties and seventies. With this illustrious tradition behind him, Dr Lewis Auerbach must have something to say about the crisis hitting the mental health services in Britain – and if it could be in language which would translate easily into a soundbite that would do nicely thank you.

Lewis kept his temper and his head. After all, didn't he know that the profession was in a state of disarray? It always had been. The split between the biological and the psychosocial camps had been developing over two hundred years. That the biological way of thinking was currently in the ascendancy together with a growing over-dependence on classification was contributing its own dangers. Blame biology or blame the family. Psychiatry needed to move on from these two polarities, to ally itself more closely both with other mental health professionals and with the people it served.

In the meantime he defended Dermot as best he might, praying that something else would happen to divert the attention of the media. A high society scandal or Whitehall cock-up would do, and the row over psychiatry would die down as quickly as it had been ignited.

His prayers weren't answered. Throughout June, additional angles on the gaping holes in the nation's mental health services spawned themselves in the press. Dermot got the worst of it. The media wanted a scapegoat, and Dermot ticked the boxes. He might not be the stereotypical over-paid clock-watching pill-pusher, but he evidently thought himself too clever by half, so busy making a splash that he hadn't done his job properly. He was too colourful, too tricksy, and journalists didn't trust him. Lewis wasn't surprised.

And now Dermot wasn't doing his job at all, shattered by so vitriolic a witch hunt, on the brink of a breakdown. He was on sick leave; Lewis began to doubt if he would ever return to public practice. Nor was it likely he'd continue with his hours at *Steep Stairs* – and here Lewis breathed another prayer, that the work of the centre would continue to escape attention. The boy Craig had never been through its doors, yet Lewis feared it was an easy target. The media was becoming rapacious for stories to feed a readership nourished on the culture of blame.

But no journalist had discovered Dermot's involvement and Dermot himself had been unusually discreet. In all the blackness of Lewis's world during these days, it was something to be grateful for. The work of the centre might amount to a tiny contribution towards alleviating childhood desolation, reaching only a handful, but it *was* a contribution, something in the tradition of his grandfather and therefore sacred to Lewis.

At home Ursula had become quiet, too quiet.

'He ought to have known. He of all people,' was all she'd said about Dermot, in a voice and manner drained of meaning. He'd expected her to be more affected. Dermot's family and her own had been neighbours if not close friends back in Dublin.

Although she rarely saw him he'd thought she would still care what happened to him.

But she was becoming detached, as she'd done before, from feeling, from expected responses. He'd seen how she dropped the newspapers unread, how her face had taken on the blunted emotion of a fragmenting and increasingly disoriented mind. He braced himself for what was coming for both of them.

The invitation to contribute to a discussion forum to be shown on Channel Four in early July came within a week of the Craig Parker story breaking. The role of psychiatry in society was up for debate; the Royal College of Psychiatrists wanted a popular spokesman.

Lewis vacillated. He'd been wheeled out before for television, but now was a bad time, too much was crowding in. The outward structures of Ursula's days might still be in place – choir practice, group therapy at the local mental health centre, a collection of adult education classes – but it was at best a fragile edifice. He'd cut back his work as much as he could these last weeks so as to be with her as much as possible. Should he take this additional time away?

Yet he wanted to accept. It was a chance to speak out about the injudicious, ill-researched and misleading accusations being made about those working in mental health at a time when cutbacks were stretching services to breaking point. He should be standing up for the contribution psychiatry should be making to a more honest and happier society.

As he turned it over in his mind, his thoughts escaped to Nell, as he pictured her watching the programme. What would she be thinking as she heard him speaking? For one forbidden moment he explored the seductive fantasy. Then, disgusted that he could indulge his selfish vanity at such a time, he quickly picked up the telephone to return the producer's call and said yes.

THIRTY-FOUR

It had been a good term, thought Clement Hunstrete, comfortably ensconced in his chair upholstered with antique gold leather, in his headmaster's office on a Thursday afternoon in early July. Nearly at the end of it now, the exams over and no major crisis so far. He swivelled himself round sideways from his desk and stretched out his legs.

The previous one had been tricky. All that business with Alastair Garwood – well, he didn't want to remember that at this juncture. The Lent term was always a problem. Too many people getting flu and the long dark evenings made for trouble in the boarding houses.

On top of that there was the need to keep everyone's nose to the grindstone so that the syllabus in each subject was completely covered and any coursework – how he loathed these ghastly modern and thoroughly misleading methods of assessment – could be completed before Easter.

One couldn't even look forward to the Trinity term, traditionally the favourite amongst staff and boys. The summer months were no longer a long enjoyable stretch of cricket matches with exams for some of the boys at the end, but an endless timetabling nightmare right from the start of term. Now that boys did public examinations for their last three years, among a plethora of different boards and papers, there was little time for civilised traditions.

The league tables – another disgraceful imposition on schools – forced both Common Room and boys into scratching about for every possible mark to the detriment of original thinking and a real education for the mind and soul. Past, present and future parents pored over the lists in the newspapers, blind to everything except numbers; every year he was under pressure to claim that Wharton was once again delighted with its best ever results.

Still, he only had a few more years at the helm, and then he could escape into a well-deserved retirement and settle down to finishing *Of Blood and Roses: the Middle Ages Revisited.* He pictured himself with his heaps of documents, searching for obscure references, trouncing inferior scholarship. This was how an academic ought to be spending his time. Some other chap could take on the headache his job was becoming.

Nearly four o'clock. Half an hour before he had to go and harangue the lower school about their activities options. Time for a bit of relaxation.

He glanced at the photograph of Eleanor on his desk. It dated from when they'd first come to Wharton, when she'd made an effort and tried to be something she wasn't. For a brief few months she'd looked the part of the wife of a headmaster of a traditional public school. A string of pearls, dignified, well-cut clothes, an expensive haircut.

It hadn't lasted. Probably a good thing, when he thought about it. The woman in the photograph could have been demanding, which Eleanor never was. He'd really been very fortunate. His hand reached contentedly for the drawer where he kept his current Brother Cadfael novel.

'Ah, headmaster. Sorry to disturb your few moments to yourself in the day. But I'm afraid something's come up.'

Something always did. But Jim North was a good man who

didn't waste your time unless he had to. Whenever Jim used the term headmaster in that ironic tone Clement knew the matter was serious. He pushed a prospectus over *The Heretic's Apprentice*, and put on his interested, colleagues-together face.

'Not good news, I'm afraid. I've had Chris Parrish – God help me – with me for the last hour. He claims Martin Darrow made a pass at him in the chapel vestry. It's a clear enough accusation. Says Zachary Shilling will back him up.'

So much for the term going well. Clement looked instinctively at his wife's photograph and found himself noticing the expression in her eyes. Was it saying, I told you so? He fingered his tie, unconsciously checking it was straight.

'Good heavens. This is a trifle unexpected. We've never had any reason to think Martin batted for the other side, have we?'

'None at all. Unless you count being unmarried.'

'Not always an infallible indicator.'

'Fortyish, isn't he? It's a bad age. At thirty a man can get away with being a bachelor, by forty people begin to ask questions.'

'*I've* never done so. Should I have?'

'Not necessarily. A man has usually settled for someone – or something – by that age. In Martin's case it's been religion. Apparently it's been enough for him, as it has for others. Though they'd be in a tiny minority.'

'The offering up of carnal instincts on the altar of sanctity? He certainly looks the part. God knows we need minorities. Important for the health of society; compassion, tolerance, all that sort of thing.'

Both men fell silent as they contemplated the ascetic image of the school chaplain. Clement was the first to break it, resentment surfacing in his mind. Last term's troubles had left him too flustered to do any more than complete a few minor footnotes to his manuscript. He'd only begun to recover from it all by the Easter holidays. Now, almost at the end of term, just when he was on the home straight for the long summer holidays, this had to happen!

'Damn it, he's the school chaplain, a man of the cloth!'

'As we all know from the tabloids, men of the cloth appear to be especially susceptible. If they've been brought up in the evangelical tradition they might be in denial over their orientation for years, because the alternative is being thrust out of heaven.'

Clement fidgeted. Jim was an Anglican of long-standing who regarded the way the Church of England was allowing itself to be torn apart by rows over homosexuality as perverseness amounting to self-destruction. It would be safer not to get him started.

'Would you say that's true of Martin, though? He's not an evangelical.'

'And never has been?'

'He might have come into the business through that door when he was a schoolboy here, but he's moved on since then. Didn't go to one of those chorus-singing theological colleges so in love with their own dogma they can't see salvation beyond it.'

'Whatever the truth of it is, not being married leaves you vulnerable in a school like this.'

This was true, Clement acknowledged regretfully. It was several years now since the governors had implemented a policy of only appointing housemasters who had wives to act as a guarantee of their irreproachable sexuality. Some of the very best housemasters he had known had been bachelors, but in the current climate it simply wasn't worth taking the risk. He looked uneasily at Jim.

'To temptation as well as allegations?'

Jim North gave him an answering look Clement didn't quite like, but which reassured him that Jim had the matter clear in his mind.

'As for temptation, who can honestly pin that down? Who in this life is immune from urges which God forbid ever extend beyond the slightest fancy?'

Clement nudged the photograph of his wife to the back of his desk, feeling the conversation was unsuitable for her ears.

'What the devil is Parrish doing in school anyway? Exams all finished. We're supposed to have seen the last of the upper sixth until Prize Day.'

'Just so. It raises certain suspicions. However, we'll have to regard these allegations in a very serious light, and if it comes to it, be seen to do so. Now, I'll need to go over the physical nitty-gritty with you, and see if you think it all sounds likely. I should have imagined the choice of vestry as a scene of seduction was a trifle hackneyed. But if it does tie up, you realise what it means.'

Clement knew exactly what it meant.

'We'll have to get Martin in smartish. Have it out with him. Might be able to explain the whole caboodle. Put it this way – Parrish! *Falsus in uno, falsus in omnibus.*'

Jim North looked at him thoughtfully.

'Been a bit preoccupied this year. Moody. Distracted. I'd put it down to all the upset over Nell Garwood. Sensitive kind of man, bound to feel for the poor girl. He sat for her, didn't he, a very fine piece of work, that portrait.'

'She certainly did him more favours than Trevor Faversham dished out to me,' grumbled Clement, still cross at being portrayed as though he resembled a multi-coloured soft toy being swirled about in a washing machine.

'Yes, that was bad luck. Still, someone had to be the victim of Trevor's love affair with a mishmash of isms. Then there's his equally abortive one with Nell. No chance there. Seen his latest installation? The piled-up contents of his bathroom cabinet. Difficult to see how any woman of sense is going to take him seriously.'

'Good God, no!' said Clement. 'The fellow's half-baked. I'd have got shot of him years ago if the art exam results weren't so good. So have you any other theories on Martin? Or are you telling me he's got something on with Nell as well?'

'No – if that were the case it would have filtered through the wives' chit-chat by this time. And it hasn't. Meredith's hand in glove with him isn't she? It's crossed my mind there could be something there. Could be mooning after her. Or she after him, and there's trouble.'

Another nasty jolt.

'My secretary? She's not that type. Doesn't moon.'

'Meaning she isn't interested in men from the romantic point of view or they aren't interested in her?'

'Never given any signs of it, has she? I'm not saying she's – '

Clement cleared his throat. He was not an ungallant man and not even to Jim was he prepared to use certain expressions, so he left the sentence unfinished and tried again.

'Not a man's kind of girl. I could have got that wrong, but – and she's got a devilish sharp tongue to boot. It doesn't go down well.'

I don't always like it myself, he might have said. It had once or twice occurred to him that she was laughing at him. And now Jim was surveying him with something of the same detached amusement.

'I presume some women might have a poor opinion of the male sex without being what you're thinking of.'

Clement pictured his secretary's unresponsive face. Out of nowhere the word iceberg floated into his head. Then he remembered it was the name for a type of lettuce and he imagined the cold crisp leaves in a cut glass bowl. Jim was right. Undoubtedly there were women who were indifferent – and this was nobody's responsibility – to bedroom shenanigans of any description. He felt pleased at having the matter so easily settled.

'She might be attractive to some. Very much so.' Jim delivered this judgment in a neutral tone which betrayed nothing. 'No pulling any wool over her eyes. Knows what's what all right.'

'An excellent woman. She fits the bill precisely. But she's hardly on the catch for a man. That was one of the reasons I gave her the job in the first place. The last thing I needed was a girl who'd be eyeing up the new intake of bachelor masters each year. She's well into her thirties now and there's never been the least sign of it.'

'For which you're no doubt grateful. Well, on the face of it, I can only agree. Pity. But *is* Martin normal in this respect? There's no doubt he's alluring to females, for all he appears to take no notice of them. Wraps himself up in a cloak of purity.'

'I hope to God he does.'

Jim levelled his sharp rodent gaze at the prospectus on the headmaster's desk, as if speculating on the nature of the paperback that lay underneath.

'When is a man ever consistent? But I've a hunch Martin isn't into that game. Something holding him back. It might be what draws him to Meredith. Makes no demands on him. And it cuts both ways.'

'A pact you mean?'

'Maybe. Or possibly she's one of those women with a secret. Not usually interested in men, but then develops an entirely irrational thing about Martin. Being unattainable adds to his attraction.'

'Good grief Jim, what have you been reading? She's not such a fool as that.'

'Doesn't love make fools of us all?' said Jim lightly.

Again the headmaster adjusted himself in his leather chair. Was Jim making an oblique reference to what Clement now assured himself was disinterested altruism towards Nell when the poor girl was on her knees? Besides, he would not have put it just like that, but even so – !

'Martin's never given us any trouble like this. He's hardly the man to embark on it at this stage.' Clement eyed his colleague uncertainly, aggrieved he was unable to convince himself. People should stay within the characters his judgment had assigned to them!

'Quite. Funny chap though. Could be one of life's slow starters. No accounting for tastes. I wouldn't have thought Parrish would be a source of attraction, even if you were inclined that way.'

Clement sighed. Sex. A hell of a snake in anyone's garden, and deadly in a public school. It had to be carefully orchestrated, given free rein in particular areas, like arranged social evenings and plays acted jointly with the neighbouring girls' school. That gave them all something to focus on and they got it out of their systems on the dance floor and stage.

It wouldn't be the first time he'd dealt with this sort of allegation. It was usually one of the music masters…and small boys sitting at pianos. If things looked bad, they would have to get Martin Darrow away before all hell broke loose. He'd give it out as sick leave, perfectly feasible after the exigencies of the term and Martin always looked pale anyway.

The end of term was only days away which was a godsend. *Fama nihil est celeries* – bitter experience as well as Livy had taught him that nothing is swifter than rumour. He and Jim must act decisively before the story got out of hand and the governors started breathing down his neck.

There was a knock at the door and Meredith put her head round.

'Oliver Benson's in my office asking for you.'

Didn't he have enough trouble for today? He didn't feel like seeing Oliver Benson, a boy whom he hadn't wanted in the school, but had agreed to take because there was no denying there was a space. The school had to be kept crammed full, the world must know that Wharton places were sought after and the bursar must be kept happy. But it had been against his instincts and now it looked as if he was going to be proved right. The boy came across as too fly by half. And bother it, he was due any minute in the hall to do his stuff with the lower school about choosing next year's activities. He'd never make it now, not if this next interruption was more bad news.

Well, he'd have to put in an appearance. He'd cut it short. No reason why the head of lower school shouldn't step in and take over, he'd enjoy that. Activity options were his pet pigeon.

'Tell Benson to come back at break time tomorrow. It can't be that urgent. I'll see him then.' He nodded to Meredith, and turned back to Jim. 'I take it you've already established that Parrish and Shilling haven't spoken to anyone else?'

Jim nodded.

'I made it clear that it would be extremely inadvisable for them to attempt it. They'll keep their mouths shut all right. But it didn't appear to be in their minds to do otherwise and that's something else which doesn't tie up.'

So there was still a small chance – Jim had a point! The frightful processes that would have to be launched if the accusation was substantiated loomed over Clement like the threat of an invading army. He made a major effort to subdue his panic at the prospect.

'Let's give ourselves until the morning before we make any decisions. Then we can interview Martin together. Buy ourselves time to mull it over and think of the best approach.'

Sweat trickled down Clement's back. The end of year governing body meeting was less than a week away.

THIRTY-FIVE

'Nell?'

It was Eleanor Hunstrete's voice on the telephone.

'Quick, switch on Channel Four. There's some controversial discussion programme that's going to blow the whistle on what's happening to mental health provision in this country. It's just about to start. I meant to phone you earlier, but Clement came in churning so I made an effort to cook an especially delicious supper. Not that it *was*.'

'I'm sorry – is there anything wrong?'

'Oh, he's probably just lost a footnote. It'll turn up. Or if it's a school thing, Jim will come to the rescue. But do watch the programme. Dr Auerbach's one of the contributors.'

Nell felt her stomach flip over. She put down the telephone and glanced across at Martin, slumped on the sofa, looking exhausted and even paler than usual in the stifling heat. She'd invited him to supper, and now they were drinking coffee, the children having disappeared to their rooms.

'Shall we watch it, I could always record it?'

'No – unless you'd like me to go – that you'd prefer to watch it by yourself – '

Had Martin guessed then? Not that there was anything – she switched on the television to hide her confusion.

'That nice Dr Auerbach from Brookner House is going to

be on the telly,' she said to Rachel, who reappeared in the doorway just then. 'He's taking part in some debate. I hadn't realised it was on. D'you want to stay and watch?'

Rachel gave her a long look.

'Not particularly. But I will, as you obviously think I ought to.'

She helped herself to another of the chocolates that Martin had brought and flung herself down into one of the armchairs.

Nell fixed her eyes on the television. Her breathing thumped so loudly that Martin and Rachel must be able to hear it. She tried to take in who were the other participants in the programme, but the screen had become a fairground mirror, distorting and disorientating.

The celebrated psychiatrist on the television in front of her and the man whose voicemail message was still saved on her mobile couldn't be the same person. This was someone in his own world, someone altogether different from the man with whom she'd wandered through St James's Park. She watched in silence, not daring to look at Martin and Rachel.

'That was certainly hard-hitting enough. Dr Auerbach will have dished up some awkward questions for the health secretary there,' Martin said when the programme finished. 'I never told you about spotting him in London – he was coming out of a building near Charing Cross.'

And I never told you or anyone else about the hours I've spent with him, thought Nell, as Rachel left the room. She wanted to listen to it all again. She was proud of all he'd said, proud of this man who was beginning to obsess her thoughts, to mean too much. He'd spoken angrily about the scandal of an inadequate and underfunded mental health service. An incisive clarity, yes, that had been there, and vision too. But not the smallest trace of point scoring. He had merely argued his case.

'The presenter made too much of how people nowadays

turn to a psychiatrist or counsellor where once they turned to the church,' Martin continued thoughtfully, perhaps noticing something and giving her time. 'But Dr Auerbach wasn't having any of that. He categorically refused to allow the separation of psychology from religion, as if the fear of life is one problem and the fear of death quite another.'

'They're all mixed up in us, aren't they? I know they are in me.'

The impression of distance faded and the psychiatrist she'd watched on the television ceased to be a stranger and became again the Lewis she knew. Nell leant forward in her chair, grappling with a crowd of ideas running like illuminated figures ahead of her, taking her somewhere unknown.

'I liked the bit when he talked about mourning for people and wasted lives and terrible mistaken choices. I didn't catch who it was – when he referred to someone else who's written about how works of art might be made out of loss – be created from an empty space, from absence. And why that's somehow important, as a kind of release, to help people find their own path out of sadness and grief. I need to try and get my head round what that might mean in my own work. The connectedness of things...the way you do jigsaws...' she stumbled, and something in his face made her add, 'I'm sorry Rachel was difficult just now. I know she likes you underneath.'

'She wasn't, you don't have to be sorry. There can't be many children who don't desperately wish their parents would get back together. They may well see any man as a threat.'

'Rachel couldn't possibly think – '

'When were any of us ever rational? Fear distorts all our imaginings.'

Nell attempted to disentangle the muddle and failed. Was there something in Martin's words giving her a warning?

'She was dreadfully rude to Trevor Faversham when he

asked me out,' she said, trying to make light of the memory. 'Sebastian was too. But that was different.'

A suspicion hit her that this was the real reason for Rachel's insistence in January that she didn't want to go to Brookner House again. She'd been afraid even then that her mother would get into another relationship. Fresh butterflies of guilt stirred and fluttered.

Then she realised what she'd just said to Martin. Would he think she was making an oblique reference to what had always been unspoken between them? She'd believed they understood each other, that he'd never wanted her to go further. Had she misread him, just as she'd misread Alastair and Juliet?

You never see things.

'Why must people be made to suffer like this, people with bipolar and schizophrenia and all the other disorders they were talking about on the programme? It's so unfair, so endlessly cruel.'

'Isn't Dr Auerbach answering the question in another way? Or rather he isn't asking it. He's working to make things better according to his own abilities. That's his answer, and it could be the only answer. I'm sorry you've lost contact with him.'

Nell looked away. She hated lying to Martin. But the longing to talk about Lewis, to say his name, was too strong to be resisted.

'I met that other psychiatrist once. The one the press are vilifying for not seeing what that poor boy was going to do. He looked at me in a way I didn't exactly like, as if he knew something I didn't. Dr Auerbach looks at people in a different way altogether. As if he sees inside them but doesn't *use* that knowledge.'

'You could be a little unjust. We all manipulate people to some extent. Isn't it an essential aspect of social skills and civilized living?'

'I wish I could manipulate myself more,' said Nell sadly, 'into not having wicked thoughts about people.'

'Alastair and Juliet?'

'You can think you're on the way to forgiving someone, and on one level you have. Then you find that on another level you haven't at all. Some small thing happens and it all comes flooding back. Sometimes it's like I still hate them both so much I'll never be free of it.'

'But you don't always feel that.'

'Not quite. A little bit of me, so little it's practically non-existent most of the time, wants to forgive them. I – I once talked to Dr Auerbach about it. He said it would come in unexpected ways.'

A shadow crossed Martin's face.

'You *want* to want to forgive. When it comes down to it, isn't that everything? To hold onto the hope of reaching an eventual and real forgiveness. That must be better than pretending to yourself and others you've done it all already. Forgiving others, yourself, God – it's a lifetime's work.'

'I think I'm just beginning on all that business. I can see now that I shut my eyes to what Alastair was – and what he wasn't. It must have been the same for him.'

'You think you would have forgiven him if he'd confessed to everything when Vail was born?'

'*He* said I wouldn't have done, that I'd have left him, and he couldn't take the risk of losing me and the children. But what's the good of him saying that now?'

Grief for all that she and Alastair and Juliet had done to each other stirred its old pain.

'For someone to truly know everything about us in love – it's like those words we say in chapel, *all desires known and from whom no secrets are hidden*. Martin, I wish *you* could find someone to love, to really love, not just watch out for others all the time.

But I suppose it's not possible for you here, and maybe it's not what you want…'

'I don't want it, I've never wanted it.'

The change in his manner was so sudden and unexpected that she stared at him. He'd gone white, his forehead damp with sweat. He was angry with her. She knew at once that she'd blundered, encroached on private territory. But why should their intimacy be always only one way? For some reason she couldn't identify she gave vent to the frustration that belonged somewhere else.

'I don't know how you can say that. It's not exactly being honest with yourself, is it? Any relationship could be celibate, if that's what's stopping you. In the programme we've just watched he said we can – ' her voice cracked and she found to her horror she might be going to cry, but it didn't matter because Martin was already jumping to his feet saying it was late, he must get back to his flat, he had a pile of work to get through.

It was because the evening was so suffocatingly hot, she told herself. It made everybody on edge, ready to tip over into overblown emotion and bad temper.

All desires known and from whom no secrets are hidden.

She shouldn't have said what she had to Martin.

After Martin had gone, she picked up her mobile. She had a reason now – the word excuse hovered – to answer Lewis's voicemail. There would be nothing wrong in telling him she'd watched the programme. It was a friendly call anyone might make.

Tomorrow was Friday. When school finished she was taking the children to London to stay with Alastair and Juliet for the weekend. She'd listen now just once more to Lewis's message, and then tomorrow evening, as soon as she was alone, she would telephone him.

She wanted to give herself to him entirely, wantonly, until there was nothing left. So what if it was immoral? She didn't care.

*

Einmal ist keinmal, Dermot Fitzgibbon had said to him.

Once is nothing. A tossed-off-the-shoulder remark, an old German saying, following some talk about Ursula.

It was the kind of thing Dermot came out with. He had a way of producing ideas apparently spontaneously with the enigmatic sleight of hand of the conjuror. Was there something in the idea that what happens only once might as well have not happened at all? If it takes a whole life to learn how to live, then it would be absurd if there was not another to apply the lessons. Someone else had said that, or something like it. Lewis couldn't remember who it was.

'Darling, we'll get through this again. Maybe in just a few weeks, and I promise you I'll be with you whenever I can – and every evening.'

Words he'd said before, on the other occasions he'd had to take Ursula to stay as an inpatient at Brookner House. In past years she'd fought him off, cried that he was her enemy and he was killing her. This time there had been no show of resistance when he'd suggested going back there. She'd only stared at him, blank-eyed and silent. He might have been her prison guard.

The deterioration he'd seen in her these last months was rapidly tipping over into full-blown crisis. He thought of the shredded sheets of piano music scattered across rooms, glass and china hurled as missiles, the upstairs window thrown wide open and beckoning. *I can't bear any more of this, don't make me go on living.* It was no longer safe to leave her alone.

Now, as he drove the short distance to Brookner House

he asked himself if he should make plans to take even more time off from his work. Already he'd cancelled a series of summer school lectures he was due to give to London psychiatry students. He could give up *Steep Stairs*, refuse to take on new cases in his private practice. Yet even this would not be enough. He knew it – and also that Brookner House was the very best place for Ursula, an acknowledged gold standard of care. Even if he gave up every hour of the day to her, abandoned his work altogether for a few months, would it help her any more?

In a few minutes, Channel Four's discussion programme on the role of psychiatry in modern society was being shown on television. He wouldn't have seen it anyway. To watch himself on the screen was distasteful to him, and Ursula, Lewis believed, had forgotten the programme's existence. She'd retreated into a splintered world of disordered thinking where he couldn't reach her.

The roads were quiet on this evening of high summer. Tall stalks of cow parsley cramming the hedges were turning brown. It had been a week of merciless, sweltering heat and there was more to come. The piercing blue of the sky was fading into eggshell; tomorrow would be another cloudless day.

He slowed down and glanced at his wife, so terrifyingly frail and remote in the passenger seat. He remembered her as she'd looked when he'd first seen her, lying helpless in the hospital bed after the car crash. Hadn't she suffered enough? Did God make up in eternity for the outrageous unfairness of so many lives?

His watchful concentration on both his wife sitting mute by his side and the road ahead of him must have wavered just then. How else was it possible that without warning Ursula had torn off her seat belt and wrenched at the wheel? He never knew. For a few horrifying seconds Lewis fought to regain control of the car, Ursula's screams filling his ears, flashing shapes spinning across the windscreen, a blow of deadly crushing pain and then there was nothing at all.

*

Love your enemies and pray for those who persecute you.

Back alone in his chaplain's flat after the near quarrel with Nell, Martin felt that Christ had no business saying such things. But there were too many things Martin wished Christ had never said.

He should never have gone to supper with Nell. He ought to have been preparing the sermon for next week's end of year chapel service. He couldn't do it. Not tonight. Not after all that had gone through his head today.

'Might not get another chance to shake hands and say our goodbyes – '

Chris Parrish, coming into the vestry after morning chapel had been wearing an expression Martin knew he needed to be wary of. It wasn't new to him, that speculative glance of invitation. But now it was both mocking and insolent. Martin withdrew his hand, aware that Chris was holding it a fraction too long. From the doorway he thought he heard smothered laughter. He looked straight into the boy's face.

'There is still the leavers' service on Tuesday,' he said quietly. 'But perhaps you have decided not to come to that.'

Later, hurrying out of his flat to go to supper with Nell, he'd almost fallen against Oliver Benson on the stairs. Oliver looked as if he might have been going to say something. Only he hadn't.

He heard again Nell's voice.

I wish you could find someone to love…but I suppose it's not possible for you here…it's not exactly being honest with yourself, is it?

She knows it all. And I – I have come to the end of myself as Wharton's chaplain.

He stared down at the jigsaw lying hardly started on the table in front of him. The Ghent altarpiece in two thousand pieces. Jan van Eyck's vision of the Last Judgement as described in the Book of Revelation, painted back in the fifteenth century.

He hadn't begun with the bleeding lamb standing on the altar, but with the surrounding crowds of people: apostles and martyrs, confessors and holy virgins; prophets, patriarchs and sages. As a boy he'd imagined St John writing down his vision as an old man exiled on the island of Patmos. He'd learnt the words by heart and he began to repeat them now but they fell meaninglessly into the silence, old and lifeless stones.

Why had Christ left so much to muddled human minds, so that men were left floundering in a sea of doubt and confusion? Life was to be lived in the dark, not just in the fear of death, but in the ever-present fear of a God who turned away. Why did he allow them to work out their path in blood and sweat, in despair and error, left only and always with the forlorn question and the dusty answer?

As a boy he'd looked up at the shining stars of the chapel ceiling and dreamed he was seeing an image of heaven. He'd been given everything at Wharton, his whole life. Given to him until the Last Judgement.

Each day for ten years as Wharton's chaplain he'd walked clothed in his robes through the great carved doors, with the inscription overhead: *Vive ut vivas*. Had he fulfilled this great injunction, to live that you may live?

He told himself he'd striven to do so, but even as he said this, he knew he'd done so only in part. Something more was required of him that he hadn't given. He'd made himself believe that he'd blotted out the hidden stain of his life, but when Oliver Benson had come to Wharton, he'd discovered that the years of deliberate and careful walking away hadn't taken him any distance at all.

Instead he'd built up a rigid and unforgiving world where the possibility of change, the redemption of the individual, was denied. He'd withheld God's grace to another man and yet taken it without humility for himself.

And *had* he taken it for himself? The whisper in his head told him that he had protected himself against its totality. Wasn't it true he'd resisted the presence of God in his understanding of that transforming year of his life? He'd shrunk in frozen terror and shame as a thirteen-year-old boy. He'd done the same in his mind ever since, denying to his God the right to accept him as he was. He hadn't believed in all its fullness that he was made in the image of God.

He'd rejected a part of himself, a part given to him by God – and in doing so he was rejecting God himself, warping the God-given power to see the whole of life as the presence of God. Something of all this he understood – and yet knew he only understood in part.

He shuffled randomly through stray pieces of fragmented painted believers. Could Piers Benson be among them? *Many who are last shall be first, and the first last.*

Love your enemies and pray for those who persecute you.

Slowly he got to his feet and went towards the door. Late as it was, he would go to the chapel. It was there, in the darkness and under the ceiling of golden stars, that he must at last make peace with the enemies who had pursued him for so long.

Yet still his heart failed him. Turning back, he looked down at the broken image on the table. Then he stretched out his hand and swept the hundreds of tiny jigsaw pieces on to the floor.

THIRTY-SIX

'Mum? You haven't *forgiven* Juliet have you?'

The train was pulling into Charing Cross station at seven o'clock on Friday evening. In just a few minutes they would see Alastair, for as usual he would be waiting by the ticket barriers. Then he would be taking the children to the mews house near Paddington (which didn't have enough bedrooms so Juliet was angling to move into something bigger and where the hell was the money going to come from?) until Sunday evening when he would put them on the train back to Wharton. Rachel knew how to pick her moments.

'I don't know.' Nell squashed her sketchbook with its study of the pug-faced lady sitting at the next door table into her bag. Half the time she couldn't have put into words what was going on in her head. 'But I want to. Or I want to want to, and that must be a start. Though I won't be able to *forget*.'

'According to Gran on the telephone last night that's because you're failing to understand God's love for you. She put on her honey voice like she always does when she's talking about religion.'

'I can just hear her.' Nell began to scrabble distractedly in her jacket pocket for the tickets, and then remembered she'd already given them to the children. 'She told me that my faith was incorrect, whatever that means. Thank goodness for Martin saying that religion is part of everyday living, more like the air we breathe. I can't cope with it as being some kind of exam.'

'Huh. Sounds like the standard crap Martin comes up with.'

'And why should Gran's version of God be right and other people's wrong?' Sebastian grabbed his rucksack from the luggage rack.

'It *is* very aggravating,' admitted Nell. 'But I guess she can't help it. Don't forget Dad says she only went like this after *his* dad walked out on her. Having him go off with someone much older and less attractive than she was must have left her feeling pretty low, like she wasn't much use even as a companion. Finding a niche in a fundamentalist church might have been the only way she could feel accepted and good about herself again.'

Sebastian eyed her suspiciously.

'You're putting on a very teacher-ish voice. I hope you're not going to turn into one of those mothers who are always saying improving things to their children just because they're getting divorced.'

'And if Grandpa fell for someone else, he couldn't help himself,' said Rachel. 'Basically everyone forgets about rules and stuff when they're in love and think they can shit on everyone else. Even you might.'

There was a question here. Or was it an accusation?

'Mum wouldn't ever – '

'Dad said that Grandpa drank himself to death so the hideous frump can't have looked after him very well,' continued Rachel, determined to have the last word. 'Or had a great time either. I bet Gran was pleased about that. She might not have been so hot about forgiveness then.'

With Pity, Not with Blame. Nell remembered the title of a battered paperback she'd seen on Martin's bookshelves. She swept the children along the platform.

'She does love us very much – and God. It's been me who's

been prejudiced, not her – and that's made me take things in the wrong way. But I'm going to change all that… Look, there's Dad.'

Alastair, emerging from W H Smith with Vail, included all three of them in the irresistible smile that always made everyone who met him feel it was especially for them – until they discovered it was handed out to everyone. He hugged the children and kissed Nell, just as he'd done on the other weekends when she'd brought the children up to London.

Nell instinctively stiffened and then made a superhuman effort. It was important for all three children. She'd made a promise to herself – and only occasionally broken it – that she would never bad mouth Alastair, or even Juliet, to Rachel and Sebastian. If she could limit the damage done to them by their parents' splitting up, she was going to try.

'Nell – ' Alastair was looking at her with his appealing small boy's face. He gestured behind him, the familiar tennis swing. She froze. Just a few yards away was Juliet.

'Alastair thought he'd take the children for an Indian or Chinese.' Juliet's words poured out in a low rush as she came up to Nell. 'I wanted to see you Nell, just you, by yourself. Please. We could go out by ourselves, only for an hour, whatever you like – I know it's unfair of me to ask and you're thinking I don't deserve it, but please say yes.'

She wants to have a sneaky talk about how they can't afford to move, and it's all because Alastair's giving too much of his money to me. Indignation flashed through Nell. Why hadn't Alastair warned her of this? But of course he'd just done what Juliet asked. Hadn't he always tried to please whoever he was with at the time? It was Juliet she would have to fight and resentment should be aimed at her.

But as she stared into Juliet's face she discovered she didn't want to give way to it. It might have been Juliet's pleading expression or the unusual lack of smartness in her clothes, or perhaps above all the questioning echo of her own too easily uttered words about forgiveness.

'As long as it's only for an hour then,' she said. 'I want to make the most of the late night opening at the National Gallery while I'm here.'

Do it with grace or not at all. That sounded like Eleanor with a pinch of Sue North.

So where did behaving with grace and standing up for yourself begin and end?

Yesterday in the art studio she'd overheard Oliver Benson calling Martin Darrow a dumb-arsed doormat who let everyone walk over him. She'd flown at him in a hot fury of indignation.

'Mr Darrow's the best person you'll ever meet – '

Oliver had only sniggered.

'Fancy him, do you, Mrs Garland? Who'd blame you?'

'How dare you say that? Go on, out. Now. Get out of my sight – ' she couldn't go on, something was catching at her throat.

She swung away from him seething with anger, but not before he'd shot her a quick look that might have been sympathy.

'Yeah, sorry, that was out of order.'

Oh God, don't bloody cry in front of a crowd of seventeen-year-olds.

'St James's Park?' Juliet queried.

Anywhere but there. It was where she'd wandered about with Lewis, telling him her secrets, wrapped up safe in his understanding.

'Something to drink then,' said Juliet, as if sensing Nell's mute refusal. She turned to Alastair and the children. 'I won't join you – see you at the house later.'

'Not Chinese,' Nell heard Rachel objecting. 'We had that last time we came.'

'I'm so glad Rachel's back to normal about food,' Juliet said as they turned towards Covent Garden.

'Yes, she is. I overreacted thinking it was anorexia and God knows what else, but it wasn't…I think Dr Auerbach guessed that from the first.' Nell walked on, seeing nothing, her thoughts losing their shape. What was she doing, falling in with Juliet's plans, just like she always had? But it was too late now, for Juliet was already leading the way into a wine bar and ordering drinks.

'It was because of me, wasn't it? She twigged somehow – I swear it wasn't meant to happen that way – and refusing to eat was a protest. Nell, you know how I love your children. I would never do anything to hurt them, anything that I could help.'

'Wouldn't you?' said Nell, not altogether meaning to sound sarcastic. Already the dull insistent hammers of a tension headache were starting up.

'Yes. I know how much I have. Please don't ever think I can forget it. But it's not that. I want you to – not forgive me, I know that isn't going to happen, but to tell me I haven't put myself quite out of reach – ' Juliet shifted the position of the drinks she'd bought for them, not looking at Nell.

'You don't believe we broke it off when you left London. But we did. For five years. Until I came to Wharton.'

Did alcohol help at all? Nell took a gulp of her wine. It tasted sour in her dry mouth.

'So when I *persuaded* you – as I thought – to move to Wharton I have only myself to blame for what happened next?'

'Oh Nell, how can I make you understand that love doesn't go away however hard you try? I'd tried for every day of those five years. That's what I want you to know. Even last summer I pretended to Al it was for Vail, that he ought to see more of the father he didn't know he had.'

She did believe Juliet now. No wonder Alastair had panicked and made sure Juliet wouldn't have another so-called mistake. He hadn't trusted himself – or Juliet either.

'And my husband fell for the trap, just as you calculated he would. You counted on it being only a matter of time before he forgot any lingering scruples holding him back.'

'Then you told me you were going to try to have another baby. I knew you wouldn't get pregnant, but I was afraid…I'd tried to con myself that if I could have just part of Al it would be enough. I could be the mistress who has it all: the career, the lover, the best friend. But from that moment I knew it wasn't ever going to be enough. I wanted Al to myself. All the time.'

'Is this why you got up this plan of seeing me today? To make me agree with you, so you don't have to feel so bad about yourself?'

'There's something else. Something I said when you found us together in my house. That I wasn't the first of Al's affairs since he married you.'

'Juliet, I don't want to know. I don't *need* to know.'

'It was a lie. There was never anyone else. I said it to frighten you.'

It was still a wound too raw to be examined. Juliet's words stole over it; the touch of a healing balm. The first year and a half, when Rachel was born and Sebastian conceived; he *had* been all hers. Something, however small, was being given back to her.

'I guessed long ago you'd decided to contrive I should discover everything, apparently by accident. Knowing that I wouldn't cope. And then when that didn't work, you let it out about Vail and – and everything else.'

'Not quite everything.' Juliet's voice was very low. 'I'm not sure Vail *is* Al's child. He may not be. I told Al I'd stopped sleeping with Newland and he believed me. It was the only hold I had over him. I used it.'

There was a long silence.

'But surely you always *thought* he was Alastair's. Even if you never said anything to anyone.'

'I *wanted* to think he was, and so I persuaded myself it was all right to let Al think there was no question. I wanted Newland to think it as well, and he was too honourable to doubt my word. He was quite incapable of telling a lie himself or spotting one in anyone else.' Juliet's expression took on her old self-derisory grimace. 'There are no limits to how far any of us will deceive ourselves.'

Nell kept her eyes fixed on the wine in her glass. Only by concentrating very hard on its jewel-rich redness could she keep her tears back.

'Does Alastair know that Vail might not be his child after all?'

'You can tell him. And there's DNA testing.'

Nell stared at her. She'd spent all these months carrying around violent urges to punish this friend who'd betrayed her. She'd wanted to make her suffer – and go on suffering. For one long moment an infinitely sweet revenge seemed to be held out to her. Wasn't this what she'd longed for, the opportunity to deal some annihilating blow to Juliet and Alastair's happiness, to smash up and destroy what they had together?

Then, as if some cool draught was offered to her from an unknown hand, the desire lessened. She felt strangely light. Something had been taken away from her and something else given. Nell didn't know what these things were, only that a change was slowly and inexorably working its way into her mind, washing away the old bitterness.

'You wouldn't have done to me what I did to you, if everything had been the other way around,' Juliet said.

Wouldn't she? Nell tried to see into herself. Could anyone ever know how they would react when push came to shove? Wasn't it arrogant of her, who hadn't been faced with the same temptation, and for whom everything had always been easy, to condemn other people's weakness or selfishness?

'I don't think any of us can ever be certain about ourselves,' she said at last. 'I don't know that I would have done anything different if it had been me.'

'I do know it.' Juliet's blue eyes met hers. 'We're made differently that way. That's why I've had to tell you the truth about Vail. I've come to see it as a kind of debt.'

'But you can't want me to repeat any of this to Alastair – '

'What do you think?' Juliet asked savagely. 'You knowing this is a punishment I want to bring upon myself, for all the unforgiveable things I've done to you. I'm glad of it.'

This was the old Juliet, blending an ironic self-mockery and self-knowledge. A picture flashed of Juliet the night they'd first met in the ladies' cloakroom at the theatre. *I haven't the heart to disillusion him. Yet.* Just then, as in a mirage within the desert of their making, she could see only the friend she'd loved for so many years.

'I know you're sorry,' she said breathlessly, the words coming from some deep inner consciousness. The beginnings of a pale light flickered into life and gathered strength. 'I shall never tell Alastair – or anyone – what you've said. For the sake of all of us. Now Vail believes Alastair is his dad, the relationship shouldn't be taken away from him. Or even questioned.' She stopped, shaking off something that was gripping and holding her close, and took a long breath.

'For I'm quite certain Alastair *is*. When I'm painting portraits, I'm staring at people's features for hours on end... I suppose I didn't recognise it before because Vail's colouring and features are like yours, but there's something in his face – '

'Oh Nell, why are you always – ' Juliet picked up her empty glass. 'It's part of the punishment. You saying things like that, because of being the way you are. Knowing that I can't undo any of it or make it any better.'

The things we have done and the things we have left undone. Nell heard Martin's voice as she'd heard it many times in the Wharton chapel. Juliet said, as if in continuing disbelief, 'I loved you so dearly. Yet that didn't stop me taking everything from you. Nothing else mattered – then.'

'You're happy – '

'Oh yes. Haven't I always loved him? Even though I know what people say, that a man who leaves his wife for his mistress will do the same to her in a few years' time. It's as though they're hoping. Oh, not you Nell,' – Juliet smiled sadly as Nell bit her lip – 'but other wives. There's a kind of justice in it that I accept. After all, shouldn't I of all people know that Alastair may be unfaithful to me in the future? Women will make it easy for him and he won't be able to resist. He might leave me. And yet I won't be able to stop loving him, though I despise myself for it. I only know I shall always take him back whatever he does.'

'That's the real difference between us,' said Nell. 'For I couldn't.'

She fell silent while something that might have been pity crept over her. Or was it shame? She'd always told herself that her love for Alastair was beyond question, but now she doubted it. Had it been a lesser kind of love than Juliet's, more selfish, expecting Alastair to be something he couldn't be? She said with difficulty, 'I've asked myself recently if there are different kinds of faithfulness – not just one way of being faithful to a person, I mean. Yours might be a way.'

Juliet fished into her handbag and took out a packet of pills.

'Here you are. You've got a hellish awful headache haven't you? I'll get you a soft drink.'

Juliet had always noticed how you were feeling. As she came back with a glass of orange juice Nell looked at the friend she'd both loved and hated and knew that it was just the same as it always was. Juliet saw things as they were. Juliet would give

Alastair what he needed, which she herself hadn't been able to do. And she would look after him.

'Has Alastair told you how I'm back on terms with my parents? Ironic really. They're so pleased I'm settled with a man at last instead of living my wild single mother life. If only they knew. It's really all about Vail of course, them not missing out, now they realise he's going to be their only grandchild.'

'You can't blame them for that.'

'No – and I'm glad I've made it up. Shall we walk together to the National Gallery?'

'I think I'd prefer to get home. Not look at pictures. They can wait.'

Back at the entrance to Charing Cross, she turned to Juliet. 'People ask me if I hate you.'

'Don't – '

'It's all right. What can anyone know about it if they haven't *been* us?'

'I'm not going to ask what you say. Goodbye Nell. One day – '

Was Juliet going to ask if she would forgive her? Could friendship ever be rebuilt after what had happened to them?

She watched Juliet disappear among the crowds. Inchoate thoughts sprang up and died. A memory of Martin preaching in the chapel about a man in the Bible. I have faith, the man had said, help me to have *more!* But what had happened to the man after that? She hadn't been listening.

Nell swallowed. She said in a small voice, 'I miss you.'

To herself she said, I will try. I *am* trying.

When she had bad dreams and woke in the night, Nell knew she was only just holding on, that the life she'd built for herself since January was a patchy affair. There were bearable days and unbearable days – and the day with Lewis. She needed to do something, anything, to get out more – an expression Hilary had used and Nell hated, but couldn't find another – not just for the children's sake but for her own.

Help me to have *more*! The strength to forgive must be a gift given by God, you couldn't do it on your own. If she was a better person, then wouldn't it be easier for God to give it to her?

But she didn't have faith, not like that man Martin had been talking about. She wasn't a good person either. Last night, after Martin had left, she'd promised herself she would make that telephone call to Lewis after she arrived home. The thought of it had been with her all through the day, a closely guarded and hidden hope of something longed for, though its full meaning couldn't be admitted even to herself. Now, as if stripped away by Juliet's clear blue gaze, something unacknowledged was revealed and she could see it in all its self-deceiving ugliness.

She was planning to run after a married man. She might delude herself there was nothing wrong in meeting Lewis again, that all she felt for him was passionate gratitude for what he'd done for Rachel. It wasn't all. She stood very still, allowing the streams of commuters to pour past. She wasn't just grateful to Lewis, the interesting and perceptive psychiatrist who'd been kind to her. She was in love with him.

And Lewis, like Alastair, was married. She slid her hand into her pocket, as if cradling the voicemail on her mobile. What had Juliet said? *We're made differently that way.* It wasn't true.

If she met Lewis again it would be with desires in her heart which must never be expressed. She wanted to give herself to him heart and soul and body. She wanted him to know that she was all his – *stop it.*

She pulled her mobile from her pocket. His message was all she had of him. All she would ever have.

She hadn't been as honest as Juliet. But she could make a start, couldn't she? Her fingers trembled over the keys.

If you were a man who would deceive your wife and have a love affair with me, you wouldn't be the man I love. She told herself this, and yet still there was the agony inside. *And if I was a woman who would knowingly have an affair with a man who was cheating on his wife I wouldn't be worthy of your love.*

She tried to force down the passionate longing that seemed to consume her whole consciousness. She had learnt to love him entirely and completely, and now she was weakness itself in the face of it.

I wouldn't be the woman you could ever love.

She couldn't trust herself. The keys of her mobile dissolved into a blur as she deleted Lewis's voicemail.

Hurrying towards platform six, she almost missed the headlines emblazoned on the stand containing the piled-up evening papers: *TV shrink car crash tragedy.*

THIRTY-SEVEN

Clement Hunstrete spent Friday morning break time in his office signing good work commendations for a stream of boys not yet cynical enough to despise these traditional school honours.

He was relieved when Oliver Benson made no appearance. The prospect of confronting the chaplain was hanging over him and he hadn't enjoyed his bowl of grape-nuts at breakfast. Jim had offered to cancel his lessons following break so they might interrogate Martin together, but on consideration Clement thought that on this particular occasion he would like to manage alone. If he made a major bish, Jim wouldn't be there to witness it.

The bell for the end of break had gone when Meredith knocked.

'It's Oliver Benson – shall I send him in?'

There was something provoking in the boy's expression. Unsettling even. Clement resisted an urge to drum his fingers on the polished mahogany of his desk and tried to keep the testiness out of his voice.

'Haven't you got a class you ought to be at?'

'Free lesson time, sir.'

'So there's something important you wanted to talk to me about? Then take a seat. The headmaster's door is always open to any boy,' he added conscientiously, if untruthfully.

Oliver had already sat down. He looked quite at home, a great deal too much so.

'It's about Mr Darrow, sir. Some of us were joshing around, looking for someone to wind up. Basically, you needn't take any notice of anything dodgy you get to hear about him, it's all made up.'

For a full minute, the effrontery of it took Clement's breath away. Was this boy, with his impudent glance and knowing mouth, actually telling him that he and his friends had thought it *fun* to make an accusation which could wreck a man's life?

'Stuff got out of hand. There was a bet and – you kind of don't want to know the rest. None of it matters so long as you believe Mr Darrow didn't do whatever some random person might say he did.'

None of it matters! Clement stared over his glasses at Oliver with mounting anger. He was on the point of pulling in his chaplain to explain some extremely serious allegations. A very nasty scandal threatened. Then he took in that Oliver evidently didn't know Chris Parrish had already told his story. He paused, unwrapping what this might mean. Already he was regretting Jim's absence.

'I take it the others involved in this *stuff*, as you describe it, didn't put you up to coming to see me? They don't know you're here?'

'Not exactly, sir.'

Clement Hunstrete allowed himself another moment of silence. Was an escape going to be offered to him? A vision of an alternative timetable for the day beckoned. No sticky interview with the chaplain, lunch with the prefects in one of the boarding houses, a sunshine stroll to watch the last cricket of the year.

'So it was intended as nothing more than a particularly unpleasant and cruel joke?'

'Yeah – that's like how it started – as a joke – '

'Which went out of control, as jokes may do in a school community. It would be disingenuous of me to pretend I don't know who else is involved. Parrish and Shilling. You appear to have been keeping regrettable company. Might I enquire as to your motive in coming to me?'

'Confidential, sir.'

'Ah yes. No doubt you would prefer this conversation to remain confidential as well?'

'That would certainly make it easier all round, sir.'

Damn it, the boy was almost patronizing! And the sir in every utterance – was there an ironic edge?

'Have you said anything about this to anyone else?'

'No one, sir.'

'Then you will continue to keep silent. Not a word to anyone, least of all Mr Darrow, is that understood? This could have been a very grave affair. It may still be. You're expecting me to straighten it out but this can't be done as easily as you appear to think.'

Clement eyed the boy's exaggeratedly casual posture with suspicion. Was it a little overdone? He couldn't tell. This was after all the artist behind that singularly distasteful caricature, an image Clement hadn't been able to erase from his mind. He twitched as he recalled its ribald and unerringly-drawn likeness. Oliver Benson was altogether too sharp. He was at the same time remarkably talented. Nell Garwood clearly thought so at any rate. And he'd stepped in to undo the damage hadn't he?

Discretion was without doubt the wisest course. Clement inclined his head judiciously and put on his benevolent headmaster's face.

'However, you have at least decided to come forward. This is in your favour.'

'No worries, sir.'

'That remains to be seen,' answered Clement, choosing to misunderstand him. 'Since you have made this attempt put things right, and provided the so-called joke goes no further, I may be able to ensure there will be no repercussions. Take this affair as a warning of the strongest possible nature. It might be the end of term, when leavers' pranks are an unwelcome fact of life, but you have another year here. I should like to see you use your time more wisely than you have done.'

'Mr Darrow can't hit back, you know, like anyone else – '

'He is also a gentleman, living among gentlemen. Let me remind you of the importance of those values.'

'Yes sir. He's kind of a legend.'

'You'd better get off to your class,' Clement said, forgetting that Oliver had claimed he didn't have one. He watched the boy amble out of his office, flicking the door not quite shut behind him with a careless hand. He heaved an inward sigh of thankfulness. Martin Darrow a legend. The last thing he would have expected from a boy like Oliver Benson. Not such a heartless Smart Alec as he'd thought. Odd how boys could still surprise you.

*

'Crisis averted, I think we can say with quiet confidence. A joke that got out of hand.'

The headmaster poured his deputy a dry sherry. It was that unsatisfactory time of the afternoon, too early for a drink, decidedly too late for tea. But it had been the sort of day when the traditional conventions could be reasonably ignored.

Jim North relaxed in his chair and took a meditative sip of his sherry.

'So Oliver would have us believe. It's likely there was more to it – there always is. Did Chris Parrish throw out lures to

Martin which were rejected, and this was his cheap revenge? Hell hath no fury and all that.'

'A tiresome flowering of hormonal play-acting, in fact. You're probably right. Well, what do you think?'

'Haul them in and get them to withdraw their accusation without any more loss of time. We'll need to pretend to believe the joke story, to keep the whole thing wrapped up. We don't want the business getting into general circulation.'

Clement shuddered.

'Certainly not. Keeping the lid on things – God knows it's always our top priority. The relentless ego of adolescents. So busy living at the centre of their own lives they never see the implications to others of their thoughtless little games. Interesting that it should be Oliver Benson who had the decency to come forward. Ever met the father? No? You wouldn't want to. Used to come to all the old boy cricket matches. Rugby too. Ghastly man. Too sure of himself by half. No self-doubt.'

Clement liked this expression. It elevated inconsistency and provided a let-out clause for timidity, of which he felt he was sometimes accused.

'Martin knew him apparently,' Jim remarked. 'Said something to me at half term. It passed me by at the time, though it shed some light on the way he reacted to the snow episode in January.'

'They may have overlapped here as boys at Wharton. Unlikely to be more recent as Benson got kicked out of the army and stopped coming to Old Whartonians Day about ten years ago.'

'Just before Martin took up the chaplaincy then. As I remember it, Martin implied the father was an ugly customer, and the son no better.'

'A nice touch of dramatic irony that, given today's revelation,' Clement nodded appreciatively. 'Benson resurfaced about eighteen months ago to say he hadn't seen his way to paying the fees when the boy was thirteen but could just about afford the two years of sixth form. The governors like to do something for sons of old boys in cases of hardship, though I had a few reservations on this one. Seems I was wrong.'

'Can anything good come out of Nazareth?' Jim quoted, his eyes on the pale liquid in his glass.

'Quite. Clearly a decent boy, against all the odds. Well, it happens. And thank God Parrish and Shilling *et al* will be out of here any day.'

'The rotten apples in the barrel. They've certainly done their bit in spreading corruption during their time here.'

'Leaves a nasty taste in the mouth,' agreed Clement. He could sympathise with his deputy head's feelings, for he also could remember various past incidents, whilst preferring to erase them amid the satisfaction of the year group's rich crop of potential Oxbridge places. 'They know all too well we can't touch them at this stage – personal statements written, A levels finished with, university offers in the bag.'

'Hmm. We'll have to trust that justice will catch up with them later in their lives. I've little doubt it will, but not before they've created further misery for those around them. A strong word with them both as a warning shot across the bow is all we can do at present. I must say it goes against the grain. They're both heading for Oxford, aren't they? I'd like to have made them sweat.' Jim's face was unusually savage.

'It's been an extremely unpleasant twenty-four hours,' agreed Clement. 'So we don't say anything at all to Martin?'

'That young Benson pulled him out of deep water? Is there any point?'

'I suppose if we're satisfied this is the end of it – ' Clement looked enquiringly at Jim, feeling in need of an expression of solidarity.

'There's a risk it won't be, but it's worth taking. Why poke about in the woodshed? He's too fine a chaplain to lose over what's most likely something and nothing.'

'We'd have a tricky job getting anyone else half as good. Especially in a hurry.' Clement revolved the cut crystal sherry glass to catch the light, grateful as always for Jim's common sense. The thought of sudden changes appalled him.

'Exactly.' Jim's tone was bracing. 'Skeletons in the cupboard: who hasn't got them? They usually lie down if they're left.'

'I would not open the windows of men's souls. Queen Elizabeth the first, you know. A good one to remember. Yes, *quieta non movere.*'

Clement Hunstrete restored his wife's photograph to its usual place. She might in reality never wear her pearls and cashmere cardigan but she was doing so in this publicly displayed image and that counted for something. Its familiar soft focus reassured him that all was as it should be.

Soon it would be time for the Friday evensong, a Wharton tradition since the school had been founded in the mid-Victorian era. Godliness and good learning had been the watchwords then, and in a sense they still were. Yes, that was it! He poured himself and Jim another sherry.

*

Standing at the window of her office, Meredith the headmaster's secretary watched the boys scurrying to chapel. Masters strode along the paths crossing the quad, pulling on gowns; rich shadows from the golden buildings crept across the velvet summer grass. Would she be rewarded by a glimpse of Martin? To have a small place in his life; this was all she hoped for. He would never offer her any more.

She was on the point of giving up when he appeared at the

311

other side of the quad, greeting boys as they raced past him. She waited, still and expectant, as that sweet-faced boy Oliver Benson loped across the grass – a privilege allowed only to prefects – and raised his hand in casual salutation to Martin. She saw Martin's answering smile, and then, quite unexpectedly, he turned his head and looked at her window. At her.

She was able to see his face for just an instant before he moved away, but it told her all she needed to know. A burden lifted from her. Whatever had been the trouble this last year, the darkness had gone.

She stood listening to the last chimes of the bells as Martin and Oliver Benson disappeared together through the great chapel doors. *Vive ut vivas.* Live that you may live.

*

Dr Lewis Auerbach, a leading child psychiatrist, was airlifted to hospital yesterday with serious injuries after a car crash late yesterday evening near his Brighton home. His wife was pronounced dead at the scene and is believed to have been the only passenger. Police state they have yet to establish the cause of the accident but that no other vehicles were involved.

Dr Auerbach is widely regarded as one of Britain's foremost thinkers in psychiatry with his study of childhood mental health disorders Who's There? retaining its undisputed place as the classic text on the subject. He is known as an outspoken and powerful critic of recent cutbacks to services within hospitals and clinics. Any connection between the tragedy and a controversial television documentary screened the same evening in which Dr Auerbach attacked the government's policy on mental health is thought to be coincidental.

A family friend has today confirmed rumours that Dr Auerbach's wife Ursula, to whom he has been married for eighteen years, suffered from long-term schizophrenic illness. The couple have no children.

All around her, commuters pushed and ran for their trains,

but Nell stood oblivious of everything, unable to move and yet doing so at last because what she had read was so terrible she must get home before she broke down altogether.

During the journey to Wharton she read the words over and over again, shivering in the hot stickiness of the train. She saw in her stunned imagination Lewis being placed on a stretcher by scurrying paramedics, the helicopter's whirring blades, the hospital theatre with its life-support machines flashing and beeping.

Oh please God, let him still be alive, even if I am never to see him again.

She remembered the photograph in his consulting room of the beautiful woman with wispy white-yellow hair and enormous eyes. A woman who was so hauntingly lovely that nobody could ever want to stop gazing into her face.

But she couldn't envy her any more. All those feelings changed into shock and pity for everything she must have suffered. Muddled up in her distraught prayers for Lewis were prayers for his dead wife. They loved the same man – death could not interrupt this, Nell believed – and their souls seemed in some mysterious way to come close together.

Would there be more information on the news? It was just after ten when Nell ran into the house and she'd missed the headlines. She switched on the television and watched in an agony of impatience, but there was nothing. A member of parliament had been having an affair, house prices had risen and an expensive face cream increased rather than reduced wrinkles. Finally there came a short announcement on the local news of a fatal car crash near Brighton, given out tersely, as though any further information must be withheld from the public.

She didn't want Martin. Or even Eleanor who'd known her mother. Certainly not Hilary. Three people whose friendship meant much to her, but there was nothing that anyone, however sympathetic, could do for her.

Yet people had tried. An elderly lady on the train had unobtrusively handed her a paper handkerchief; the ticket collector, perhaps seeing her reddened eyes, had curbed his habitual cheeriness; a rowdy tangle of teenaged boys had stood aside for her, letting her first off the train when it arrived at Wharton.

'You don't look as though you've had a fun weekend,' commented Sebastian when Nell went to meet the children at the station on Sunday evening. 'As we aren't going to America this summer, will we have two holidays, one with you and the other with Dad?'

'I don't see why not. You and Rachel decide where you want to go.'

There's no money for us to go *anywhere,* she was thinking, but she couldn't tell the children that. Sebastian searched her face.

'Rachel and me don't mind, about America, I mean.'

Rachel said nothing. She had dark circles around her eyes.

'I know you don't. But we'll find somewhere we can afford, I promise. The painting of the quad for Mr Hunstrete's office could lead to more well-paid commissions, so Eleanor's hoping. And that'll be on top of the portrait of Mr Thingy I've been asked to do after the Mall Galleries exhibition.'

'There's the three thousand pounds you got for winning that prize – '

'Mum ought to spend that on herself, not us,' interrupted Rachel. But after supper, when Sebastian had disappeared upstairs, she hung around the kitchen.

'Mum, you might not have watched the news, but something awful has happened. Dr Auerbach, he's been in a car crash.'

Nell bent over the dishwasher, afraid she was going to betray herself.

'Yes, I did know – I wasn't sure when to tell you. I saw it in the paper on Friday night.'

And I have been with him every minute since then.

'I never said a proper thank you to him. He understood about things – and made them okay. But then when you and Dad split up, I stopped you taking me there – ' Rachel gave in, sat down at the table and started to cry in the same over-tired and hopeless way of last winter.

Nell crouched down, cradling Rachel's head. Hadn't Lewis known everything? Except how much she loved him. Oh God, only let him live and I will never even try to see him again.

'He's not *dead.*' Rachel accepted some torn-off kitchen roll and wiped her face. 'But so dreadfully injured he's got to be in hospital for ages and his wife was killed and I wanted to say I was sorry – but I can't because the stressy receptionist at Brookner House wouldn't tell me anything. Not even how I could – '

Nell, pressing Rachel to her, stammered, 'Brookner House? You rang there? But darling, why – '

'Juliet told me to. When we heard about it on Saturday. She said it was important to know things for certain. Then she rang somewhere else and found out more for me. It was weird, but Mum, it was like she did kind of really mind, and just then I couldn't hate her at all – '

Nell tried to take in what Rachel was saying, but for one timeless moment she held on to the one thing, that Lewis was going to live. A slow surge of thankfulness crept through her. She wanted to say she would never be able to hate anyone ever again, but her whole body was shuddering and no words came.

THIRTY-EIGHT

'I've had Martin Darrow with me giving me the extremely upsetting news that he wants to make a move,' said Clement Hunstrete to Jim North at the beginning of the Michaelmas term in September. 'Something about his conscience – naturally I didn't like to probe – and doing God's work elsewhere. It's the most infernal nuisance.'

'It's certainly disappointing.' Jim looked his sympathy rather than his surprise. 'I'd hoped we'd tied the knot on that one last term. However, there's no arguing with God's will – or what a man thinks is God's will. Has Martin given in his notice formally?'

'More or less. And as to that, I told him he'd been doing God's will here for ten years – hasn't Wharton been his whole life? – and there was no earthly reason why he shouldn't continue with it. I didn't get anywhere with that argument.'

'I don't imagine you did. I can still hear echoes from his quite remarkable sermon at the end of year chapel service. Smacked of some kind of epiphany. Then he took himself off to a retreat house over the summer, or so I heard from Meredith. It set a few of my alarm bells ringing. Not going over to Rome, is he?'

'Nothing like that,' Clement assured him hastily. 'Though obviously the same idea occurred to me.'

'*The Parting of Friends*,' murmured Jim. 'Newman's last sermon as an Anglican. He still has an extraordinary allure.'

'The man seemed more concerned about Nell Garwood than how I was going to find someone else half reasonable to take his place. He even asked me to look out for her!' Clement spoke with some indignation. 'I informed him that headmasters weren't entirely lacking in chivalry, even in the twenty-first century. I've had Eleanor fussing too, insists Nell's hiding something.'

'Which is only to be expected in the circumstances.'

'Eleanor said it must be about some man but then she accused me of not listening – hardly fair when I'm preoccupied with the start of a new school year – and wouldn't say any more.'

'Probably cut up about Martin. I've no doubt he's confided his whole story to her first. Made short work of Trevor Faversham's pretensions, didn't she?'

'Yes, thank heavens,' agreed Clement, who still hadn't forgiven the art master for his portrait of him. He glanced with satisfaction at the grandiose painting of the quad buildings, hung over the fireplace. Nell had done a splendid job. Quite a number of prospective parents had made admiring comments. A very nice piece of public relations for the school; he could give himself a pat on the back for thinking of it. Or had it been Eleanor's idea?

'More strong-minded that you might think, if you ask me. Pity we weren't able to persuade her to stay full-time. Getting her divorce, moving house, by all accounts working round the clock on portrait commissions. Put the Alastair business behind her with more grace than might have been expected.'

'And more than he deserved,' said Clement, enjoying his image of Nell as a delicate climbing rose in need of a sunny wall to cling to, even though she'd proved that she could manage perfectly well by herself.

'Well, as to Martin, it looks as if our suspicions were right after all. Sad for Meredith, but I've no doubt she's long accepted the inevitable.'

'Suspicions? Did we have any to speak of?'

Jim made a significant gesture.

'Good grief. Are you sure about this?' The question was rhetorical. Clement never doubted his deputy's sharp animal instinct. As he adjusted his thoughts, his eyes rested for a moment on the gilded nakedness of the putti supporting the clock face. 'So we've been skating on alarmingly thin ice and getting away with it.'

'Yes. We can count ourselves fortunate.'

Clement swung his headmaster's chair round, thinking of the potentially hideous scandal they'd escaped.

'You're not suggesting the Benson boy – '

'No reason to think that. In fact, definitely not. More likely Martin's had some kind of Damascus moment. God setting him free to pursue a way of life he would never contemplate here.'

'Assuming that's what he's after,' said Clement, not quite convinced.

'As to his future role within Anglicanism, we'll have to hope for an enlightened bishop. What have you agreed with Martin?'

'Says he'll stay until I'm happy with a replacement, the whole year if needed. But it's no good, his heart won't be in it. And after your comments' – Clement gave another swing to his chair – 'there can be no question about it. Think of the risks, we'd never sleep at night. We'll have to let him go at Christmas. Any sooner, such as half term, would look smoky. People would think we had something to hide. It'll be the devil of a job replacing him.'

'It will indeed. Idealistic young ordinands don't perceive that working among well-heeled youth can be a worthy vineyard in which to labour. They're all too inclined to dismiss it as a backwater job, a convenient nest for comfort-lovers fighting shy of the real world.'

'Comfort! They've got that wrong.'

'Entirely. I'd have said that between the contempt or indifference of the majority, and the zealous and prescriptive activities of the God Squad, a chaplain in a public school has to steer a hazardous course. Martin's got it right all along. Human enough to be approachable by anyone, substantial enough spiritually to have something to offer. Even when the need is unexpressed, as it so often is.'

'So we can expect a lot of lily-livered applicants,' grumbled Clement. 'The ones with any fire in them are too busy burning themselves out in inner city parishes. That's if they aren't being swept off to some cranky sect in America, and coming back claiming to be prophets and self-styled workers of wonders.'

'It might be worth phoning Graham Saunders at Oxford to see if he has any reasonable candidates hidden away who could start in the Lent term. Some chap not yet decided on his future, awaiting God's call.'

'We don't want anyone like *that*!'

'Same breeding ground as Martin Darrow, you know. We'd be sure of a sound theology.'

'A headmaster's job is becoming increasingly that of a manager,' said Clement crossly. 'I'm not a human resources facilitator, as I believe is the modern expression, but an academic. It hasn't felt like it these last few terms.'

'Well, we've had ten years of benefit. A man of unusual holiness and self-denial, that's beyond doubt. A whole generation of boys will go through life never guessing how much they owe him…did you get any idea of what he means to do with himself next?'

'I hardly liked to enquire too closely,' said Clement, who'd forgotten to ask.

'Ah yes. Personal reasons. Could be a delicate matter.'

'*Nec scire fas est omnia* – it is not permitted to know all things,' Clement declared, adding the translation in case Jim was not as well up in Horace as he ought to have been.

'Certainly not about the consciences of chaplains,' agreed Jim in his driest tone.

*

Nell loitered by the telephone in the kitchen. She wasn't waiting for Lewis to ring her, he wasn't going to. Why should he? She'd never meant anything to him. She could admit that now.

Term had started. In the summer holidays she and the children had moved to a rented newly-built townhouse, chosen not just because it was cheap, nearer to the station and convenient for the children going to London for weekends, but for its integral garage which she'd converted into a painting studio.

It was a relief to move away from school property and dependence. She was creating a new home – and a new life. She'd borrowed the money from the bank and signed up for a part-time course starting in January to train properly as an art therapist. She worked punishing hours in her studio. She was starting to hope that in the years ahead she might get somewhere as an artist, produce work that meant something, even make a name for herself.

It was only when she was ready to drop with exhaustion she allowed herself to think of Lewis. It was more than two months since the horrifying accident in which his wife had died and he had so miraculously survived. More than two months of hoping he might turn to her; of telling herself that such hope was obscene, almost blasphemy in the face of his loss.

The holiday with the children in a cramped and remote

cottage in gale-swept Cornwall hadn't helped. It only enforced a week's break from googling Lewis's name. She knew every entry now; she'd read each article he'd written, stared hungrily night after night at photographs of him on the screen and on the back cover of her copy of *Who's There?* She still couldn't stop doing this, saving it up for the end of the day, before she switched off her laptop and went to bed alone and ashamed of behaving like an infatuated schoolgirl.

You're different, Juliet had said to her in July. Nell knew this wasn't true. She didn't know who she was any more.

To go on with a futile hope or to give up, which hurt the most? Juliet had said to Rachel it was better to know things for certain.

Nell picked up the telephone and dialled the number for Brookner House.

'I wonder if it's possible to speak with Dilys Cole, Dr Auerbach's secretary? I would like to find out if – '

She'd tried to make her voice sound authoritative but the receptionist cut in, coolly polite and impersonal.

'I'm sorry, Dilys Cole doesn't work here any more. Dr Auerbach no longer has a clinic at Brookner House.'

Nell put down the receiver with a shaking hand, suddenly aware that Rachel had come into the kitchen and was standing in the doorway.

'Why are you ringing Dilys Cole?'

'I just wanted – '

I needed to hear his voice one last time, that's all. But she couldn't say that to Rachel whose question held a note of accusation.

'Mum, you know you sent Dr Auerbach a letter to say you were sorry about his wife dying – '

'Yes darling. And you wrote something too, didn't you?'

'He might have replied.' Rachel glared at Nell as if it was her fault. 'Not just sent that printed card, the same as everyone probably got.'

Nell remembered with pain the stilted phrases she'd copied out so carefully, lest he should think that now his wife was conveniently out of the way she wanted to get into his bed. Not to anybody, not properly even to herself, could she admit the thoughts which invaded her mind.

'People don't necessarily respond individually to condolence letters. Perhaps he's not up to writing. They said just now he wasn't working at Brookner House any more.'

Again the measuring expression. What was Rachel thinking?

*

Words, Martin had learnt, should come out of silence. There was too much empty talk, too much sound bite comfort. Most of it bounced back unheard, or offered a temporary stopgap followed by further emptiness. Marshmallow religion. If God was sold too warm and sweet, people were left hungry in the end.

'I can't bear to think I shall never see him again.'

Martin watched the expression of infinite sorrow settle on Nell's face, as she sat hugging a mug of tea in the armchair opposite his own. He prayed inwardly he would know how to say any words that came.

The term had started more than a fortnight ago but he'd seen almost nothing of her. He supposed that now she was working flat-out on portrait commissions as well as teaching she no longer had leisure for dropping in to his flat.

'I wish you weren't – but I want you to be happy,' she'd said when he told her, just before the beginning of term, that he was giving up the chaplaincy. He hadn't explained. He didn't need to. Didn't her portrait of him – and her last words to him on that hot evening in July – show she understood it all?

Today she'd appeared unexpectedly bringing it with her; a

322

present, she said, for his parents. He'd tried to pay her, but she refused, as he'd known she would.

It was the day of the Wharton lecture, and he thought this could be the reason why Nell had finally felt able to tell him she loved the man who'd come for the same occasion a year ago. But why hadn't he seen what was happening to Nell for himself? Not even after watching the discussion programme on the mental health crisis when she'd said – he knew the answer and castigated himself. He'd been careless of everyone's feelings apart from his own.

'It's as though however much I try, I'll never be able to stop loving him…and then I keep thinking of his poor wife,' said Nell, with a catch in her voice. 'How completely they must have loved each other. He's so kind and good, and she must have been – Oh Martin, where *is* God when people take their own lives?'

More than anything he wanted to find something to wipe that look off her face, but the only thing that came into his mind was the memory of seeing Dr Lewis Auerbach with another man coming out of a building in that little side street somewhere off the Strand. That had been almost a year ago, and yet their snatch of conversation came back with unbroken clarity.

Einmal ist Keinmal, the other man had said in a strong Irish accent.

Once is nothing. If we only have one life to live we might as well not have lived at all. For a long time the words had stayed with him, inert, waiting. Now something of recognition came upon him, a kingfisher's flash of colour, as if for a moment his mind's curtain twitched to reveal a fleeting glimmer of the light of God's presence in the world.

'He's with them still,' he said. 'All that unfulfilled promise in a life, we can be quite sure that God will keep his hold on it. Nothing will ever be lost to him. And in eternity we will go on learning the lessons of love.'

He saw her serious grey eyes had filled with tears. He could have cried himself. At the end of the term he would be going away from the place he loved most in the world. But this was as nothing. Nell was unhappy.

'I thought – once – that he cared about me,' she said. 'Not loved me, but cared enough to – but he would surely have written or something if he still did. *If* he ever did.'

He was silent. He thought it possible that Lewis Auerbach loved Nell as she loved him, but so much had happened to this man, perhaps too much.

'The psychiatrist friend of his I met, I remember he said when Lewis got an idea about something he stuck to it. Don't look like that. You see, Martin, it works both ways. He's a man who would feel guilty about being unfaithful, even the idea of it, and he'd feel it even more now.'

'It sounds as if you understand him more than you understood Alastair.'

'I've never admitted it before. But it's true. Juliet understood Alastair better than I ever did – and loved him more. That's something I've learnt at least. It was about time.'

He looked away to the portrait propped up in the corner of the room. He must be very careful with what he said.

'You also know more about yourself. More than Lewis does perhaps, in this matter. Tell him,' he insisted, seizing on the words as conviction came to him, 'tell him what you've told me. That you love him.'

'When his wife has been dead not three months? She was *ill*, Martin, they didn't say in the papers that it was suicide but they hinted at it. It would be like cashing in, grabbing at something that shouldn't be mine. I'd feel *smirched*.'

'It may be offered to you,' said Martin. 'And then it'll be yours to accept with clean hands and a clear conscience – and a grateful heart. Lewis possibly had to give up a great deal for his wife. But she did something for him in the end. She gave him his life back. God allowed this to happen, didn't he? Are you so proud that you won't condescend to take what God gives you, just because it doesn't come packaged up with a pretty ribbon in the uncomplicated way you want?'

She'd turned away her face, but now she shot him a look of anger and denial.

'God *does* restore things to us.' Martin heard the new firmness in his voice. Nell must not go on running away. 'We have to wait. Sometimes for many years.'

Half a lifetime. But it mustn't be like this for Nell.

'Remember Lewis's grief may have lasted for a long time, not just since July. Stop deceiving yourself and other people. Tell this man you love him, tell him soon, confident that the right moment will be given to you.'

At Christmas he would be going to stay with his parents. After that – but he didn't know yet. Only that life was always and everywhere to be offered to God.

And Oliver Benson? Just another boy, an unfinished mix of good and bad – not half so sure of himself as he'd like others to think, at odds with his father – and belonging like the rest of them with all the company of heaven.

A long-forgotten chorus from his school days here at Wharton came unbidden into his head.

He brought me into his banqueting house…and his banner over me is love.

God had always been there even when he most appeared to be absent, and so he would always be. He could be quite sure of this now.

THIRTY-NINE

Why hadn't he done this before? There had been time, too much time. But he'd avoided it, and then allowed himself to procrastinate. It was almost December now, short days of half-hearted light, and he'd been out of hospital for over three months. It must be done, and it was surely a job like any other from the endless list that filled his life since the day his wife had killed herself.

Her clothes. He'd started with these when he first came home. Friends and neighbours had offered to help, but he'd resisted. He preferred to do these things himself, that nobody should observe him as he pressed his cheek against cloth that had once lain against her skin. An efficient driver from the Mind charity shop had collected the bags of carefully folded garments, with much-repeated thanks and avoiding looking him in the eye.

Each weekend he worked, tidying away the lives he and Ursula had lived here. By Christmas the house would belong to someone else. A young family was moving in. Small children would run up and down the stairs, and kick balls into the neighbours' gardens.

Now there was just this one room left. The nursery, said the estate agent when they'd bought the house, and neither he nor Ursula had said anything, each of them perhaps knowing by then there wasn't going to be a baby. Instead it had become a place where things could be kept out of sight and therefore forgotten: half-finished craft projects which Ursula had abandoned, unused art materials, books of music she'd long ceased to play.

As he'd returned to consciousness in the hospital ward, he hadn't needed the compassionate faces of the medical staff around him to tell him that Ursula was dead. He lay there day after day, silenced by the shock and grief that consumed him. A profound tiredness lay on him like a stifling blanket, as if all hope of life and renewed energy were forever withdrawn.

As the weeks went by and his body gradually recovered from its injuries, he found his mind reliving the horror of those final moments in the car. Ursula's image swam before him in fast moving fragments; dazzled him before slipping away into a blur of confused noise and colour. Then his thoughts would drift over the years of their marriage, and he would re-pace each memory, where joy had been so cruelly interwoven with sorrow.

When he left the hospital, the jagged scar running across his temple and the more frequent return of his childhood stammer were the only outward signs of what had happened to him. In psychiatry he might again find meaning and purpose. Despite the fatigue that stalked him, he threw himself back into it. He put the Brighton house on the market; increased his hours at *Steep Stairs;* gave up his private practice outside London. There was work to be done and he was still equipped to do it.

It was mid afternoon and the daylight fading when Lewis found the doll. It was wrapped up in white material, hidden among spare linen in the built-in cupboard running along one wall. A baby-sized doll.

The room all at once felt cold, his breathing strained and unnaturally loud in the near empty house. He undid the softly knitted shawl, and looked down at the exaggerated chubby limbs, the sky blue eyes opening in mute surprise at this intrusion.

When had Ursula bought this doll? Not during those first few years of marriage when they'd lived on a shoestring squashed into a tiny flat in Camberwell. He hadn't finished his medical training but she'd been eager to get pregnant. She'd been disappointed month after month.

He ran a trembling finger across the doll's baby-smooth face as the answer came. She'd done so when she'd sensed the change in him, when he'd first woken to that grey dawn of fear that the mood swings when she became disorientated and unreachable were not just emotional fragility, but presaged something far more serious.

The truth had slowly and painfully seeped into his consciousness, and after that he'd taken his own precautions. She ought not to have children. Not yet.

He heard again her screaming at him during those years. He was her enemy, he was preventing her having the child she needed. Then she would fall into the hysterical crying fits which were to become an established pattern, and he would console her, saying that when she was better then that would be the time to think again about starting a family. That time had never come.

His wife had kept this doll hidden here in the cupboard on the other side of the wall to where they had slept. Had she stolen here in the night to cradle it?

Very gently he smoothed the crumpled material of the dress, the colour of pink icing on cheap cakes, and retied the once jaunty bows on the bright blond hair. They were limp and wilted; the doll had been lying here for too many years. Fringed glassy eyes accused him. You stopped my life. You didn't want me to be born.

A car drew up outside. Lewis went to the window. It was Dermot Fitzgibbon.

'A week later and you wouldn't have found me here,' he said, as he let Dermot in. 'I can give you some coffee, but not much else.'

'I haven't come for the drink,' said Dermot. 'I called in at Hampstead, to your mother's flat. It wasn't hard to guess you'd be staying there. She told me you were here packing up. You've changed your mobile number.'

'I had to get the press off my back, didn't I?'

'And everyone else, so who's blaming you? Haven't I done the same myself?'

'I've sold the house. Going to buy somewhere in central London.'

'Too many memories?' Dermot's voice contained the faintest touch of derision.

'Too many memories,' answered Lewis steadily. He led the way into the kitchen, now stripped bare of its old clutter, and switched on the kettle while Dermot watched him in silence.

'That woman I saw you with,' Dermot said unexpectedly. 'In Flavio's, wasn't it, back in May?'

Lewis stiffened.

'You're making a mistake.'

'Oh, stop playing games with me, what's the bloody use? As for making a mistake, yes I have. It's why I'm here.'

Lewis handed him a mug of black coffee.

'There's no milk.'

'I've done you an injustice,' said Dermot, easing his skeletal frame onto one of the chairs around the table. 'I ought to have spotted it. I got it wrong with Craig Parker. Don't you be telling me I didn't have it coming to me.'

'I didn't defend you because you were an old family friend of my wife,' said Lewis, with a faint smile, leaning against the sink. 'I didn't believe – and still don't believe – that anyone could have prevented that particular tragedy. You're a damn good psychiatrist.'

'You might not have been so generous had you known I'm a little more than an old family friend,' said Dermot. He looked up at Lewis, with his familiar magician's mockery. 'You've not guessed, have you now?'

A premonition of pain worse than any he had already suffered crept over Lewis. Its dark agony was coming for him, but as yet he was aware only of its certainty.

'Ursula and I were childhood sweethearts back in Dublin,' said Dermot. His eyes, too large in a face that had become gaunt and wasted, flicked to the steaming mug of coffee in front of him. 'I'd started at medical school in London when she told me she was pregnant. She was only sixteen. I gave her the money to come over for an abortion and fixed it for her.'

For a moment the words made no sense. Lewis struggled to understand their implications but was conscious only of an image of a doll, lying lifeless on the floor upstairs.

'Ursula aborted your child – '

'She did – '

'And you – ' Lewis fought to thrust away whatever Dermot was saying and lost. 'You *arranged* it – a schoolgirl – before ditching her –'

'I'd already embarked on a relationship of a different kind,' said Dermot. 'There wasn't anything more we could do for each other, given its nature. I'm thinking you wouldn't care for me to go into details.'

'It doesn't take much imagination.'

'She wasn't in the way of wanting me after what had happened. She fell into a succession of jobs, stayed on in London and made me promise to bury the whole business. Not just from her family either, but from everyone and for always. No surprises there, the family had never been in the way of coping with her, they couldn't deal with the stigma of mental illness and what their church friends might be saying. Hasn't she been dead as far as they're concerned ever since? She kept her distance from me for a couple of years and then I got a call to say she'd been in hospital. A car crash. If I say I wasn't surprised you'll be thinking I'm a brute, but it's the truth you're wanting now. I'd heard something about the kind of company she'd been keeping.'

Dermot swallowed some coffee, allowing a tiny pause.

'She was in love with someone, she said, and went on at me about my promise. Afterwards, when I learnt it was you, and you were marrying her – to be sure we might be fellow medics, but there was nothing beyond that in the way of friendship. I didn't owe you any more than hoping to God Ursula would come clean about her past. But she never did, did she?'

Little girls played with dolls. And women too when –

'About eight years ago, just before you moved here, she came to see me. She said they'd botched the abortion and she'd been left unable to have children.'

'She can't have thought that – ' Lewis broke in harshly.

'She wanted to believe it, that's the truth of it. Don't all our misfortunes have to be someone else's fault? She'd been seeing specialists on the quiet but they wouldn't have told her that, abortions didn't do that to women, not even twenty years ago, and trust me Lewis, it wasn't a backstreet job either.

'It was an obsession all right – like the promiscuous lifestyle she took up in the years before you came here. Sleeping with anyone and everyone. Well, it goes with the territory, doesn't it? Or maybe it was just about wanting a kid. You never caught her at it, did you?'

Lewis stared at him without speaking. Oh God, what had he done? A dead baby hidden in a cupboard, a living doll in a mind falling apart.

'You didn't have to tell me any of this,' he said at last. 'What difference can it make now?'

Again he fell silent as he thought of the course his marriage had taken. He'd struggled to defend this man, and yet for all these years Dermot had known more about his wife than he did himself. Something of bitterness came over him at having been so deceived, at Ursula having escaped from him before he could put it right with her. As he thought about how he was left to deal with this final sting, he felt he hated them both.

But as he became calmer he began to acknowledge in his heart that Dermot, in keeping his promise to Ursula to the end, had not in truth injured him. Nor was Ursula's final act connected with Dermot's involvement in the Craig Parker tragedy. Suicide had been waiting in some dark imagined future, an inexorable hand waiting its moment to strike. He'd lived with the unmistakable warning signs all these years. It was too late to hand out blame to anyone else for the long shadows cast by old sins.

'I can see the shame in your face,' said Dermot savagely. 'You'll go on whipping yourself for not curing her illness. Aren't you a man who delights to blame himself? You've tied yourself up so tightly in guilt and self-condemnation you'll be ruining the rest of your life if you don't face up to a few truths. You didn't do enough for her, you're thinking, and you're planning to spend the rest of your life trying to make up for it.'

Lewis had sat down, but now he leapt up again, unable to endure the recriminations with which he'd tormented himself. He stood gazing unseeingly out of the kitchen window. Each day he'd searched his mind for what more he could have done for Ursula and he'd whispered there was much. Had he done and been everything possible for the young wife he'd promised to love? Had there ever been, buried deep in his consciousness, a thought – a wish – that one day she would die?

Now here was this man, another psychiatrist, living and dying with the mistakes of his life, telling him something. They both knew, with their psychiatrists' training, of the baseness hidden in every human being, to what depths anyone may sink. And yet alongside his despair at the endless grief he must always carry with him, he could be thankful the pity and tenderness that Ursula had always evoked in him had never faltered.

He said, as if testing the truth of the words, 'I loved Ursula – I still loved her to the end – in a way.'

'And she loved you. In so far as she was capable of it. But you're not God Almighty, you can't make lame people walk or give the blind their sight. Ursula wasn't fit to be a wife, let alone a mother. There was the question mark of psychosis hanging over her as a young teenager, before you even met her. She'd seen doctors in Dublin. All that was kept from you, wasn't it, not just by her but by her family, and you married her before you'd time to see her more clearly. Why don't you allow yourself to be human and try for some ordinary happiness instead of thinking you've got to atone for the sins of the world?'

'That's my affair.'

'Have it your own way. Are you thinking I can't guess what happened in that car the night she was killed? You did your best for me over Craig Parker. I've an idea I owe you something after all, even if it's just telling you not to make a mess of your life.'

Resentment at the man's arrogance flared. Dermot had no right to take it upon himself to prescribe for him like this.

'Is that why you came? One bankrupt psychiatrist speaking to another?'

'For God's sake, Lewis. You're still alive, aren't you? Half your life ahead of you? I came because of that grey-eyed girl in Flavio's. She loves you, I'm telling you. It was written all over her face. Try telling me you're not in love with her yourself and I'll not believe you.

'I'll lay my life you haven't contacted her since Ursula died. All because you're too stiff-necked to forgive yourself. You feckin' eejit. Isn't that for the person who loves you to decide? To have you for better or for worse, like you did with Ursula all those years ago?'

Lewis didn't reply. He looked into Dermot's hollow eyes.

'And you? What will you do?'

'As for myself, I'm going back to where I come from, for however many years I've got left. I'll be letting you down at *Steep Stairs,* but it'll survive without me. I've blotted my copybook here – and there's as much madness in Dublin as in London, wouldn't you say now?'

At the door he touched Lewis lightly on the shoulder.

'Goodbye old fellow. Remember that word of wisdom about the heart having its reasons which reason knows nothing of.'

'Nell,' Lewis said suddenly. 'She was called Nell. She said you must be a good man if you were a psychiatrist.'

Dermot laughed before he turned away with something of his old swagger.

'And I was thinking she was a perceptive lady. Aren't we shrinks all as mad as hatters?'

Lewis went back upstairs. The doll lay on the floor, its pink prettiness unheeding of the pain of the living. Picking it up, Lewis held it in his arms and found he was crying.

FORTY

Nell hadn't wanted to go to London for her birthday at the beginning of December but the children had insisted.

'We might as well take advantage of it being a Saturday which won't happen again for years,' urged Sebastian.

'Thank goodness you've decided you definitely don't want to go to Wharton next year with its stupid Saturday school,' said Rachel. 'We'll still be able to go to London together at weekends – so long as Mum doesn't get too dug into her art therapy stuff.' She turned to Nell. 'You could wear your dress. The one you've got squashed at the back of your wardrobe. It must have cost a fortune and it's been bloody well wasted.'

'It's the wrong weather for it.'

Was everything on this day going to lead inexorably to memories of Lewis? All through the summer she hadn't been able to bring herself to wear the white dress with its rash of scarlet poppies she'd bought on her birthday a year ago. She felt her face flushing as she remembered sitting on a bench in the winter sunshine, the beautiful dress in its carrier bag at her feet, and daydreaming – but not of Alastair.

'You couldn't skate in a dress,' pointed out Sebastian, who had suggested Nell might enjoy the Somerset House ice rink as part of her birthday treat. She and Martin had laughed over this but she'd been pleased when both children asked if Vail could join them.

They were just leaving the house when the telephone rang. It was Juliet.

'Nell – it's me – '

'I can recognise your voice.'

'I wanted to say happy birthday...I wish I was seeing you today as well as Vail. We've shared so many birthdays in the past.'

'Yes. In the past. But thanks for the great card and the amazing collection of paints. I've never used some of those colours. It'll be good to try something new – '

Did you know Alastair sent me a pair of pearl earrings? The words almost said themselves. There had been moments since the arrival in the post yesterday of the little package when she'd relished the saying of them in her head, but now the impulse died.

'Guess who I bumped into yesterday? Actually you never will so I won't make you. It was Newland – and do you know, he kept me talking for twenty-five minutes about a play he'd just seen – the kind where people talk philosophy all the time and nothing ever happens.'

'Maybe he took his wife to it,' Nell said, not without emphasis.

'Ouch. He might not have married. Though actually he's just as attractive. But it didn't *look* like it. I didn't ask.'

Naturally not.

'You never did read *The Age of Innocence* – about Newland Archer – did you? Why don't you try it? It's Eleanor's favourite novel. But I must go – the train. Is Alastair bringing Vail to Somerset House?'

'Vail's finding his own way. He can, you know.'

Yes, and you've arranged it like this. But Nell put the phone down with a sense of freedom.

336

My darling Nell, he'd written in a scrawled note, tucked in with the earrings and looking as though it had been written in a rush. (Had that been deliberate or just Alastair?) *If only I could give you an undiscovered Vermeer! As that isn't possible, it will have to be these pearl earrings – with love as always, Alastair.*

She hadn't yet thrown away the note, but already she knew she would, and soon. A part of her would always love Alastair, but he didn't belong to her any more. She didn't want him to. A different kind of relationship must be allowed to grow between them – and Juliet too – containing something of a necessary detachment and yet sustained by everything that would always hold them together.

The exhibition of visionary landscape artists in the National Gallery had been Rachel's idea. Nell was surprised and touched; she'd wanted to see it very much. But after the initial excitement she became too restless to concentrate on the paintings. The boys, tired from skating and oversized pizzas, lolled on seats and fidgeted. Rachel, apparently preoccupied with sending and receiving texts on her mobile, asked if she could explore the rest of the gallery by herself.

Tell this man you love him, Martin had said.

'Would you mind if we went round the corner to the National Portrait Gallery? I'll text Rachel to tell her where we are – '

'Can we go to the cafe while you're looking at stuff?'

' – and have some money for the shop?'

'Be as long as you like – we like it there.'

Nell left the boys in the gallery's basement cafe and went upstairs pretending she was going to look at old favourites.

It was no good. Even Gwen John's self-portrait, which she'd always loved for its muted tones and unlikely self-assertiveness, withdrew itself and didn't speak. With a thumping heart she hurried to the room where she knew she would find the little Rembrandt painting Lewis had given to the gallery last year.

It was even smaller than she remembered. The eyes of Thomas Daintree stared into some endless depth of human experience which Nell could only guess at. The real passions of his life were locked tightly into that mysterious gaze; to those who came after him they would always remain an enigma.

Did Lewis remember that this time last year he'd been with her, eating cakes in the cafe downstairs?

He *must* remember. He *did* remember.

She turned quickly. Inside her bag, her mobile vibrated.

*

Dilys Cole came into one of the rooms in the *Steep Stairs* building carrying a cup of tea.

'There's a girl downstairs asking for you.'

Lewis, sitting at a desk writing up case notes, said sharply, 'A girl? Did you get her name?'

'She wouldn't give it to me. Or listen when I asked what she wanted. Came in off the street and won't leave until she's seen you.'

'I should hope she didn't listen. Isn't seeing people off the street what this place is all about?'

His secretary smiled as if to say she'd heard that one before; that overworked consultants needed protecting from themselves as well as the ever-demanding and needy public. She put down the cup of tea by Lewis's elbow.

'She might have come to Brookner House. I've seen her before, but there's no saying when. A girl with a mother – '

'They do usually have mothers,' Lewis said, more impatiently than he meant to. He went down the stairs to the reception area in the hall.

A girl with hair the soft brown of a ploughed winter field was sitting bolt upright in one of the chairs. She shook it away from her face, her expression a mixture of defensiveness and defiance. It was Rachel Garwood.

'I didn't stop coming because of not liking you,' she said before he could say anything. 'Because I do. I really, really do. It was just that – '

'That's okay. I know it wasn't.'

'Mum tried to ring you at Brookner House. She didn't know – ' she faltered, and ended lamely, 'if you'd got her letter.'

'I did.' Lewis unconsciously lifted one hand to touch the breast pocket of his jacket and the much-creased sheet of paper. 'And yours. It was very good of you both. Thank you.'

He hated the brittle formality in his voice but he couldn't help it. He stared down at this girl who expected something from him, feeling himself at a loss.

'I thought if I could see you again – '

A shot of terror rushed at him.

'What's happened? Rachel, where's your mother?'

'Nothing. Mum's with my brother – and Vail. You remember about him. He's a kind of real brother now.'

He heard only the first word. Nell was all right. He steadied himself, looking into her serious face with its thick eyebrows over wide apart eyes. They were exactly like her mother's and they were frowning at him.

'How have you come here? You're not alone?'

'No – not exactly – ' Rachel swivelled her eyes to the door. 'I don't have much time. But Mum won't know if I'm quick – '

'Rachel, where is she?'

She edged away from the question with an expression on her face he didn't know how to interpret. He tried again.

'Is she at least here with you in London?'

'She's in the National Portrait Gallery. Five minutes away. Please don't be angry. I needed to ask about something.'

He caught the expectant note. Ursula too had needed

something from him and he hadn't given it to her. He'd betrayed her trust, as a doctor and a husband. He'd given everything to psychiatry and failed the people he loved. A kaleidoscope of grief and remorse wheeled before him and he wanted to fall down and weep for everything that was gone. But he must not frighten this child. Dear God, hadn't there been tears enough?

'Martin – Mum's friend – told me he'd seen you coming out from here,' Rachel fixed her eyes on him and twisted a strand of hair round a finger. 'I asked him about you and he said – but he's leaving Wharton at the end of term. Mum says he has to.'

Martin Darrow, the school chaplain, the man whose portrait Nell had painted. Lewis had spent too much time dwelling on the hours of intimacy Nell must have spent with this man, hours in which she'd learnt to love him. He heard again in his head her careful insistence: *he's a very unusual man. Almost a perfect man.*

And Nell wasn't the only one to think so. Hadn't he made some enquiries about the Wharton chaplain after he'd lectured at the school and worried about the boy with the stammer? He'd been assured that Martin Darrow was known for his soft pedal faith and undemonstrative rectitude, trusted by even the most difficult and wayward of teenagers. So why was he leaving and why did Rachel want him to know it?

'I had to find you. You understood about stuff before and Mum won't ever – '

The instinctive tenderness which troubled children always aroused in his heart flooded through him, but still he hesitated. What was she really asking of him?

'Rachel, you must ring your mother and explain to her where you are before you do anything else.'

She gave him the obstructive scowl he remembered from their first meeting.

'I can't. My battery's flat. Couldn't you do it?'

Why don't you allow yourself to be human and try for some

ordinary happiness instead of thinking you've got to atone for the sins of the world? He shut his mind to the words he'd whispered in his brain since Dermot had come to his house. What did Dermot know?

He took out his mobile and handed it to her.

'You can use mine.'

You're too stiff-necked to forgive yourself.

*

'I hate all this for Nell,' Eleanor said to Sue North, while pretending to watch the first fifteen rugby match on Saturday afternoon. 'Why does love have to cause so much unhappiness?'

'You don't *know* Nell is in love.'

'Oh Sue! What else could be the reason for that look in her face when she thinks nobody's noticing?'

'If the man she's apparently in love with is available, then no doubt he'll come to return her sentiments.' Sue spoke in her usual brisk manner. 'Splendid, we've scored another try. I should have thought she'd do better to concentrate on her career just now. I gather she's deluged with portrait commissions.'

'I have a lowering suspicion he must be married. That's the trouble with having principles. After Alastair letting her down in the way he did, I should like Nell to find someone who deserved her.'

'It's not a good idea to run from one man to another. A woman needs to grow up, show herself and other people that she can do without one in her life.'

'But Sue, she *has* done! And anyway don't you think Nell is *designed* to make a man – and children – happy? Don't mind my saying so, but this talk of women having to find themselves by going off and being all independent is a worn-out cliché really.'

'Or rather it's not a valid journey for all women? All right,

I'll give in. And add that it's very tiresome about Martin Darrow. That could have been so suitable.'

'I think she'll always be *fond* of Alastair, without having any illusions about him, and that must be a good thing,' continued Eleanor, following her thoughts in her usual haphazard fashion. 'Remember how nice he always was to everyone. The way they've got their divorce so quickly shows it *can* be done without all the squabbling over money and children that one hears about with other couples. What's so strange is the relationship with Juliet. You wouldn't have thought friendship of any kind could be resurrected after such a betrayal. Yet *something* obviously has been.'

'They'll end up closer friends than ever. Especially when Alastair starts straying, which must be regarded as inevitable. As for any future romantic attachment, Nell has doubtless learnt to show better judgement next time around. A more cautious and pragmatic approach go a long way towards a happy marriage, especially a second one.'

'But there are so few available men, where do they all disappear to?' said Eleanor, dissatisfied with this prosaic viewpoint. 'All these excellent women on their own. The problem gets worse the older we get. Don't we know dozens of women who would be more comfortable having a man to love? I almost feel it's my duty to die so Clement can make at least one of them happy.'

Sue looked sceptical, as if weighing up whether this sacrifice would be to any woman's discernible advantage.

'I do hope I'm wrong about Nell being embroiled in an unhappy love affair,' Eleanor went on, brooding on the unfairness of life, and then smiling fondly as she caught a glimpse of Clement on the far touchline making valiant efforts to talk about rugby to a group of parents. 'I've been tactful for once and haven't asked but I can't help thinking I should have done. It's her birthday today, she's taken the children up to London. Thirty-five – I wonder if that's either young enough or old enough to get over it?'

*

Nell, still clutching her mobile phone, stumbled through the doors of the *Steep Stairs* building, choked, and fought for breath. A woman with a tired face was sitting at a desk. She said something into a telephone and then nodded at Nell.

'Rachel has gone to the cloakroom to wash her hands. I'll go and tell her you're here.'

Nell stared wordlessly at the woman, weak and shaking with relief. She tried to speak and found she couldn't. Beyond the reception desk was a flight of stairs and Lewis was coming down them.

He was older, much older. The image she'd carried in her head these past months swayed and fell apart. His once black hair was faintly streaked with grey and a scar ran across his forehead. She remembered how the inscrutable expression which was habitual to him would soften with the smile that lay deep in his eyes. Now his face had lost its default setting of resolute impassivity, as if the will to maintain it was no longer available to him. Something of assurance had been taken away. But even in her agitation she knew it hadn't been assurance, she couldn't have said what it was, only that it wasn't there.

'Thank you – Oh God, I can't thank you enough – but I don't understand – '

'Everything's all right. Rachel's fine, there's nothing to worry about.'

'I didn't know she was coming here – '

'So she said.'

' – or that she'd ever heard about it even – '

343

'Martin Darrow told her.'

'Martin?'

Her cheeks flamed under the harsh strip lights. *Tell this man you love him and believe that the moment will be given to you.*

She'd been so certain. But the man in front of her was retreating into himself, withdrawing into the disciplined reserve of the consulting room.

'I'm so terribly sorry. I would never have – ' she lost her way and said confusedly, 'After everything you've been through. We should never have troubled you like this, not when – oh, if only I'd known what Rachel was thinking of doing!'

'It doesn't matter at all. It's what I'm here for.'

Why must he look at her with the same grave and formal courtesy as when she'd first met him at Brookner House? She struggled for the words which wouldn't come, stammering so badly she was almost incoherent, 'I have to go – I've left the two boys in the cafe. Lewis, I – '

She thought a light appeared in his dark eyes but couldn't be sure.

'You once said I could tell you anything, that it wouldn't be – '

He must know. He must be able to see it in her face. She'd never been able to hide anything. Why was he so still, so guarded? *I love you, I love you, I love you.* He made the slightest of movements as if towards her, but at that moment a door opened and she saw Rachel and Dilys Cole coming towards them.

*

'I'll make you another cup of tea,' Dilys said, following him up the stairs. 'Seeing as the other one has gone cold.'

'Thank you.' He did his best to sound appreciative, remembering his earlier sharpness.

'Looks just like her daughter, that mother, doesn't she? Had a nice way with her, it's all come back to me. A Friday's child, I used to say at the time.'

'Yes,' he said, almost stupidly. 'Yes, she's like her daughter.'

'On second thoughts Dr A, I should push off home, if I were you. Chances are it's going to stay all quiet here.'

He perceived that his secretary was scrutinising his face and offering him the only comfort within her power. She probably guessed the whole sorry business. He might have minded this once, but he was beyond caring now, aware only of her mute encouragement while he picked up his things. Dilys was, in her own way, a good woman.

Outside the daylight was fading and it was spitting with rain. Lewis hurried along the Strand towards Charing Cross, knowing he was turning his back on all hope of happiness and yet driven by an obstinacy that had become impossible to relinquish. He plunged on in the gathering twilight, fighting an image of Nell last May running away from him across Trafalgar Square.

That grey-eyed girl, she loves you, I'm telling you. But Dermot had got it wrong. In Nell's mind he'd been merely the friendly psychiatrist, someone at a safe distance.

I had to find you, Mum won't ever – Rachel too had misunderstood.

As he lingered by the lights, looking up at the church of St Martin in the fields, he thought again of Martin Darrow. It crept into his mind that he was missing some clue about the chaplain, something Nell had unconsciously revealed when she'd painted his portrait.

As though in a dark mirror he saw again the intensity of emotion in the layers of pigments and vivid colour. With her instinctive depth of human empathy, she'd exposed something hidden behind the sitter's eyes, had delineated the suffering created by some inner conflict.

He stood motionless, the soaring walls of the church

reaching above and beyond the mass of hurrying human beings below. Droplets of rain flickered in the street lamps, trickling off his thick hair, and at last he thought he began to understand some part of it all. Nell had simply painted the truth. *Almost a perfect man.*

A life without pain would, in the end, be a life outside the movement of everything that matters, Lewis had once read. The suffering of the Jews in the twentieth century had been at the heart of his grandfather's redemptive work, and shaped his own inheritance. Lewis, caught up within both Jewish and Christian ideas, had taught himself to think that pain, accepted and endured with faith and hope, was part of what it meant to be included in the purpose of God, but it came to him now that Martin had gone further than this. He'd known that Christ's suffering could in some mysterious way be completed by human beings.

Lewis turned away from the shadowy façade, all at once certain nothing else mattered so much as telling Nell that he loved her. He must for this hour put everything that had happened to him into the past where it belonged and push aside the destructive doubts and scruples that crippled him.

This much he must do – and believe that he *could* do. He swung around the corner, crossed the flow of traffic and hurried into the National Portrait Gallery.

For a moment he stared around him in dismay, for there were so many rooms and hundreds of people in the building. But Nell was here somewhere. His heart began to beat with strong, painful thuds. Thankfulness for all he'd already been given and might still be given in the future swept through him.

He ran up the escalator. He knew where he would look for her first.